The Blue Monster

Mike Roche

Resort Readers Publishing

Cover design by Stuart Bache and The Books Covered Team

ISBN: eBook: 978-0-9835730-1-2

Print: 978-0-9835730-0-5

Contents

Blurbs

"I immensely enjoyed The Blue Monster. Mike Roche knows the world he writes about. His will be a strong new voice in crime fiction."

Michael Connelly, N.Y. Times bestselling author of the Lincoln Lawyer and Harry Bosch
novels.

"The Blue Monster is a solid crime novel by newcomer Mike Roche. It's filled with authentic dialogue and scenes that make the reader feel like they're right there. Roche delivers the goods."

Jim Swain, bestselling author of the Tony Valentine series

This book is dedicated to my wonderful family, who have provided support, inspiration and love.
A special thank you to my first FTO Jack Matlock and my first Sergeant Grady Anthony. They showed me the way and how to be a good cop.

Chapter One

M aximilian Kress opened the front door to the darkness he feared would consume his life. He stared at the police officer with desperation and said, "Oh, thank God you're here. We think our daughter is in danger."

The dark blue uniformed officer stepped into the entryway of the elegant home, where three anxious faces stared at him, searching for hope.

The well-built officer raised his large hand in a calming gesture and said, "I know you're upset. Let's start from the beginning."

"I am scared. Our daughter, Jennifer, is missing," Maximilian Kress said.

The officer nodded, gave a reassuring smile, and asked, "How long has she been missing?"

"A couple of hours. I was talking to her on the phone as she left work. She said she was on her way home. It should have taken her no more than twenty minutes to get here. She just turned seventeen. We are worried sick."

The officer asked all the details about their missing daughter, including the description of her black Audi sports car. He nodded to the responses and jotted some notes in a small memo pad.

He looked up and said, "Mr. and Mrs. Kress, we get hundreds of reports like this. Most times, they come home later. She is at the age where she can get sidetracked. Sometimes, they will go out for a quick bite with a friend and lose track of time, or the battery goes dead in her cell phone. I know you are anxious, but most times it's nothing to get too worried about."

Mr. Kress looked at the ceiling, blew air through his lips, and said, "As I was saying, Jennifer is not like that. She is very safety conscious, and she's very responsible. This is so unlike her. She is an honor student and a model child. I can sense that something is wrong. This is Luke Shugard over here." He pointed to the young athletic framed young man. "He lives down the street. He is like a family member and sometimes he meets her for a burger or ice cream, but he has not heard from her either."

The officer gave an impatient nod in acknowledgement towards Luke.

Luke said, "That's right. I haven't talked to her today."

The officer asked, "Did she mention any plans to meet with anyone, or does she have a new love interest?"

Luke and Marge Kress answered in unison, "No."

"Any disagreements or fights?"

They all shook their heads and answered, "No."

"We'll broadcast a lookout for her, and I'll have the unit near the mall make a pass around. Stay by the phone in case she calls, or we need to ask some additional questions. You might call her friends and co-workers to see if anybody knows anything about her plans."

The well-tanned Marge Kress threw her hands up and said, "We are just supposed to sit here? What about detectives and a search party?"

"Ma'am, I am aware of your concern. I will issue a notification to all units in the City and the County. The missing person's detective will be in touch with you. I understand what you are saying about Jennifer, but most of these missing persons show back up a few hours later, or are runaways."

"I can assure you, she is not a runaway."

"I know she doesn't fit that model, but until we find some evidence of foul play, we are limited in what we can do."

Luke said, "You're saying you're not going to do anything until you find her body?"

"No, I am not saying that. We are actively looking for her. We will look at the mall and checking with mall security. The sooner I leave here, the quicker I can put out a broadcast on the radio to all units. I am sorry, but I need to act on this now. I have notified Detective Alexander, the on-call missing person's detective."

Marge said, "When will we hear from him?"

"Detective Alexander is a female, and she should call sometime tonight."

The officer walked outside and left them alone with their emotions.

Chapter Two

As requested, Officer Jeb Parker drove through the parking lot of the mall. It was common to have cars left in the mall parking lot. Some employees carpooled, while other employees go out on a night on the town after work and leave their car behind. He checked each car judiciously. One black Dodge pickup truck parked on the same side of the mall where Jennifer Kress worked at, drew his attention. The truck had a Georgia license plate. He thought the owner could be a student or someone who had just moved to the Tampa area. It was out of the ordinary to find an out-of-state tag on a car left at the mall. The mall is a great place to dump a stolen car and pickup another.

He saw headlights headed in his direction. He slowed down, hoping to get lucky that it was Jennifer Kress returning. The car slowed, and he realized it was a green Ford driven by a lone detective. As the window lowered, he recognized the driver as Detective Kate Alexander.

She yelled out to him, "Hey, Jeb, what do you think?"

"What brings you out?"

She hooked her brown hair behind her ear and answered, "I just locked up a runaway in juvy and was heading home when I heard the broadcast."

"I'm impressed. Kick Ass Alexander rides again."

"Yeah yeah."

"I was just about to check out this pickup truck."

She cocked her head back, looking at the rear bumper. "Georgia plates. A long way from home. Why don't you run it, and I'll take a look."

She put the unmarked car in park and stepped out, while Jeb typed on the computer terminal. She shined her flashlight through the windshield of the truck and observed the ignition punched out. No doubt stolen.

Jeb leaned out the window and said, "The plate comes back to a red Chevrolet Impala from Valdosta, Georgia."

"This is a long way from the color red. The ignition is punched too. I'll get the VIN." Kate read the vehicle identification number through the windshield and wrote down the series of letters and numbers on her pad. She walked over and handed the sheet containing the VIN to Jeb. He typed in the numbers and letters as Kate leaned through the window. The computer display reported the pickup was stolen in an aggravated rape yesterday in Pasco County, Florida. Less than an hour north.

Kate said, "That's not good."

"No, it's not."

Kate stood up and shined the flashlight towards the asphalt surface of the parking lot. The beam of light caused a glimmer on the ground about twenty-five feet away. She walked over and discovered a chrome cell phone on the ground. She kneeled down for a closer look and heard the repeated short buzz of the voice mail alert. Her eyes focused on the ground in the area of the phone, and she found a black stem. She leaned closer and could see it was a broken heel to a woman's shoe. The leather frayed on the stem and scrapings deposited in the pavement indicated a struggle. She continued to focus on the pavement and noticed a few drops of what appeared to be blood. Kate took a deep breath and turned to Jeb, who was stepping out of the cruiser. "Call for a supervisor and a crime scene unit."

While he made his notifications, Kate, suspecting foul play, followed protocol by calling for the on-call homicide detective, Blake Hamilton. "Blake, it's Kate. We have a missing person from a stabile family. At her place of employment, we have a stolen truck linked to a rape in Pasco and evidence of a struggle. We also have a cell phone on the ground and there appears to be blood as well."

Blake responded, "Well sweetie," Kate rolled her eyes, "that doesn't mean it's related to your runaway. It also doesn't mean a violent act has occurred. If you get something more, like a body, give me a call. Someday, when you work your way up to the homicide squad, you'll understand."

"First of all, I'm no sweetie of yours. Second, she is not a runaway, but a missing person and third, I'm documenting the time of notification. If you don't want to come out and want to stay at home with whatever sweeeeetie you're bedding down, fine. I'll let you know when we find the body." She ended the call and said, "Jeb, I'm going up to the parents and interview them. I'll be back before crime scene is finished."

"You got it."

As she walked to her car, Kate felt emptiness and an uneasy anxiety. She transferred to missing persons a few months earlier. She had seen many broken homes and runaways. Being an advocate for the runaways, she is often the lone voice echoing in the abyss's darkness of the juvenile justice and social service system. It bothered her to see dysfunctional families. What bothered her more were cops who didn't want to do their job, like Hamilton. She knew in the pit of her stomach that something terrible happened to Jennifer Kress, and it would be up to her to take the lead.

Chapter Three

Deputy Dallas Smith had just completed a call to a family in Wimauma in southern Hillsborough County. Wimauma was a rural community comprised mostly of migrant farm workers and people that enjoyed the space. It was rich in oranges and in methamphetamines.

Dallas, a deputy for three years, enjoyed living in a similar area with his wife, Anne, and six-month-old son, Jason. They lived in a doublewide trailer on an acre of land. He liked the serenity of not living on top of his neighbors.

Idling on a dirt road off Highway 674 next to a patch of trees, he could watch the minimal traffic. The trees obscured the marked unit from the approaching eastbound traffic. The dirt road with two ruts from tires led to the Fellowship Primitive Baptist Church and Cemetery. The presence of the cemetery behind him would reduce the chances of someone walking up behind his car. No one likes to walk through a graveyard in darkness. At 2:00AM, there was little traffic. He cracked his window and let some citrus scented humid air mix with the air-conditioning. He could hear the tree frogs croaking in a rhythmic harmony.

The deputy looked at his watch. At 2:05AM, it was time to eat. He twisted to his right and, with eager anticipation, unzipped the top of the blue soft-sided lunch cooler to see the contents of the dinner that Anne packed for him. The glow from the computer screen provided enough light so that as he pulled out the sandwich baggie, he smiled to see it was roast beef, his favorite.

A mosquito flew in through the window. He swatted it against the dashboard and rolled the window up, when he heard a car coming from the east. He looked up and saw the black Audi A-4 eastbound on 674. This was not the norm. Most of the rural inhabitants had no inclination to own a foreign sports car in an area populated with dirt roads and farms. It was more likely some rich kids coming down from one of the trendy clubs in Ybor City. They were looking for meth or some trouble. He tossed the roast beef sandwich back into the cooler.

As the Audi approached, he decided the sports car earned a closer look. He pulled out without his headlights on, hoping to close the distance before the Audi took evasive measures. As he closed the distance to about fifty feet, he turned on his headlights, illuminating the license plate. Before he could get the entire plate, the Audi increased its speed and pulled away. At seventy-five miles an hour, Dallas engaged his overhead blue L.E.D lights that lit up the dark sky like a laser light show. The Audi's speed continued to increase as Dallas turned on his siren in the yelp mode and picked up his radio microphone.

"Two - Charlie - Seven, I'm in pursuit eastbound 674 towards 39 behind an Audi. You better give Polk County a call because I don't think anyone else is close."

The dispatcher called out for any units in the area. The radio was silent. Dallas knew the response before asking. He was alone, with no help. He was a nine-mile drive to the county line. Knowing he was about to engage in an adrenaline-pumping ride, Dallas would share the same thrill as the risk takers on the downhill drop of the steepest roller coaster at Busch Gardens. The laser light show and yelping siren increased the excitement. He had driven this road hundreds of times and always enjoyed the views of sleeping cattle and the structured rows of orange trees illuminated by the moonlight. At 100 miles an hour, he noticed nothing outside the focus of the road in front of him and the streaking black Audi. The broken white lines in the middle of the road seemed almost solid at this speed.

The sergeant's voice called over the radio, "Two-Charlie-Seven, what do you have him on?"

"Traffic only at this time, sir."

The dispatcher interrupted and saved Dallas from a supervisor, terminating the chase for safety reasons.

"Tampa is working a possible abduction. The victim's car is a black Audi. The license matches the first three characters of Charlie-Seven's suspect vehicle."

"10-4, be careful and start some additional units in that direction, and call Polk County and FHP, and see if they can help."

"Polk County has advised they have a unit south of Mulberry on 37 heading south, but they are about 12 miles away."

Dallas said, "I just passed Fort Lonesome at 39. Still on 674 eastbound, looks like he's heading towards 37."

Without notice, the Audi slammed on his brakes. Dallas locked up his brakes to avoid the imminent collision and the exploding airbag as the lunch cooler tumbled to the floorboard. His cruiser wiggled and, ever so slightly, the back end started sliding to the right. Just before impact, the Audi accelerated blowing out the residue in the exhaust. Dallas straightened the cruiser. Now driving in a two-footed manner, he released the brake and slammed his right foot to the floor on the gas pedal. The Dodge Charger responded like an F-18 leaping off the deck of the USS Enterprise.

"Son of a bitch."

His heart was thumping out of control, and his neck muscles were tighter than a cover of a drum. His white knuckled grip on the steering wheel tightened like a vise grip, as the Dodge's speedometer again reached triple digits. He closed the distance, but gave a larger cushion after the near miss. The Audi's brake lights illuminated again and Dallas lifted his right foot off the gas pedal.

"He is slowing down. Looks like we're going to be northbound on Bethlehem Road."

As he watched the Audi turn left, the front end of the fleeing car dipped off the side of the road. After striking a "No Truck" sign, the driver overcompensated and steered across to the left side of the road. The car slid back to the right side of the road and then came to a bone-jarring stop as it hit a tree stump hidden in the ditch. A cloud of dirt and debris blew over the top of the motionless Audi.

Dallas yelled into the microphone, "He's crashed!"

Dallas unlatched his seat belt, slid to a stop, and pulled on the door release as he observed a figure emerge from the wreckage. He pushed the door open and rolled out of the patrol unit. The suspect's stumbling dark figure turned towards Dallas and lifted his right arm. Dallas saw the flash from the barrel before he heard the bang from the handgun. The bullet struck the windshield, entering the driver's compartment and striking the seat cushion where Dallas had been sitting.

Dallas, already pulling his pistol from the holster, tightened his finger around the trigger. He knew he was in peril, and his only thought was if he was going to die, he was going to take this son of a bitch with him. He was leveling his weapon when the impact in his left shoulder felt like someone punched him. The gunfire continued as Dallas lost his balance and fell to the ground behind the open driver's door. His mind flashed to his wife, Anne, holding Jason in her arms. He would not die. He would not die. Pushing himself up, he used the car for cover. He inhaled through his mouth and exhaled through his nose. Dallas had to control his breathing. He looked over the top of the hood, fired six rounds toward the flashes, and continued firing at the now fleeing figure. There was silence and the powerful odor of gunpowder hanging in the air.

He could hear his heavy breathing and the radio traffic. He lunged into the car, pulled the microphone out, and shouted, "Two-Charli-Seven, shots fired! Start an ambulance. I've been shot. The subject has fled on foot northeast."

Reaching up, he pulled the shotgun down from its rack at the top of the cage separating the front and back seat. He could hear anxious chatter on the radio. Dallas uttered the words no cop wanted to hear on the radio. He knew everyone was on their way, including other agencies. A brother was in trouble. He knew residents were dialing 911 to report the sounds of gunfire. Help was coming.

There was a tingling sensation in his left arm. There was no time to check. He must live. He must get home to Anne and Jason. His fight-flight autonomic response engaged, as his blood was redirected towards the major organs away from the skin to reduce potential bleeding. The brain stem that houses primitive impulse behavior and modulates the fight-flight response had kicked into overdrive. His heart was pumping five times faster. His eye acuity increased. All for basic survival.

He ejected the magazine from his pistol and inserted a fresh one while saving the partially used one. Using the uninjured right arm, he jacked the slide of the shotgun, while balancing the butt of the weapon on the ground and depressing the slide release with left hand. He thought about staying where he was, but he knew help was a long way off, and this guy could come back and kill him.

He ran around the back of the car, trying to remain in the darkness and trying not to silhouette himself with the flashing lights in the background. He thought about turning them off, but decided they would be like the lighthouse, guiding distant sailors to safety. The responding units could find him. He controlled his breathing while his heart was pumping like a locomotive. He entered the orange grove away from any cover. The unripened fruit hung from the trees. He again smelled the citrus in the air. The trees provided little concealment or cover from the gunman. He knew he might have only one chance with the shotgun. If he missed, he would have to go back to his pistol. He walked with caution through the tall grass. It crunched under his boots.

As he exited the orange grove, suddenly floodlights illuminated the property in front of him and a barking German Sheppard raced out of the simple home. The headlights of the Audi peered through the orange trees towards the home. Dallas was careful to stay away from the streams of lights. He observed a figure in the field stand up and staggered forward. As the dog closed the distance, Dallas witnessed the muzzle flash directed at the dog. Dallas raised the front of the shotgun with his injured arm and pulled the trigger with his right. The blast rocked Dallas. He dropped the shotgun on the ground. Drawing his handgun from the holster, he rushed toward the suspect and the barking dog.

He could not see the figure hidden once again by the weeds. The dog was holding its ground ferociously, barking and defending its territory.

The homeowner was calling out to the dog, "Brutus! Brutus, come here."

The dog seemed confused. Brutus ran towards the house, stopped and turned towards the suspect, who was on the ground. His tail was in constant motion. Dallas closed the distance with caution as he placed one foot in front of another. His pistol was in the ready position with both hands clasped around the butt and his arms extended. He focused his stare on the figure on the ground. If the suspect moved, Dallas was prepared to empty his magazine from the Beretta 92F. As he moved to within ten feet, he could see the subject on his back in a patch of flattened weeds.

Dallas shouted, "Police, don't move or I'll shoot you again! Don't even think about it!"

He could see the pistol still gripped in the suspect's hand. He was not moving. As Dallas got closer, he could see the suspect look up with frantic eyes. He tried to speak, but only gurgled through his throat. Dallas removed the weapon from the suspect's clenched hand.

The shirtless property owner standing on the raised wooden porch hollered,

"Deputy, you, all right?"

"Yeah, yeah, I think so. How about your dog?"

"Brutus is ok."

Dallas could hear the sirens in the distance.

"Thank you, sir. You and Brutus saved my life. Thank you."

"I called 911 too. I didn't know what the hell was going on out here."

The seasoned EMT said, "You're a very lucky man. That bullet just hit the edge of your vest and ricocheted across your shoulder. It will hurt like hell for a few days. We'll get a doctor to take a look."

They stopped talking and covered their faces as the Med-Flight Helicopter lifted off the ground from a field across the street. Dust and grass blew across from the prop wash of the chopper. It labored into the air, carrying the wounded suspect. The front tilted toward the ground and moved towards the safety of Tampa as it gained elevation.

The EMT said looking up at the helicopter, "Good shooting. He is not doing too well. He could go either way."

Sergeant Jim Cassidy said, "Dallas you did good, man. Jennifer Kress, that poor girl he abducted from the mall in Tampa, didn't make it. We found her body in the trunk. Looks like he killed her before you found her. He was probably looking to dump her body out here somewhere. We might never have found her or caught this piece of garbage. You know, it looks like you hit him three times before the shotgun took him out. He must have been hyped on meth. It wouldn't let him go down. His name was David Stilts. He had some priors for drugs and a not guilty of attempted kidnapping. I wish I had the same judge for my divorce. Our homicide folks are on the way and two TPD homicide detectives." He strained to read his writing and said, "Detective Alexander and Hamilton."

The reality hit home. Dallas's voice cracked with emotion. "I just want to go home and hug Anne and Jason."

"I know." Cassidy took a deep breath and repeated, "I know."

He placed his huge hand on Dallas's shoulder and continued, "I know you felt alone out here. You were." There was a long silence. "I'll get someone to ride with you to the hospital. Why don't you give Anne a call in a few minutes and let her know you are all right? I've got Sampson on the way to pick her up. She doesn't need to be driving alone."

Chapter Four

MONDAY - TWO YEARS LATER

The driver of the black Escalade drove with eager anticipation, as he glanced over at the smiling blonde. He guided the expensive status symbol toward the ritualistic site of their sinful pleasures.

It was one of those Mom and Pop motels long since forgotten by the interstate highway system. The Pirate's Cove Motel was announced by a weathered sign of a patched eyed pirate, whose once black accents were now a bleached gray from the hot Tampa sun and driving afternoon heating showers. The formerly manicured grass in which the sign stood was now a jungle of weeds. The sparsely used parking lot surrounded the "U" shaped motel.

Scraping the undercarriage on the driveway, the black Escalade turned into the driveway apron and paused. The passenger door opened and a shapely blond stepped out of the black SUV. Her stiletto heels click across the asphalt parking lot to the glass doors. A neon sign illuminated "Vacancy Office." The Escalade continued to the same spot it always entered in front of room number sixteen. The last room in the back was difficult to see from the road. The drooping and overgrown oak trees that once provided shade to the deserted swimming pool now provided discreet camouflage for their noon tryst.

Raj Patel, the middle-aged desk clerk, flicked his straight black hair off his forehead as he watched *The People's Court* on the 12" TV screen. As the attractive visitor approached the glass door to the office, Raj looked away from Judge Milian, rendering a decision. The hotel owner recognized the frequent visitor and was relieved it would be a temporary interruption. He smiled and handed her the silver key with the attached green plastic oval embossed with the white number sixteen. She returned the smile, handed him thirty dollars, turned, and walked out without a word. Raj turned back for the final verdict on the *People's Court*.

As she approached room number sixteen, the driver exited the car and chirped the alarm pad on the key fob. He admired the curvy blonde strutting with confidence towards the den of sin. She raised her right arm, and holding the key, she jingled it like a bell. He returned the anxious smile, as he admired the smoldering beauty. The driver joined the blonde at the room door, as she leaned down to insert the key into the door. He stared at her bulging chest. The rarely oiled and over painted hinges creaked as she opened the door. He followed her into the cheap room. The musty odor hit the nostrils, and the sunlight illuminated the dark room.

He eagerly waited for the disrobing, as a child anticipates ripping the paper off a birthday present. He pushed the door closed and switched on the button to the room air-conditioner to high. He turned, grabbed the blonde around the thin waist, pulled her toward him, and began kissing her passionately. In moments, they freed themselves from their clothes, littering them on the soiled maroon carpeting.

She pushed her lover sideways across the full-size bed and crawled like a cat after its prey. She sat on his hips and ran her hands through her blonde wavy locks as she closed her eyes and moaned with pleasure. He heard a crack. Suddenly, the blonde collapsed forward and tumbled to the floor. He sat up and called out to her, "What the hell? Are you all right?"

There was no response. The panic raced through his mind like a person falling off a cliff. He jumped out of the bed. He reached down and shook the shoulders of her naked body.

"Oh God, no, oh no, oh God."

In the dimly lit room, a dark tar looking fluid now matted her blonde waves. He touched the fluid and looked at his fingers in disbelief. The blood pooled on the carpet next to her lifeless body. He screamed, but his voice froze with his fright. His heart raced like a greyhound coming into the final stretch. His knees buckled, and he collapsed to the floor. Everything appeared in slow motion. He could not hear a sound. He looked around and observed daylight peeking through a finger size hole in the brown curtain shielding the window.

He frantically dressed and peered out from behind the curtain like a nosy old neighbor. He noticed the hole in the window glass. He grabbed one towel from the bathroom and wiped the door handle and everything else he touched. He dragged open the creaking door, as he peered out like a criminal peering out of an alley. He detected no movement.

He bolted for the Escalade. He hit the door open button and jumped into the leather seat, and hit the ignition before the door closed. He slammed the shift in reverse, as he stared at room number three and glanced back at his vacated room. Without hitting the brake, he slammed the shift selector into drive and pushed the gas pedal with his wobbly foot. He screeched onto Nebraska Avenue as Raj Patel continued to watch the last segment of *The Peoples Court.*

Chapter Five

S ergeant Alfonso Stewart answered the phone with a soft voice that contradicted his large frame. "Homicide, Sergeant Stewart." The former football linebacker scribbled some notes and ended the call. He made two additional phone calls. He stepped out of his office and looked up at the whiteboard that adorned the front wall of the squad room. The board contained a list of the previous homicides for last year and the current year. He didn't need to read the board. He had the list memorized. The squad room looked like a narrow pool hall. Eight desks looked like pool tables waiting for the next customer. Various police patches decorated the far wall. A blank white wall was opposite to a wall of windows overlooking the city skyline. He decided on the next victim.

Detective Kate Alexander dropped her black gym bag with the PBA logo under her desk. She picked up the purple Gatorade and began gulping. Beads of condensation dropped from the bottle. She savored the grape flavor.

"Kate!"

She looked over at the imposing figure standing in his office door as she flicked her brown bangs off her face.

"Yes, sir."

"You're up. Have a double at the Pirate's Cove Motel up on Nebraska. I just called crime scene, and the M.E.. Take Bridges, Rollins, and Duffy with you. I'll be out there shortly."

Kate looked at her watch and noted the time of 2:36PM. She picked up the black phone and punched in some numbers.

An older female voice with a southern drawl answered, "Hello"

"Hi Mom. I'm going to be late, very late."

"Do you have any idea?"

"No, not yet. How is Britney feeling?"

"She has her ups and downs. Don't worry."

"Mothers have a right?"

"Yes. An obligation."

"Remember to give her the antibiotic at bedtime and kiss her good night for me. Thanks Mom and I love you."

"Okay and I love you too baby, and be careful."

"I will."

Kate hung up the phone and looked out the long bank of windows at the skyline of downtown Tampa. Sometimes she questioned the demands of her job. She had been a cop for almost ten years. She enjoyed the job. She loved the excitement and the occasional rush of adrenaline. The brotherhood of cops was a constant source of entertainment, and companionship in a lonely world. Once again, her daughter was going to bed without her mother tucking her under the covers. Sure, she was going to solve another person's premature death and arrest the perpetrator, but was it worth the personal cost to her daughter? Most of the victims were not much better than the dirt bag that killed them. It was a thinning of the herd. Two mopes off the street. One in a coffin and one in shackles. Despite her cynical view, she still viewed her position as the final voice for the deceased. An advocate for the dead and everyone of the victims deserved to be heard. She walked past the memorial to two homicide detectives, Randy Childers and Ricky Bell. It was always a reminder to the dangers of the job. They did not make it to the end of the shift, dying in a hail of gunfire.

Chapter Six

K ate stepped out of the black Charger with Kyle Bridges. Officer Jimmy Severands walked up with a big smile accented against the dark blue uniform.

"Kate, how are you doing?"

"Happier than the only cheerleader in a football locker room."

"Well, you won't be so happy after this one. I hope you're up for a good one."

"Remember, my initials 'K.A.' stands for Kick Ass."

"How could I forget? You're going to have to do some ass kicking today. The manager calls to report a body dead from a gunshot. We get here and find not one but two corpses. One in two different rooms. Here is how it went down. It looks like one, Thomas Maguire, he has been a tenant for a couple of weeks, took one execution style in the head. There was a second round fired. It went through the window and traveled across the lot and through the window in unit number sixteen. It hits this good-looking chick inside the room. Looks like maybe she was pumping a John. Bad day for her. Her John left without a word. When I first arrived on scene, I thought Maguire tried to blow his brains out, but the weapon grew legs and left. Then the manager runs over to me and points to Blondie's room. He tells me he has found another body. He was going to clean the room. The manager, Raj Patel, pulls a Sergeant Schultz on us. I know nothing."

"Thanks Jimmy. Oh, any idea what time this happened?"

"After 11:30. Miss Blondie checked in. I already checked. No registration card. She comes in a couple of times a week, pays cash and always stays in sixteen. She drops the key off an hour or two later. Raj gets suspicious after a few hours and comes to make sure she is gone, so he can change the sheets. Bingo. He finds her stiffer than a poker. We get here and find the other corpse. Checked for other witnesses. There was a guy in number ten sleeping off a hard night, but he was pretty well out of it. I'll leave it up to you to canvass across the street."

"Thanks Jimmy. Good seeing you again."

"Always my pleasure."

Kate walked toward the first crime scene room, number three, as she reached into her messenger bag and pulled out cloth booties and latex gloves.

Chapter Seven

The slender but athletic figure of Detective Lester Rollins stood in the doorframe and peered into the interior of room number three, absorbing some of the air-conditioning. He flipped his notebook open and said,

"Hey, Kate."

She was leaning over the black trash can in the unassuming motel room, stood up and looked at the door.

Rollins waved his hand past his face and said, "Whew! This place smells like an old locker room."

"Yep, it's ripe for sure. We might find some mushrooms growing."

"I checked on the tenant. Thomas Maguire, resident dirt bag. He has been in and out of trouble for the last fifteen years. Typical escalation. Simple thefts, to burglaries, to robberies. In between some drug charges tied to meth. Looks like he has been out of Starke Penitentiary for a year on a robbery conviction. Did a little probation wake-up for a couple of months in the county and he has been out for a few weeks."

"Yep, that makes sense. He has already made up for lost time. He was definitely back on methamphetamines."

With her hand shrouded in blue latex, she reached into the trashcan like a magician sticking his hand inside the hat. She held up a syringe and said, "He ripped someone or failed to pay a debt. Looks like the shooter came, and they had a discussion. No signs of forced entry, so he let the shooter come in. Someone Maguire knew. Looks like they have a disagreement and struggle over control of the gun. The first round goes through his left hand. Since his watch is on his left hand, he is right-handed. He probably has both hands wrestling with the gun. His strong hand being the right, grabbed the meat of the gun, and with the left he grabbed the barrel and it discharged."

"You know, he screamed like a cat being pulled by the tail."

"Yep. Maguire probably lost control, and the shooter puts the gun up to his head and lights out. You can see the tattooing of the gunpowder and star around the wound. Therefore, it was within a few inches. The first-round travels through the window across the courtyard, hits Blondie, and takes her out as well. It has to be the shot of the decade. Our own snipers couldn't have done that. Two shots and two kills."

"Even with all the training those hut-hut boys do, they couldn't make that shot."

"All right, let's find out who his probation officer is, and check with the jail, and find out if he had any beefs and who his cell mates were. He pissed someone off. We know he grabbed the gun, but maybe he scraped some DNA off his killer. The carpet was like a sponge. It is a good reference mark. There was no movement after he fell."

"Yep, D.R.T. Dead Right There."

"For sure. It looks like the head shot was an in and out. Let's look and see if we can find the round."

They stepped over the body wearing their protective booties on their feet. Kate shined a hand size black flashlight and said, "It looks like it hit the chair."

She examined the back of the seat and observed the fabric protruding from the path of the bullet. Her flashlight illuminated a bullet pancaked into the cement block wall. "Here it is, but it won't be much help. We'll let crime scene dig it out of the wall. Either the shooter picked up the shell casings, or he used a revolver."

"You don't see many revolvers anymore."

"Maybe he is old fashion or careful. Let's say the shooter was facing the victim here. The casings would have been discharged to the right, towards the door or the dresser."

Kate shined the light along the baseboard and behind the dresser. Rollins and Kate pulled the dresser from the wall to allow more room. Gum wrappers, popcorn kernels and other trash littered the ground. The flashlight illuminated the cobwebs attached to the wall. Still no casing.

Chapter Eight

S tepping back into the bright sun, Kate walked across the searing asphalt, heading toward room sixteen. The air smelled like rain. She heard the thunder and looked up, squinting. In the distance, percolating clouds the color of charcoal advanced towards the crime scene. Great, that's just what she needed. An afternoon torrential downpour, while they run back and forth with rain gear that never seemed to keep them dry.

As she entered the next death room, Kyle Bridges and Frank Duffy were examining the crime scene. Duffy, squatting like a catcher, looked up at Kate as she entered the room. Tucked inside his white starched shirt was his bright blue tie with equally bright orange accents. This kept one of his noted ties from accidentally becoming a sponge.

Duffy said, "We don't have a clue who Blondie was. We can pass her photo around with Intel and Narcotics. Maybe they will recognize her."

Kate said, "She looks too clean to be a working girl or a stripper."

"I agree, but she wasn't tanning herself in here. There are a couple of places up the street we might check."

"The ahh, ahh, ..."

"The Gypsy Lounge and the Candy Factory."

"Duffy, now why did I know you would know the name of the place?"

"Because I am always a wealth of knowledge."

"Yeah right. I don't think she is going to fall in with the usual cast of characters or working girls. I think she was doing someone, and they were looking for a little privacy. She comes in twice a week and always gets the same room. We are not talking about a beach view at the Ritz. You can hardly see out on the road because of the trees, weeds, and fence." She pointed to the discarded garments and said, "Her clothes are not from a discount store. She was wearing Kenneth Cole shoes and an Antonio Melani suit. Most working girls couldn't afford that."

Frank smiled, shook his head, and said, "Kate, you are quite useful to have around. I had my doubts when you first came to the squad, but now I know your usefulness. Next time my wife's birthday is coming up, I'll take you shopping."

"I'd love too. Spending someone else's money. How exciting! Because the only way I know these brands is window-shopping. I am sure Bridget tires of the useful gifts from Home Depot."

"Hey, last year, she loved that vacuum cleaner."

"I'm sure she did. Blondie either left her high-priced purse in the John's car or he took it. Allow me to point out another thing that most men would not pickup on." She pointed with her index finger. "She is wearing a nice wedding set. That's a full carat marquis cut. Not exactly cheap."

Kate thumbed the ring finger of her own right hand. She touched her wedding set on her right hand. She felt the vacant spot on the left hand where she once proudly displayed her commitment to marriage.

"Someone should claim her before the day is over, unless she is wearing the rings to keep the deadbeats like you away."

Frank sighed, "You see. This is what I'll never understand. What was that book, Men are from the Moon or something? I have given up figuring you ladies out, and I live in a house full of them."

"It's Mars, and let's get the medical examiner to roll her prints."

Kate walked outside and called her mother. She again apologized, but after assessing the scene, she knew it would be a very late night. She then called Sergeant Stewart to check what his estimated arrival time would be. She jotted a few notes and walked back inside.

Deborah Shook, an experienced crime scene analyst, was crouched down holding a dusting brush and looking closely at the door handle, while her partner Jason Wade snapped photos of the room.

Kate asked, "Deborah, how's it going?"

She stood up and tossed her head back to flick her platinum locks off her face. "Not well. It looks like he wiped all the surfaces. You can see the lint from the towel. We have collected the used towels and sheets for DNA and fibers."

"Good. So, someone is trying to cover their trail."

Duffy's jovial face beamed as he said, "I am glad to hear you used an asexual term."

She bowed in feigned respect and said, "We'll have to check with Mr. Patel and see if any towels are missing. I am sure he counts them like gold heirlooms. Thanks Deborah."

The on-call Medical Examiner, David Tresswick, arrived. The light reflected off his bald spot on top of his head. He jotted some notes, asked some questions, and snapped a few photos. With the help of Duffy, they slowly rolled the naked body. The back of her head had a bullet hole at the base of her skull. They observed two other identifying marks. A tattoo with jumping dolphins inscribed on her lower back at the waistband. A second tattoo would be more beneficial. A heart with the name Chuck inscribed on her right butt cheek.

Kate said, "I feel sorry for Chuck."

Frank sighed. "Maybe Chuck was old news. I don't understand the thrill of these tattoos."

"They call them body art."

His eyebrows lifted. "You have one?"

"No reason." She shooed a fly out of her face.

Duffy stood up and arched his back. He brushed his hand through his thick brown hair and looked down at the victim.

"You know, whoever was banging her had good taste."

"Thanks for you input Frank."

"Hey, remember, I am here to help. Homicide all the way. Our day begins when your day ends."

"You know you should show some compassion."

"Yeah, like she did for Chuck or whoever her husband was."

"She still didn't deserve to die."

The silent Kyle Bridges came out of the restroom, adjusted his black-rimmed glasses and said, "The bathroom looks clean"

"Thanks, Kyle."

"You're welcome, Kate."

Sergeant Stewart arrived carrying the foam carrier tray with four Starbucks for everyone. The scent of the robust coffee acted as an air-freshener.

He asked Kate, "What have we got so far?"

Kate filled him with the known and unknown details. She told him of the investigative leads.

Tresswick pushed his black-rimmed glasses up his nose and said, "Yep, she is dead." He winked at the detectives and walked outside.

Kate shot back, "Big help, thanks."

He waved as he hustled across the parking lot to the medical examiner's van.

Chapter Nine

The four detectives walked back to room number three as the first fat raindrops pelted the pavement. The wind blew at their backs with strength. As they entered the room, Lester stood up, holding a driver's license, and said, "You know this dirt bag's birthday is tomorrow."

Duffy, with a sinister grin, said, "Ah, that's a shame. Why don't we sing him happy birthday?"

Sergeant Stewart quietly protested, "Oh man, that's not right. That's cold."

Frank Duffy kneeled down on the floor and pulled Maguire's upper and lower lip like a veterinarian examining a horse.

"Looky here. Meth mouth."

It was one of those sights where you would lose your appetite looking at the advanced decay of the yellow and brown teeth.

Lester Rollins walked outside to use his cell phone. The storm disrupted the phone coverage as Rollins angled his body to achieve more bars on the phone display. He cursed in defiance, popped open a black umbrella overhead and continued to complete the telephone calls. Shaking off the rain while collapsing the umbrella, he stepped back inside the room.

He said, "Maguire's P.O. is gone for the day. His supervisor said he will be back in the morning."

Kate, with her hands on her hips, struck a defiant pose and said, "I am sorry, but that's unacceptable. I would like to be at home with my family. We have a double homicide and they're telling us to take two aspirin and we'll see you in the morning. Well, that ain't going to fly. If we have a name, we will go knock on his door tonight."

Duffy said, "Yeah baby, that's what I am talking about!"

Rollins rubbed his fingers over his mustache and goatee and said, "It's Ralph Sanchez. I'll work on it. I have a list of Maguire's cellmates. There are ten. One is dead of a heart attack, four are in the penitentiary, four more are still in county and one is out."

Duffy said, "That leaves, what, four to talk to?"

Bridges said, "Five."

Duffy ignored the correction. "Who is the one that is out?"

"Octavious Singleton."

"I know Octavious Singleton. I popped him back when I was working dope. He has a mean streak. He wasn't a very good shot unless you were in the backdrop. He used to throw them bullets out of the gun while he was hanging on to his pants. I chased him on foot once."

Rollins laughed, flashing his brilliant white teeth, shook his head, and said, "I would have paid to watch that one. Some old fat white dude chasing a brother that is a fleeing felon."

"Well, smart ass. For your information, it was a short chase. His baggy shorts fell to his ankles, and he fell face first. He tried to get up, but he fell again. His wheels were spinning faster than a truck stuck in mud, but he wasn't going anywhere fast. So, this old fat white dude caught the brother." As he patted his softening stomach with pride, he said, "It took me nearly forty years to sculpt this body. It simply was not a single night of success. Now, getting back to Octavious, before I was so rudely interrupted, I could see him popping someone in the head over a debt. We can go pay him a visit. He was staying with his girlfriend in the Robles Park projects. We can call communications and see if they can get a more current address."

Sergeant Stewart spoke, "All right, let's go find a good address for Octavious. In the meantime, I agree with Kate that we should make a house call to Maguire's P.O.. Since this is one shooter, it's one case with two homicides. It's all yours Kate. Duffy and Rollins, you guys knock on doors across the street and see if anyone saw anything."

Kate put down her coffee on a table and roughed out a quick crime scene sketch. The crime scene folks would complete a detailed sketch using a mapping system.

This was the part of the job that jazzed Kate. She got into the zone. It was an adrenaline rush to put the pieces together, come up with a clearer picture, and come closer to solving the crime and thinning the herd. She enjoyed hanging out with "the guys" and the constant banter back and forth.

She enjoyed the respect she earned from her male counterparts. It wasn't always easy. Duffy was the tough one. The ex-New York Cop was her biggest critic, not belligerent, but in a scrutinizing way. He was now a banner waver for her. She proved herself repeatedly. She could hold her own at Hattrick's Pub. She didn't care for Guinness, but she ordered it for the first time as her own initiation into the club. She drank it with pride, ordered a second round, and saluted Duffy. His Irish smile and red cheeks beamed back at her. She was in.

Chapter Ten

K ate Alexander and Kyle Bridges walked up the sidewalk towards the probation officer's simple one-story house. The white blockhouse with the nearly flat roof was in a quiet neighborhood just north of Lowery Park Zoo. Like the zoo, there were bars on the windows.

The thunderstorms had moved on, leaving clear skies and an air thick with humidity. She looked over at Bridges shuffling along in his penny loafers in need of shoe polish. His thin, short-sleeved white shirt was damp from perspiration.

She thought it would be nice if he would wear a t-shirt under his dress shirt, if you could call it that. She admired his indifference to competing with some others in their high-quality stylish suits. He just didn't care. As a former reporter for the Toledo Blade, he wanted warmer weather and moved to Tampa fifteen years earlier. He possessed great report writing and analytical skills. Someone remarked that his tenure with the Blade was writing the obituaries and his personality was right for the job.

She knew the P.O.'s carried huge caseloads for low State wages. Many start out believing they are making a difference, but in short order they fall victim to burnout from frustration. Many use the job as an entry-level position to another law enforcement position. She noted the red tricycle on the side of the small house. She softened her hostility at working late and being away from Britney, while this person was at home with his kids. Why should everyone be miserable?

They knocked on the screen door. A late twenty something man with dark hair and skin opened the door. Two rambunctious boys played in the background. Something smelled good in the kitchen.

"Hi, Ralph Sanchez? I'm Kate Alexander with TPD and this is Kyle Bridges. I would apologize for disturbing you at home, but we had a double homicide in which one of your case files is six feet under."

"That's okay."

"His name was Maguire."

"Yep, he's one of mine. In fact, I just received a notice of his rehabilitation that he was back-out. Well, that is one more I can cross off my list."

"What can you tell me about him?"

"I have to look at his file. He was a cranker. He went through one period where he looked like he was going to be okay. He was working as a landscaper. However, he fell off the wagon and came up with some dirty urine. The surprising part was he always had a public defender, but that time Melvin Storms represented him."

"Thee Melvin Storms?"

"It was like having a battleship show up to blow up a raft. I don't know if Storms was doing some pro bono work or not. Maguire didn't have that kind of money."

"Did you ask Maguire?"

"Nah, I thought about it, but once he went back in, he was no longer my problem. I have a lot more just like Maguire and the State will not pay the overtime that you folks get."

"Any next of kin or associates?"

"I don't think so. I think he's from Alabama or Mississippi. He was a transient type. He moved around between here and Polk County. I don't think he was ever married. I would have to look in his file."

"Thanks for your help."

"No problem."

They walked down the uneven sidewalk to the car in silence.

Bridges drove towards the projects to meet up with Duffy, Rollins, and Stewart. The sky now looked like a kaleidoscope of colors as the sun set on the city.

"What do you make of Melvin Storms?" asked Kate.

"He is an attorney. That's all you need to know."

She said, "He is not some bottom feeder. He may be a sleaze bucket like most lawyers, but he does not come cheap. Maybe one of Maguire's family members hit the Lotto. Storms is usually working with the heavy hitters, organized crime, cartel types, or dirty politicians."

"You think Maguire prior to falling off the wagon, somehow got connected?"

"I just don't see it. Maguire is a low-level mope. Someone was putting the money up."

"Why?"

"That is the $64,000 question." She said.

Chapter Eleven

B ridges pulled into the parking lot of a convenience store down the street from the projects. Duffy, Rollins, and Sergeant Stewart were standing outside their cars. The three unmarked cars caused the locals to give scrutinizing stares as they walked in and out of the store and slipped their money under the Plexiglas enclosure.

Duffy handed out photos of Octavious and said, "I confirmed he is either staying with his girlfriend or his momma. Neither one is official, because they don't want to get kicked out having him as a permanent resident. He will rabbit on us. We had better have an air unit, and we have a couple of uniforms on the way. Narcotic's is busy and can't help."

Two marked units arrived. Sergeant Stewart gave out the assignments. They would split-up and half would go to the front door, while the others would watch the back. The assignments in the rear would have greater exposure to harm's way. He made sure everyone was wearing a ballistic vest.

"Let's rock n roll. Ready set break! I am sorry I still get flashbacks to the huddle."

They all smiled at the attempt to cut the tension.

Kyle drove, with Kate following one of the marked patrol units. They would go to the front door. As they drove down Central Avenue, they passed the rows of two-story pink buildings surrounded by four-foot white iron fencing. The parade of cars turned on Lake Street. Every resident's eye locked on the patrol unit and then on the white Dodge. Groups of residents instinctively shuffled apart, not knowing where the attention of the police would focus.

One such group under an oak tree lost their smiles as the caravan approached. Kate's eyes locked onto one youth with a long goatee, who looked away.

"There he is. Stop the car!"

She jumped out of the car and yelled over to him. "Octavious don't even think of running!"

It was too late. Octavious clutching his waistband was striding like an antelope across the grass towards the parking lot and towards freedom. He failed to realize a cheetah was chasing him.

The patrol unit stopped. He had to back up through oncoming traffic, oblivious to the common sight of the overhead red and blue lights lighting the darkness. Kyle, also on foot, was on his handheld radio barking out a foot pursuit and requesting air support. Rollins abandoned the driver's seat of his car and was in full stride to help Kate.

Duffy, acknowledging his inability to catch the fleeing Octavious, ran around to the driver's side and took control of the car. Sergeant Stewart took command and ordered all unnecessary traffic to stay off the radio. Kate's hand-held radio lay in the front seat of the now abandoned unmarked car.

One of the youth's wide eyed and smiling, said, "Look at that bitch run." Kate yelled at Octavious, "Police stop!"

She yelled loud enough so that everyone in the neighborhood could testify that she announced who she was and what she wanted before she shot him. He did not stop, and he continued to run like the pursued antelope, rapidly changing directions. Youth and fear were his advantage. Every time she yelled, "I'm going to shoot you," he would look back over his shoulder. He continued clutching his baggy pants to keep from tripping. Fashion has its price. She closed the distance.

She no longer heard the jeers from the residents, many who were now stepping outside to view the spectacle. It was just about the time the helicopter lit up Octavious with the spotlight that he jagged back to the right, and Kate tackled him just like her Sergeant had crushed many a running back in his pro football days. Octavious hit the ground with a thud. The marked unit that was having trouble navigating through uncooperative motorists pulled up to assist Kate. Rollins coasted to a stop and helped Kate cuff Octavious's two wrists that she had locked behind his back.

"Damn girl, you can run. You're almost as fast as me." Rollins said.

As she gasped for air, she said, "Thanks. Coming from you, that is quite a compliment."

The youths were all laughing at Octavious. "You fool a poleece women out ran you man!"

"Shut up!"

The helicopter hovered overhead like a gunship in Afghanistan. It was a different war zone. Kyle finally caught up. He was huffing and puffing like an old cigarette smoker, and his shirt was again soaked in perspiration. He helped Octavious to the back seat of the police car for transport back to the office.

Kate looking over at Duffy as she sucked wind into her tired lungs and said, "That is another reason I don't wear Kenneth Cole shoes"

Chapter Twelve

S lumped down in the sterile gray metal chair of the interrogation room of the homicide squad, Octavious almost fell asleep. He looked bored as he stroked his goatee. Duffy and Kate entered the room. She pulled her flowing brown hair into a ponytail.

Octavious sat up, leaned forward, and said, "What am I charged with? I want my attorney. I ain't sayen nothin. I'm just minding my own business and you all go to jumpin on me for no reason. I need to go to the bathroom. My civil rights been violated."

Kate, ignoring Octavious, said, "You know Octavious, you run like the wind. I thought I would never catch you. If you weren't hanging on to your pants, there is no way I could have caught you. You must have played some ball in the day."

"Yeah."

"I also know if you had done something wrong, you would have been a lot faster than me. I could tell it was hot, and you were thinking I ain't going to waste my time running from something I didn't do."

"You got that right." He sat taller.

Duffy admired Kate's approach. She is smooth. She let this guy save face and he is going to talk. Duffy smiled and jumped on board.

"Octavious, I have chased you before."

Octavious looked at Duffy in bewilderment. "I ain't run from you."

"Yes, you did. You sold me a rock."

"Oh man you Mr. Duffy. I know you."

"Yes, you do. I agree with Detective Alexander. I have seen you run when you are motivated. You were either hurting tonight or not in the mood."

"Yeah man."

Kate said, "You know we planned to ask you some questions about a friend of yours and let you go home, but now you said you wanted an attorney and don't want to talk to us, so we will charge you with fleeing and work it out between your attorney and the State Attorney."

"What kind of questions? If I answer your question, will you let me go?"

"As long as you tell us the truth."

"Start asking Mrs. Detective."

"Thomas Maguire."

"He ain't no friend. That cracker ain't nothing but a tweaker."

"He is a dead cracker. We know you shared a cell with him in the county."

"All I know is he'd been braggin about a big score. People say that all the time. It's like people sayin I am inside jail cause they made a mistake. He was like me. We're street people. We don't do big scores. Man, I'm just trying to survive. It's like people dreamin of hitting the Lotto. It ain't never going to happen. I asked him what kind of score, but his lips were sealed. I figured he was full of it."

"Do you know who his connection was?"

"I ain't into meth man, and we wasn't exactly the United Nations. If you catch my drift."

"I appreciate your help. Just like I promised, I'm going to get a patrol car to take you home."

"Are you trying to kill me? They all think I've been giving the 411 down here."

"All right. I get an unmarked car to drop you off wherever you would like inside the city."

"That's cool. You ok, Mrs. Poleece Lady."

Rollins and Bridges returned to the squad room from the county jail after interviewing Maguire's last cellmate, Rolando Salinas.

"Well, how did it go?" asked Kate

Rollins took his jacket off and hung it on the back of his chair with care. He traced the outline of his mustache and goatee with his thumb and finger.

He said, "Maguire told Salinas he was working for a landscaper and was making connections with big people. No specifics. One of them talked to him about a big caper. Again, no specifics."

Chapter Thirteen

A t the urging of Duffy, the two detectives walked down the stairs to narcotics. Frank felt that if this was drug related, one of his old partners might come up with some information.

Clyde Billings was sitting at a desk writing some notes while talking on the telephone. He knew more about drugs than most pharmacists at CVS. His long brown hair on the sides compensated for the lack of cover on top and almost obscured the dangling buccaneer earring. The proud illustrations of a local tattoo artist adorned his thick arms. Due to his appearance, he blended with the 1-percenter motorcyclists and the trailer park variety of meth heads, tweakers, crankers, or whatever else you wanted to call them. Clyde worked narcotics for fifteen of his nineteen years on the department. The hard life of a narcotics detective had not been kind to his face. He looked older than his forty-three years.

Kate said, "Did you get a tax deduction for the artwork on those arms?"

He looked up at Kate. His skin looked like parched mud flats with plenty of cracks and wrinkles. He put the telephone down. "No, just the earring, but that is a good point. I'll have to check with H & R Block."

"Are you ever coming out of here?"

"Nope. Not by choice. Where else can I ride a Harley and hang out in bars all night while being paid? I think after I have my time, I might retire and get a job as the sergeant of arms for the Hells Angels. Besides, with the new policy of the Chief, I would have to have these tats lasered off or wear sleeves."

Frank shook hands with his old friend. Their smiles of recognition were also signs of the respect that each cop had for one another and the hallowed ground they shared.

Clyde said, "Dude you better give up those M&M's. You've put on a couple of pounds."

Frank shuffled and blushed slightly and said, "Yeah, with everything going on at home, I haven't been hitting the gym and combined with too many pulls on Mr. M&M."

Clyde's face tightened as he asked Frank, "How is Bridget?"

Franks smiled dulled as he reflected about his wife and said, "She starts chemo next week. They are going to wait to do the implants for a while. I guess to make sure they got everything. It spread pretty good. Ole Bridget said she is going to look like Dolly Parton after it's over."

"Good for her." Clyde turned towards Kate. "Hey, does he still have those post-it notes all over his desk?"

Kate said, "Absolutely."

"It was amazing how I could ask him about someone and he would go through all these post-it notes that he had in some disorganized order and find what I was talking about."

Frank changed the topic. "Are you still with Mary?"

"No, she threw me out six months ago. I am learning. I don't marry them anymore. It's a lot easier."

"And how is Kevin?"

"He is in his fourth year at Annapolis. Can you imagine me showing up for his graduation?"

They all laughed at the mental picture with the white caps thrown in the air and Clyde standing amongst all the neat crisp young midshipmen.

Clyde said, "Hey I know you guys are not here to check with the human PDR about some illicit narcotic."

Kate said, "PDR?"

"You know the Physicians Desk Reference. Well, anyway, what can I do for you?"

Frank asked, "Thomas Maguire, ring a bell?"

He looked up as if he was checking his brain and then shook his head. "No, I don't know him. Meth?"

"That's his favorite."

Clyde rubbed his stubble on his chin. "Nah, Sorry."

Kate said, "We would like to know who his supplier was?"

"Give me his info and I'll check around. Is he a victim or suspect?"

"Victim up at the Pirate's Cove."

"Oh, that was the one where the broad was banging her paramour and caught an alibi in the head."

"You got it."

"Isn't that amazing? I don't think I have ever seen anything like that before."

"One other thing, when he went away on the probation violation, his attorney was Melvin Storms."

"Man, that is some serious jack. These people don't have those types of resources. That should be easy to ask about, but it may take a few days. Was he a biker or wannabe?"

"Neither. Not that we know of."

"Okay, I'll get back to you."

Frank said, "Thanks. We'll have to do lunch."

"You buy I'll fly. Later."

As they entered the stairwell, Kate sprinted up the stairs, as Frank labored behind. She smiled as they returned to their desks.

Chapter Fourteen

Sergeant Stewart stepped out of his office, leaned his arm against the door frame and said, "We just received a missing person report from District Two on a female that just happened to be blonde. It could be our victim. Here is the address. I told missing persons to hold off until they hear from you. Patrol is still out there. Kate and Lester, you go talk to him. I am heading home. Call me to let me know."

As Kate shifted the Charger into drive in the police garage, Rollins said, "If we are riding together, we are going to have to turn off this country stuff." He reached over and turned off the radio.

"Excuse me." As she pushed the power button. "What would you like to listen to? Cardi B, Megan Thee Stallion, Big Sean, or some other hip hop back yo ass up crap."

"No man. I don't like that stuff either. I appreciate better music. Like Lou Rawls, God rest his soul, Barry White, the Righteous Brothers are good for white dudes or Ryan Farish. It is musical foreplay. I am telling you I put that stuff on the speakers and the girls are dropping their clothes."

"You're full of it. You never been married, have you?"

"Why get married? I have an entire harem. If one causes problems, I just fire them and find a replacement."

"Just like that?"

"Yep, just like that."

"You're just a piece of work. Don't you ever feel like growing old together like that couple over there?"

She pointed towards an elderly couple holding hands, walking past Sacred Heart Church. Hordes of homeless men huddled in the doorway overhang. Too comfortable to get up from their shelter, they begged the couple for money from a distance. The couple growing old together politely declined. Kate never heard the response from Lester as she looked down at her empty left ring finger.

"Girl, where are you?"

"Huh oh, ah punch the second button that will give you 98.7 Smooooooth Jazz."

"So, you do have class. Now speaking of that, you looked like a world-class sprinter chasing Octavious. Where did you learn to run like that?"

"Cross country. I ran at Duke. I got a patchwork of scholarships and a good education. Didn't you get a scholarship?"

"Yeah, but not at a blue blood school. I went to FAMU in Tallahassee. I played second base and an education. I am the first one in my family to get a degree."

"You grew up over here in Central Park?"

"I tell you I would ride my bike almost five miles to Lowery Park Zoo every weekend to work at one of the concession stands. Billy Tubbs was the manager. He tried to shoo me off by telling me I was too young and needed a work permit from the city. So, I rode to city hall, got the permit and rode back to the neighborhood, got my momma to sign it and went back to Billy. He couldn't believe it. He gave me a job on the spot. Billy let me set my schedule around football and baseball. When I went to FAMU, he would let me work during the summers. And look at me now." As he spread his arms and shined his teeth.

They grinned in unison.

"You're a success story. That's great."

"I know."

"While they tore down the projects, you have risen above ashes. Where's your mom living?"

"Seminole Heights."

"That's nice."

Chapter Fifteen

K ate parked the Charger behind the marked unit. The officer in the dark blue uniform briefed them and said that Chuck Morris was expecting them and to let themselves in. What made this death notification worse was that not only was the husband receiving a crushing blow that his wife was dead, but now he would learn she was not the faithful wife he probably believed her to be. There would be no getting around it. As they walked up the driveway to the newer beige stucco house, Kate looked at Rollins, walking with an air of confidence. His suspenders provided a classy look as he slid his arm into his jacket. What a contrast between Bridges and Rollins. This was how he got the nickname Luster. He flicked a toothpick into the mulch.

He looked back at Kate and said, "It is not like you can say your wife got tired driving home, and pulled over to get a room, and some guy was knocking the bottom out of her, and oh by the way she caught a bullet in the head."

They knocked and let themselves in. After the initial introductions, the anxious-looking Chuck Morris asked, "I understand you may have a lead on Wendy?"

They ignored the question and deflected the inquiry. "Mr. Morris, do you have any recent pictures of Wendy?"

"Yes, I believe I do. I'll be right back."

They sat down on a soft brown leather sofa and looked around. Kate felt the smooth, soft texture that reminded her of the sofa at home. The two detectives scanned the interior. One can tell a lot about people by their decorating. There were several candle arrangements and trendy floral arrangements to complement the potted palm and ficus trees, but no family pictures. This was a clear sign that not everything was delightful in Camelot. Most people like to personalize their home. The Morris house, decorated like a builder's model home, lacked personality.

Rollins whispered to Kate, "Ken and Barbie, but nothing is as it looks. It's all an empty façade. It looks good on the outside, but it's empty inside."

She nodded in agreement.

Chuck Morris strode back into the room; his tight buttoned shirt barely contained his muscular figure. His thick hand carried a photograph. Kate snapped a picture of the photo using her phone.

Lester asked, "Do you happen to know what she may have been wearing, or any jewelry that might be unusual?"

They would milk this for all they could before breaking the news to him. There was no telling what his reaction might be. He could become a blubbering idiot, go into a catatonic state, squeal like a high school girl, shake uncontrollably, or thrash around like a kid wanting to break everything in his reach. He could go through all of these phases on a rollercoaster ride. As a possible suspect, Chuck would be a remote consideration.

"I just can't remember what she was wearing this morning. Wendy always dressed nice. She enjoys shopping. It was a double-edged sword, but she didn't always understand. I had to work as much as I could to maintain our standard of living. I think sometimes she would dress nice as I was going to work, to make me sorry to leave." He chuckled nervously.

Kate thought it was natural for people to expect to see each other at the end of of the day and often take life for granted. No one expects to die suddenly. They forget to notice the sunrises, the birds chirping, or what their spouse was wearing.

Kate asked, "Mr. Morris, when was the last time you saw her?"

"When I left for work at 7:00AM. I work in sales. I enjoy organization, so I get there early before making my first calls. Today, I was in a training class for a new software program. I was there from nine to four. They brought in lunch so we could condense it."

"You never left?"

"No. Not until after 6:30PM. I wanted to check my email and messages before I came home. It also allows traffic to thin out on I-75."

"Where is your office?" asked Kate.

"It is in Brandon."

Kate noted Brandon was on the other side of town from the murder and there would be plenty of witnesses to confirm his whereabouts all day. His email account could confirm he remained late. She knew the chances of any connection to the two murders were nearly nonexistent. As Lester said, nothing is as it seems.

Resuming the questions. "Does your wife work as well?"

"Yes, she is an administrative assistant for an insurance company."

"And you're in insurance as well."

"Yes. We met at a conference a few years ago. She didn't have to work, but it kept her busy. I told her to go to work for a charity, but she liked the work and the people she worked with."

"Have you and her experienced any problems lately?"

"No. Well, no more than most people." He started wringing his hands.

Lester asked, "What would be your definition of no more than most people?"

"I work a lot of hours. The pay is good. Before we got married, I thought she understood that. I guess she was hoping it would change, but if anything, I increased my hours. I am one of the leading producers and she enjoyed the fruits of my efforts. She just felt I didn't give her enough attention all the time. We argued over that from time to time. I would come home early if we had plans. I think she was adjusting to my schedule. But when I arrived home today, I could tell she had not been home all day."

Kate asked, "Why is that?"

"The mail was in the box, and the lights were not on. We finished a bottle of wine last night and she had not uncorked a new one. Wendy enjoys a glass of wine when she arrives home."

"Do you own any guns?" Kate asked.

"No. I have a knife, but no guns."

"Did she have any problems with any neighbors?"

"No, we kind of keep to ourselves. Occasionally we socialize with them for someone's party."

"Did she tell you about anyone following her or any altercations?"

With a look of bewilderment, he said, "No."

Kate started to lower the boom as they were running out of questions. "I know this is difficult, but did you suspect any relationships that you may have considered inappropriate?"

"No. Absolutely not. Like I said, during the week was difficult, but we made up for it on the weekends. I think most everyone she worked with was a female outside of Nick, her boss, who was also married. She was close to Cindy Oltman at work."

"How would you describe Wendy?"

He smiled softly and said, "She is very outgoing and loves life. She is the life of the party. Wendy is exciting to be around. She is my alter ego. I think that is why we hit it off. I am safe and conservative. She likes to live life on the edge. Here is a picture of her from two weeks ago at her birthday party."

"What about her jewelry, like her wedding ring?"

"It was a full carat that was kind of pointed on the edges."

"A marquis cut?"

"Yes, that's what she called it."

"Were there any engravings on the rings?"

"Yes, it has my initials and hers with our wedding date."

"What kind of purse did she carry?"

"I... I don't ...I just can't remember."

"How about tattoos or any scars?"

"She had two. One was dolphins jumping in the water in the small of the back. The second was a heart with a ribbon through it with my name written on the ribbon."

"Where was that located?"

"It is kind of embarrassing. We had them matching. I had her name on mine. They are on our right cheek."

"The buttocks?"

"Yes."

"Do you know any private investigators?"

"No. I don't think so."

"Have you ever hired a private investigator?"

"No, never. What for?"

"Has Wendy ever mentioned to you anything about the Pirate's Cove Motel on Nebraska Avenue?"

"No, I am not familiar with it."

Kate's body tightened as she said, "I am sorry to tell you, Mr. Morris, but I believe your wife met someone there and it resulted in her death."

His head pulled back. "What do you mean her life?"

"This afternoon we discovered a woman who was killed at the motel. The picture you have looks very similar. The wedding set also matches the description, and the same tattoos."

Chuck's voice deepened and became tight. "No. No, you must be wrong. She would have no business there at that motel."

"I am sorry Mr. Morris."

"Someone must have kidnapped her and taken her there against her will. She would have put up a fight. She is spunky. Wendy would never go along willingly. It couldn't be her. She must have gone out with some friends and forgot to call and she has just lost track of time. She'll be home. You'll see. You are wrong."

"Is there anyone we can call for you?"

"Her sister is on her way. You'll see. Wendy will call in a little while."

"Mr. Morris, I wished I could have told you better news. We do not know how she landed up at the motel. We'll find out. Mr. Morris, we are very sorry for your loss. Thank you for your cooperation. Here are our cards if you have questions. We'll be in touch."

Chuck collapsed onto the sofa and buried his face in his hands. Kate put her hand on his back and again asked, "Can we do anything for you?" She knew it was hollow. He wanted his life returned, as he knew it. She could not return to normalcy, but she could bring justice. He shook his head in silence. She left her business card on the table and they headed for the door.

They walked outside into the humid night, the sounds of air conditioners humming to cool the interiors down to sleeping temperature. Kate's mind drifted back to the time when the roles were reversed and she received the notification. She visualized the car pulling into the driveway, the uniforms, the bite in the stomach, the sudden wave of despair, the denial, the fear, and finally the loneliness.

Rollins interrupted her thoughts as he said, "What do you think?"

"I think he is clean. Clueless but clean. Like many husbands. He is working his tail off bringing home the bacon and he thinks she is happy to spend his money. It doesn't work that way. If he had given her more attention maybe, she wouldn't have strayed. He was talking about her in the present tense and still calling her by her given name and not referring to Wendy as her or it. You heard him say she liked to live on the edge. Today she fell over the edge. Tomorrow, he falls with her because he won't understand how it happened. He wonders why she betrayed him. Then he will have to plan for the funeral."

"Yep. You're right."

"Tomorrow, we'll talk to her coworkers and confirm his alibi."

"He might want to get an eraser for her name on his tattoo."

"I don't think it's that easy. Well, I am calling it a night. I'll drop you at the office and head home."

"I think I'll cruise by South Howard and see what's shaking."

"Luster, you amaze me. You're going down there to shag some poor, unsuspecting young thing."

"There ain't one unsuspecting young thing hanging out on So-Ho. Everyone is looking for love."

"Love, yeah right. Just like Chuck wanted someone to love."

"See, I am not like the rest of you. I have no worries and no responsibilities other than to myself."

"That's probably why when the bell rings, you are always ready."

"Plus, I am in peak physical condition. Just check me out, Kate. I am cut, I am tight." As he patted his midsection with his long slender hand.

Not showing the effects of delivering a death notification, she laughed and said, "You are a piece of work."

Chapter Sixteen

It was nearly midnight as Kate turned the unmarked car down the dark road. She cranked up Carrie Underwood on the radio. She was tapping her hands on the steering wheel like a drummer in the band. Her headlights assisted the moon in the dark. Kate peered into the darkness, looking to avoid any wildlife that might dart across the road. She turned into the driveway of the ranch style home. The coach lights were casting shadows from the house.

Kate stepped out of the air-conditioned car into the warm, humid night, looked up at the stars, and listened to the chorus of tree frogs, crickets, and no traffic. She admired the peacefulness of the country night and she listened to the hooting of an owl in the distance. As she walked up to the front door, she could feel the heat from the warm red bricks. She unlocked the door and reset the alarm system. Her mother was in the brown leather recliner, sipping on a diet Pepsi and watching Jimmy Fallon interview some pretty celebrity that Kate did not recognize.

"Hi Mom."

"Hi Honey."

"Hey, I am proud of you for setting the alarm."

She rolled her eyes and said, "It's after dark."

"You should always set it when you're inside."

"I know. You worry too much. We never had an alarm in our house."

"Times have changed."

"I suppose. Can I get you anything? Are you hungry?

"No thanks. I'm beat. How is Britney?"

"She is doing well. No fever and her congestion seems a lot better. She wanted to go to the stable tomorrow, but I don't think it is a good idea."

"I agree. Anything else going on?"

"Orthodontist bill came in."

"Do I want to know?"

"$2500 and that's with the discount."

Kate sighed heavily. "I guess I need to find some extra duty jobs to help with the cash flow."

Her mother flicked her auburn bangs off her petite but smoothed skin face. "You're already working too many hours."

"I know. I am going to go to bed."

"Was it bad?"

"Yes. Senseless. One mope is an addict and someone he knows shoots him. Maybe over drugs, or money, or girls, or sneakers, or maybe they just looked at him the wrong way. One bullet travels across the courtyard and hits a girl who is cheating on her husband, who appears to be a great guy." Her right thumb rubs her wedding set. "I just broke the news to him."

"Kate, I don't know how you do it sometimes."

"Mom, sometimes I don't either."

She opened the door to Britney's room. The hall light illuminated the room more than the Barbie night light. Kate heard Fallon cracking a one-liner that created laughter in the studio audience. Britney was flat on her back, arms raised overhead, as if she was under arrest and her mouth wide open. She was breathing hard, but steadily. A stuffed Winnie the Pooh kept her company. Kate stood for a few moments, admiring the innocence of her nine-year-old daughter, and smiled with pride. Reaching over, she brushed Britney's soft brown hair off her daughter's forehead and felt the skin with her hand. It was cool to the touch. She kissed her supple cheek.

Kate whispered, "Goodnight, my princess. Mommy loves you."

She stood back and looked at the framed picture of her grinning, camouflaged, fatigued husband holding baby Britney in his arms. She turned off the ceiling fan and closed the door, as she headed to her own king-size bed to sleep alone and to sleep fast. Tomorrow would be a busy day.

Chapter Seventeen

TUESDAY

In the homicide squad room, Duffy walked up behind Rollins, pulled on his elastic suspenders, and gave them a quick snap.

"Luster, I love you, man. It gets me all excited to do that."

Rollins dropped his head and shook his head with a huge grin.

Duffy continued, "If you were a girl, and I did that, I would be fired. But it still gives me that same thrill."

"You know you need counseling."

"I have known that for a long time."

"Let me see your tie today." Rollins craned his neck.

"It's the Harley Davidson tie. It's a collage of various license plates about Harley Davidson. It works well picking up chicks at the biker bars."

"I didn't know you were a biker dude."

"I'm not. I just like American institutions and the bikes excite me. I keep trying to get Bridget to dress up like a biker babe and get some tattoos. She won't have anything to do with it. I am too scared to ride one. I worked too many wrecks involving motorcycles. I remember one, where this poor bastard slid for two hundred feet on his ass. It was in January and he had scraped so much skin off his ass, there was steam coming from where his insides were spilling out." They both cringed. "It was nasty."

"How is Bridget?"

"Hanging in there. She starts chemo next week."

"Let me know if you need anything. I'll keep you in my prayers."

"Lester, I appreciate that."

Frank Duffy sat down at his desk and began retrieving his messages from voice mail. With each pertinent message, he scribbled on a yellow post-it pad, peeled the page off, and stuck it in an organized order with the other messages. The important ones were reserved for the fluorescent green post-it pad.

Kate walked up behind Frank and put her arm on his back. "Hey, how is Bridget?" She noted that one of the bright green post-its was written, "Moffitt Cancer Ctr. confirm chemo."

"She is hanging in there."

"And how is Duffy doing?"

He gave an uneasy laugh and shook his head in the affirmative. He took a deep breath, trying to control his emotions.

Kate said, "As President Clinton would say, I feel your pain. I know how tough it can be. Let me know if you ever need to talk or if you want to have another Guinness contest."

"Thanks."

She thought that was the fewest words she ever heard from Francis Xavier Duffy. "Hey, could you go with me to interview the coworkers of Blondie? Rollins has court today and Bridges is going to handle the autopsy for me. Wendy worked over in the Beer Can building. We can walk over and hit Eddie and Sam's for a slice on the way back. My treat."

"What, no PB&J today."

"No, today is PB and pretzel, but it will keep."

"Pretzel?"

"It gives a little crunch."

"So, does glass, but you don't put that on a sandwich. Since you're buying, how could I turn that down?"

The smile lit up his jovial Irish face. He stood up, tightening the tie against his collar as the once muscular neck spilled over the top. He ran his fingers like a comb through his thick, dark hair. Only his hair stylist would notice the few gray specks.

Chapter Eighteen

B ridges parked in the lot at the nearly anonymous beige brick building of the Hillsborough County Medical Examiner. It was a vast improvement over the archaic building downtown. As he stepped on the pavement, he could hear the squeals of laughter from the nearby Adventure Island water park. He could see the purple top of a tube ride. The thrills of life had escaped the occupants of the M.E.'s building.

The medical examiners perform 1,500 autopsies each year to bring closure to the families, unattended deaths, victims of violent crimes, and identify anonymous bodies. As he pulled the glass door open to the one-story building, the prevalent odor of disinfectant hit him in the face.

Thomas Maguire's naked body was already on the first stainless steel table in a room with too many similar tables. Wendy presumably was still in a body bag on the next table. Maguire's face and gaunt body were a testament to a hard life. He looked years older than his actual age. The body bag and the clean sheet removed. The clothes were removed and now saved for evidence. The x-ray showed no bullet fragments. The slender assistant, Walter Lovelace, snapped photographs of the body, assorted tattoos, old scars, and close-ups of the wounds. As the strobe of the camera flashed, the Medical Examiner, David Tresswick, removed the paper bags covering the hands. He inspected the left hand. With his own hands shrouded in latex, he scrutinized the webbing between the thumb and the first finger. There was significant damage with multiple fractures of the hand bones near the wound. The wound in the shape of a star striation, gunpowder burns, and residue showed it was a contact wound. He scraped the fingernails with a pointed wood stick, which he dropped into a manila envelope along with fingernail clippings to preserve any DNA. The clipped nails might provide evidence, since it appeared Maguire struggled with his assailant.

Tresswick lowered his face shield, braced himself against the table with his hip and gripped the shoulder of the corpse with his left hand for leverage. Using a large scalpel in his right hand, he slowly cut through the skin and made the infamous Y-shaped incision on the torso. Without the heart pumping, the blood was minimal. The arms of the Y extended from the front of each shoulder to the bottom end of the breastbone. After completing the Y incision, the M.E. peeled the skin, muscle, and soft tissues off the chest wall.

He fired up the hand-held saw. The spinning blade made a small rooster tail of bone matter as he sliced through the rib cage to gain access to the cavity. After switching back to the scalpel, he excised the organs from the body. The odor of food matter digested and undigested escaped from the cavity. The examiner picked up each with his hands. Like a lump of roast, he scrutinized, weighed, and dissected the once vital organs.

The head was next. The slick headed Tresswick made an incision across the scalp and folded it away from the skull like peeling a blanket to expose the mattress. As with the torso incisions, this one was deep, cutting all the way to the skull. Tresswick guided the squealing saw towards the head. The blade sliced through the skull from behind one ear, over the crown of the head, to the opposite ear. Lovelace assumed his position with the camera and clicked away, recording the naked skull and measurements of the entry wound through the forehead and exiting the base of the skull. The M.E. wiggled his fingers under the skullcap. With a good grip, he tugged it away from the brain. This created a distinctive sucking sound, like a cork pulled from the drain of a bathtub.

The now severed spinal cord freed the brain from the body. The brain that once made good and bad decisions for Thomas Maguire now lay dormant. The silent brain spoke to the examiner. Photographs documented a rod slipped through the brain, illustrating the path of the bullet. Since the brain is so soft, string hangs it up in a large jar of formalin solution for a couple of weeks to help it become firmer and easier to handle.

They made biopsies of each organ for future microscopic examination. Tresswick placed the small slices of organs in a jar filled with formalin. They placed the containers into evidence and saved until after the case was over. The odor of blood or old meat was now widespread throughout the examine room. Lovelace began tidying up the remains. The veteran M.E. peeled off his scrubs and face shield, revealing an unemotional facade. This face has seen thousands of sad stories.

Prior to starting on Wendy, Tresswick spoke to Bridges and said, "On the frontal aspect of the right side of the skull there is a circular pattern of blackened powder or soot, approximately 10 centimeters in diameter. This is consistent with a gunshot wound. We can tell the shooter discharged the weapon from about twelve inches due to the powder burns. The bullet traveled on a diagonal path through the brain. The scalp surrounding the wound is blood-covered and there is significant fracturing of the cranium beneath. At the exit point near the base of the brain, portions of the bone and brain have been evacuated, consistent with a blowout wound such as a gunshot. The exit wound is irregular shaped and fragmented, measuring 11 millimeters across. The gunshot wound to the hand looked painful. There is severe trauma to the wound site. I don't think there is much room for error here. Homicide it is. Tell Kate that I am upset she didn't drop by. I was going to share my peanut butter sandwich."

"Too much going on. We split the duties."

"I am on to the next. I understand I might retrieve a bullet."

"You should."

"Tell Kate I am skipping my lunch to knock this one out."

Kyle adjusted his glasses and said, "I'll tell her."

Tresswick performed the second autopsy much the same way as the one on Maguire. Aside from the shape of the cavity incision, he was now looking for a bullet and any fragments that would identify the firearm. He discovered the bullet had struck the base of the skull, entering the cerebellum and stopping in the medulla oblongata. That severed all communication with the autonomic functions. She was dead before she hit the ground. The bullet, a .357 magnum, looked in good shape for identification. The FDLE Crime Lab would conduct the examination of all the evidence collected, including the bullet.

Chapter Nineteen

The phone interrupted his thought pattern. "Homicide, Frank Duffy."

Clyde Billings said with a raspy voice, "Hey hero, I am off today, but I wanted to let you know what I found out. I would check with a Seamus Joyce. He is an Irish Traveler from the grifter clans in South Carolina. He worked as a carny for the circus one season and settled in Gibsonton last year. Running a few roofing scams on some elderly people, he skated on the charges after they received restitution. I am sure the victims were just the tip of the iceberg. He moved up here and fancies himself as a wannabe Pablo Escobar of meth dealers. He is pretty smart and resourceful. I heard he was getting some financial backing from the travelers like a Wall Street investment. The word is that Joyce was Maguire's main fix before he was popped. Irish on Irish crime, right?"

Duffy pushed down on the blue M&M candy dispenser. The saxophone-playing toy filled his open palm with the rainbow colors.

"Yeah."

"He is a real conman. Don't believe a word he says. I heard his wife is not a day over 17. You can get married at 16 with parental consent in South Carolina. Maybe I'll move there after I retire."

"I thought you weren't going to get married again."

"That's for sure."

"Thanks buddy. Go back to sleep." Frank tossed the candy in his mouth.

Sergeant Stewart was placing one of his prized orchids in a bucket of water to soak the roots as Kate walked in, wishing him a good morning.

He said, "Hey, I sent Canseco and Dietz to speak with Melvin Storms to see if he has any insight into his former client."

"That ought to be interesting, sending Dumb and Dumber over to one of the best legal minds in the state. I believe this is checkmate before they get there."

In a mocking tone, he said, "Now, let's be nice. It is Tuesday morning. There are too many leads for the "A Team" to run out. I know it is your case, but the JV needs to help out."

"Understood. I'll get started on some of the paperwork."

As she walked back to her desk and sat, the wooden frame of the chair creaked. Duffy walked over to Kate, shaking M&Ms in his hand like a dice player in Vegas. He popped a couple of the candies in his mouth. She could smell the chocolate.

"Clyde called me and told me that Maguire was scoring his meth from a Seamus Joyce. I checked Joyce in the system. There were several reports. Nothing that raised my eye, but the county has one report of interest. He was the subject of a report, in which he got into a fight with another patron at the Lucky Cabaret on SR 60. Neither one wanted to file charges. The other person involved was, who do you think?"

"Maguire?"

"Correct-o-mundo."

"The manager was the one that called it in. I thought before we went to talk to Joyce, I would talk to the manager."

"You know you could just call the deputy that wrote the report to save time, or is it the pole dancers you want to talk with?"

"It is purely an investigative lead."

"I have a sinkhole for sale as well."

He popped the rest of the M&Ms in his mouth and said with a partially obstructed mouth, "Actually, I am too busy. See if Rollins and Bridges are interested."

Chapter Twenty

Howard Canseco and Conrad Dietz strolled through the door. Kate looked up at the two detectives and thought of Hector, the bulldog protecting Tweety bird. Canseco was the bulldog and Dietz was always slumping behind him. Canseco was a good-looking fellow with his dark hair in one of those short-cropped cuts. You could tell he spent a lot of time in the gym and thought a lot of himself. No one else did. He hit on Kate in the gym once and she repulsed the attempt. He could not mask his discontent for Kate after she rejected the come-on. After serving on and earning a good reputation on the Tactical Response Team (TRT), he arrived in homicide a year earlier. That glory faded once he got to homicide, where he had exceeded his competency level.

Dietz resembled a big oaf. He was frumpy, looking like he never grew out of his baby fat. His shaved head and double chin earned him the nickname of Uncle Fester from the Adams Family. He always appeared to be huffing and puffing about something and never appeared to have control over even mundane tasks. Although Dietz had been in homicide longer, Canseco was the brighter of the duo of Dumb and Dumber.

Kate said, "What did you find out from Storms?"

Canseco's smile dissipated. He turned towards Kate's voice and said, "Storms said it was attorney client privilege. He's a jerk. He kept us sitting in the lobby for forty-five minutes. He said he was with a client."

"So, let me get this straight. You two spent forty-five minutes in his lobby and got zip for information. Now you're going to spend the next hour and half at The Wing House harassing some waitress that's trying to pay her way through college. Then you get your hour-long pump at Gold's and Dietz admires you flexing your muscles and telling you how great you look."

Canseco pulled out the well-chewed gum with his fingers, tossed it in the trash bucket, and said, "Hey, up yours."

"Hey Howie, why don't you inject another steroid and tell that to the victims' family?"

Dietz rubbed his shaved head and said, "Hey, like Howard said, we tried. That guy is a jerk."

"You shouldn't call Howie a Jerk."

"No, I'm talking about Storms."

"Oh, Okay, I didn't realize that."

Canseco said, "By the way, it's Howard.... Katie."

"So, it took you over an hour to find out nada, zip, nothing, and by the way, Uncle Fester, you dribbled some, ahh, maybe jelly from a jelly donut on your shirt."

Dietz looked down at his shirt. Realizing he was fooled, he tried to make it look like he was checking his shoes, and bent down to retie his left loafer.

"You might consider Velcro. That's what my daughter uses." Dietz looked up with a sneering look.

Kate walked over to Rollins and said, "I hate those guys."

"They ain't worth it. They are nothing but fools."

Kate had little use for ineptitude, especially blind incompetence. She didn't enjoy working with those people. What makes them so dangerous is they think everyone else is screwed up. Just like this one task. They were too stupid to press Storms and sat there wasting everyone's time. Someone would still have to speak to Storms.

Rollins reached down, pulled open the bottom drawer of the desk, and pulled out a book. Kate hooked her hair behind her left ear.

Rollins said, "You need to read this."

Her head tilted back as she let out a large laugh and said, "You're right, this is what I need. *Don't Sweat the Small Stuff*. I wish Alfonso would get rid of them."

"His hands are tied. Lieutenant Rizzo likes them."

"And what's up with that? The L.T. is no rocket scientist either, but you would think she would want smart people around to make her look good."

"Actually, the opposite is true. I just read a book called the *Idiot Boss*. They feel empowered by surrounding themselves with other idiots."

"I never looked at it that way before. Perhaps that is why I have never been in her good graces."

"Why do you say that?"

"Rizzo hardly gives me the time of day. When my husband was killed, she said how's it going? How's it going? Most people say, hey I am sorry for your loss, or just plain, I'm sorry, or is there anything I can do for you? I could have forced her to explain herself, but

I just wasn't up to it. Then she said to me that she knew I was entitled to take time off, but staffing was low and could I come back early? I looked straight in her eye and said absolutely not. I have to care for my daughter. She just said okay and walked away. She is weak."

"Your right. When you finish that book, you need to read *Up Up Up in A Down Down World*."

"Do you really read this stuff?"

"Yep. I have to. Food for the soul, baby. How do you think I made it out of the projects and survived here? In fact, in a few weeks, I am going to hear the motivational speaker Les Brown speak. Just like me, he scratched and clawed himself out to success."

"You never cease to amaze me. Hey, I have a huge favor to ask?"

"Fire away, my dear."

"Could you cover a lead at some strip club on SR60 with Kyle?"

"Twist my arm. I am all over that."

"I bet."

Kate and Frank walked the few blocks to the "Beer Can." Its actual name is the Sykes Building. It received its nickname from the tall cylinder architecture of the beige building. As they entered the lobby, the air-conditioned comfort refreshed their sweaty skin. Frank removed a monogrammed handkerchief from inside his breast packet and dabbed the perspiration from his face.

They entered through the glass doors of Florida Business Insurance Specialists. The receptionist's eyes were red and puffy and a cubed shaped box of Kleenex sat on her desk. The bad news had made it to the office.

The phone rang. She sniffed, and answered, "Florida Business Insurance Specialists. How may I direct your call? Yes, hold please." She looked up and feigned a futile attempt to smile. "May I help you?"

"Yes, I am Detective Alexander with the Tampa Police. We would like to speak to Cindy Oltman, please."

"Yes, one moment please."

A woman came out to the lobby to greet the visitors and introduced herself as Cindy. Her light hair looked like a parted curtain, revealing a sad face. The diminutive women escorted them to her office. Through the windows, they could see a few blocks away to the dark blue tiles of the police department building.

Kate said, "Cindy, we are sorry about the loss of your co-worker."

She hated saying that. She heard that so many times from people who did not know what to say, yet she repeated the same obligatory statement many times herself.

"We are investigating the death of Wendy Morris. Do you know where she went to lunch or with whom?"

"No."

"Does she go out for lunch or frequent any favorite places? Some people like to go to one of a few places for lunch. It is their comfort zone, so to speak. Does she eat alone or with others from the office?"

"No. Normally, she goes out by herself."

Frank, with his deep voice, said, "That's unusual. I understand she was very outgoing. Was that contrary to her lifestyle to eat alone?"

Cindy's eyes looked down, "I don't know."

Kate said, "Cindy, we'll be right back."

Duffy and Kate stepped outside her office, where Cindy could not hear them.

"Frank, give me a couple of minutes with her. Woman to woman."

He gave a pouting look. She put her hand on his shoulder and said, "It will be okay, Frank. I promise I won't be long. Now be a good boy while I am gone."

Kate entered back into Cindy's office and closed the door. Frank began questioning the other employees.

"Okay, Cindy, here is the deal. You did not ask to be involved in this. You merely work here and try to mind your own business. I am going to interview everyone in here, so whatever you tell me, no one will know. You cared about Wendy. I can tell you are a caring person. You have pictures of your children on your desk. They must be a sense of pride to you. I know that as a mother, as I am very proud of my daughter. They grow up so fast. It seems like just yesterday they were in diapers and now look at them. Like most mother's, we care for others."

Cindy nodded, and her face brightened at the thought.

Kate continued, "You are working here to give them things you didn't have. I am in the same boat. My husband died a couple of years ago. It forced me to keep a job with stability. Jobs are scarce and you may not love this job, but you like the stability of helping to support your family. No one wants to jeopardize that stability. I know Wendy was a little on the wild side, and she was screwing around on her husband. I am sure you did not approve. You know Chuck is a hard-working, decent man, but she was stepping out on him. I think it was Nick."

Cindy's head dropped. Her eyes looked towards her desk.

"He might be a decent boss and a decent person, but they were making a mistake. Now, one is dead. Did they leave together or did they take separate cars?"

"I didn't say they did."

"You didn't have to. We will find out with you or without you. Can I be honest with you? Nick is not in any trouble. He may have been having an affair, but that is not a crime. I know he did not kill her. I think he has information that may assist us in identifying who killed her. We would like your help. I know you did not approve of what they were doing. We are not the moral police. I am not here to pass judgment on them. I only want the truth."

"Yes."

"I am sure if anything ever happened to one of your children, you would hope and pray that someone would come forward and provide information that would bring closure to you. It helps to know who was responsible. We owe that to Chuck, and especially to Wendy."

Her head dropped again for the second time. Kate leaned forward and touched her shoulder with her right hand.

"It's all right. I know it's difficult. I would feel the same way, but you will feel better getting it off your chest."

Cindy looked up with tears in her eyes and sniffed as she dabbed her eyes with a tissue. She cleared her throat and said, "I knew there was some hanky-panky going on. I don't think she was getting enough attention at home. She came in here dressed to kill. She was in great shape, and she liked to display her attributes. It wasn't just Nick. Wendy turned all men's heads. I think Nick's resistance wore down. They would take lunch about the same time. They were careful. They would leave a few minutes apart and take separate cars. They would return about the same time. She would give an excuse that she was going shopping or running an errand. She would stay a little late to make up the time or come in early.

"What about Nick?"

"Nick would never provide an excuse, except to say he was on his cell phone. Sometimes they would come back and you would see his hair was messed up or hers. You could see the way they looked at each other. We went to her birthday party a couple of weeks ago. Everyone was having a good time, and I noticed both Nick and Wendy were missing. Just like at work, Nick came in and a few minutes later Wendy came in. I couldn't believe they would fool around in the house. She made a few passing comments about Chuck that he was always working so hard and was never around. I could tell she was frustrated and lonely."

"Tell me about yesterday."

"Nick left around 11:30 am. She left about five minutes later. He came back at about 2:00 pm. He called about 12:30 and said he would be out in the field for a while. He sounded a little excited. His voice pitch was a little higher and his speech was short and choppy."

"What exactly did he say?"

"He said, Hey Cynthia, that's unusual. He usually calls me Cindy. He said I'm busy. I'll be back later. Okay, gotta go. A few minutes before he came back, he called and asked if anything was going on. I didn't think it was all that unusual. He came in looking as white as a ghost. He kind of had this blank stare. He's an outgoing person, but he was very quiet. About 3:00 pm, he asked where Wendy was. I tried to cover for her, but I could tell he wasn't listening to my response. I tried to call Wendy on her cell phone. No one answered, so I left a message. He left right after that and said he was not feeling good. I asked him if it was something he had eaten. He just nodded no and left. He came in this morning and asked again where she was and he seemed to be good. Mary came in and told us about the story in the news. We were all in shock, even Nick."

"Cindy, I want to thank you. No one from this office will know what you told me."

Kate conferred with Frank, briefing him on the conversation with Cindy.

Frank said, "Shall we have a chat with Nicky, baby?"

"Yes. Why don't we."

"Allow me to take the lead this time."

"Have at it."

Kate loved interviewing people. It was like a chess game. Intellect against intellect. It was an art form. After the completion of a successful interview, it was almost like a shot of adrenaline. Good detectives had to be excellent interviewers. As confident as she was in her abilities, she always respected Frank's ability.

Chapter Twenty-One

They knocked on the door to Nick Tortorino's office. He was looking at some papers, but looked like he was expecting their arrival. They displayed their badges and introduced themselves. Nick's office overlooked the winding Hillsborough River. They sat down in modern upholstered chairs.

Frank sized up Nick. His well-tanned skin contrasted with the white shirt. He was wearing an expensive looking blue suit and stood a few inches shorter than six feet with a trim figure. His hands displayed a gold wedding ring, a gold watch, and a gold bracelet.

This pal liked himself. Frank decided on his strategy. He opened with a quick compliment and put him on the defensive immediately. Use shock and awe on him. Don't give him time to become comfortable in his own office and have time to come up with a plan. If this approach failed, Kate could come in and save the day by utilizing her female charm to exploit his weakness to females. He loved this aspect of the job, breaking down some asshole.

Frank started, "Hey nice tie," pointing at the bright blue tie.

With a voice from the diaphragm, he said, "Oh, thank you."

"Being a connoisseur of ties, I like that."

"Thanks."

"Where did you buy it?"

"It was a gift."

Frank thought that Wendy might have been the gift giver.

"Whoever bought it has good taste. Most of my gift ties I discard in the bottom drawer."

Nick gave an awkward smile. He nodded as if he was interested, but his face was tight. He picked up a paper clip and played with it in his hands.

Frank thought to himself, hold on Nick here is the first salvo, "Nick, I am going to be a little forward and ask you if you were with Wendy yesterday when she was killed?"

Nick stopped playing with the paper clip.

"What? Killed? What would ever give you that idea?"

Frank noted the lack of a direct answer to the question. "Perhaps because you were having an affair with her."

His hands trembled. He picked up the paper clip and twisted and pull the clip apart.

Nick shifted in his seat. "An affair? I am happily married. I have two kids. That girl was married as well. In fact, most of us here were at her birthday party two weeks ago. Cindy, Taylor, and Mary were all there at her party. Do you think I would go to her party at her house if I were having an affair with her? I don't like your accusations. I think you should leave. I know your type. That poor woman is dead and you're looking to pin her murder on someone. So, let's go after the boss and say they were having a romantic fling. Well, I did not kill her."

Frank was enjoying this. "Where were you yesterday afternoon between 11:30 am and 2:00 pm?"

"I went to lunch."

"Where did you eat?"

"I don't remember. I think it was a Cuban joint over near Nebraska."

"Do you remember where?"

"I think it was La Casa."

"What did you eat?"

He looked right at them. "It's what you always eat at those places. Rice and beans and a Cuban sandwich."

"Did you eat inside or out?"

"This is ridiculous. Inside."

"How did you pay?"

"Cash." He put the mangled clip down, pointed his finger, and leaned across his desk. "I don't like this line of questioning. When do the bright lights and jumper cables come out?"

He leaned back in his chair and spread his arms wide. Frank grinned at Nick's weak attempt to go on the offense.

"Okay, so how long were you there?"

"I don't know, maybe thirty minutes. Let me answer your next question. I went shopping. After going to her party a couple of weeks ago, I thought I would surprise my wife with jewelry. So, I went to the International Plaza. I parked by Dillard's, walked around to a couple of different stores, and looked for jewelry. I was looking for a gold chain necklace with sapphires and diamonds. You know? Something in a 24-karat gold. I looked in Dillard's, I looked in Nordstrom's, and Tiffany's as well. I decided not to buy anything."

Frank was laughing on the inside. Batter up, jerk-off. Let's see how you can handle this one.

"How much were the necklaces you were looking at?"

He hesitated and said, "More than I wanted to spend. You can appreciate.

that." Nick grinned.

Frank thought, strike one and knew that Nick was looking for an alliance.

To this point, he obtained several dangerous lies that showed deception. Who needs a polygraph? This was more fun.

"On our salaries, we can't just spend money. I am sorry if we upset you. I know this is upsetting to everyone. This must be surreal. A girl who works in here turns up murdered after going out to lunch."

"You've got that right. I know you are just doing your job."

Now he is trying to placate me. "You've got that right. Hey, you wouldn't mind taking a polygraph test, would you?"

"We'll... I ... ah... I don't know. I heard they are not very accurate. I have high blood pressure, so I don't think it would be very accurate."

Frank leaned forward. His blue eyes were like tracer bullets staring at his adversary across the desk.

"Nick, they are deadly accurate." Frank watched Nick's Adam's apple go up and then dropped like an elevator in freefall. "This is not one of these dime store variety lie detector tests. They take a good three or four hours. They want to get an accurate reading."

"We'll, I don't have three or four hours to spare."

"You know, most men have a high degree of integrity. You look like an honest person. I think you would want to prove your integrity like most men. They want to be counted on and believed."

"I know I am telling the truth."

"I heard you went home early."

"I felt like the flu was coming on, but I went home, took some Advil and went to bed early. I woke up feeling good. After this kind of abuse, I am starting not to feel so good anymore."

Frank thought it's time to take him to the mat. He leaned forward more and said quietly, "Can I be honest with you?"

Nick leaned back, trying to put some space between them and said uneasily, "Sure."

Frank dropped his smile and stared right at Nick, who again swallowed hard.

"I don't believe you."

Nick's eyes widened like a kid at the top of the rollercoaster before the

plunge downhill. Frank was now going to unleash the second wave of shock and awe, knowing that Nick felt he had beaten them off on the first strike and was feeling confident. He started with one of his trademark statements. He told Kate once this would show he was about to get out his can of verbal whoop ass.

"Let me explain something to you, Nick. I am going to make a project of you. I am going to become a proctologist and climb so far up your ass; you'll start to choke."

Nick pulled back, his eyes expanded in fear and he swallowed.

"I know you were getting a little on the side." Frank said, "You were balls deep into her. One of our detectives is going to go to La Casa and pull their deposit. They will have every bill checked to see if your fingerprints are on any of them. The detective will show your photo to the employees to see if anyone recognizes you."

Nick protested.

Frank held up his hand like a cop stopping traffic and said, "Quiet. I want you to listen to everything I am saying. I am going to pull the surveillance footage of every jewelry counter in every store at the mall, as well as the main mall and parking lots. I am going to check with all the clerks. I am going to pull your cell phone records to see all the calls you made to Wendy. Not just "that girl" as you call her, but Wendy. Your indifference to her indicates to me you want to distance yourself from her. She was a human being full of life until yesterday. Now she has a husband in mourning. I will also check Wendy's cell phone records. I have checked the DMV records. I know you drive an Escalade and I am going to check with Cadillac Onstar to see your GPS location at the time of the murder. Yeah, that's right. How do you think Onstar knows how and where to send help? I am going to the clerk at the Pirate's Cove and show your photo. I know you think Wendy was the one that went inside. All the times you went there for your afternoon gymnastics session, he has gotten enough glimpses, so that he can identify you. After all that, I am going to interview your wife."

Nick's eyes panicked.

"I will have the medical examiner check for your DNA on the body and the sheets. I will charge you with obstruction of justice under Florida Statute 843. Therefore, Nicky baby, the ball is in your court."

There was silence. Nick slumped his shoulders and his head lowered. He avoided eye contact.

"I did not kill her."

Frank wanted to jump up and pump his fists in victory but quelled the urge and said softly while gently touching Nick's knee, "I know you didn't. If I thought for one moment that you did, I would have done all this other work first. Then I would have come here with a warrant in my hand, and I would have arrested you. I know you are just trying to protect your family. I know this was not your fault. She was lonely and not getting enough at home. You're a handsome fellow in a powerful position. I am sure she caught you at a weak moment. The way she dresses. She had that nice figure. She was in here flaunting herself around like some prom queen. Every day, you look at her showing more cleavage than Sofia Vergara. Those jacked up heels. Who could blame you?"

Frank needed to become an ally to Nick. He despised Nick as a womanizer man-whore. He had to put that aside to solve this case. He wanted to minimize and substantiate the conduct that Frank abhorred.

He continued, "Any man with the scruples and character like you could resist for just so long before you succumb to her advances. She wore you down. It was her fault and not yours. Therefore, you're having a little fun. No one is getting hurt. Then bam a shot hits her in the head. You had nothing, and I mean nothing, to do with that. You knew you couldn't save her. She was dead. You left to protect your family and work. That is admirable. I don't want to charge you, we just want to know what you saw when you were coming and going. I think you saw something and you might not be aware. You see, someone else was murdered at the motel. The bullet hit Wendy accidentally. You may have seen the other person or their car or heard something. That is all I want. Then I will leave, and this is over between us. I won't charge you."

"I think I need an attorney."

Frank had to steer him away from the attorney word. "You can get one. That is up to you. I am looking to cover some ground. I can't move ahead while you retain an attorney and the State Attorney's Office negotiates. While you are out there spending your money to get legal advice, I am going to continue my investigation. Right now, you are in my way. If you cause me any extra work that delays my identifying and arresting the person responsible for killing Wendy, I will charge you. Right now, I don't care about you. You made a mistake. You were thinking with the wrong head, like many men. Now is the time to think with the head on your shoulders. You have my word and this detective as a witness that I will not charge you. The train is pulling out of the station. You can get on it or you can be left standing on the platform and watch it leave without you. Your attorney and you will stand there waving goodbye at your best shot. Your choice. I'll give you two minutes. I'll step outside. When I return, I want a one-word answer. Yes or no."

Chapter Twenty-Two

T hey walked out in the hallway and were like two high school kids trading answers to an exam outside the classroom.

Kate said, "I enjoyed it when you leaned forward and whispered that he was lying and how you were going to be a proctologist. When he went into the whole thing about the necklace and all the details, I knew he was lying. He was just throwing a bunch of smoke to make us think he bought that necklace."

"I knew he had no idea how much the necklace was unless his wife had shown him a picture."

"He'll cave. He knows he is screwed. Let's go finish."

They resumed their seats in the blue armchairs.

Nick let out a gasp of air and said, "I'll cooperate if you don't tell my wife. I don't want to hurt her or the kids. She'll throw me out."

Frank said, "Stop! I said yes or no. You are not in a position to negotiate. I will not speak to your wife. There is a good chance she will find out from the over eager media. You should have thought about her feelings before you pulled the one-eyed snake out of your zipper. If you are a Las Vegas gambler, you can roll the dice and hope she doesn't find out. You can have a 'she didn't mean anything to me conversation' on your own terms. I am a busy man. Yes, or no?"

There was a pause and Frank started to stand up, knowing this would appear that the deal was going out the door.

Nick shouted, "Yes!"

"I want the entire story, not what you want to tell."

"Okay, okay. Wendy was hot. As you said, she dressed provocatively. We all went out after work one night to celebrate a sales achievement. You know, just dinner and a couple of drinks. Everyone left except the two of us. I asked her why she was staying out, and she said her husband always worked late and kind of ignored her. I just tried to provide comfort and said something like, wow, how could he ignore a great-looking girl like her? She smiled and touched my hand and said how sweet it was to say that. We talked about relationships and spouses. I walked her out to the parking lot, she kissed me and the next thing I knew, she was all over me. I used to be known as the Italian Stallion."

He chuckled with bravado that changed to an uncomfortable chuckle when the two detectives gave a simultaneous, "you have to be kidding stare."

He continued, "A couple of weeks later, she asked me if I could go with her to Staples for supplies because her car was having trouble and Cindy was on vacation. We loaded up the supplies. We stopped for lunch and she ordered a bottle of wine. I resisted at first, saying we needed to get back to work. She told me we would have one glass and keep it our own secret. We finished the bottle and left. She asked me to drive by to see a friend who left a box for her in her room. She said the friend who was going through a divorce was staying at the Pirate's Cove. I was a little suspicious. She knocked on the door like someone would be there and she pulled out the key from her purse. Once inside, she was on me like Velcro. I'll be honest, I didn't resist too much. She did things to me I didn't know were possible. I felt like I was in college again. We would get together once or twice a week. We would park her car somewhere and I would drive to the Pirate's Cove and drop her off at the office and park. The room I paid for with cash."

Frank asked, "Why the Pirate's Cove?"

"She lived on the edge. She liked the sleaziness of it."

"What happened yesterday?"

"It was just like any other day. We went inside, I turned the A/C to high, I turned, and we embraced. She enjoyed being on top. I wasn't paying attention to anything other than her. Then I heard a pop. Suddenly, she fell over to her right and hit the floor. I jumped up and saw the blood oozing out of her head. Her eyes were staring straight ahead. I started freaking. I cared for her. Not like loved her, you know. Wendy was incredible."

Kate said, "Continue."

"I was in a panic. I looked and saw a small hole in the window and I knew someone had shot her. I thought her husband found out. I grabbed my clothes and got dressed. I grabbed a towel and wiped the door down and the A/C. I ran out and jumped in my car and hauled ass so I could get out before someone killed me. This scared the hell out of me."

Frank said, "Did you see anyone or a car?"

He shook his head to the side. "No, I didn't see anyone or hear anyone. There was a dark colored car in the lot, but I couldn't tell you what kind or the color."

"What did you do with her purse?"

"I threw it in a trash bin behind a shopping center off Westshore. I couldn't tell you which one. I was just in a panic."

"Now, don't you feel better there, Nick? Getting it off your chest?"

"It was an enormous burden."

"Now, you can go talk to your parish priest and confess your sins." Silence. "Thanks for clearing this mystery up. Would you mind allowing yourself to be hypnotized? It helps with the memory to recall events in a clearer manner."

"Yeah, I suppose it would be all right."

"We'll call you if we need anything else."

"Like what? Just don't call me at home. Here is my cell phone number."

"Thanks. Like Columbo. I always think of something else after I leave. Don't worry. I won't shatter your delicate marriage. Speaking of marriage, does your wife suspect any indiscretions on your part?"

Panic crossed his face. "No! No, I know what you are thinking. She was watching our kids' choir performance at school."

"So, while you were banging your co-worker, she was doting over your kids. We'll check it out."

With desperation, he said, "How?"

They walked out without a word and stepped into the elevator.

Kate said, "This gives us a glimmer of a lead."

"Yeah. I could use a shower after talking to Nick. What a sleaze."

"Definitely. We still on for pizza?"

"Absolutely."

Chapter Twenty-Three

They stopped at Eddie and Sam's N.Y. Style Pizza for the promised slice. Kate and Frank walked under the large green, white, and red awning. Frank opened the door for Kate and she thanked him. As they muscled into the narrow pizzeria and stood in the long line of hungry office workers, they watched the employees work like a precision drill team, efficiently moving the line along. The sweet aroma of tomato and garlic lingered in the air. She picked up her single slice.

Kate spotted a vacating party and descended upon the still warm seats like a holiday shopper after the last toy. Kate pulled a hunk of napkins from the black dispenser and dabbed the oil off the top of the pizza. Frank sat down with his back to the crowd and folded one of his two slices longwise. He held the slice with determination and took a large bite, pulling the excess cheese with his fingers like taffy. He wiped his fingers on a napkin to remove the slick olive oil.

Kate said, "I enjoyed watching you break Nick."

Frank, talking through his mouthful of pizza, said, "I can't tell you how much fun I had in there. When you are in the zone, you're jazzed. I could tell he was big on himself. I had to put him in his place."

"I thought he was going into the fetal position."

Frank glanced side to side to make sure an eavesdropper didn't occupy the cramped tables. Good, both tables were consumed in their own tales.

He lowered his voice. "The reality of the interview is that we still don't know who killed Wendy or Maguire. We are not much better off than before talking to Nick."

"I know, but it was still a good interview."

"Thanks. I have no use for a man cheating on his family. It's not just the wife, but also his kids. He had the photos of the happy family. From that perspective, I guess it was a success to break him down. You might consider using a hypnotist. He has already agreed to it."

"Do you think it will work?"

"Like Wayne Gretzky, the hockey great said, you're guaranteed to miss one hundred percent of the shots you don't take. Of course, some people look at hypnosis like voodoo. What do you have to lose? It might work. Anything is better that nothing, unless the crime scene unit comes back with some revelations. You don't want this to go into the unsolved pile. There is a person at USF that does it. Call him and set up an appointment. Just run it by Al."

One of the pizza workers bellowed, "Large supreme to go!"

"You're the only one that calls him Al."

"We're friends. I respect him as my supervisor and I am very loyal to him. I'm just not big on titles."

She nodded and hooked her hair behind her ear and gave a smile of approval.

"Al and I go back a long way. We were on the same squad for a while. We were in narcotics for a little while before he went to homicide. He could be a captain if he didn't fight for us. He can look at himself in the mirror with a clear conscious. There are not a lot of folks in the Blue Monster that can do that. With all the time that I took off for Bridget's surgery and recuperation, he has been great. I would walk through a ring of fire for him."

"I would walk with you. When Jake was reported missing in Afghanistan, I was a basket case. The Sarge wasn't in my chain of command, but he called and said he was praying for us."

"He meant it."

The hustling employees continued to bark out the pickups, "Sausage roll and two cheeses."

"I believed him. When they located the helicopter crash site and recovered Jake's body, I remember feeling so lonely. At the church, I couldn't believe the turnout from the department. The Sarge was there and I could see tears in his eyes. This former football player, tough guy, has such an enormous heart."

"Not to change the subject, but how about coming over to the house and have dinner with Bridget one night? She would love to see you again. What are you doing this next weekend?"

"I am taking Britney horseback riding, but maybe Saturday night or Sunday."

"Ok, I'll get back to you. So, what did you do this weekend?"

"I had a judo class in the morning and I took Britney shopping. Then I hosted a sleepover that meant no sleep and then went to Bush Gardens."

"Wow! Where do you get the energy? Is Britney the thrill seeker like mom and loves the roller coasters?"

"Absolutely."

"Well, let me know if you are free. I have a recipe for a macadamia nut crusted mahi mahi with a crab relish I would like to try."

"Sounds wonderful."

"How is the judo going?"

"Great. I test for my second-degree black belt in two weeks."

"Good for you. I am still waiting to watch you unleash that on someone."

"I use it every day to maintain the discipline to keep from killing Dumb and Dumber."

"I hear ya. Well, good luck with that."

"Thanks. I should do all right. Remember my initials K. A."

"Yeah, yeah, I know."

"What about Maguire's landscaping boss? You want to hit him on the way home this?"

"Sounds good."

Employees barked, "Two pepperonis to go."

Two diners hovered over Frank, waiting to sit down. "It's all yours. I kept the seat warm for you."

They strolled back to the Blue Monster along Lykes Park. A homeless man who appeared very comfortable sitting on the ground was extending his thin, well-tanned hand, forming a cup and asking for money. The breeze blew the odor of stale urine past them. The two detectives ignored the impoverished man.

The Blue Monster was a nine-story, dark blue paneled building. It looked like it was formerly an old abandoned bank building. It was. Many of the 1960ish blue panels were faded, while other panels were bright. It was an ugly building. The yellow letters attached to the front let everyone know it was no longer a bank. The letters spelled "Tampa Police." Affectionately and un-affectionately, it was called "The Blue Monster."

The two detectives returned to the homicide squad. They checked messages, gathered their necessities, and Frank grabbed a handful of M&M's and his car keys.

"Shall we visit Maguire's drug connection, Mr. Joyce?"

Chapter Twenty-Four

F rank drove the black Ford towards the guard gate.

"I love these guys. This piece of garbage is living in a gated community, so he can keep the riff-raff out. I bet his neighbors would love to know they are living next to a conman turned drug dealer." Frank said.

The acne faced guard with a sloppy uniform and carrying a clipboard stepped out. Frank held up his badge and identified himself.

"Hey, how are you doing? Tampa Police."

The young guard inspected the credentials and said, "What address are you going to?"

"I am sorry, we're on official business."

"This is a private community and I need to know your destination."

"Let me explain something to you, pal. I have identified myself as a police officer, and I have told you I am on official business. I am not here for a picnic."

"Well, I am not supposed to let anyone, including the President, drive through here."

"Well, I am not the President, so open up."

"I am sorry sir...."

Not letting him finish, Frank leaned his head out the open window and said, "Now you have two choices, pal. You can open the gate and let me through, or I am going to get out and place you under arrest for obstruction of justice, and I'll handcuff your ass to the gate. I'll pick you up on the way out."

"I am just doing my job." As the guard put his palms out.

"Ditto, right back at you, pal."

Duffy stared at the guard. "Your choice." The black railed gate groaned as it swung open and Frank sped up without a word.

"Kate, would you get the plate off that guard's car?" He pointed to a beat-up Nissan in a parking area. "Can you believe that guy? I would never have the guts to say that at his age. I would love it if he had a warrant on him. We could cuff and stuff him on the way out. In one way, I will give him credit. We could use him up at my place. This guy will probably let a carload of gang bangers through, but he is going to jack up some cops. Unbelievable."

"I'll bet you were the bully in the school that stole everyone's lunch money."

"I was the kid whose lunch money was stolen."

"Like I believe that."

They stopped next to the curb in front of a spacious stucco one story home. The red brick walk cut through a lushly landscaped yard.

"Isn't this great? They are trying to keep the cops out and let the mopes in."

Kate closed the cell phone and said, "Communications checked the boy genius at the front gate. He is clean."

Duffy shook his head in disappointment.

Kate pushed the doorbell that chimed a loud melody. A weathered faced thirty something male opened the crystal glass door. He was wearing a bright Hawaiian silk shirt with shorts and flip-flops.

"Yes?"

"Seamus Joyce?"

"Yes?"

"Tampa Police. Can we come in?"

"Sure. Have a seat." Joyce pointed towards the formal living room.

Their steps echoed on the tiled foyer. They sunk into the green overstuffed sofa overlooking the glistening swimming pool. The breeze from the spinning ceiling fan felt good. There was a hint of vanilla in the air from a nearby candle. A young blonde wearing a black bathing suit top and denim shorts strutted into the living room like a fashion model on the runway.

Seamus said, "Honey, would you get these fine public servants something to drink?"

Kate said, "No, we are fine, thank you."

The girl, presumably Mrs. Joyce, left the room like a dispatched servant.

Frank asked Seamus, "Did you know a Thomas Maguire?"

"I don't believe I do."

"Well, there is a police report that say's you got into a fight with him at the Lucky Cabaret."

"Oh, was that his name? That was nothing. Someone jumped the gun and called the cops."

"We have several people who say you were his meth connection."

"Detectives, I don't know what you are talking about."

"You know he was murdered?"

"I didn't do it. I don't have anything else to say. I am calling my attorney."

"Who is your attorney?"

"Melvin Storms, have you heard of him?"

"Mr. Joyce, I don't need to ask any more questions, especially since you have invoked your right to council."

He pushed himself out of the sofa and looked down at Joyce.

"It is good that you have a famous attorney, because you are going to need one." They walked towards the door and Duffy continued. "I have just decided to make a project for you. That could be bad for business."

"I am not worried, and I don't care about your threats."

Frank opened the door, allowing the humid air to slap them in the face like a wet blanket. A green lizard scampered for protection.

Kate stepped outside. Frank smiled with an evil grin and said, "I'm not worried either, and it wasn't a threat. Enjoy the pool."

Joyce's face tightened, and he closed the door without comment.

Chapter Twenty-Five

T he ringing telephone greeted their return to the office. Kate picked up the receiver and said, "Homicide, Detective Alexander?"

"Detective Alexander, this is Linda Stout. Please hold the line for Attorney Melvin Storms. He would like to speak to you."

"Hello, Detective Alexander, this is Melvin Storms. How are you today?"

"Fine, Marvin."

"Ah, that's Melvin. Melvin Storms."

"Oh, okay. Could you hold just a moment?"

"Certainly."

"Guess who is on hold?"

Frank Duffy said, "Santa Claus? You know I need to ask him for a new car."

"No. It's Melvin Storms. I am going to leave him on hold until he calls back. His secretary called first, as if it's such a bother for him to talk to me. Then he gets on the phone acting like we are long lost buds. I'll let him listen to the recording by the chief saying what a great department we are, and how we are fighting crime and have a diverse department."

A few minutes later, the phone rang again. "Detective Alexander? This is Mr. Storms again. You put me on hold and I think we were disconnected."

"I am so sorry about that Melvin. I guess you are calling to apologize about the two detectives that you kept waiting in your lobby this morning." She felt like the angler casting just the right bait to score the big fish.

"That was unfortunate, but that comes with the territory. When you become successful, you don't always control your time. If only they had called ahead of time, I would have seen them. But as I told them, the information they were seeking is protected under the attorney client privilege."

"Yes, that's what they told me."

"The reason I am calling is you visited Seamus Joyce today."

"Yes, that is correct."

"Perhaps I could arrange a meeting with you."

"Melvin, I know you are a very reputable attorney, but I think you may have a conflict of interest."

"What do you mean, Detective?"

She just felt the first nibble on the line. "Your client, Seamus Joyce, is a person of interest in the murder of Thomas Maguire. This is the same Thomas Maguire that you earlier invoked your attorney-client privilege. Now, I am not an attorney, but I don't think you can represent the man that killed your client. Especially since, I think Seamus paid your fee to represent your dead client, Thomas McGuire. In fact, Melvin, you might want to get your own attorney, because you and Joyce might be in cahoots."

"I resent the insinuation, Detective."

She just hooked the largemouth bass. "I am so sorry. I didn't mean to offend an officer of the court. As I told your current live client, Mr. Joyce, that the Tampa Police Department is dedicated to crime reduction and service to the community. We will *thoroughly* investigate your client, so he can avoid prosecution for something he did not commit. In addition, if along the way we uncover something else he is involved in that has nothing to do with the investigation, wouldn't that be a shame? Oh, and by the way Melvin, I am preparing a subpoena request for your bank records to identify who paid your fees for Maguire."

As he protested, Kate said, "Gotta go Marvin, talk to you later."

She hung up the phone and high fived Duffy and Rollins as if she just scored the winning goal for the Stanley Cup Championship. It felt good to put a top-notch attorney in his place. Storms did not know she was bluffing all the way. She knew that the State Attorney's Office would never issue a subpoena on a private attorney, unless he was dirty. She also knew she had no time to make Joyce a project. She merely wanted to rattle the cage.

Chapter Twenty-Six

Rollin and Bridges parked in the heat baked gravel parking lot and looked up at the sign. At night, it glowed with neon flashing lights illuminating the shamrock and the figure of the dancing girl on the side of the yellow corrugated building. The Lucky Cabaret populated a commercial and warehouse district on SR 60 just east of downtown. As they stepped inside, it took a few moments for their eyes to adjust to the darkness of the interior and their ears to adjust to the loud thumping music.

"Can I help you fellows?" said a brunette from behind the counter with more makeup than a commercial for Revlon.

Bridges said, "Tampa Police, we would like to see the manager."

"Are you vice detectives?"

"No, homicide."

"Homicide, oh, I'll get him for you."

They looked at two lonely souls sitting at the bar, keeping the barmaid company. Two construction workers sat at the round table around the stage as a topless red head with 6" pumps, slithered around the gold pole to a thumping beat. One of the construction workers stood up, waving a folded dollar bill, drawing the dancer closer.

A short, thick man approached the detectives. He was wearing a black guayabera and a large gold chain around his thick neck.

"Gentlemen, I am Silvio Romero, I am the manager here. Can I get you something to drink?"

Bridges said, "No sir. Is there someplace private where we can talk?"

"We can go to my office."

As they ambled down the hall, they pressed their backs against the wall of the narrow hallway to make room for a short-haired brunette wearing a black silk kimono robe. She smiled at them as she walked by. Inside the cramped office, they sat down on two stained blue banquet chairs while Silvio took his position behind the crowded desk.

"Candy told me you are homicide detectives."

Bridges said, "That's right. We are investigating the death of Thomas Maguire. He was a patron here on February 22. He got into a fight with a Seamus Joyce."

"Yes, I know Seamus, he is a frequent customer."

"Here is a picture of Maguire."

"Oh yes, I remember. They got into quite a fight in the club. I was back here and someone called the police. I heard it was over a woman."

"Who said it was over a woman?"

"It was one of the customers or one of the girls. I can't remember."

"Was the fight over one of the dancers?"

"I don't think so, because I think I would have remembered that."

"Have you seen Joyce's wife in here?"

"Oh no. She is too young to come in here. She is not twenty-one."

"Oh, so you have seen her?"

"Just in the parking lot. She came and picked him up one night. He was too drunk."

"I am sure you like to run a clean club here?"

"Absolutely. Just ask the Sheriff's Office."

"We have."

Silvio seemed a little surprised.

Rollins spoke, "I know most of the dudes in here are just having a couple of beers, watching the talent, and massaging the inside of their pockets. Is there any action going on in the parking lot?"

"I don't believe so. The bouncer checks the lot periodically. The only action out there is some couple that comes in here, and they can't wait until they get home. I am sorry I couldn't provide any more info."

"Are you aware that Mr. Joyce might be what is known as a pharmaceutical entrepreneur?"

He hesitated. "Ah, no, I was not. I only know him from the club."

Bridges said, "Thanks for your time."

"Hey you fellows should drop in while you're off duty. I'll waive the cover."

"Thanks."

Chapter Twenty-Seven

K ate dialed a number and cradled the phone in her neck as she flipped through the pages of *"Don't Sweat the Small Stuff,"* that Rollins gave her. After a few rings, a male voice answered. Kate put the book down and said, "Deputy Stepanski, this is Detective Kate Alexander, TPD. I understand you responded to a fight at the Lucky Cabaret in February. The two subjects were a Thomas Maguire and Seamus Joyce."

"Yes, I remember. They were both liquored up pretty good. They got their Irish up about something. It must have been quite a donnybrook. They put quite a few licks in on each other. I can't remember which one was which. The one said that the other made a move on his wife, and he was putting him in his place. The other one, I can't remember which one he was by name, but he denied it. They left separately. I could have charged them with being drunk, but they weren't causing me any trouble. Neither one wanted treatment, nor to file charges. They each claimed the other started it. One left in a cab and the other one left with a girlfriend."

"Were they mad enough to kill each other?"

"I didn't think so, but you guys know some of these people will kill over a pair of basketball shoes."

"Yes, you're right. Thanks."

Melvin Storms strutted through the door and straight towards Kate. The tall, impeccably dressed attorney, in a light gray suit, walked with confidence. He was carrying a distressed leather satchel. His almost white hair slicked back behind his ears, and his locks flowed over his collar.

Kate said, "Mr. Storms, what a surprise. Have a seat." She motioned with her hand towards the chair.

Storms placed the satchel on the floor next to the chair, adjusted the knot on his bright red tie, and tugged on his suit sleeves to cover the gold cufflinks. He ran his hand through the long white locks. If she didn't know better, she would have thought he was in front of a mirror.

Without introduction, he said, "There is no conflict. I could go into the chief and complain about your threats, and I would have a judge issue an injunction against your subpoena. I am busy, so let me clarify a few things. With Maguire dead, there is no conflict. I represented him on a probation violation. I received an unmarked envelope in the office. They dropped it off with our receptionist. I believe it was a courier, but you can check yourself. The envelope contained $3,000 in $100's and a type-written letter asking me to appear personally at his probation violation hearing. The letter did not contain a signature or a name. It was very bizarre. I placed the letter in his file. Get me a subpoena and I'll turn it over to you. I represented his interests at the hearing. It lasted all of thirty minutes and I never saw, nor heard from him again. Regarding Mr. Joyce, he vehemently denies being involved in the murder of Maguire. He is concerned that you might disrupt some of his business operations and therefore, being the good citizen that he is, he would like to cooperate. I will set up a meeting of mutual convenience with you at my law offices."

"Melvin, I appreciate you coming in here. We have already been out to see him, and we have been to see you without good results. If you don't mind and since your client is now in a more cooperative mood, perhaps he could come here. Especially now, since you know how to come here."

"Very well."

He stood up, picked up his satchel, and said, "My secretary will be in touch."

As he walked out, Duffy looked at Kate and said, "You played him like a cheap drum."

Her smile could have lit up Times Square at night.

Duffy, in a mocking tone, said, "Very well, I'll have my secretary contact you to schedule a meeting."

Everyone broke into laughter. Even Dumb and Dumber couldn't suppress their smiles.

Duffy dispensed a handful of M&M's and handed some to Kate. "Your reward, my dear."

She knew there was always a cat-and-mouse game between cops and lawyers. Sometimes a mutual distrust resonated with hate. She respected most lawyers and knew they had a job. She also knew she had a job. It was a human chess game monitored by the judge. If she did her job properly, it would remove many options for the lawyers. She knew some were absolute lizards. Storms was shifty, but honest. She thought if she needed a criminal lawyer, she would hire Melvin Storms.

Chapter Twenty-Eight

K ate sat alone at the traffic light at Bruce B. Downs and Fletcher Ave. tapping the steering wheel like a drum and lip-synching to a Taylor Swift song. The light turned green, and she turned right on Fletcher Avenue and entered the parking lot for the Louis de la Parte Florida Mental Health Institute at the University of South Florida. She stepped out on the wet pavement from the latest afternoon thunderstorm. An oil slick appeared across the top of a puddle. The temperature cooled to the upper 80's, but the pavement emitted humidity like moist vapors of a sauna. She walked back into the crisp, air-conditioned building and located the Department of Mental Health Law and Policy.

She found the office she was looking for on the second floor. She knocked as she entered and smelled a pleasant cologne in the air. "Dr. Trent Sellers? I am Detective Kate Alexander from TPD. We traded voice mails."

Dr. Sellers said, "Ah yes, I would prefer if you call me Trent. I am not real big on titles."

"Okay, Trent. You sound like my partner. I understand you are a forensic psychologist?"

"Yes. Well, yes, I am. I am also a professor. I am also a terrible cook, and I am also a Gator fan."

"I won't hold that against you. I went to Duke myself."

"No kidding. So did I. I did my doctoral at Duke with a forensic fellowship. They have a Federal Correctional Institute at Butner that is for those incarcerated that may have mental health issues. I made my way down to the Florida State Hospital at Chattahoochee for a little while before landing a faculty position here at USF."

"What do you do at the Department of Mental Health and Law?"

"You forgot the Policy part. The official poster says that we conduct research and training on the relationship between the legal and the mental health systems and develop innovative approaches to mental health and related services within the criminal and civil justice systems."

"That's a mouthful." She smiled pleasantly.

"I cut and paste it often enough. What can I do for a lovely detective with the Tampa Police?"

Trent had a soft-skinned face with comfortable features and a gentle smile that instantly made you like him. He had well-groomed hair with a tinge of gray mixed with light brown. His khakis and buttoned-down sport shirt added to his comfortable nature and reflected a man that still maintained a fitness program.

"I understand you do a little hypnosis from time to time."

"When the occasion calls for it."

"Do you have your gold pocket watch?"

"You have been watching too much CSI."

"That's my line."

"Most people think hypnosis is like the Vegas stage shows where they make people run around barking like dogs or clucking like chickens. Hypnosis is a trancelike state in that the persons characterized by extreme suggestibility, relaxation and heightened imagination. The person is alert the entire time. It is kind of like daydreaming, or when you read a great book and you become so absorbed, you lose awareness of your surroundings. Do you have children?"

"Yes."

"Have you ever had your children talking away, but you are ignoring what they are saying and you're focused on something that happened at work?"

"Sure."

"That is kind of like a hypnotic trance. We have to be very cautious because there is a level of suggestibility and that's where we can run into trouble. Take people that want to quit smoking or lose weight. That is nothing more than behavior modification. Through hypnosis, we get the client to associate bad things with the associative behavior they want to change or good things with compliance. The concept in forensic hypnosis is that many times people observe more than they are aware of or that they consciously remember. My job is to put them in a state of relaxation without inhibitions and open the door so that anything that the mind has suppressed through trauma or stress is within the range of recall. The conscious mind takes a step back and allows your subconscious mind to take the primary role.

"I have heard of it used in investigations in the past."

He nodded. "It is not uncommon that witnesses in homicides have difficulty recalling key facts that the unconscious brain has suppressed. Surprisingly, the unconscious brain covers seven-tenths of the brain. We have to be careful not to accept everything uncovered as gospel, and to tread carefully as not to fill the voids with our own wants. It is an investigative tool, no different from a polygraph or an eyewitness account. You will have to corroborate the information. You know the Fugitive, with Sam Sheppard, the Boston Strangler, and in the case of Ted Bundy?"

Kate leaned closer. "Sure."

His passionate eyes jumped like ballet dancers. "They used hypnosis to help with recall of the witness's observations in those cases. There are many snake oil salesmen that took a thirty-hour class off the back of a matchbook cover and now they call themselves hypnotherapists. I have taken three hundred hours of training and the American Council of Hypnotist Examiners and the National Board certified me as a Certified Clinical Hypnotherapist. I am not trying to impress you, but there are a lot of quacks in this business."

"Whether or not you tried, I am impressed. It is fascinating. My minor was in Psych. I find it exciting to get in someone's head."

"The mind is uncharted. There is so little we understand. Hey, maybe I can hypnotize you. That would be a wonderful demonstration."

"Not on your life." She smiled and looked down. She looked back up and said, "I could use your help on this case."

"I worked an excellent case with ATF a few years ago."

"Really? What was that involving?"

His hands became like illustrators on a canvas. "There was an arson case with negligible leads. A husband and wife observed a car across the street from the bar. After hypnosis, they provided a more accurate description and a partial Louisiana license. It was enough to identify what section of the state the license plate originated. The next witness was even better. She was a cashier at a Wal-Mart and sold a hotplate and a water jug. Under hypnosis, she could provide an excellent description of the suspect and recalled him drinking Pepto Bismol right out of the bottle. The cashier could provide enough information that a police artist could draw a sketch of the suspect. ATF put out a bulletin in that area of Louisiana. Low and behold, a deputy called and said he arrested a fellow a couple of years ago for arson. The suspect looked just like the drawing and he suffered from ulcers, hence the Pepto. The suspect's mother owned a car like the one described. Now, sometimes we come up empty. We are not miracle workers. If they did not see it, they can't remember." His hands collapsed into his lap.

"I am impressed. This case involves a homicide over on Nebraska Avenue. It was in a motel. One murder was an execution killing. In the apparent struggle, one errant round traveled into another room and killed a woman. Her boyfriend, who was a cheating husband and her boss, freaked and decided to get out of Dodge. He can't remember observing anything. I would like to see if he saw anything."

"Sure. Could I read the reports so I know what to ask and where he is going?"

"I'll send them in the morning. There is a bit of a rush on this. Can we do it tomorrow?"

"I am free in the morning after 10:00."

"Great."

"I am also free right now if you would care for a drink? I can provide further insight into the criminal mind."

She crossed her arms and smiled, "I am sorry I need to get home tonight. Thanks anyway."

"Maybe some other time?"

"Maybe. I'll see you tomorrow."

"Looking forward to it."

As Kate drove out of the parking lot, she looked at the empty ring finger gripping the wheel. She thought Trent seemed like a pleasant fellow. Maybe he was a little on the studious side, in a sexy way. He looked comfortable and stable. Since Jake's death, she never really allowed herself to have feelings for anyone else. As a working single mother, she had other priorities. She considered the possibilities. He was on the outside of the cop world. She was tired of the employees of the Blue Monster hitting on her and the associated gossip. Cops gossiped more than a group of bunco card players. Trent could be her intellectual equal. She started humming to a Jake Owen's tune.

Chapter Twenty-Nine

K ate and Duffy drove separate cars so they could go straight home after interviewing Maguire's boss. They drove down the uneven dirt road into the Serenity Lake Mobile Home Park, kicking up dust as their cars jostled down the road. Kate thought she should have driven her Jeep Wrangler to navigate this road. This was not some doublewide heaven. Foot tall weeds surrounded many of the trailers.

They passed an old green Lincoln on blocks. It was well past the days of being a status symbol. Kate thought, unlike the name of the park, there was no lake and there was nothing serene except the canopy of oaks. The branches of the oaks looked like the arthritic fingers of an old man and cast a gloomy mood. They finally came upon a mildewed white and turquoise trailer. The number eighteen was spray painted on the exterior shell.

Kirk Sussex was as thin as a blade of grass. His greasy brown hair was protruding from a camouflaged ball cap and his face had a few day's growth of beard. There was an earthy smell, punctuated with body odor. He examined the oil dipstick on a riding lawnmower. The lawnmower rested in a trailer attached to a shiny black Chevy pickup that looked out of place. Toby Keith echoed from the truck stereo. A large number 3 decal covered the back window.

Duffy and Kate walked up to Sussex and identified themselves. He stood up, pulled a long drag from the cigarette, and blew a long cloud of smoke upward towards the oak trees.

Kate said, "NASCAR fan, huh?"

"Yep."

She pointed to number three in the rear window and said, "Earnhardt fan?"

"You know it."

"It's been twenty years since he died."

With a two pack a day voice, he said, "Still a legend."

Kate nodded, "I like Aric Almirola myself."

"I can live with Aric. He's a local boy."

"Indeed. Kirk, we would like to ask a few questions concerning one of your former employees, a man named Thomas Maguire."

"What he do this time?"

"He died. Died of unnatural causes."

"No shit he was murdered?" he said, as he let out a congested laugh and a wet cough of non-surprise.

"Yes. When was the last time you saw him?"

"Not since his P.O. pinched him for dirty urine."

"Did you know he was using?"

He rubbed his stubbly face. "Understand, this is hard work and not always very steady. It's hotter than balls in the summer. We have to worry about thunderstorms and there is little work in the winter. So, it's hard to keep people."

"I understand that, but back to my question. Were you aware he was using?"

He took a deep drag on the cigarette and talked while the smoke spilled out of his mouth. "I don't run no convent here. What they do on their own time is their business."

With impatience, Frank said, "Mr. Sussex," raising his voice, "did you know he was using drugs?"

"Oh sure, he was a meth head."

Kate asked, "How did you know?"

"You guys are detectives, right?"

"Yes, but we're asking you."

"He was always jumpy. Kind of like a whore in church. His complexion was bad and so were his teeth."

"What kind of employee was he?"

"He was okay. I had better and I've had worse. When he showed up, he worked real good."

"Did he do any side jobs for any of your clients?"

"Not that I know. If he had anything on the side that was cutting into me, I would have fired him and beat his ass."

An old blue short wheel base Dodge minivan rumbled past. Latino music bellowed from the stereo. A pit-bull strained the strength of a chain as he barked ferociously at the passing van.

Kate said, "What about his drug connection?"

"I have no idea. I am not into that scene, and it's not like we would hang out together. Sometimes we would split a six-pack at the end of the day, but that was it."

"Could we get a list of your clients?"

"What are you going to do? Call all of them and tell them I hire a bunch of ex-cons and Mexicans? These people are clueless about life. They don't care about me or my employees as long as their lush green yards are mowed so they can play golf."

"We don't plan to call them. We would like the information, so if their name comes up later, we can call them. When he was picked up before, did you spring for an attorney or his bail?"

"Do I look like I am nuts?"

"Did he try to contact you after he got out of jail last week?"

"I had no idea he was out until you showed up."

"Can you get us that list?"

"Yep."

"Where were you yesterday at noon?"

"Same place every day, cept Sundays. Cutting grass."

Frank looked at the number three decal in the back window and said, "Is your mother alive?"

With a puzzled look, Kirk said, "Nope."

"How come you don't have her name in the back window?"

"She didn't win the Daytona 500."

"Yeah, sure, that makes sense." As he arched his eyebrows.

Frank nodded and walked towards his dust-covered car. He looked at Kate and said, "I just don't get that whole racing thing running around in circles."

"It's called racin and I wouldn't expect some Yankee to understand the complexities of drafting, sling shotting, getting clean air, and rubbing."

"You're a winner."

"Thanks. I'll see you tomorrow."

Chapter Thirty

WEDNESDAY

The smiling Duffy walked whistling and carrying his newspaper and coffee. He was wearing a light gray suit and black tie with what looked like exploding blue grapes. Kate was sitting at her desk reviewing reports.

Kate asked, "New tie? Are those grapes?"

"No, and no. One question at a time, counselor. The pattern is called testosterone. I thought it would be subliminal in a planned confrontation with Storms and Joyce."

"Like you need any more testosterone."

He slyly smiled. As he reached his desk, his smile dropped like an anchor into the sea. His M&M candy dispenser was gone. In its place, a neon yellow post-it note partially covered a photograph. The note read, "Help me! I've been kidnapped." He pealed the post it and saw the blue M&M was sitting on a workout bench in the gym. He placed the paper and coffee on the desk. His smile returned as he prepared for his rescue mission.

As he started out the door, Kate said, "Hey macho man, where are you going? Maguire will be here in a few minutes."

Duffy left in silence. Everyone exploded in laughter. Duffy exited the rickety elevator on the ground floor and walked with a purpose towards the gym. Bursting into the gym, he walked to the weight bench. He found another printed photo of the candy dispenser in a circular trashcan.

"Hey Duffy, lose something?"

Frank had not noticed, but turned around and saw Willis Holmes smiling and dabbing the sweat off his face. Holmes had biceps the size of most people's thighs.

"Yeah, funny Willis. I know you and Luster are in cahoots."

Holmes put his hand up in a surrender position.

Frank asked, "Where do you get the energy to pump iron after a midnight?"

"Testosterone, Dude."

"That's the name of my tie."

"Good luck, Frank."

He walked back into the squad room and found a trail of M&Ms on the floor leading to his desk. The colorful trail continued across his desk and stopped at the edge. The trashcan sat below where the trail ended. He reached into the receptacle and grabbed the dispenser.

Kate said, "I hear you have to be led to the evidence like a blind man in the dark."

"That, my dear, is an oxy moron. A blind man can only see darkness and they are referred to as visually impaired."

"Mr. P.C. I guess they would call you, finding evidence impaired."

"I'll show you impairment. Let's go talk to your boy."

They entered the small interview room. It smelled like a locker room at the YMCA. Meant to accommodate two detectives and a suspect, it was now crammed with the addition of Seamus Joyce's attorney, Melvin Storms. The attorney immediately asked if they could move to a larger room.

Duffy, playing the bad guy, said, "Sorry Melvin. The tax collections were down last year. This is as good as it gets."

Melvin looked at his Rolex and huffed.

Kate started, "I am going to read you your rights, and I will have your attorney witness the form. You are free to leave here at any time." After reading the rights form and obtaining signatures on the waivers, she asked, "How long have you known Thomas Maguire?"

"About one year."

"How did you become acquainted?"

"Around. You know I would see him at different places. We weren't tight. You called it. We were acquaintances." Joyce used his hand to form air quotes.

"Did he ever mention what his line of work was?"

"He was in landscaping. He said he wanted to start his own business. He asked me to front him the money. I told him I was not running a bank, and I sure in hell wasn't the Salvation Army."

"Did he mention to you about having a job with someone lined up?"

"He said something about a score lined up through a client that would pay off well. People are always talking smack. I didn't ask what it was concerning. I told him if it was such a good score, he could fund himself in his own business. He made that U-Turn and went back to the County jail. I didn't know he was out until I saw the article in the Times about the murder. It is such a terrible thing to meet such a violent end to a life."

"What kind of a person was he?"

"He was okay. He ran a hard and fast life. I wouldn't say he was prone to violence, but he would fight and get drunk."

"Why did you get into a fight with him at the Lucky Cabaret?"

"We were both drinking and trashed. I was ready to leave, so I called my wife to pick me up. She came in to let me know she was outside. Maguire talks trash to her right in front of me. I hit him and knocked him on his ass. The fight was on. Someone called the cops, and that was that. I don't think I saw him again."

"Did he buy drugs from you?"

Storms interjected, "My client will not answer that."

"Did you kill Maguire?"

He leaned forward, looked into her brown eyes, and said, "No, I did not. I whipped his ass that night. I might hold a grudge against him for talking trash, but I wouldn't kill him. I might have killed him that night, but I wouldn't wait six months later to kill him."

"Did you hire Mr. Storms to defend him?"

"Oh, for God's sake. No. Why would I spend the money to defend someone that offended me and my wife?"

"Do you own a gun?"

"My client will not answer that."

"Did you hire anyone to kill him or have any knowledge of anyone else involved in killing him?"

"No."

"Where were you on the day of the murder?"

"I was with my wife."

"We would like to speak with her."

"Sure, as long as she has representation. I always want to help the police reduce crime in my adopted community. This time, you can interview her at my attorney's office. I will not subject my wife to sitting in this hellhole."

Frank said, "Speaking of crime, I know you are a traveler from South Carolina. Most of you and your friends are scam artists. Maybe you have an occasional slugfest. I am surprised you came down here and set up shop selling drugs."

Storms said, "I believe this interview is over."

"One additional question. Would you be willing to take a polygraph examination?"

Storms speaking on behalf of his client, "Not a chance."

Kate said, "Thank you for coming in."

Melvin said, "Detective Alexander, you can meet Mrs. Joyce at my office at 1:00PM. You can leave Detective Duffy behind. He might scare off the clients."

"I'll be there and I believe Detective Duffy has a conflict this afternoon."

"See you then."

After Joyce and Storms left, Kate said to Frank, "You enjoy pissing off people, don't you?"

"Only assholes."

Chapter Thirty-One

Trent Sellers walked out to the reception area and extended his hand towards Nick Tortorino. They shook hands and exchanged pleasant smiles. Kate smiled warmly back at Trent.

"Hello Mr. Tortorino, I am Doctor Trent Sellers, but you can call me Trent. I appreciate you coming in here."

"I am a little nervous about this."

"I promise I won't make you bark like a dog."

Nick's smile dissipated.

Trent said, "I am sorry. That was a joke."

Tortorino gave an uneasy laugh as Trent escorted them into the conference room. Kate sniffed at the lavender candle.

She said, "Nice candle."

"Aromatherapy. Lavender calms the nerves."

Kate nodded in surprised acknowledgement. She was impressed. Aromatherapy. Few men would know the first thing about candles.

Trent turned to Nick and said, "If you have no objections, I will video record the entire procedure for validation for the court if it goes that far. I know you have been through a tough situation. I am here to help. I know you are here for the same reason. Together, working as a team, I believe we can help the police. Have you ever been hypnotized?"

"No."

"That is good. I want to dispel any myths or false information that you might have concerning hypnotherapy."

He explained everything concerning hypnosis to Nick. Trent then asked Kate to return to his office and wait. He turned on the video camera set on a tripod and spoke into the microphone stating the date, time, location, and identified himself and the examinee. He sat down facing Tortorino and engaged the metronome commonly used by musicians to keep the beat.

Trent said, "I would like you to close your eyes and relax. Have you ever been anywhere that you found as a complete escape from the stress of life?"

"I took a cruise a couple of years ago to the Bahamas."

"Why was it relaxing?"

"There were no phones or computers and it was just me and my family. It was nice."

"What kind of cruise was it?"

"It was a Disney Cruise."

"So, then you stopped at their private island."

"Yes."

"I want you to continue to relax and keep your eyes closed. Do you hear the beat of the metronome?"

"Yes."

"I want you to think about the private island. I want you to think about relaxing in the chair. The warm tropical breeze is blowing across your face. You are curling your toes in the cool soft sand. You're sipping a pleasant drink of your choice. Can you still hear the metronome?"

"Yes."

"You can hear the sounds from a steel band playing Caribbean music. It is so relaxing. Children are playing in the water. The waves are rolling across the beach and you can smell the salt water. You should feel yourself getting relaxed now. You can feel all of your worries draining out of your body. The top of your head is becoming more relaxed. You can feel your heart slowing down and your breathing becoming more relaxed, shallower. Your forehead is becoming more relaxed. You can feel the wrinkles relaxing and your eyelids becoming more relaxed."

Trent continued the progression through the entire body until he reached the toes and regressing to the beach and the metronome. After nearly thirty minutes, Trent finally thought he had achieved the hypnotic trance. He asked the test question of raising the arm.

"Your arm is very heavy. Can you lift it upwards?"

Tortorino lifted his arm in response to the command.

Sellers said, "I am going to take you back to the Pirate's Cove Motel. You enjoyed such wonderful times there with Wendy. She pleasured you. You have not felt like that in a long time. You are feeling ecstasy. What do you recall?"

Nothing changed concerning his previous statement provided to the police. Trent slowly progressed to the point of the shooting. As Nick described running out of the motel room, his breathing was deeper and faster.

"I was freaking out, man. I jumped in my car. I just wanted to get away. I'll never do that again. I swear. She meant nothing to me."

"In the car. What do you do?"

"I start the car. I slam the shift into reverse. I punch the gas and before I come to a stop, I smash the shift into drive and hit the gas. I just want to get away. I want to live."

"Who are you trying to get away from?"

"The killer is in room number three."

"Do you see the killer?"

"No. I see a car?"

"What kind of car?"

"A black car. It's a new Cadillac XT4."

"Why do you say a new Cadillac?"

"It was shiny and they look sharp and I own a Cadillac."

"Are there any bumper stickers or any other stickers?"

"No."

"Are there any dents or scratches?"

"No."

"Can you see the license?"

"Yes."

"What state?"

"Florida."

"Can you read the number?"

"I think it is X, ah 6, ah I think another 6, ah I can't see the rest."

"Why can't you see the rest?"

"That is all I saw before I hit the gas."

"Did anyone come out of the room as you were leaving?"

"No."

"Did you see anyone look out the window?"

"No."

"Was that car there when you arrived?"

"No. I only saw an old blue pickup truck parked in the middle of the parking lot. It was backed in."

Satisfied that Nick had related all thoughts related to the shooting, he brought him out of the trance.

"All right Nick, you have been very helpful. I want you to think about the beach again and the soft sand with the breeze blowing."

He brought him out of the state gradually.

"I am going to count to five. When I get to five, I want you to open your eyes and the session will be over. Do you understand?"

"Yes."

He concluded the session and said, "I think you have provided some useful information. I'll get Detective Alexander."

Nick said, "I feel great. No barking, right?"

"No barking."

Kate walked back in and thanked Nick for coming in. She sat down and began watching the video from the session.

Kate took notes and said, "Can I get some popcorn and Junior Mints?"

"Hey, this is not Muvico."

"Well, you'll just have to buy me lunch."

"You're on."

At the conclusion of the video recording, Trent ejected the SD card. He pulled out a silver marker, initialed, and dated the card for evidentiary purposes. He turned it over to Kate, who used his marker to initial and date, as well. Kate called back to Alfonso and asked him to have someone run the partial license of X66 through the computer and pull all the Cadillac XT4's with that partial. Now they could start looking at all the cars registered within 50 miles of the homicide and work out from there.

After Kate hung up, she said to Trent, "That was very interesting. It's amazing how the brain works."

"We have very little overall understanding of the brain compared to the heart. It is an interesting case. I hope the partial license helps."

"It's more than we had before."

"Hey, it's almost lunch. You made me promise."

She regretted her offhanded invitation. She put him off.

"Can I get a rain check? I need to get back and place this in evidence."

"You still have to eat. How about we lock it in your trunk and eat someplace where we can monitor your car?"

She looked at her watch and squeezed her lips together, hesitated and knew she owed him for at least the hypnosis and said, "I guess we could have a quick bite."

"Great. How about Subway?"

"That will work."

He handed her a manila envelope to hold the SD card, and they headed for the door.

Chapter Thirty-Two

T rent felt exhilarated. What a day. He conducted a great session of hypnosis that might be one piece of solving a murder. Now he was having lunch with a lovely and interesting young lady. Trent eagerly held the door open as she walked in. The aroma of warm bread wafted through the air. They approached the counter. Kate ordered a chicken wrap, and Trent ordered a turkey sandwich. Trent stepped forward and paid for both tickets. They sat down in awkward silence, neither knowing what to say. Trent stepped out from behind cover and, like a tennis player serving the first shot, he spoke, making a glancing blow by asking a question.

"I'll bet your job is very interesting and challenging, isn't it?"

She volleyed back, "Sometimes, but yours is to get inside the thought process of the human brain. It is intriguing?"

The volleying back and forth concerning job responsibilities and individual war stories continued. Trent was feeling comfortable and his confidence was growing. As they traded stories, he admired her comfortable, unassuming smile. Modest dimples accented her face. She was naturally pretty with little makeup, not like a beauty queen pretty, but a wholesome simple pretty. Her brown eyes were captivating. They were the type that exuded warmth. He finally went for the hard serve and sent one past Kate.

"So, you spoke of children earlier, but I noticed you're wearing the rings on your right hand, divorced?"

The smile evaporated from Kate and she looked down at her near empty plate and broke a potato chip in half. He recognized he hit a nerve.

"I am sorry. I didn't mean to get too personal."

She curled her hair behind her left ear and looked up at him. "Jake was killed."

Oh great, now you did it. Here you go. The beginning of crash and burn. He could write a book on how to fail in romance.

"I am sorry I didn't..."

"No. Ah.... no, it's all right. He was in the Army and was killed in action while in Afghanistan. It was unexpected. I just never expected to see that car pull up and see the major and the chaplain come to the door. It's kind of like when I show up at your door. Your day is pretty well ruined. Jake and I were soul mates. I heard the victim's husband say she liked to live on the edge. Jake and I both did. That is why we were so much in love. We did everything together. We loved being together. I still have a part of him in Britney, our daughter. She is nine and looks just like him. She has the same spirit."

"Perhaps she has some of your spirit as well."

"Perhaps. Well, I guess I should get back to work."

"I am sorry I brought that up."

"I am sorry I unloaded. Thanks for lunch."

"My pleasure. Maybe we can do it again sometime."

"Maybe." They exchanged smiles. Hers was a quiet one. They shook hands and parted.

That was a middle of the road response. Not good, not bad. It was hard to tell if she was interested. They were having fun, but Trent felt like he just stepped on a roadside bomb. He did not know if he had gotten to first base. Lunch dates almost guaranteed getting to first base. He made too much of an assumption with the rings on the right hand. What an imbecile. He knew he should have stepped a little softer. He should have started by asking about the children and working. Then ask, what does your husband do? Nooo. He had to ask, are you divorced? What a slap to a woman who lost her husband through a tragedy. He may as well have slit his wrists. That was his luck with women. He may have been an expert on the human thought process, but when it came to talking to women, he was as cumbersome as a newborn giraffe trying to stand for the first time. He went back to his office feeling empty.

Chapter Thirty-Three

K ate returned to the office. Frank had not returned from taking his wife, Bridget, to the doctor. She pleaded with Lester to accompany her to Melvin Storm's office. After a mild protest, he agreed with a white-toothed smile. Rollins agreed to meet her downstairs in the lobby.

Sergeant Stewart stepped out of his office and quietly asked, "Kate, have you seen Dumb and Dumber?"

"No."

"Dad Gummit."

He turned and walked back into his office. Kate stood up and followed him into his office. He was inspecting the crawling stem from an orchid sitting in a bucket of water.

"Is that a new orchid?"

"It's a jewel orchid."

"You keep it up and the water department is going to cite you for violating the watering restrictions from the drought."

"You're right. Where are those two dopes? I text them. I should check The Wing House or the gym."

"What's going on?"

The phone ringing interrupted his response.

"Where in the heck are you? Ahh huh, ok, ah, huh? Is your sidekick with you? There is a shooting at an ATM at the Plant Bank on Platt Street. No, write this down. Not Plant Street. Plant Bank on Platt. You got that. Looks like a UT Student was killed. I need you two to step up to the plate. Crime Scene is on the way. Let me know if you need anything. I'll be down shortly."

Kate asked, "Sarge, why do you keep those idiots around?"

"It was like when I played football. Some players are better than others. The more gifted athletes would pick up the slack and compensate for the less athletic individuals. At some point, all players had to play as an entire team to expect consistent success. I reached a point where I was no longer the standout. The problem comes in when some inferior players thought they were better than their abilities. We have to play as a team here as well. Sometimes the administration gives you a player you don't like, but you still have to play them and hope they won't cost you the game. This should be an easy touchdown for them. A girl walks up to the ATM and some gang banger pops her. I am sure the shooter didn't work at NASA as a rocket scientist and it won't take one to figure this one out. With Canseco and Dietz, their problems come in when they think everyone else is stupid."

Kate nodded in agreement and headed downstairs to meet Rollins.

Chapter Thirty-Four

Sergeant Stewart stopped his white Ford outside the secured crime scene. The marked white Dodge Charger with blinking blue lights blocked Platt Street. Yellow plastic crime scene tape stretched across the road. Reese Crenshaw from the Tribune stood behind the tape. He was surrounded by a crowd that looked like they were at Disney waiting for the park opening in the morning. The uniformed officer was in no mood to keep the reporter entertained, and thus sat in his car working a crossword puzzle.

Crenshaw had been covering the police beat for what seemed like forever. All the cops knew him. He stood out with his thick head of white hair pulled back in a ponytail and a neatly groomed white beard. A small fake diamond stud adorned his left ear. He always wore a sport coat and blue jeans. A photographer snapped pictures with a long-range lens and the local NBC affiliate news truck had just parked. Reese and Alfonso nodded at each other.

"Reese, how are you today?" He waved his large hand.

"Good Alfonso. Good to see you today. Is the PIO on her way?"

"Yep. I'll brief her when she arrives."

"Thanks, Alfonso. Anything at all yet?"

"Nope. You probably know more than I do. I'll find out as quickly as I can."

"Thanks."

Alfonso sauntered up to Detective Dietz. Stewart always thought the detective reminded him of a Shar-Pei dog with a wrinkly head.

Dietz said, "Thanks for coming, Sergeant. I always feel better once you get on scene."

Alfonso's face revolted like he had just sucked on a lemon at the attempt to suck-up, "Shut up. What happened?"

"It looks like some brother, ah, an African American male. He was wearing a yellow Gecko Unlimited hooded sweatshirt with the hood up over his head. Baggy jeans and he was wearing more gold than Mr. T. It looks like a crime of opportunity. A witness saw him jog up, put the gun against her head and bang. He ran back the way he came. It looks like she was withdrawing a twenty. The receipt was hanging from the machine, as was the cash."

"Do we have an ID on the victim?"

"A Lori Applebaum. Man, he is bold, hitting like this in broad daylight. I'll check the recently released prisoners and similar robberies. I'll get the witness with the artist to workup a sketch. This is her car, the black Beemer. The car was still running. Crime scene is checking it out. The shooting is pretty straightforward."

"Remember, nothing is as it seems. You make a lot of mistakes making assumptions and coming up with theories too early."

"Yes, sir, you're absolutely correct. I won't leave any stone unturned."

"Save it. Just find the shooter."

Alfonso walked up to the ATM. He stood in stoic silence, examining the blood spatters against the terminal like a visitor to an art gallery. There was a five-inch concentration of blood on the ATM. Another three inches of smaller spatters extended out in an uneven pattern from the middle. The spatters got smaller the further out from the center. He looked at the impact from a bullet in the stainless-steel ATM. It appeared to be a larger caliber hole. Maybe a .45 or a .357. The round may have sustained so much damage that it might be useless for comparison. Heavier fragments of skull and other matter landed on the ground in front of the ATM.

Alfonso looked down at the lifeless body with a hole in the back of her skull and a larger hole in her forehead. Crumpled over on her side, the girl looked like she laid down to go to sleep. Her brown eyes were open and stared too nowhere. Judging from the spatter concentration, the shot was fired from close range. The bullet had some oomph behind it to go through the skull and to have enough velocity to imbed in the frame of the ATM. The head is a small target for someone jacked up, committing a crime, and is out of breath from running. They were either a good shot or lucky. Lucky for Lori Applebaum that she never knew what happened. She was watching the money come out of the dispenser and lights out. If there was a blessing, she did not suffer. There would be a lot of suffering for her family.

He looked at the young, lifeless girl and thought of his daughters about the same age. How do you really keep them safe? There was so much hate and death in this world. This was why he worked homicide. He couldn't help the victims, but he could help the future victims that would never know he saved their lives. He called over to Dietz.

"Hey Dietz, have you found a shell casing? It should be here to the right."

"No, I looked."

"They either picked it up or used a revolver. A random act mope won't take the time to pickup a casing. If it was a revolver, it had some kick to it."

Dietz and Canseco nodded in agreement.

He saw Becky Godfrey, the PIO, duck under the tape and leave Reese Crenshaw with all the other newsies asking unanswered questions and speculating. He was glad he could brief Becky and leave. He was looking forward to going home and hugging his girls.

Chapter Thirty-Five

Frank behind the wheel glanced over and asked Kate how the meeting went with Mrs. Joyce.

"As we figured. She confirmed her husband's version. She made me giggle. Maguire came on to her and said that he wanted to get in her pants. She said that she already had one asshole. Why would she need two? He called her a bitch, and the fight was on."

"Spunky?"

"Definitely."

"I wish I was there. Why do you want to go back to the motel?"

"I want to go back to see if anything comes to mind."

"Sure, no problem. Do you mind if we swing by and pickup a Cuban sandwich after? I am starved."

"Sure. How did the appointment go?"

"Fine."

"Was that fine good or fine bad?"

"Just fine. That chemo makes you sicker than a dog."

"You should have taken off the rest of the day."

"Work is a distraction for me. My mother is with her."

"It's not like the job is going to say, hey thanks for coming."

"I know. It's for me. I am well beyond expecting gratitude from work."

"If you need anything, I know I can't touch Frank Duffy in the kitchen, but I can buy a mean pizza."

Frank slowed the car to yield to an approaching red fire truck, lights flashing, siren wailing, and air horn blasting. A pumper truck entered a storage complex. The siren stopped. The pumper hesitated as the manager frantically pointed the truck in the emergency's direction. The truck followed the bellowing black smoke.

Kate said, "Wow. Wouldn't that be a bummer to have your stuff in there and another unit catches fire and burns up all your stuff? I'll bet most of those people don't have insurance."

"It's probably a bunch of stolen stuff, anyway."

"Mr. Compassion. Hey, there goes Jimmy Severands."

The SUV with the overhead red and blue lights bounced into the parking lot.

"After the motel, let's go back and talk to Jimmy."

"Your wish is my command."

Kate stepped out of the car in the parking lot of the Pirate's Cove Motel. She looked at her Timex sports watch and made a mental note that it was 1:30 PM. She looked around and looked up at the hazy, heat-seared sky. The fragrance of freshly cut weeds lingered in the air. She watched the flow of traffic past the motel. She imagined the black Escalade driving into the lot. How Wendy and Nick were in a jovial mood, eager to get to the room for their tryst. They were happy. They had no clue that within minutes their lives would be inexplicably changed. Wendy would be a client of the morgue and Nick's philandering life was forever derailed.

She could not identify with their passion. A long time had passed since she'd experienced the anticipation of a lovemaking session. She recalled the time she and Jake drove to the Keys for a diving expedition. They could hardly wait to get into the room to ravage each other. She could not imagine what Wendy and Nick were feeling as cheating spouses. Despite their adultery, Wendy did not deserve to die.

Maguire made bad choices in life. Drugs consumed his life and caused his death. If he died by overdose or drug related disease, that was his choice. There was no choice in murder.

She squinted into the scorching sun. She thought about all the families long ago traveling along U.S. 41, better known as Nebraska Avenue. They traveled roads like this on summer vacations before the interstate highway system. No air conditioning in the hot station wagons and the kids looked forward to jumping into the pool and splashing in the refreshing water. Dirt now filled the pool. Weeds flourished where the water once glistened. The area was once a destination for family getaways, drive-in movies, and putt putt golf. Now it was tired and populated by cheap hotels and prostitutes.

Nothing stood out concerning new leads. She felt their deaths. She was more determined to find Wendy and Maguire's killer.

As she slid into the fabric seat, she smelled the ham and pork. She looked over at Frank's lap, now covered in crumbs from the crispy Cuban bread, as he dabbed mustard off his mouth with a napkin. He swallowed a bite of sandwich.

He said, "Anything?"

"No. But I can feel it now."

Frank nodded his head in agreement, rolled up the sandwich in the wrapper, and shifted the gear selector to drive.

Chapter Thirty-Six

F rank guided the Dodge over to the storage facility. As they opened the car doors, the acrid odor of fresh smoke slapped them in the face. Kate brushed her hair back with her hand and yelled, "Jimmy!"

"Hey, it's Kick Ass. What can I do you for?"

"What have you got going?"

"It's a regular who done it. One of the storage units has some shifting of boxes. A jug of oil falls over and starts spreading under the door. The manager becomes concerned that it may have gotten into the adjoining units. He pops this one open and realizes that all is not copasetic. He said it looks like someone is living inside. It's set up with an easy chair, a sleeping bag, and carpet. He said it was immaculate. There were some candles, a laptop, and some electronic looking equipment. There was a milk crate with files and some photographs on the wall. He thinks that at least two of the photos have a big black X through them. Ding ding ding. He knows something isn't right. He runs to the office to call the police. He gets back, and he sees all the smoke and runs back to call the F.D. They get here first. They said it appears there was an alarm system of some sort that was wired to a napalm bomb."

"A napalm bomb?"

"That's what they said. Therefore, whoever was the occupant here didn't want the contents examined. A tall mustached man with his protective fire equipment walked towards the group."

Severands said, "This is Lieutenant Graphton."

Graphton said, "I have the Fire Investigation Division en route. It appears there was an alarm system wired up with an outgoing cell phone to call the monitoring location. It used the light socket as a power source. Another cell phone used from the outside called the detonating cell phone to initiate the explosive device. This was somebody who knew what they were doing. It looks like napalm. They add soap or polystyrene to gas to make it a gelatin. It burns a lot slower than gas and thus meant to burn everything in here. We used foam on the fire. The remaining storage units, we could use the conventional fire hose."

Kate said, "This is strange."

"Very. I can say, I have never seen this before in Tampa. I've been here for fifteen years. I have only read about similar devices."

"Maybe we'll talk to the manager and see what he has to say."

"Be my guest. He motioned toward the office.

"Thanks, Lieutenant."

She briefed Jimmy on the updates for the Pirate's Cove case and asked if he had heard anything on the street. He told her the street was quiet and pointed them towards the manager's office.

They entered through the glass door. The door chime announced each visitor as the door opened. The office reeked of overpowering cologne. Behind the Formica counter was a neatly organized desk. They mounted a bank of color monitors on the wall behind the desk. Duffy waved at the camera and gave a goofy smile that was projected on one monitor. It was a nice deterrent for robbers. The manager was on the phone but quickly ended the call and gave a big sigh.

Kate said, "Mr. Cruz, we are with the Tampa Police. The fire department's investigation division is on their way. They will investigate the arson. We are curious about the photos you saw with the X on them. Could you identify who they were?"

"No. They didn't look familiar to me. It was just somewhat weird. There were also some photos without an X."

"What size were they?"

"Maybe 8x10's."

"Were they portraits?"

"Sort of. It was more of the face shot, but it didn't look like they were posing."

"Were they female or male, young or old?"

"I didn't study them too long. I am glad I didn't. I could have been blown up and turned into a crispy critter."

Frank said, "Yes sir, you cheated death today. Hey, the Lotto is up to 15 million. You might buy a quick pick."

Kate said, "Mr. Cruz, back to the photos."

"I think one was maybe a teenager, another was an older woman with short hair, and one was definitely an older man. There were more, but I can't remember."

"That's okay. I know it's very traumatic. How do people access their unit?"

"We provide 24-hour access. They punch in a code."

"Does everyone have their own code?"

"Yes."

"Does your computer maintain a log of the codes?"

"Yes."

"Do you have a file on the person who rented the unit?"

"Here is a copy of his driver's license. Albert Lias."

Kate and Frank looked at the poor quality black and white copy. The subject in the photo had a heavy mustache. Frank took the copied driver's license to the telephone to run the name.

Kate asked, "Do you have surveillance cameras?"

"Yes ma'am. We have 16 cameras with a 30 days storage capacity. It cost a lot of money for the system. This is not some fly-by-night operation."

"I can see that."

Frank said, "I checked the D.L. Number. It comes back to someone else. The address is one of those mailbox places. There is no criminal history on Albert. I think he is having a little fun. Albert Lias or Al Lias or perhaps put them together to make Alias. Get it, ha ha ha."

Kate said, "Can you pull the logs and see the last time someone used that code to enter the property?"

"Sure."

"Do you remember what this guy Lias looked like?"

"He looked like his picture wearing a ball cap of some kind. He wore sunglasses the whole time."

"What kind of sunglasses?"

"Those tear drop type."

"You mean like the aviator type that pilots use?"

"Yes exactly. They kind of stood out because they were a little big and he wore them inside."

"How did he pay?"

"One year of cash upfront. Many of our customers don't have the best of credit, so they don't want anything to happen to their belongings. They may stiff the phone company, but not the storage company."

The phone rang the same time the door chime sounded. Kate and Frank turned. A good-looking fellow with short black hair walked through the door wearing a blue jumpsuit and fire boots.

"How you doing? I am Rex Hampton with FID. What's homicide got to do with this?"

Kate said, "We happened to be coming by to talk to the uniform concerning another case. Your lieutenant suspected arson and Alex Cruz here told us he saw some photographs with an 'X' through it."

Rex said, "It doesn't mean it's homicide." He crossed his muscular arms as he looked over the edge of his nose.

Kate could sense some hostility. She wanted to launch damage control and keep this fellow an ally. Besides, he filled out the jumpsuit nicely and had rugged good looks.

"No, and we have no intention of stepping on your toes. We wouldn't know the first thing to look for inside that crime scene. Therefore, we backed off once we heard you folks were coming. Actually, we have no jurisdiction at this time. This is your case. Alex is going to pull the entry logs to see if they have any video on the tenant. I am not too optimistic that the video will give a clear picture. He tried to cover his tracks and hide his appearance. Look at the copy of his D.L. His name is Albert or Al Lias. Alias, get it?"

Rex smiled and nodded. "Got it."

"We have a few unsolved homicides. One was an execution and one was collateral damage. It's kind of coincidence that this person has photos with X's. Who knows, maybe he is an assassin."

"An assassin?" His arms dropped to the side.

She wanted dramatic effect to raise the alarm and importance. She really did not know if there was a connection. He would feel privileged to have some inside information.

"Yes, or a serial killer, but people start spazing when they hear serial killer. An assassin has an agenda and if this Alias has anything to do with those, it confirms my suspicions that he is hunting for human prey for some reason not known to us. When it comes to arson scenes, we don't know our ass from a hole in the wall. You're the expert and you have been through the training and police academy as well. I am sorry if we stepped on your toes."

"Hey, no problem," Rex said. "I'll let you know what I come up with."

"We would appreciate it. Here is my card."

As they were driving out of the facility, Frank said, "I would have told him to kiss my ass. They have a chip on their shoulder. Firefighters are all the same. They screw off most of the time waxing their trucks or playing cards waiting for the ding ding ding. They only work for the city for the insurance. They all have full-time gigs on the side, like carpenters or plumbers."

"It never hurts to be nice. I would rather have him with us instead of being an adversary. Besides, no one wants their job when they get the ding, ding, ding and have to slide down the pole."

Kate thought that, at times, Frank could be too insolent and too principled. You get more bees with honey. It wouldn't hurt to put the jealousies aside so they could achieve a common solution and put a killer away.

"Kate, you are a 100 percent right, but he can still kiss my ass."

"Besides, he was kind of cute."

"It would never work. Cops and firefighters. It's like oil and water."

"Haven't you heard opposites attract?"

"Yeah sure."

"Frank, can you pull over at the CVS up the street? I need some Advil. My head is killing me."

Chapter Thirty-Seven

They stopped at the CVS. He could see Kate was deep in thought and said, "What are you thinking?"

"I don't know. It's odd."

"Alias didn't want anyone to have a look see inside the unit. He really is trying to cover his tail. But, I'm stumped."

Kate walked into the drugstore and Frank unwrapped the last of his sandwich, once again dropping crumbs. As Kate walked out of the store, she hesitated to answer her cell phone. When she ended the call, she returned to the car.

"That was Rex. He said he has some preliminary findings for us. So, we can go back to the storage facility."

"Oh good, I get to see Kate Alexander gush over the cute strapping fireman."

"I think they prefer to be called firefighter."

"Yeah, whatever."

After they returned to the storage facility, they could smell the stale odor of fire. The fire trucks were gone, but the water puddles remained. Hampton stepped out and peeled off a pair of rubber gloves covered in black soot. Black streaked his perspiring face.

Hampton said, "The alarm system was not too sophisticated. Looks like maybe a sensor on the door and you can see the infrared beam at calf high. A rat would not set that off, but someone walking through would. The alarm is wired into an automatic dialer that dials out on a cell phone. I didn't know if there was a listening mike or not. It looks like another cell phone was wired to the device. When it rang, it completed the circuit."

Frank interrupted and said, "Good thing he didn't use my cell phone provider. It would have dropped his call."

Rex, with a look of annoyance, continued and said, "The circuit was wired up to a battery, and two lines went out to two separate initiators that created the explosions in three, one-gallon jugs of a petroleum-based fuel."

Kate asked, "Was it napalm?"

"Yes, I am sure it was, but the lab will confirm it. I still need to collect samples. This dude knew what he was doing. He is not some kid who read this off the internet. In that 10' x 10' room, he spread out three gallons of fuel on that carpet. He wanted to make sure nothing survived. There was a laptop in there that is toast. If you want the laptop, maybe someone can image the hard drive and see if any of the data survived. You know how fast the hard drive can crash under everyday situations. I would not be too optimistic. There was one thing that survived."

"What's that?"

"It was one of those generic white plastic shopping bags. I found a receipt in the bag from the Da Boyz n Girlz Hip Hop Fashions. It was for cash."

"How did that survive?"

"It is amazing the things that survive sometimes. You just scratch your head. My money is on Alex opening the door and it blew out. On the other hand, it has nothing to do with this and was just blowing around outside. In the fire department, we would call that a clue."

Frank asked, "Well, Mr. Fire Investigator, what about the cell phones?"

"There is not much left. I would suspect they are prepaid phones. If he is trying to cover his identity, that would be the most difficult to trace. I'll send the documents recovered over to the FDLE lab to see if they can recover anything from them."

Kate said, "What do you mean?"

Rex explained that sometimes the paper doesn't burn clean. Paper is composed of wood pulp and water. In a flash fire, it doesn't have time to completely dry in order to burn one hundred percent. Occasionally, paper can be recovered and processed. It's dried using a low humidity heat. Then they remove the soot and expose the writing underneath. It is tedious and therefore time-consuming. Kate was intrigued at learning about a new area of crime scene investigation.

Rex added, "The shopping bag might contain fingerprints. I know they can get them off trash bags, so why not this?"

"Your right. All right, Rex, good job. I'm impressed."

Rex said, "Coming from you guys, that means something."

Frank said, "Let's not start getting all sappy here."

Rex said, "No, I'm not. I know we don't always get along with each other, I mean between the P.D. and the F.D., but we're on the same side, and I have pride in doing a good job."

Kate said, "I'm convinced. If you don't mind, we can copy that receipt in the office and you can log everything into evidence."

Rex said, "Do you think this is connected to these killings?"

Kate said, "I just don't know. It's definitely weird enough. Let's stay in touch."

Kate and Frank walked away from the fire fighters toward the Dodge. Kate said, "We might want to hypnotize Alex Cruz and see if he remembers anything else."

"You just want to use that as an excuse to see your USF honey."

Her cheeks turned a crimson color as she looked down at the ground.

"No, I don't. It is purely for investigative purposes."

"Yeah, sure, and I just hit the 15-million-dollar Lotto. When is the last time you went out with someone?"

"I go out."

"With a man?"

"Yes, I go out."

"You didn't answer the question, Little Miss Investigator."

"I am invoking my rights."

He pointed his finger and raised his inflection. "Kate, you have carried that torch too long. You have a life. If anything happened, I would want my Bridget to carry on and see the one or two good-looking guys' leftover after me."

"You're not dead."

"You know what I mean."

"I know what you mean and I am again invoking my rights to not answer any additional questions."

"Hampton was okay too."

Ignoring his statement, she said, "Mr. Cruz probably didn't see anything other than the distorted appearance of Alias. That may not be conducive to hypnosis."

"Sorry, now you're going to have to come up with a different excuse to call the good professor."

"To quote the great philosopher, Francis Xavier Duffy, yeah, whatever."

She thought she really needed to get out more and have a life. She had become such a homebody. All her social outings were associated with the police. Trent was a definite possibility. So was Rex. He was gorgeous. However, she was right back in with an investigator and cop type work. She lived cop work eight hours or more a day. Trent gave an intellectual deviation to the cop world. He was nice. What's wrong with nice? He may not have the hard edge, but it was worth taking the ride for a while. She was looking forward to a smooth ride as opposed to a wild ride.

Chapter Thirty-Eight

C hanging the subject, she looked over at Frank and asked if he had the list that she gave him from DMV. This provided the local registered owners with the first letters of the license plate on the suspect's car at the motel that Nick recalled in his session with Trent. If they struck out, they could widen the search to include all dark colored Cadillac's and enlarge the geographic search.

Kate said, "Let's go down the list."

Frank read aloud from the list, "The first one was totaled in a wreck. The second one, the owner, was arrested in the early morning before the shooting and the car was still in impound. The third one was stolen a week before and has not been recovered."

"Really?"

"Yep."

"Why take the chance he might get stopped driving a stolen car?"

"Well, you just say, oh it was recovered, and I forgot to notify the police."

"Okay. We'll put a question mark on that. If we come up dry on the others, we can go back to that one."

"All right, who is next?"

"Let's see. The next one, Dumb and Dumber, checked and said it was a soccer mom. Next, is a Maximilian Kress. That sounds like a real blue blood name."

"Did you say Max Kress?"

"Yeah, do you know him?"

"Sure do. My husband and Max were coaches in little league baseball. In fact, more than that, when I was in missing persons, I rolled on his daughter Jennifer. She was murdered a couple of years ago. Some piece of shit grabbed her outside the mall and killed her. A deputy shot the suspect. Blake Hamilton caught the case. He wouldn't come out at first until they found the body. I made the notification. It was probably the hardest one that I made."

"None of them are easy."

"Nice family and nice kid. They didn't ask for that."

"That's why we do our job. To save the next victim. How was Hamilton to work with?"

"A slug."

"That's why Al forced him out. Back to Mr. Kress. Is he a killer?"

"No, no way. He was a sweetheart."

"That's what they said about Ted Bundy."

"Max was a civil engineer. He made some money and started buying up land and using his engineering knowledge to subdivide and sell the developed land to builders. He did very well, and what started out as a way to make a little money on the side, turned into his own land development company. He played some minor league baseball, and that's why he enjoyed coaching baseball."

Kate thought of David Stilts, the murderer of Jennifer Kress. He was a predator preying on a defenseless victim. Jennifer had so much potential in life. David Stilts ended that.

Chapter Thirty-Nine

T hey drove in silence as she looked out the passenger window, viewing the world go by and not seeing anything. She remembered the little league baseball games that Jake and Max coached. They were opposing coaches teaching young boys not just a game, but lessons in life. All the little boys were having fun. She had at one time wanted a son of her own. Deprived of that opportunity brought sadness. She was just happy to have Britney.

Frank turned the car down Tampa Palms Boulevard, lined with the towering palm trees. Different communities branched off the main drag. Some moderately priced and some posh neighborhoods hidden by gates. It was in one of those latter neighborhoods that Max Kress lived. Frank viewed the elegant stucco homes with Spanish tile roofs.

"Max must do okay for himself." Frank said.

They drove past a woman pushing a stroller and Kate said, "Nanny or resident?"

"Nanny. The shoes gave her away, and she had no makeup."

"Frank, I'll make you into a good investigator yet."

"Yep, that's the problem in some of these places. They farm out the child rearing, while mom hangs out at the club, playing tennis, and golf, and talking about their next Botox injection."

"That's a sexist comment."

"Guilty. Report me. What are they going to do, transfer me to homicide and call me out in the middle of the night and on weekends?"

"This is his house up here."

They looked at the enormous house and observed an older frail man who appeared to be in his 60's. He was standing in the driveway with his hands in his pockets, talking to a good-looking fellow, who appeared to be in his early twenties with short, dark hair. Frank stopped the car against the curb and the two men turned their attention towards the Dodge. Kate opened the car door and felt the heat rise from the street.

Kate said, "Max, how are you doing? I don't know if you remember me."

He looked with bewilderment.

She said, "I'm Kate Alexander."

His face brightened and said, "Yes. I remember. How are you doing? Are you still with the police department?"

"Yes. I am. How have you been?"

The smile was absorbed back into the sad face. "Getting by. Somehow, I sense this is not one of those, I've-been-in-the-neighborhood-and-decided-to-drop-in."

"No, it's not."

He touched the shoulder of the young man and said, "This is Luke Shugard. He is a longtime family friend."

"It's nice to meet you."

"It's a pleasure as well. Hey Max, I need to run, so I'll see you later."

Kate said, "I hope it wasn't something I said?"

"Oh, no ma'am. I was just getting ready to leave, anyway. Bye," Luke said as he waved his arm and headed for a small silver car.

Max said, "Nice boy."

"Yes, he seems it."

"So, what can I do for you?"

"We are running out some leads in a case. Someone was able to get a partial license plate on a black Cadillac."

"I don't drive too often. When I do drive, it's up to Publix or to eat."

"Do you know where the Pirate's Cove Motel is?"

He shook his head and said, "No. I don't."

"It's up on Nebraska."

"Oh no, I don't get over that way. I have everything here in Tampa Palms."

"Have you had the car serviced or left unattended?"

"No, not lately."

"Does anyone else use the car?"

"Sometimes, Luke. He helps to keep the tires from rotting. He never drives very far and certainly not over to Nebraska Avenue. He just runs local errands."

"What is this about?

Kate said, "Oh, it's nothing Max. It had nothing to do with you. I just needed to check you off the list. Don't worry about it. How is Marge? Is she inside?"

"No, she's not. I guess she is okay. She left me a few months ago."

"I am sorry to hear about that. Is everything else okay?"

"Oh, I suppose."

"Well, it was good to see you again, Max."

"Same here. Be careful."

As they drove away from the large home, Kate said, "Boy, has he changed. Max was a very outgoing and a likeable person. Now he has a flat affect. No personality. He looks ten years older than he is. I guess he never got over his daughter's death."

"I don't think I would if something happened to Erin or Anna. It's a father's or a parent's worst nightmare. No one wants to get that phone call or knock on the door. I would fall apart. No parent should outlive their child. Maybe that's why I like homicide so much. It's my contribution to keeping my girls safe. I take bad guys off the street. The thinning of the herd."

"Yes. Makes sense." She said as she thought about the knock on the door and the delivery of bad news. She had delivered death notifications, as well as being on the receiving end.

Chapter Forty

D umb and Dumber parked in front of a large two-story gray and white trimmed home in Hyde Park. It was one of those stately older homes with a huge covered porch. The house was on a street lined with a canopy of oaks and dangling Spanish moss. They stepped onto the porch as it creaked under their weight. The white rattan rockers and the porch swing sat empty. Dietz pushed the doorbell and heard the chime. He watched a bee buzzing around some fragrant, red, flowering rose bushes in front of the house. An older looking man with glasses came to the door. He was smiling. He pulled the glass door open.

"Hello Mr. Applebaum, I am Detective Dietz and this is Detective Canseco and we are with Tampa Police Homicide."

"Homicide?"

"Ah yes sir, I am sorry sir, ah I am afraid we have some bad news about your daughter, Lori."

"No, no, it must be a mistake. She should be on her way home from school. She is a freshman at the University of Tampa."

"I know, sir, but she was at an ATM at Plant Bank. Apparently, ahh, someone shot her trying to rob her. She ah didn't make it, sir."

He stepped back as if he was trying to put distance between the bad news and himself. He said, "No. It can't be. This must be some mistake."

"I am sorry, sir. We found her identification at the scene."

"Who would do this to her? Why? Oh, my God. No, this can't be happening."

"I am sorry Mr. Applebaum. I know it is a shock. I hate to break this devastating news to you."

"Who would do this to her?"

"I'm sorry to say it happens. It is usually some thug looking for money for his drug habit. They prey on innocent people like your daughter. Between these judges putting these people on probation and the state attorney not wanting to file charges, it's not safe to walk the street in broad daylight."

"My God, how could this happen?"

"Mr. Applebaum, is there anyone we can call for you?"

"Has anyone contacted my wife?"

"Ah no. Where would we locate her?"

"At the County Court House. She is Judge Judith Levy."

"Your wife is Judge Levy?" Dietz said incredulously.

"Yes."

Canseco thought this poor guy. Then he thought of a judge's daughter? In addition, not just any judge, but Judge Levy-them-out-of-jail. He realized they had just stepped into a steaming pile of crap. He remembered the saying, big cases, big problems. Little cases, little problems. No cases, no problems. This was a huge problem.

Dietz said, "Oh ahh, ahh, ok. We'll get someone over there."

Mr. Applebaum stepped to the rocker and struggled to maintain his balance as he sat. The rattan made a stretching sound as it rocked. His hands covered his face as he leaned forward in the chair. He rubbed his face with his hands.

"Are you positive about Lori's identity?"

"I am sorry, sir. Yes, we are."

"I can't believe this is happening again."

"What do you mean, sir?"

"Her older sister, Rachel, was killed a year ago in an automobile accident."

"We are so sorry, sir."

Canseco shook his head in disbelief. This old man has his two kids killed. He can't get a break.

Mr. Applebaum shook his head in disbelief and said, "Why did he shoot her? Did she resist? She was a pacifist. She would have given him the money. She had such a kind heart. She volunteered at the soup kitchen for the homeless."

"It doesn't look like she had a chance. She had no idea what happened. She did not suffer."

"I need to call her boyfriend David. Oh my god, I can't believe this."

"I know, sir. I am very sorry."

Chapter Forty-One

D umb and Dumber returned to the squad room and checked in with Sergeant Stewart. Alfonso dropped fish food in the aquarium. He dipped his fingers into the seventy-six-degree water to rinse the flakes off his finger. He dried his hands with a blue hand towel.

Dietz spoke, "Nice fish tank."

"It's an aquarium. It's a marine community. This is how I survive here. I surround myself with God's gift of nature. It helps to filter out the trash."

"I always wondered why you kept all these plants in here."

"They're orchids. What's going on with the Judge's daughter?"

"I have Bridges notifying the judge. I checked with the Department of Corrections to see if any robbers got released who are prone to violence."

"I would check all of them regardless of violence. If he is a habitual, he may not want any witnesses."

"Good point. Three strikes and you're out and you go away forever. That's why you are the Sergeant."

Stewart shook his head in disgust and once again held his hand up and said, "Stop."

"I checked with Blake Hamilton in robbery and they said there was a similar shooting at an ATM in the county. The detective on that case hasn't returned my call."

"What is similar?"

"The victim was popped without warning, but she survived. They said the suspect was wearing a yellow hooded sweatshirt."

Stewart tapped the side of his head with his index finger. "Ding Ding Ding, that's what we would call a clue. Do you realize this is a judge's daughter and not some mope? We're talking about a circuit court judge who has lots of connections and juice. You call that detective and go to his sergeant and to his captain and to the High Sheriff if you have to, but find out what they have or don't have."

"Yes, sir."

"What did the parents say?"

Alfonso thought he would not want these two idiots investigating his daughter's homicide. He had no confidence in either detective. It was the hand dealt to him. He would have to watch them close. That was not his style. He liked to give his detective's room to operate.

"Well, the father was pretty broken up and since it is a random act of violence, there was no point in upsetting him more by asking questions. They would not know the answers to."

The Sergeant rolled his eyes and extended his arms. "Oh my God, please give me patience. How do you know unless you ask the questions? Do you know if this shooter was an Anti-Semite, or exacting revenge on the Judge, or maybe stalking the girl from school, or she had boyfriend problems?"

"She had a different last name and would not have been associated with Judge Levy. No, her father said he planned to call the boyfriend, so obviously they were on good terms."

"But you didn't ask, did you?"

"Ahh, no he was."

The traffic cop signal was again invoked, "What about the ATM surveillance video?"

"I have not had a chance to call the security guy."

"Have you checked area business to see if they have surveillance cameras that might have picked up something? A lot of those are not on the cloud and therefore, you can lose the images. Many times, the quality is not that good, but who knows?"

The bearded forensic artist stepped in, handed a copy of the original and some additional copies, and said, "Here you go, Dietz. If you need any additional copies, let me know. The original is in evidence."

Dietz said, "Thanks. This ought to do it."

The artist, who still plied his trade the old-fashioned way, using his hand and chalk, walked out.

Canseco, who had remained silent through the entire episode, looked at the sketch that the artist had so meticulously created and said, "That looks like the Unabomber."

Alfonso looked at the sketch and nodded in agreement, looking at the thin face with a bushy mustache, oversized aviator sunglasses, and a hood framing the face. Something caught his eye.

"Wait, a second, this dude is white."

Dietz said, "Must be some mistake. Mr. Jenkins, the witness, told me he was black."

"What is the witness's telephone number and name?"

Sergeant Stewart pushed the speakerphone button and dialed the number. A male voice answered and after the introductions, Alfonso asked the witness the question he already knew the answer.

"Mr. Jenkins, we have some confusion as to the race of the suspect."

In a high-pitched voice, he said, "No. He was definitely white."

"Did you tell the detectives?"

"Yes, I corrected him two or three times, but he wouldn't listen. I told him the clothes looked like a rapper. He said oh he must be black coming across the tracks. I said no, he was white with a big bushy mustache and gold jewelry. He read it back to me, and I told him he was white, but it looked like he wasn't really listening. He just said, okay, okay."

Alfonso could feel the rage building inside and said in a flat tone, "Mr. Jenkins, thank you for your time."

Alfonso disconnected the call, leaned forward, and stared like a pit-bull before it bites.

"That is why African Americans are afraid of the police and why they get arrested and wrongly accused."

"But."

The traffic cop signal went up. Sergeant Stewart stood, walked around his desk, and left his office without a word. Dumb and Dumber sat stunned in silence, contemplating their career choice.

Dietz and Canseco slowly walked out of the sergeant's office. Neither one spoke. Kyle Bridges had just returned from the death notification to Judge Levy. He pushed his black-rimmed glasses up on the bridge of his nose and booted up his computer.

Dietz asked, "What happened?"

"Nothing much."

"What do you mean, nothing much?"

Bridges turned in his chair and glared at Dietz.

Dietz backed up and said, "You know, I was just wondering what happened. You know how she took it."

"She just had her second daughter killed in the last fourteen months. She has outlived her children. How do you think she would take it? The same as I would. She was not aware of any stalkers, problems with ex-boyfriends, current boyfriend, or suspicious activity around the family."

He turned back to the computer screen.

Dietz, now wearing a smirk, said, "I always heard she is as cold as ice. I always wondered if it was the atmosphere in the courtroom or that she was a bitch?"

"It's all in the approach and how you treat people."

"So, it is her?"

Without looking at Dietz, he said, "She is a mother who has lost a daughter to violence. I did not find her difficult. I found her very cooperative and now she is grieving for a child. Maybe it's your approach to interpersonal communications." Kyle Bridges resumed his typing.

Chapter Forty-Two

THURSDAY

A lfonso walked into the Lieutenant Rizzo's office. She was on the phone. She gave a subtle nod of recognition and gestured for him to have a seat while she continued her telephone call. He rubbed his fingers over the smooth upholstered cloth. He sat there looking at her. "I love me, wall." He wondered how much she dropped on framing all this worthless crap. It looked like every seminar and every civic organization that ever gave her recognition was papering the wall. He was looking for the eighth-place flag football trophy from the fourth grade. He recalled having fallen into the same trap. Cops have a bad habit of wearing their accomplishments on their sleeves, or in this case, the walls.

He remembered once moving offices and a yellow paper tie with a blue ribbon and blue sparkles emblazoned with #1 DAD was on top of one of his boxes. He realized at that moment nothing else mattered. That was his identity. He was Alfonso the father, Alfonso the husband, Alfonso the parishioner, Alfonso the gardener. His job was a cop, but that was only part of him. He realized how important that was. So many forgot that and their home life was a train wreck. He left all the awards in the boxes and took them home, where they remained in his garage. His walls now contained photos of vacations and family pictures.

He looked at her college degrees on the wall. Her bachelor's and master's in sociology. She was intellectually smart. As a result, she gained little experience on the street before moving to an admin post and so on. Detectives did not respect her. She had never been one. Some non-detectives made good supervisors. It all depended on managing people. Her IQ was high, but her investigative quotient was at the other end of the scale. The desk jobs had not always been kind to her. Gravity caused her pear-shaped body to conform more and more to the breadth of the chair. Alfonso always enjoyed a good relationship with female supervisors. In fact, he preferred them. Unfortunately, in the two months since Rizzo arrived, they'd had a less than friendly coexistence.

She turned and folded her hands together under her chin and flashed a phony smile. She presented a smug attitude.

"Alfonso, I am sorry to keep you waiting." She provided no explanation for the personal phone call. "How is the body count?"

"Well, we have some problems. Kate is burrowing through on the motel killings." He noted her smile evaporated at the mention of Kate, but reappeared as he mentioned Dietz and Canseco. He said, "We have a problem."

"Ohhh?" She now moved her hands from under her chin and steepled the fingers to a point.

Alfonso leaned toward her desk, "As you know, the victim is the daughter of a judge. Dietz and Canseco have made numerous oversights and mistakes. They have enough time in the squad not to be making such crucial errors. They are a liability to this department and me. I would like both of them moved elsewhere at the first opportunity."

She then pointed only her index fingers in the form of a gun barrel. "Sergeant." He knew this was not good with her becoming formal. "Perhaps you have failed to provide the necessary oversight and training to these junior detectives. Perhaps they could use additional help. It is a shame this girl was murdered. The media will be all over this. I expect you to personally supervise this and devote all the necessary resources to assist them. Come on, Sergeant, the motel shootings are involving a philandering wife and dope head. Kate can handle that by herself."

"They are still human beings and no, Kate can't work it by herself. Her case looks like it has more to it, and it always takes two detectives to interview someone. You should know that."

He thought if she had investigated anything more complicated than a traffic crash, she would know.

"Well, fine, then give her someone to help hold her hand, but put everyone else on the other case."

"Don't you realize if the investigation of the Judge's daughter is screwed up, we will have egg on our face?"

She dropped her hands flat on the desk and leaned forward. "No Sergeant, you will have egg on your face. Dietz and Canseco are both doing a good job. They just need guidance."

He wanted to scream and tell her to pull her egghead out of her enormous ass. He knew that no matter what he said, it was his entire fault, especially bringing a problem to her. The emperor didn't like being told she was naked.

He stood up and walked toward safety.

"Oh, and one more thing, Sergeant. I need a team player here, not a shop steward. If you can't be a team player, there is a line waiting to replace you."

He felt like the boiler on the USS Maine and he was about to explode, but a sudden calm overcame him. He smiled and said, "Lieutenant, you are right. I have played football since I could almost walk. It required teamwork to win. One thing that always remained consistent for the success of a good team was that the team depended on a great coach. I witnessed good teams fail because of a lousy coach. Good or bad, I never played football for a coach who never played a down of football." He walked to the frame of the office door and said, "Oh, and one more thing, coach. You might extricate yourself from that chair and lead by example."

He continued out of the office, leaving the speechless lieutenant. It felt nice to be in the position to retire.

Alfonso ambled back into his office and closed the door. He looked up at the family photographs and stared at the fish aquarium. He turned the stereo on, closed his eyes, and listened to the new age music of the Ryan Farish that Duffy gifted him. A calm smile engulfed his peaceful face as he thought about the wonderful times with his family and his pride in his daughters. He took several deep breaths and worked on the biofeedback relaxation techniques he learned many years ago. He started at his scalp and worked his way to his toes. Once completed, he felt rejuvenated and opened the door to the real world. He walked over to inspect his orchids.

Bringing in the return of the hostile outside world, Kate said, "I saw you in the L.T.'s office. Did she have any words of wisdom?"

"No words of wisdom. Only words of stupidity. You and Duffy are flying as the dynamic duo on this. It's all hands-on deck for Dietz and the ATM shooter."

With her hands on her hips, she said, "This is not fair. Because I am competent and do a good job, I get no support. Dumb and Dumber screw up an investigation and they get all the help. What's up with that?"

"You think I am not any help?"

"You know what I mean."

"Kate, life is not fair, and it's not always on the level. Just ask any of the victims on that white board. You know that better than anyone."

Kate rubbed her wedding set with her right thumb.

He continued, "We are not doing it for the front office. We are doing it for the victims and ourselves. Don't ever confuse the two. Focus on that."

"Your right. I am sorry."

She walked out the door. Alfonso closed his eyes and took another deep breath.

Kate dropped into her chair and let out a long sigh. She shook her head in silence with her lips clenched.

Frank interrupted her thoughts and said, "I was watching American Idol the other night."

"What?" She was slightly annoyed at Frank for interrupting her hostile thoughts with some inconsequential story.

"I was watching an old American Idol..."

"You, Frank Duffy, actually watch that?"

"It was on the DVR. Bridget records it. I had nothing else to do or watch. I know there is nothing socially redeeming about the show, BUT it can be entertaining and it is interesting to observe the dynamics of human interaction. Look at the judges. One is brutally honest, one is an apologist, and one dances back and forth. Like some of our bureaucracy in the Blue Monster. The amazing part is you have these yahoos getting on national television. They make complete fools of themselves. The judges tell them they are appalling and their feelings are hurt. They are in denial that they are bad. Either no one has the guts to tell them they are bad, or they are under the delusion that they are good enough to win. It suddenly occurred to me they are no different from Dumb and Dumber. Those two actually think they are competent. They are so pompous and arrogant to believe that they are good, but ALL of their peers, except the stupid L.T., know otherwise."

"You are absolutely right."

Chapter Forty-Three

Dietz walked into the office like an out of breath dog looking for a bowl of water. He looked over at Duffy who was writing on a post-it, but stopped writing at the sound of the huffing Dietz. Duffy looked up at Dietz and gave a head bob of acknowledgement. He picked up his Styrofoam cup of coffee and took a sip. Bridges was reading the Thursday edition of the Wall Street Journal and Canseco was eating yogurt sprinkled with grains. Dietz dropped his jacket in a pile in his chair. He walked to Canseco, tapped his broad shoulders, and hooked his thumb toward the hallway. Canseco licked the spoon and walked out to the hallway.

Dietz snickered and said, "I got the shooter." he laughed in a sinister manner.

Canseco leaned towards him and lowered his voice and said, "Who?"

Dietz looked around to make sure no one was within an earshot and said, "His name is Troy Unger."

"Never heard of him."

"He just got out a few weeks ago. He is a Billy Bad Ass. Since he was sixteen, he has been in trouble. He has quite a few domestics, a restraining order from his ex-wife and ex-girlfriend. A few assault and battery charges. He just completed a stint for armed robbery at Starke. Guess who the sentencing judge was?"

"Levy?"

"Yep, and he was in Starke at the same time as Maguire. I'm going to call the Department of Corrections and see if they shared any quality time together."

Canseco asked, "How did you figure the motel shootings are connected?"

"Just a hunch. Here is the best part. I checked with his P.O. and Unger is working a few blocks away from Plant Bank as an auto mechanic."

"Really? Oh man, that's good."

Dietz said, "I figure you and I can go grab him and lean on him. Do the good cop bad cop routine and break him open like a walnut."

Canseco watched how Dietz's mind always ran off like a deflating balloon sailing through the air. There is no clear direction. He says, "Wouldn't it be better to do some more homework on this guy?"

"We don't have time. We don't want that bitch, Alexander, to scoop us on the motel shooting. I'd love to catch her with her skirt around her ankles. Lieutenant Rizzo hates her anyway. Hasta la vista, baby. Back to patrol. We'll be the shining stars. That smart-ass Duffy will be flatfooted, too. This is going to be great."

"Here comes Kate now."

Changing the subject, hoping to conceal his intentions from Kate, Dietz said, "I don't know if the Lightning can keep the team together with the salary structure."

Kate walked by without a word and entered the squad room.

Dietz looking around and said, "We'll leave separately, so no one becomes wise to us. I'll meet you in the garage in fifteen.

"Are you going to put anything in the murder book?"

The murder book was a three-ring binder created for every homicide. The lead detective kept the book updated with the details of investigations, leads to be covered, lab reports, crime scene information, and other items of interest. At anytime a detective could pick up the book and check the status of the investigation. Kyle Bridges had the best reputation for his organization skills. Dietz had the worst reputation.

"Screw that. Then they'll all know and steal our thunder. Stewart doesn't like me. He'll tighten our leash. If we get out there, he won't know until we drag Unger in here in cuffs. I'll see you in the garage."

"Okay."

Canseco knew this was not a good idea, but it was also intriguing to think they could throw a net over this Unger and solve three homicides. He could picture himself standing next to the Chief at the press conference. A lot of face time.

Standing in the noisy, hot parking garage, Canseco, with his well-developed biceps folded across his chest, was in a cheerful banter with a young blonde female officer. Dietz came out of the elevator, winded as though he just descended the stairs. His shirt collar was open. The necktie hung crookedly, too short to reach the belt line. Sweat rolled down his shaved head like lazy rivers. He looked over at Canseco.

"Hey, lover boy, we have bad guys to arrest."

The female officer sucked in her midsection, hiked up her gun belt, and pushed out her chest, highlighting her abundance. She did not need the padding of the ballistic vest.

Dietz, speaking to the female officer, said, "I hate to break up this meeting, but you're talking to the next co-officer of the month."

She answered, "Really?"

Canseco said, "Give me a call."

"You know how to find me, cowboy."

He yelled to Dietz, "Hey, you're not driving."

"Why not?"

"I think you spent too much time in the DUI squad. You drive like a DUI."

"I don't think my driving is bad."

"That's because you're not the passenger. Since you know where we are going and who we are looking for, I'll drive."

"All right. I still don't think I am a bad driver."

Chapter Forty-Four

C anseco eased the car around the corner and parked against the curb down the street from Manny's Automotive. Dietz pulled out the binoculars. He could see three men in dark blue mechanic's uniforms talking in a group outside one of the bays. They were all drinking from Styrofoam cups. It was difficult to see their faces through the cumulous cloud of cigarette smoke. He could see another mechanic working under a car raised on the lift. Two of the mechanics were not Unger. That narrowed the field by fifty percent.

Dietz said, "I can't see the one with his back turned and there is one more in the garage."

"How about if I lay on my horn for a second and see if the one turns around?"

"Nah. How about we make a pretext call and see if we can get him to the phone?"

"Sounds good."

"Hand me your cell phone."

"Use your own."

"I want to keep Stewart off my ass and not be able to see my activity."

Canseco reluctantly handed his phone over to Dietz, who dialed the number. They watched as one of the three trotted into the office.

"Hello, Manny's Automotive, how can I help you?"

"Can I speak to Troy?"

"Troy, yeah, hold on. Hey Troy, phone call."

They watched the one with his back walk towards the office. Dietz disconnected the call. His voice was now elevated with excitement.

"That's him. Let's go."

Canseco put the car in drive and accelerated towards Manny's. As he turned into the parking lot, the car behind them honked at the displeasure of the sudden slowdown. It had the desired effect Canseco had initially hoped for by honking the horn. The two mechanics, smoking and drinking, turned towards the horn. Unger walking out of the office displayed a puzzled look over the empty dial tone on the phone. The car honking changed his focus.

Unger looked at the Ford and, seeing the two white men in dress shirts and ties in the hot summer, he put two and two together. He exchanged stares with Dietz through the windshield. Unger dropped his coffee cup and cigarette and ran down the right side of the garage. Canseco slammed on the brakes. Dietz jumped out of the car, gun in hand, and yelled at Unger, "Police stop or I'll shoot!"

Dietz followed the route of Unger, glimpsing him as he ran behind the building. The fleeing suspect barreled through a stack of tires, scattering them like dominoes. Dietz tightened his body and lifted his leg like a hurdler. His toe caught the inside of one tire. He stumbled, and he fell to the ground, landing on his right shoulder and displacing the Glock from his hand. Canseco raced down the side and looked like an Olympic hurdler as he began his leap over the prone Dietz, who had got up on one knee. It was like a Mack truck hitting a cow in the middle of the road. There was a large oomph from the impact. The two detectives fell to the ground. Canseco scampered to his feet and ran to the corner. There was no sign of Unger.

He looked back at Dietz, who was pulling up his pants and trying to tuck in his shirt, now stained by grease and grass. Dietz smelled like a gas station. He looked pitiful with a tear in his pants at the knee and a smudge on his baldhead.

Still breathing heavy, he said, "I told you I should have driven. Now he has gotten away."

"I'll call for the chopper and some additional units."

"No way, man. Stewart will be up our ass like a proctologist for not sharing and playing nice in the sandbox. This is our secret, and we will find Unger as soon as I change clothes."

"Clothes? Someone might call this in. We need to update Stewart, and what about the murder book?"

"I'll update Stewart and the book later."

Canseco shook his head in defiance, "You know Stewart has one hand in a rubber glove about us not updating the book and if he hears of our misadventure, he will not only have the second glove on, but he will have those both lubed with KY Jelly."

"Don't worry."

"I know we're protected, right?"

"Yep. Rizzo will cover for us."

"Are you banging her?"

"Hey, don't worry."

"You are, aren't you?"

"She merely has respect for my superior intelligence and investigative skills."

"And I have some land for sale in the Everglades."

"Okay, Mr. TRT, let's go to my place to change clothes and clean up."

Chapter Forty-Five

U nger's listed address was The Tabernacle of Everlasting Life Bible Church. The church was symbolic of the Seminole Heights neighborhood it occupied. The area was once a thriving area of Tampa, then forgotten and now split in half by I-275. Now, the area was experiencing a renaissance. The rundown bungalows were now chic and in demand by preservationists and investors. The building the church occupied was once an appliance store selling color TV's and console entertainment centers. It morphed into a used furniture store and then replaced by the storefront church. Above the sanctuary were several rooms for rent.

Dumb and Dumber pushed open the Plexiglas door and looked at rows of padded banquet chairs, a simple wood stage with a podium and a replica of Jesus on the cross attached to the wall. There was a subtle scent of incense. A well-dressed man in his early forties, wearing a welcoming smile and elongated goatee, approached the visitors.

"I am the Reverend Feroeshus Lamb." Dumb and Dumber exchanged glances, believing the name was bogus. "How can I help you, gentlemen?"

Dietz said, "We're looking for Troy Unger."

"Are you police officers or bill collectors?"

"Yes, we are with TPD." They flashed their badges.

"Have you tried Manny's Automotive?"

"Yeah, but he developed fast feet and ran."

His face now looked like a mortician. "What did you do to him?"

"We didn't do anything. We pulled into the parking lot and he ran."

"I find that difficult to believe, gentlemen."

"Are you calling us liars?"

"Not at all, gentlemen. I am a clergyman who looks for the good of in people. Troy came to me as a lost soul. He is a personal salvation of mine. He is a believer in Jesus and has repented his past indiscretions."

Dietz said, "The only thing he believed in today was his feet."

"Why is it that the Tampa Police Department would like to speak with Troy?"

"There were some crimes in the neighborhood and we know he was recently paroled."

"I see. A leopard never changes its spots. You are castigating him for having made mistakes in the past and for obtaining a job in an area that is besieged by the criminal element. He mentioned he was concerned for his own safety after that poor girl was murdered in close proximity to his place of employment."

"What did he say?"

"I see how this is working. That poor Jewish girl, the daughter of a judge and born into affluence, is putting some heat on you folks. Therefore, you look at rousting one of my flock. I am sure Troy felt the same way and decided it was best if he left and got legal counsel before talking with you. Sometimes discussions can be misconstrued, and he merely wants his best interests protected."

"Would you mind if we look at his room?"

"Troy has nothing to hide. Seeing that he pays rent for that room and I am a self-educated legal mind, I believe you will need to get a search warrant. If you have any substantive evidence outside of a hunch, getting that legal authority should not be too difficult. Now, if you will excuse me, I have religious missions to fulfill."

"Just let him know we are looking for him."

"May god bless you and guide you both." He bowed ever so slightly.

They walked outside and Canseco slid his Oakley sunglasses over his eyes and said, "Well, I guess he is in the wind now. We can hit The Wing House before we go to the office."

"Are you nuts? We can't go back to the office. The entire office will laugh at us. Look, it's Dumb and Dumber. Ha Ha Ha. No sir. I am calling his P.O. again and we will go look at his file. We have to shake the tree. He will show up somewhere. Forget the Wing House. We can grab a Cuban sandwich on the go."

Canseco hated when Dietz was like this. He would become like a rabid dog and lose his judgment. He was in pursuit of recognition. Even when he was in the DUI squad, he had a reputation that he would write his own mother a ticket.

Chapter Forty-Six

C anseco guided the car onto I-275 south, towards downtown. They exited downtown and parked inside the chain link fenced parking lot. The tall State Office Building surrounded by a moat of obscurity, looked down upon the highway with a lonely scowl. The well-worn elevator groaned as it delivered them to the ninth floor of the State Probation Office.

They stood in the cramped cubicle with the bushy headed George Demetrius, Troy Unger's probation officer. Demetrius said, "What do you mean, he ran?"

Dietz said, "Just like I said. He ran from us."

"Did he know you were cops?"

"He knew who we were."

"I am just saying. His defense attorney will bring it up."

"Look Demetrius, I told him on the phone that we were the police and to come out quietly. Instead, all we saw was ass and elbows."

Canseco's blood pressure increased. He had just listened to Dietz lie to another law enforcement officer. He had gone crazy. He was so convinced that Unger was the killer, he would do anything to arrest him. As a partner, he would back him all the way. That is, unless the flames were licking at his ass. Then he would have to save himself.

The P.O. said, "Well, that will be enough to send him back. I'll swear out a warrant this afternoon."

"We checked the church and talked to the Reverend."

"Oh Feroeshus?"

"Where do they come up with these names?"

"He made it up after he found God while he was doing a stretch for manslaughter in Starke. He actually runs a tight ship. Think what you may about his storefront bible thumping church. He keeps them under tight reins. He has a few rooms upstairs that he rents. They have bible study classes and he has a curfew. He hand picks the parolees."

"Do you think he is on the up and up?"

"I have no reason to believe he isn't."

"George, do you think it's possible he is running a crew that reports to him?"

"Anything is possible, but I doubt it. I have seen nothing to show that. May I caution you? Feroeshus Lamb is politically connected. He received a Governor's Pardon."

"The Governor? I'm impressed. I guess he needed some votes. We'll go see Unger's mother."

"Good luck. She is a hard woman. You'll see."

"Ok, let me know when you get that warrant."

They walked outside and peeled their sport coats off. Dietz's head was beaded with sweat. He said, "I think he has been drinking the Kool-Aid from The Tabernacle of Everlasting Life Bible Church. They always think their parolees are reformed. They don't see what you and I see. Most of these perps are hopeless. I took classes with some folks that became P.O.'s and most of them think they are going to change these lost souls. You and I know better."

"True, but if he got a pardon, it means he has some juice. What was that lying to the P.O. about?"

"Hey, he knew we were cops. No one else ran. I'm just coloring the story a bit. Let's go see momma."

Chapter Forty-Seven

T he two detectives stepped up onto the gray wooden porch. They could hear a soap opera blaring from the TV and the smell of cigarette smoke was wafting through the screen door. They could see several cats doing their own thing. Dietz knocked on the wood framed screened door. It bounced back and forth in the frame with each knock.

A gruff sounding female yelled, "Yeah, who is it?"

"It's the police."

"Christ." The female voice paused and a congested sounding cough followed. They heard shuffling toward the door. "What the hell do you want?"

They looked down at the short women wearing a yellow flowered housecoat and pink slippers. She pulled her wiry gray hair back behind her leathery face. A cigarette balanced on the lip.

"Is Troy here?"

"Let me see your damn badges."

They both displayed the silver and gold accented detective shields. She put a pair of glasses on her face that were hanging around her neck with a string and studied the badges as if she didn't believe them.

"What he do now?"

"We would just like to talk to him about a few things."

"Bull shit. You would have called on the phone or talked to him at work or that make-believe Holy Roller church if you wanted to talk to him. You're looking for him if you came here. I knew he couldn't keep his ass out of trouble. Just like his father. Always dreaming and talking a good game. I ain't seen him in a week or two. He's been a pain in my ass since I got pregnant with him, and his no-good father skipped town. Just give me your card and if he comes by, I'll give it to him. I'm missing my show."

She unhooked the screen door, took the card from Dietz, and closed the door.

"Would you mind if we looked around?"

She stared at them, took a deep breath, and said, "You can look around all you want, but unless you have a goddamn warrant, you ain't coming here. Now git off my porch." She closed the inside door. The window air-conditioner turned on.

The two detectives walked back across the mostly dirt yard towards the car as Dietz stumbled on an exposed root from an oak tree.

Dietz said, "With a mother like that, you can understand why he is a thug."

"I suppose."

Dietz's cell phone rang. He reached under the girth and pulled the phone off his belt with a groan. He sat down inside the car. Howard Canseco chewed on a piece of gum, watching two Sandhill Cranes fly overhead. He pretended he had a rifle and aimed at the large-winged birds gracefully gliding through the sky. His attention was distracted by the muffled sounds of Dietz yelling at him. It was hot. He fanned himself with the notepad. Dietz covered the phone with one hand while the phone rested in the crook of his neck. The free hand motioned to turn the key in the ignition. Canseco walked over to the driver's door, spit the gum into the thin weeds, and pulled the door open.

"Hey slick. Turn the car on. It must be a thousand degrees in here. Now I know what a basted turkey feels like stuck in the oven."

"No, you don't. You'd have to fill it with stuffing first."

"Real funny, Slick. I am actually starting a diet."

"Starting or started?"

"Well, smartass, I am starting the keto diet next Monday. So, I start the week fresh."

"You're like most other people grazing from one diet to the next. You just need to do some push aways from the table, eat healthy, and get more exercise."

"That's easy for you, Mr. Gold's Gym."

"I follow my own advice." He recalled Dietz had always been flabby, but now he was carrying quite a tire around the midsection. He had failed at every attempt to control his weight.

Dietz said, "That was a call from the Department of Corrections. He said that Troy and Maguire were in Starke at the same time. They didn't share a cell together, but they probably took the same pottery class and license plate making lessons."

"And probably the same social club as well." Canseco added.

"Yeah. I guess we should head in and deal with Stewart."

"Unless you have a mouse in that pocket, there is no we in you."

"Thanks for your support there, Slick. Maybe we should pickup a new orchid for him."

"Not so much."

"Let's get this A/C cranked up too high."

Dietz pulled the file he had accumulated on Unger. The pages were ragged, with edges bent and wrinkled. He thumbed through the records copied from the P.O.'s file.

"Here is the report from the county on his last arrest. He robbed someone that was walking out of one of those Chex R Us places. Uniform gets him a few blocks later on a traffic violation and realizes this person fits the description and not to mention the dumb ass left the gun on the passenger seat. They got him for two other similar types."

"They're not ATM's."

"No, but it's the same style of waiting for people to get their money."

"Why do you think he capped the victims?"

"No witnesses. He is facing the bitch and has nothing to lose."

"Why would he shoot her before she got the money?"

"He jumped the gun. No pun intended. He was probably all hopped up on meth and wasn't thinking clearly. Maybe he got scared."

"Maybe. What did the County say about the other ATM shooting?"

"I checked with Bridges. He checked with HCSO. They have squat. They have a lot less than the Dynamic Duo here." As he motioned between the two.

The cell phone rang and Dietz looked down at the caller ID and said,

"Stewart is calling me. I'm not going to answer. I'll tell him about Unger when I'm ready."

"He'll call me next."

"Just pull the you're breaking up. I can't hear you. Can you hear me?"

"He is no fool. He'll know what we are up to."

"Screw him. He is just out to protect sweet cheeks, Kiss Ass Alexander. He is looking for anything to make us look bad. We are the best investigators he has. He is just too stupid to realize it."

"He is probably intimidated by us."

As he flipped through the pages, he pulled out a single sheet. "Oh, here is something else. When Unger first got out, he worked at a car wash pretty close to the Lucky Cabaret. I overheard Duffy bloviating about that drug kingpin hanging out at the Lucky Cabaret. I wouldn't doubt that the kingpin gets his car washed there or Troy walks over to the Lucky. Let's get a photo pack together and take a ride out there. I wouldn't mind looking at a little T and A."

"We'll have to wait until everyone clears out of the office."

Canseco's phone rang, and he answered.

"Hello, sir."

"Where in the heck are you two?"

"I am sorry, sir, you're very scratchy. Are you asking how the investigation is going with Dietz? He is here with me."

"I know he is...."

"Sir, can you hear me? I'll move to a better location. Can you hear me?"

"Yes, I can...."

"Hello, hello?"

Canseco ended the call.

Dietz smiled and said, "That was great. That ought to frost his ass. Now just let it go to voicemail like we are in a dead zone."

"He'll know."

"Who cares?"

"Let's run by the vitamin store. I need to pick up a few supplements and then we can go to the office after everyone leaves."

"Sound like a plan."

They snuck back into the office like a couple of cattle rustlers in the night. The sinking sun provided enough light through the row of windows that they could avoid turning the lights on. Canseco looked down at the deserted sidewalks and modest traffic volume. Like the Flintstones, when the whistle sounds at five, the race is on for the suburbs. Canseco sat in front of his computer and surfed the internet. Dietz left a voicemail for Stewart apologizing for leaving his phone at home and not being able to update him, but he would see him first thing in the morning. He pulled up Unger's photo from the computer and allowed the computer to match five other similar looking photos to prepare the photo pack to show to witnesses.

Dietz said, "Come on, Slick, let's go."

He gathered up a stack of disorganized papers and shoved them under his arm as they left the office. Canseco checked his image in the reflection of the windows. He smiled.

Chapter Forty-Eight

They pulled into the Lucky Cabaret. The happy hour crowd had filled the parking lot on the way home. Entering the strip club, the two detectives began grooving to the rhythm of the music. The skinny girl standing inside the door stood up and flashed a bright lipsticked smile at Canseco. He flashed a smile back.

Her smile evaporated when Dietz said with urgency, "Hey, how are you doing? We're with TPD. Could you look at some photos and see if you recognize anyone?"

She looked back at Canseco and smiled again. "I guess I could."

"Have you seen anyone in these pictures?"

"Nope."

"Are you sure? How about number three? Does he look familiar?"

"Maybe."

"Okay, could you initial this black and white copy?"

"I'm not going to have to go to court, am I?"

"No darling. It is just to say I showed it to you, so my boss knows I was out here."

"Oh, okay."

Canseco looked around with contempt at the wasteland of humanity. They lack the charisma and looks to attract their own women. They get some cheap thrill looking at girls they can't touch. He could tell Dietz was in the same group.

They walked around amongst the sea of inquisitive stares and hostile tension, asking each employee the same question. No one recognized the photo of Unger. Dietz gave a hard look at the strippers on stage, plying their trade. As they walked to their car, the sun was just about gone and the streetlights were warming up. The parking lot was clearing out.

Canseco said, "Well, we struck out there."

"A maybe is better than a no."

"That was a doubtful, maybe."

"It's a probable cause, maybe. We'll get in early. Stop in to see the L.T. before the sergeant gets in."

"Okay. Are you up for a cold one?"

"Sure, why not?"

"Let's go to South Howard and see what's happening."

Chapter Forty-Nine

FRIDAY

On Friday morning, Dietz and Canseco met in the garage and walked straight into Lieutenant Rizzo's office. They planned to play Rizzo against Stewart. They knew the chances were good if they got in early enough and went directly to her office, they could sidestep the sergeant. She was reading her email on the computer screen. Conrad Dietz knocked on the door. Her serious look changed as her eyes looked at the door. Her face brightened like a springtime dawn.

"How are my favorite detectives doing? Connie, what brings you in so early in the morning?"

Conrad Dietz spoke first. "Like I always say, Lieutenant, the early bird gets the worm. Criminals never rest, nor should we."

Canseco thought he had heard no one refer to Conrad as Connie. He was wondering how much sappier this could get. What a suck-up, but Dietz was pulling him along. His name was on the movie marquis in front of the Lieutenant. They were on the front burner.

Dietz continued, "We wanted to bring you up to date on the investigation concerning the Lori Applebaum homicide. We stopped at Sergeant Stewart's office, but I guess he wasn't in yet. I really wanted to talk to him first."

"That's all right. You're on the trail of a killer. You don't have the time to make office hour appointments." She winked at Dietz.

Canseco felt nauseas. He felt Dietz was definitely knocking the bottom out of the L.T. He quivered as he thought of that scene. He had no tolerance for people who did not take care of their bodies. Their heart locks up and suddenly, they want to know what happened.

Dietz said, "I have to tell you I made an awful mistake yesterday and forgot my telephone at home. I was also in a foot chase and tore my clothes hurdling over a stack of tires."

"I'm impressed."

Canseco thought that since Rizzo never chased a criminal from behind the various desks' she had been riding during her career, she would be impressed. What a liar. Dietz never hurdled anything in his life.

"So, I went home to change, and I forgot my phone. Unfortunately, Sergeant Stewart tried to call me several times. I'm sure he was getting frustrated and tried Howard, but we were in a dead spot and Howard couldn't hear him. We worked late last night. I left a voice mail for him."

"If you don't see him before you leave, I'll bring him up to date."

"Oh, that would be great."

"I'll see him at the 9:30 staff meeting. I'll put you both in for unlimited overtime. I want this case closed."

"Yes ma'am. Thank you. Is that a new blouse?"

"Why yes, it is."

"It's a nice color on you."

"Well, thank you." Her cheeks flushed with red.

Canseco again thought this was over the top. He probably bought the blouse for her. *I am sitting between two idiots. I am swimming in a sea of sharks.*

Dietz said, "Well, here is the deal. A Troy Unger gets out on parole for robbery. He pulled the same style of robbery, not an ATM, but catching people as they left after cashing checks. He works just a few blocks away from the ATM. He is a habitual offender, so he doesn't want any witnesses. We went to talk to him yesterday, and he ran from us. And get this, he was in Starke at the same time that Maguire was there. He is the mope that was smoked at the Pirate's Cove and Unger also worked down the street from the Lucky Cabaret where Maguire frequented. One employee thinks they have seen Unger in there. That is where Maguire got into a fight with his drug connection. I don't know the guy's name, but Duffy knows it. We checked a couple of places yesterday looking for Unger. I think he is good for this one and maybe the Pirate's Cove."

"Wow, you have been busy."

"His parole officer is putting out a pickup on him. I'll put out a BOLO for him with your permission."

"Absolutely. This is a high-profile case. We need to put our full resources to work."

"Canseco and I still have more work to do, but we are getting close."

"Good, keep up the good work."

Howard thought he saw her purse her lips in an imaginary kiss. Now he was sure that something was going on between the two. Dietz and Rizzo needed the lonely-hearts club. Perhaps they were just perfect. Except he was her subordinate. Canseco really didn't care, as long as their relationship was benefiting him. If things went south, he would fall into the middle of a cesspool.

As they walked back down the sterile white hallways, Howard said, "You are putting the meat to her, aren't you?"

"Don't let your imagination get the best of you. We are golden right now. So, let's ride the wave and grab the glory, baby."

Chapter Fifty

K ate researched the archived stories of the murder of Jennifer Kress on the newspaper website. She knew the story all too well. She did not know or did not remember other revelations about the murderer, David Stilts. He was a known tweaker, who had on his previous arrest had attempted to pull a woman into his car. He said he thought she was suicidal and was about to jump into traffic. The witnesses couldn't contradict Stilts. The girl had some minor issues with depression. Judge Levy was the presiding judge, and she found him not guilty. One detective stood up and pleaded to the judge to reconsider her decision. Levy chastised him and called his supervisor. There had been a lot of controversy with the decision of Judge Levy acquitting Stilts. Kate had not realized that Levy was the presiding judge. Now her daughter is dead.

She continued reading that Stilts snatched Jennifer after she finished work. HCSO chased and shot him. AeroMed airlifted him to Tampa General in critical condition. Frank walked over to Kate's orderly desk, interrupting her and said, "Kirk Sussex, the landscaper emailed in the list of his customers. For a million dollars, guess who is on the list?"

"Who?"

"Is that your final answer?"

"Yes, who?"

"Maximilian Kress."

"No. Really?"

"Yep."

"Let's go talk to his ex-wife, Marge. I just read that Levy was the presiding judge that let that dirt bag out before he killed Jennifer."

Frank nodded in surprise and said, "Isn't that interesting?"

Chapter Fifty-One

K ate and Frank pulled into the Palm Bay Condominiums close to Max's house. The walled and gated complex was very upscale. The percentage of BMW's and Mercedes was a tip-off. They walked up to unit 233.

Frank said, "It looks like Max came out a winner."

"How so?"

"He gets the house, and she gets an apartment."

"It's a condo."

"These were apartments before they went condo. You can call it what you want. It's only a wall separating you from your neighbor."

"Or in your case, they are separating themselves from you."

"Yeah, right?"

They knocked on the door. "Hello Marge."

An eager smile spread across her botoxed and tanned face. "Kate? Kate Alexander?"

"Yes, you remember."

"Sure, how are you doing?"

"I am all right and yourself."

"I am doing as well as can be expected."

"How did you know I was here?"

"We saw Max yesterday."

"Oh. Come on in."

Kate looked around and thought it looked like the inside of a Pottery Barn catalogue.

"Marge, this is Frank Duffy. We work together."

"Nice to meet you."

Frank said, "Yes ma'am."

Kate said, "This is a nice place."

"Thanks. I wanted to stay in the neighborhood and to keep an eye on Max. This is low maintenance. I need this."

"I am sorry to hear about you and Max."

"Thanks. That's sweet of you. It has been tough. You remember, Max was always the life of the party. He had just never recovered from Jennifer's death. He neglected the business. He finally sold it for a fraction of what it was worth when he cared. He improved after the doctor prescribed antidepressants. He didn't like the way they made him feel. So, he would stop taking the medication."

"That happens frequently with folks on antidepressants. Does he own any firearms?"

"Yes. I'm not good with guns. It's silver, maybe a .357? Is that right?"

"It could be."

"He kept it for protection. Are you asking because you think he might be suicidal?"

"No. Although what you are telling me, I guess he could be. The other reason is that a car similar to one he owns was parked at the scene of a homicide. I doubt he was involved. I just have to cover all the bases. You know, keep the bosses happy who review all the reports."

"He would never be involved in something like that. He may have issues, but he would never hurt someone intentionally."

"Trust me, I hate to ask these questions, but I have to keep my lieutenant off my case. Do you know where he keeps the gun?"

"No. He keeps it in the car sometimes. I told him someone might break in and steal it someday, but he wouldn't always listen. I don't know where it is anymore. He might not know where it is. His life is in shambles. You know how he was involved in the little league and at church. His business was going well. He loved Jennifer so much. His whole life revolved around her and me. After her murder, he withdrew from everything. I don't think he has been in a church since. Like I said, the business fell apart, and I just had to get out."

"Do you know the landscapers?"

"Yes, we have used them for a while. Since Jennifer died. Max used to take pride in the yard, but he couldn't be bothered anymore."

"Do you remember a man named Maguire who worked with the landscaping crew?"

She shook her head. "No. I didn't know any of the workers. Most of the time, they were from Central America and didn't speak any English."

"Do you think Max is capable of violence if someone pushed his button?"

"I don't think so. He never raised a hand towards me. He rarely lost his temper. The only person I saw him get mad at was that Judge Levy. She was the one that dismissed the case against that animal that killed Jennifer. Max blames her for Jennifer's death. I do too, but he would obsess about her." Marge said.

"In what way?"

"He would send her letters and he would go into a hysterical rage when he read her name in the paper. He would scream and call her names and throw the paper and start crying. I would leave. Give him space. On Jennifer's birthday and Christmas every year, he mailed a card to the Judge. I tried to get him some help. I tried to get him into counseling. He went once or twice to Dr. Rushdi, but Max called him a quack and refused to go back. I dragged him to meetings at the Child Protection Education of America and Families of Missing Loved Ones. I was hoping to turn our tragedy into a positive and help be an advocate to these great organizations. I used my time constructively to organize fundraising for these groups in Jennifer's name. I found strength in our faith and to be with others that shared the same nightmare. He couldn't deal with it and gave up. He had no place to go but down. I would not go with him. At first, I was concerned about leaving Max by himself. I hoped that my leaving would encourage him to seek help. He just won't do it. One of the neighborhood kids, Luke, keeps an eye on him."

"We met him yesterday."

"He is a nice boy. We stay in touch to make sure Max is all right."

"At least Stilts wasn't given a second chance at justice."

"He at least suffered in pain. He died in the hospital about a week after they shot him."

"Did he have any relatives that were upset about him being shot? You know, sometimes people's relatives come out of the woodwork saying they denied him his right to justice and all that."

"No. I don't remember any of that."

"Did you know that the judge's daughter was killed a couple of days ago?"

"Oh my gosh, no. You don't think Max had anything to do with that?"

"I hope not. Do you think he would be capable of that?"

"No. He might be sick and depressed, but I don't see him plotting to kill the Judge or, worse yet, her family."

"Thanks for your time, Marge. Here is my card, if you think of anything else."

"You were so helpful to us after Jennifer died. I'll never forget that."

"There is nothing worse than the tragic loss of a child. I couldn't prevent her death, but it was my way of helping."

"Kate, you be safe and it was nice to meet you, Frank."

Kate and Marge embraced, and she shook the hand of Frank as the two detectives walked outside. Kate exhaled deeply, as if releasing the anxiety like a deflating balloon.

As they waited for the gates to open, allowing their escape, Kate said, "Okay, a car matching the description of Max's car is spotted at the scene of a double homicide. Maguire, one victim works for a landscaper that works at his house, and he tells people he has a big score lined up from a customer. We found out that Judge Levy released David Stilts, who killed Max's beloved daughter. That same judge had her own daughter killed at the ATM, and another daughter was killed a year earlier in an automobile accident. Max also owns a .357."

"Maybe a .357."

"Yes, you're correct and that is the type of weapon used in all three killings plus a fourth shooting at the ATM in the County to make this look like a serial robber and cover the true intentions. Now we get the arson at the storage facility. The receipt for hip-hop fashions. The shooter in the ATM killings was wearing a hoodie and baggie jeans."

"Most kids wear hoodies."

"The shooter and the arsonist are both described wearing aviator sunglasses like the Ray-bans. I think he wants the Judge to experience the same loss and pain he has endured. He is over the edge now. His business has collapsed and his wife has left him. He has nothing. I'll lay money on it; he is going to be gunning for Levy."

"Slow down there Nancy Drew."

"The description of the person renting the storage facility was young. Not someone in his fifties."

"All right, Sherlock Holmes. I don't have it all yet, but do you have a better suspect?"

"He is up there. Just keep your options open."

"I will. And we can't forget Dumb and Dumber have someone that they feel good about."

"I don't think Dietz has felt good about anything since the backseat of his mother's car after the high school prom."

Chapter Fifty-Two

Kate said, "Since we are close to the mall, let's go to the Da Boyz N Girlz Hip Hop Fashions. You know that was the mall that Jennifer Kress was snatched."

"Interesting."

They walked into the clothing store populated by several youthful customers. The speakers bellowed hip-hop music to provide a little ambience to the bargain basement décor. They identified themselves to the clerk, who was wearing a retro afro hairdo.

Holding the copy of the receipt, Kate said, "Can you tell me what this item number pertains to?"

The clerk looked at the receipt and typed in the number.

"Yeah. It's an ECKO Hoodie."

"Does it give you a color?"

"Yeah, man, it's yellow. They also bought a pair of Akademik jeans."

Kate looked back towards the front of the store and noticed that all the customers had left the store. She pointed toward the ceiling.

"Is that camera hooked up to a surveillance system?"

"No. It ain't even working."

Frank said, "What clerk made this sale?"

"I'll have to check with the manager if I can give that out. You know I don't want to get in trouble."

"Well, is the manager here?"

"No."

Frank wanted to manipulate this putz before the manager got involved. They might have some corporate policy that would require police to get a subpoena.

"I understand. I know you don't want to get into trouble, but this is not confidential or protected information. I am not some irate customer. I am conducting a criminal investigation into a murder. Wouldn't you want someone to cooperate if your loved one was injured or killed?"

"Yes, but I need this job. I don't want no trouble from my boss."

Frank leaned across the counter and said, "Let me explain something to you, pal. Your manager doesn't have to know, and I don't have time to screw around with you. While you are trying to track down your manager, I'll get a grand jury subpoena for him and everyone else that works in this store and every former employee. That will shut down this business until the grand jury questions everyone on this matter and anything else they feel like asking you about related to this case or not. All that time, you are sitting without pay. The owner will fire you for costing him so much money. I don't want to get you in trouble, but I think your boss will be pissed at your lack of cooperation and judgment. So perhaps you were mistaken. What is the clerk's name?"

"Lashondra, but they fired her last week."

Kate said, "What was she fired for?"

"Stealing."

"Where she stay at?"

He shrugged his shoulders. Frank looked at his nameplate.

"Delvin, why don't you find out before I start explaining things to you again?"

"I know she be staying over at some apartments by USF." "Why don't you check and see what her number is? Look on the phone list."

"The manger keeps that with him."

"Now, why don't you call the manager?"

Delvin got the number for Lashondra, and the two detectives were glad to escape.

They stepped out into the mall, and Kate called the number for Lashondra. After two rings, she heard the intercept recording that the number called was either disconnected or no longer in service. Kate pulled back the phone to confirm she dialed the correct number.

Kate said, "Okay, let's go to the mall security and see if they have video and how far back it goes. If he walked in here, he should be on camera in the mall. The sheriff has a substation in here. They may have Lashondra's info if they ever responded to a shoplifting."

"There you go again putting your thinking cap on."

They contacted Corporal Janakowski with the Hillsborough Sheriff's Office. The husky voiced Corporal said, "Let me see here. Running the store name, we come up with ten hits. Four are for alarms, these kids come in, they have a five-second brief on the alarm, and they set it off by accident. Six are shoplifting reports. You say Lashondra?"

Kate answered, "Yes."

Pointing with a thick sausage sized finger he said, "Okay, here she is, Lashondra Watkins. The deputy that wrote the report only listed the store address, not her residence. I have her identifiers so you can check through DMV and public records search. If you would like, I'll check for you in the spirit of cooperation," flashing a wisecrack grin.

"Thanks, that would be great. Do you have any idea how long the recording loop is on the camera system for the mall?

"Forever on the cloud. They focus more on the parking lots. That's where we have the biggest problem. The mall leaves it up to the stores to enhance their own security."

He hit the print icon and pulled a sheet of paper from the printer, and said, "Here is her last reported address."

Chapter Fifty-Three

They drove to the address for Lashondra. The address was in an area of a high concentration of apartments servicing the students of the University of South Florida. Some apartment complexes were nice, and some were not so nice. At the Frontier Apartments, they searched for an open parking spot.

Many of the residents who were awake migrated outside to avoid the heat inside. Several units left the doors open and you could hear either the stereo thumping the beat of hip-hop or the TV sounding some reality show reruns. Kids were playing like kids. Running and chasing each other.

Frank gave a forceful knock with the pound side of the palm on door number 37. Kate stood on the hinged side and Frank on the knob side. They were both in a position to draw their weapons. Cops never knew if the person they just wanted to talk to about something as minor as being a witness could, in fact, have a meth factory inside the apartment. Life was unpredictable. Many dead cops could attribute the end of their lives to complacency in similar settings. Kate listened in for sounds of noise. Silence. They knocked again and announced their identities. Just in case, she was ducking a bill collector. No answer. Kate slid one of her cards into the door jamb with a note asking Lashondra to call regarding a customer at the store. She might respond to the card, but probably not.

"Hey, what ya'll want?" Bellowed an overweight woman with her red hair pulled back. It looked like she was wearing a blue nightgown. She stepped out of apartment thirty-nine.

Frank answered, "Were bible salesmen. We're just trying to spread the word."

"Na ahh. You the poleece."

He put his finger across his lips, simulating the quiet signal. "Hey, don't say that too loud. You'll blow our cover."

She smiled big, exposing a mouth like a hockey player and mirrored his finger across her mouth.

She whispered, "Lashondra ain't here."

Frank whispering back said, "Do you know where she is?"

"Nope."

"Would you tell her the poleece wants to talk to her about a customer from the old store she worked at?"

"She ain't working at the Boyz n Girlz no mo?"

"Nooo."

"Man, I hate to hear that. She used to bring home clothes and sell em cheap."

"Tell her she ain't in no trouble. Or if you want to be like an undercover secret agent for us, you could just call us when she comes home."

Her face grinned again. "Just like on TV?"

"Your codename is Angel. Here is my card. You call me, Angel."

"I sure will."

Kate smiled as they walked away. "You have no shame, do you?"

"You do what you have to do?"

"I'll bet you were quite the lady's man. You really wowed Angel there. I could see the chemistry."

"What can I say? I am a regular chic magnet. How about we grab a bite to eat at Panera's so we're still in the area in case my Angel comes through?"

Chapter Fifty-Four

They arrived at Panera Bread across from the University for lunch. Frank inhaled deeply, pulling the odor of fresh-baked breads through his nose. They ordered their sandwiches and listened to the classical music.

Kate said, "I called the Professor to come meet us."

"Today is our lucky day. I get Angel and you get the Professor."

Kate's face glimmered with excitement as she watched Trent Sellers pull open the door and looked around. She knew he was interested. He was pursuing her, and she did not mind. The feeling was mutual. It had been a while since someone was as determined to develop a relationship with her. He smiled in recognition as he waved at her and walked up to her booth. She felt wanted.

Trent leaned towards the booth and said, "I have already eaten. I am going to get a cup. Can I get you something?"

"No thanks, I am good to go."

Frank said, "He seems like a pleasant fellow."

"Stop. I thought I would pick his brain concerning Max."

"Oh, okay. I am sorry. That was awful presumptuous of me to take a leap like that after seeing your face light up like a kid's face on Christmas morning."

"Not true."

"Afraid so."

"I have other priorities."

"Sure, you do. You need to look out for Kate."

Frank purposely remained on the edge of his seat so that Trent would have to slide in next to Kate. Trent returned holding a cup of coffee and hesitantly sat next to Kate as she slid further to the inside.

Trent said, "What brings you into the neighborhood?"

Kate answered, "Frank found an angel. It's an inside joke. We are still working that motel homicide. Hey, could you put your professor hat on?"

"Oh, I see. You're looking for some free advice. I am going to have to send you a bill. You know my hourly rate is high. Of course, I would be willing to discount it if I could buy you dinner or lunch."

Frank said, "That is a spectacular idea. What a class guy."

She frowned at Frank and turned to Trent. "We have a guy whose daughter was killed a couple of years ago. The killer was out because of a judge's decision. The judge kicks the killer loose, and he goes out and kills this person's daughter. The father never gets over it. He has a land development company that goes belly up, or at least he has to sell it for less than it is worth. His wife leaves him. He sends a birthday and Christmas card to the judge each year. When he read about the judge, he goes into a rage. He is depressed, has been on medication, and is not taking them anymore. Counseling in the past has not been a success."

"Are you asking me if he could be a killer and is after the judge?"

"Yes."

"He could be. Being noncompliant with meds is quite normal. The patient thinks they are getting better and they don't like the side effects, so they quit. Then the symptoms become exacerbated and they have to be committed and re-medicated. It's a never-ending cycle for many. Most subjects involved in targeted violence do not contact their intended victims. They want to get away with murder. No pun intended. They want to be successful. I would not discount him. In addition, he is in despair. He views his life as going down the tubes and blames the judge for ruining his life. If he can formulate a plan of attack and remain focused, he might do it. There are a couple of thought processes that may explain his actions. One, is he thinks he is about to take his own life and figures to take her with him, as his ultimate punishment to her. He attaches significance to his now meaningless life. The second belief is that once the judge's elimination occurs, he can rejoice. He believes she is causing the pain, and he believes he can recapture his wife and business again once the dark cloud of the judge evaporates. Vengeance can be a real catharsis. It cleanses the soul. Don't you love it when you lock up someone that pisses you off?"

Kate smiled, listened, nodded, and said, "If I understand you correctly after that detailed dissertation, you don't know if he could or did it."

"Kate, you have a wonderful ability to cut it down to simpler terms."

"What about killing the judge's daughters?"

"Yes."

"Yes what? You can elaborate if you would like."

"How about lunch tomorrow?"

"We'll see."

"He would look at transferring his pain to the judge so that she experiences the same pain he has lived with. A judge in Chicago suffered a similar fate."

Frank gave an exasperated look as he reached down and snatched the cell phone off his belt. He held it at a distance, squinted at the display, and nodded with approval.

"Is this code name Angel calling? You are vectored and cleared to talk."

He winked and everyone at the table could hear the giggling on the other end, followed by a female voice.

"So, she is back? What kind of ride does she have? Angel, you have served your country today."

He ended the call and said, "I need to make a call. You two take your time and I'll meet you outside."

Trent and Kate watched Frank walk outside and hold the phone to his ear.

Trent said, "What about lunch?"

Kate looked to her right at Trent and said, "We just had lunch together."

"No, you ate lunch. I drank coffee. Listen, if you want to keep this strictly professional, I can live with that. I may not like it, but that is your decision. The psychiatrist in me tells me that because of the pain you experienced, you are reluctant to commit or you're in avoidance ..."

"I am not. You don't know me. My focus is on my daughter. You have no right, nor have you been around me long enough to judge me."

"I'm sorry. You're absolutely right."

"I'm sorry. I was out of line."

"No, I was. I forgot to take my lab coat off. I am not asking to marry you. I am asking to have lunch."

She laughed and looked down. She was embarrassed at being overly protective of her romantic interests. After Jake died, the cops were hovering like vultures to come and help the young widow. She fended them off, but now she was always in a defensive posture toward men.

He continued, "Who knows, I might not like you. We have a few things in common, and I would like to get to know you better. I'll leave it up to you. I won't bother you anymore. I'll see you around. Call me if you need any additional help on this or any other cases."

"I know what you're doing. You're pulling back like you have lost interest and blowing me off, so I'll come running back and say no, it's not you, it's me and I'll feel guilty and cave in."

"Is it working?" He smiled.

She reciprocated the smile, "I'll see you Saturday at 10:00 am. As long as you don't mind spending time with my daughter and me."

"Ten o'clock it is."

She handed him a business card with her home address written on the back. As they walked outside, Frank ended the call.

"Hey, Professor. You do better work than the FBI."

"Thanks, Frank. Their behavioral unit develops a suspect profile, where I have the advantage of having the suspect. They do pretty good, considering what they have to work with. I know there are a lot of complaints about how broad the descriptions are."

"Yeah, they will tell you it's a white male between 20 and 50. I could use a Ouija board and get better than that."

"The mind is very difficult to predict. They may call it science, but it's not exact."

"Good seeing you again Doc, and remember; perseverance. Don't give up." He winked at the professor and Trent returned the gesture.

Chapter Fifty-Five

F rank guided the car into the parking lot of the Frontier Apartments. He looked for the beat-up brown Buick with trunk damage and no hubcaps that Angel described. He spotted the car easily. Parked facing in, the car stuck out like a wart on the face. The parking lot was not as crowded as before lunch. He drove around the complex and approaching the car for the second time. He observed a young thin black female hustling towards the Buick.

"You think that is Lashondra?" Frank said.

"I'd say so. This makes it easy."

"Yep."

Lashondra looked over at the newer Dodge with two white folks and it didn't take long for her to recognize the car as an unmarked police car. She took off in a sprint toward the street.

The Dodge came to a stop. Kate jumped out and took off on foot, quickly closing the distance, while Frank slammed the selector in reverse, threw his arm across the seat, looked out the rear window, and punched the gas. As he accelerated, it became more difficult to steer the vehicle. Every slight variation of the steering wheel resulted in what appeared to be an amplified response. He glanced back toward his partner, who had caught her prey. He eased up the pressure on the gas pedal. Then he felt the jarring impact and could hear the crunching of metal. He had plowed into a white Pontiac pulling out of a spot. A tall, thin black male with dreadlocks stepped out, sucking on a joint. Reggae thumped from the car stereo as the cloud of the pungent weed floated with the breeze.

The driver said, "What the hell are you doing, man? Backing up like a rocket ship. Where is your space suit, Mr. NASA Man?"

"Shut up, you dirtbag, before I arrest you for possessing weed and obstructing justice."

"Justice man. I'm minding my own business, and you plowed into me. I hope you got a lot of insurance because my neck is hurting."

"Your balls are going to hurt more after I finish kicking them up to your throat. You failed to yield the right away. I had the right away."

"You was backing up, man."

"Still had the right away. You were in a parking space. You have to yield to me."

Frank looked up and saw Kate escorting Lashondra with her arm locked behind her. Kate looked a little hot, but was hardly out of breath.

"What in the hell happened to you, Frank?"

"What's it look like? Bob Marley over here pulled out in front of me. Is she saying anything?"

"Another of those, I am running because I am scared, but I didn't do anything."

"Mr. Marley, have a seat. I'll get to you in a minute. I'll check her purse. Bet she's holding."

He pulled out a baggie of marijuana and dangled it like a fisherman showing off his trophy catch. He opened the bag and inhaled the aroma of the cannabis. He rubbed the leafy stuff between his fingers and sprinkled it back into the bag.

Kate said, "Now Lashondra, you can answer our questions and we can pretend like the wind blew this out of Detective Duffy's hand and he lost the evidence or you go to jail. Your choice."

"What questions?"

"Concerning a customer at a store you worked at."

"That's it?"

"That's it."

"Why didn't you say so?"

Kate asked, "Look at this receipt. Do you remember this sale?"

"I remember. The manager fired me that day. They fired me because I was a good salesperson and they wouldn't give me a raise. So, I took out my bonus in merchandise. They owed me."

"What do you remember of the customer?"

"He was a white dude with big sunglasses. I asked him what he was wearing them inside for. He said his eyes."

"What about his eyes?"

"I dunno. He just pointed and said his eyes."

"What else about him?"

"He had a big, bushy mustache and baseball cap."

"What kind of hat? Color, or did it have a logo?"

"Maybe the Yankees. I am not sure."

"Young or old?"

"I don't remember. Average maybe."

"Average? Was he as old as Detective Duffy over there or younger than me?"

She looked over at Frank, who gave a sarcastic pose. "No, not that old. Maybe your age. Oh, and he had a twitch, too. Right here at the corner of his mouth."

She pointed to the right side of her mouth. "It would jump like someone jabbed him."

"All right, thanks for your help, Lashondra."

"Can I get my dope back?"

"No."

Frank winked at the waving Angel and called for a patrol supervisor to work the accident. He notified Alfonso as well. He thought of all the paperwork.

Mr. Dreadlocks said, "Hey man, how long have I got to stay here? I got places to be."

Frank answered, "Just shut up and sit in your car. You're lucky you're not sitting in jail."

Kate said, "Well Crash, shall we go back to the office? I can update the murder book and you can fill out all the accident forms in triplicate."

"You're a regular comedian, aren't you?"

"I try. With her description of a younger man, who we now know is connected to the storage facility by the receipt and the clothing description and witness description of the ATM shooter, I am becoming more interested in Max's young friend Luke."

"Very interesting. I would agree with that. He had access to his Cadillac."

Chapter Fifty-Six

Dietz sat on the passenger side of the car and looked over the printout on Troy Unger, trying to get a lead on where Troy would hide.

"Let's try this address over on Emma Street. Gator Koons lives there. One of his old pals. Gator? Where do these people come up with these names?"

As they pulled up on the address, they observed a slouchy figure shuffling down the walk from the house.

"I'll bet that's him."

As the figure shuffled by their car, Dietz showed a cat like ability not previously displayed by the overweight detective. He sprung out of the car gun in his hand and showed a quick burst of speed typically seen on Sunday afternoons in NFL. He grabbed Gator by the shirt collar and thrust him onto the hood of a nearby car. Dietz put the barrel of the gun to the right side of the surprised Gator's head.

"Police don't move or I'll blow your brains out. Are you Gator?"

Gator snarled, but didn't move. Dietz winced at Gator's bad breath.

"Where is Unger at?" Silence. "Where is Unger?"

Gator said, "Or what, you're going to blow my brains out? Up yours, I don't know where he is. Even if I knew, I wouldn't tell you."

"We could arrest you."

"For what?"

"Pissing off the police."

"Go ahead. I could use a few free meals and a firm mattress."

"I'll let you go for now, but let him know we're looking for him."

"Sure. Give me fifty cents and I'll be sure you're the first person I'll call."

"Don't be a smartass." Dietz said as he re-holstered his gun.

"Thanks for the charity, big man." He sauntered off in no hurry.

Canseco said, "He called your bluff, tough man."

"He got the point. He'll spread the word."

"Whatever you say. Any other bright ideas?"

"Let's go sit on the Tabernacle Church and see if Unger pops in."

From a distance, they blended into a parking lot with the air-conditioner on high and Dumb and Dumber watched the church. The gaze of the binoculars scrutinized every car and person who piqued their interest. After three hours, Canseco looked down at the discarded subway wrappers, potato chip bags, and candy wrappers at the feet of his partner and said, "What happed to the Keto Diet?"

"You gotta eat, and I drank a diet coke."

"You showed real restraint."

"Remember, I am not starting the diet till next week."

"Oh, I forgot. Then next week it will be the next week."

"You'll see."

"I can hardly wait."

As they watched the moon ascend into the sky, they sat in the darkness soaking up air-conditioning, gas, and overtime, but accomplishing little.

Canseco asked, "Did you want to go out for a couple of pops after?"

"Where?"

"Hyde Park Café?"

"Every time I go there, I bump into Rollins."

"So, what? It's not like he's asking to dance with you."

"He always acts like the deer hunter who makes fun of you catching a four pointer while he drags out an eight pointer. He gives that little nod and you know he is giving a report card to Duffy and Alexander. My philosophy is to go ugly, go early. If they take a shine to you and everyone is happy, what difference does it make? I would rather go to Four Green Fields."

"Not as much action."

"There is more of a chance to rub elbows with someone with juice. The powerbrokers are in there. That's who you need to hang with."

Canseco listened to the king of suck-ups. There is more to life than kissing ass. You're only as good as long as that person has control. A true politician balances on the tightrope and knows when to jump into the safety net. He answered, "Okay, we can hit Four Greeners and finish up at the Hyde Park Cafe."

"No can do tonight."

"After all that, and you can't go. Why not?"

"I have plans."

"Rizzo?"

"I have plans."

"It's Rizzo."

"I have plans."

"That is dangerous water you are swimming. Be very careful."

Canseco dropped the gear selected into drive and steered towards downtown and the Blue Monster.

Chapter Fifty-Seven

SATURDAY

O n Saturday, Trent's heartbeat increased, as he turned the silver Camry down the long driveway to the simple one-story red brick home. After he stopped, he smiled, glaring at his teeth in the rearview mirror to make sure he didn't have anything stuck in the gaps. He inspected his nose, making sure no hairs were sticking out. Confident he was good, he popped a mint into his dry mouth, took a deep breath, and opened the car door.

As he approached the front door, the door sprung open and a young pigtailed girl with braces dashed out.

"Hello Mr. Trent, I am Britney. It's so nice that you like horseback riding." She ran to the jeep.

"Horseback riding?"

Kate stepped out wearing jeans, a bright blue Lightning t-shirt, and a black ball cap with her hair threaded through the adjustment strap. Wow, she looked good. Casual wear was very becoming to her.

Looking at his face of surprise, Kate said, "I am sorry. I didn't mention we were going to the stables. You ride, don't you?"

"Well, ah, I suppose I can learn."

"I just assumed that you knew since you lived in North Carolina. That's like you assuming everyone in Florida knows how to fish. I am sorry Trent. We can do something else."

"And what, disappoint Britney? I'm not wearing the label of the person who ruined her day. I'll watch. Maybe they have one horse that I can stick a quarter in and get a feel for it."

"If you're sure, let's go. I'll drive."

"Is this your Jeep?"

"Yep. What were you expecting?"

"I am not sure, to be honest with you. Maybe a Volvo station wagon?"

"Yeah right."

"I'll bet you have a Harley, too."

"Nope, not anymore. It sat in the garage. No one to ride with."

"Well, you see, we could have ridden together."

"You ride?"

"Absolutely. How do you think I stay in such great shape?"

"Oh, you're toying with me. Maybe you could bring your bicycle down here next time and we can ride together."

They turned down the road to the Maverick Stables. Kate parked in a space near the stables. As soon as she shifted into park, Britney, who was sitting in the back, unfastened her seat belt, leaned around Kate and jumped out as soon as Kate opened the door to the two-door Jeep. Britney ran towards the stables like a kid running for the Christmas tree on Christmas morning.

Trent smiled and said, "She is cute. Loves life like her mother."

Kate smiled. They stepped out to the jeep and Kent thought it smelled like the circus.

He said, "It must be difficult raising her on your own. It looks like you're doing a wonderful job."

"Thanks. It is tough. My mother is a blessing. She could move down here permanently and is like a full-time nanny. So, my mom should get a lot of the credit."

"She must be talented. She raised you and you turned out okay."

Her face flushed with redness. "I'm all right."

"I'll bet she still has some significant memories of her dad?"

"She does, but certain memories fade with time. She remembers him giving her horsy rides, and reading books especially, *Oh the Places You'll Go* by Dr. Seuss. Jake couldn't remember *This Little Piggy* Went *to the Market,* so he substituted the local grocery stores, Publix, Winn Dixie, Whole Foods and Fresh Market. Then he'd say, and this piggy went wee wee wee all the way home and he would tickle her on the ribs."

"Sounds like he was a great father."

"He was."

"Does anyone keep in touch with you from the military?"

"Christmas cards. They kept in touch for a while and then tapered off. They moved and their lives changed. I don't blame them. I have my support system here."

"What was he like?"

"He had an A/B Switch. He could be as macho and full of testosterone as anyone. He was an adrenaline junkie and loved living on the edge. That's what cost him his life. I know he died with a smile. One moment he was oorahing with his fellow stud puppies and then he would switch and became so gentle, kind, and thoughtful."

"Like how?"

"Well, anyone can buy chocolate, flowers, or jewelry. Not every man knows what size their wife wears."

"You were very fortunate. Most people live an entire life without experiencing that joy."

She stared at him and said, "You are right. Yes, you are right."

He could see her mind contemplating the statement and he brought her back. "Why did you become a cop?"

"I joined the police department because I wanted to share the adrenaline rush that he liked. I couldn't get a rush from the corporate world. Now and then, I could spot someone lying in a job interview and get a little jazzed, but nothing like catching a mope and taking him off the streets. Jake was a warrior. He was noble. Jake said while most people run from danger, a warrior runs to it. That initially attracted me to the job. Maybe I wanted to identify with him. Along the way, I also learned that I enjoyed helping people. Those that are sick, hurt, in danger, or with this recent murder, to seek justice on their behalf. Were these victims' good people? Probably not, but they didn't deserve to die either. I will be their knight. Take the motel shootings. Those two people had a right to leave a legacy. Good or bad, they had that right. They were cheated of their legacy. Jake was cheated of his legacy, too."

"He left Britney and impacted you."

"Yes, but he was deprived of the ability to have a dramatic influence on her."

"You are impacting her. He is an influence everyday through the impact he made on you."

"I suppose."

"You have a fulfilled life. Not only as a great mother but also as a police officer. It has to be rewarding."

"Sometimes. I always felt good pulling up behind a stranded motorist and turning on my lights and calling for a wrecker. For that brief time, that motorist feels safe. On Christmas, while everyone was off and at home celebrating the birth of Christ, I was out there on patrol, keeping them safe. I would have a certain sense of exhilaration, as I pulled out of the parking lot on to the street and went 10-8. That feel good feeling might last until the first call of the day to a family disturbance. I still love the job. It is the politics and bureaucracy that I hate."

He thought about inherent risks. Without being chauvinistic, he still thought it was a tough job for a woman, especially a single mother whose safety was paramount to Britney. Could she separate from the job setting to the social setting without always being in charge?

Trent looked at her said, "It must get scary out there."

"Sometimes, I fear if anything happened to me, how much she would remember me? She knows her father through me. I have complete confidence in her wellbeing if something happened to me. Cops are a family. We take care of each other. When someone hears an officer needs assistance over the radio, everyone races to the rescue. Regardless if you dislike that person or they are your best friend, because it could be you. We are a family of blue. There was an officer who had Lou Gehrig's disease. He'd been on maybe a year and well liked. He had to move and by this time, he was in a wheelchair. Sixty officers show up to move him to a smaller house. That is something most people would never experience. I think it comes down to the closeness with death that we live with. Listen to me rambling. I guess you could charge me a therapy fee, right?"

"I am sure we can work something out."

"Shall we check on her?"

"Yes."

Britney sitting tall in the saddle wearing her helmet looked so confident atop the black stallion, Knight.

"Mommy, look, Knight is smiling. He is happy to see me."

"Yes, he is."

"Duke is waiting for you."

"I am not going to ride with you today, sweetie. I am going to watch and talk with Mr. Trent."

He asked, "Duke?"

"Duke is mine."

"You own these horses."

"Yep. We were going to build a barn. It's just easy for consistency to house them here. It is hard enough to care for Britney and my mother without worrying about if the horses were fed, exercised, and brushed."

"What kind of horses are they?"

"Quarter horses. Knight was Jake's horse and over there is my pride and joy, Duke."

They strolled over to the stall for Duke. He was caramel color with a white diamond on his forehead. Kate reached up, stroked his forehead, and put her other hand up to his mouth. Her hand moved from his forehead to his mane and to the side of his head. He responded by licking her hand.

"There's my boy. You're a handsome beauty. I missed you. Maybe next week I'll take you out. Wouldn't you like that? We'll go for a long ride with Knight. That's my boy."

Duke's eyes blinked gently, and the tail swished. She bent down and pulled out a red apple from a paper bag. She put the apple to his mouth, and he took it tenderly with his teeth and gave a throttle of appreciation.

Trent stared at Kate, admiring her simple beauty. With her hair pulled through her ball cap, there was a kind of casual elegance to her. He watched her smile warmly at the horse and how affectionate she was with Duke. He'd seen her beam with pride as she watched Britney on top of Knight. He knew this would take a lot of patience and time on his part to breakthrough to Kate, but he admired what he saw. It would not be a sprint, but a marathon. She displayed a deep and driven spirit. A commitment to loyalty almost to a fault. Who could blame her? This was her survival shield. She turned to look back and caught Trent admiring her.

She gave a "caught you," look and said, "Isn't Duke handsome?"

"Yes, he is. I was just admiring how you touch him and care for him."

"You are observing the kindler and gentler Kate. The non-cop."

"You have a job to do. An admirable one."

"A lonely one."

"How so? I thought you just talked about the esprit de corps?"

"Oh, I don't know. Women in a man's world. You always have to prove yourself."

"Frank acted like he respected you."

"Frank didn't always care for me, but yes, he supports me. Most of the others in homicide trust me. Some of the higher ups and newcomers cast an eye of suspicion on a female homicide detective. Sometimes I wonder if Britney suffers while her mother proves herself. I could work 9 to 5 with weekends off."

"As a trained professional, I must warn you that in my esteemed opinion, I notice no lasting psychological damage to your daughter. In fact, she acts like any other nine-year-old having fun. This is her frame of reference. This is the only world she understands. It's like a poor person not knowing what it's like to be rich. This is her comfort zone. In fact, if you switched to a corporate job, she might actually feel some anxiety during the change."

"You think?"

"Yes."

He looked into her eyes. For the first time, she did not divert her gaze, but instead mirrored his gaze. The corners of her mouth eased up slightly. Slowly, he leaned in towards her. He felt she was finally softening her shield of protection. He stepped forward and leaned in closer. He could smell her perfume. He inhaled the pleasant citrus and vanilla scent through his nose. Her brown eyes displayed emotion. Her smooth pale skin was soft looking, with just a hint of makeup.

She turned to the left and said, "Did you have any lunch plans?"

Disappointed, but willing to be patient, he said, "No, I cleared my schedule."

"Do you like BBQ?"

"I know I was a disappointment to you being a Duke boy who doesn't ride horses, but I love good BBQ."

"There is a place in Brandon called First Choice that has wonderful BBQ. We can go there after Britney finishes riding."

"Sounds great. Let me ask, do you like the theater?"

"What do you mean, do I act?"

"I have tickets for next Saturday's performance at the performing arts center, if you're interested?"

"It has been a while since I have seen a play. Can I let you know on Monday?"

"That's fair enough. I'll be anxiously awaiting your call."

She smiled.

He admired her assets from behind as she walked toward the safety of the riding area to watch Britney. The jeans hugged the curves and accented her fit body. He thought he would have to be persistent. At some point, her protective façade would collapse.

"Hey Kate, can I get you something to drink?"

"How about bottled water?"

"What about Britney?"

"The same thanks."

He stepped inside the office where the vending machine was located and asked the scrawny teenage girl behind the counter, "Do you give riding lessons?"

Chapter Fifty-Eight

MONDAY

On Monday morning, sitting at her desk, Kate examined the TPD report on the fatality accident involving the judge's oldest daughter, Rachel Applebaum the previous May. As she read the reports, she gently tapped the end of a yellow highlighter on the desk.

Rachel was driving southbound on Dale Mabry Highway at approximately 10PM. An unknown vehicle struck her right side, resulting in her losing control of the red Chrysler Sebring convertible she was driving. Her vehicle left the roadway at the Hillsborough Avenue overpass and rolled multiple times, crushing the roof and killing the driver. Rachel died at the scene. She experienced a moment of terror and then she was dead with a broken neck. Kate rubbed her chin and thought, what a senseless loss of life. She died because she was the daughter of a judge. Rachel was just experiencing life.

A distant ringing phone interrupted her thoughts. She heard, "Homicide Detective Dietz, may I help you?" His sour look disappeared. "I enjoyed that too. Oh, you know it. Tonight? Sure, what time? Count on it."

Canseco put another piece of gum in his mouth and was just working it when Dietz said, "Let's blow this pop stand while the gettins good and go find a murderer."

Kate, listening to the conversation, said, "I'll let you know if I see any."

Dietz sneered and left.

Kate resumed concentrating on the file and looked at numerous photographs of the crime scene. It was obvious the convertible didn't stand a chance in a rollover accident. There were all the technical pages involving measurements to determine the speed of her vehicle, tire marks, the drag coefficient of the road surface, and all that. The suspect vehicle fled the scene southbound without stopping. One witness described the suspect vehicle as a light-colored SUV. They advised it was difficult to determine if the SUV veered unintentionally or intentionally into Rachel's lane. Rachel's blood contained a blood alcohol content of .03. This would have caused minimum impairment, but could have impaired her response if someone, without warning, hit her car.

She read the statement of Sandy Fields, a friend of Rachel. Fields said they were studying at Sandy's apartment in the Carrollwood section off Dale Mabry Highway. They shared a bottle of wine. Fields said Rachel consumed only two glasses of wine over two hours while they studied. There were all the follow-up reports of attempting to locate the driver and or the suspect vehicle. The investigators checked with all the body shops, sending out a flyer to all the bay area law enforcement agencies. Crime Stoppers offered a reward. A billboard was posted near the accident, asking for help. The Sheriff's Office set up a roadblock the next week hoping to locate a witness that traveled at the same time perhaps, getting off work that might have seen something. They checked with rental car companies, police impound lots and abandoned vehicles in parking lots. They asked the airport police to check all the garages. They checked stolen car reports. Nothing. Case closed unless additional leads were developed.

Kate wondered if they would have done all this for an ordinary person, or were they were catching some heat because the death involved a judge's family member? She was impressed with their fortitude. She picked up a picture frame on her desk. She smiled at the photo of Britney riding Knight and the caption underneath read, *"Priorities - a hundred years from now it will not matter what my bank account was, the sort of house I lived in, or the kind of car I drove, but the world may be different because I was important in the life of a child."* It was so easy to forget your priorities sometimes. As she looked at the file of Rachel Applebaum, she thought here again was a life deprived of a legacy. She could only hope Rachel's parents had been a positive part of her brief life.

She picked up the telephone, called Sandy Fields, apologized for opening old wounds, and asked, "Did you recall any suspicious activity around the apartment, or did you hear of any crime in the apartment complex?"

"No, I don't."

"Is your complex gated?"

"No, it's not."

"Did Rachel confide that someone may have been following her?"

"No, I would have remembered that."

"Did you always study together?"

"Most of the time. We made it a point to get together on Thursday nights for a study session because exams were on Fridays."

"Were there any other rituals she followed?"

"No, other than going to class."

Kate closed the highlighter with her pen, jotted some notes, and thanked Sandy.

Chapter Fifty-Nine

F rank walked over to Kate's desk, shaking M&Ms in his hand and crunching some in his mouth. The scent of sweetness floated out as he spoke. "You will not believe this, but your suspect, Maximilian, killed himself yesterday."

"No way."

"Yep," as he tossed the remaining M&Ms in his mouth.

"Dig him back up. Put some cuffs on him. He is the one."

"Nope. I talked to Dupree over at HCSO. He said it looked like it was the old gun to the temple while he was sitting in his car contemplating life. He said they bagged his hands. It won't matter much if he was sitting in the closed car. The gun residue covered the inside. The gun is a .357. I asked him to get the FDLE lab to check the bullets from the ATM shootings and the Pirate's Cove. If I was at the Seminole Hard Rock Casino, the odds would be on my side of the house that all bullets came from the same gun."

"Where was he that the County took the hit?"

"Found him in his car in Wilderness Park."

"Which entrance?"

"Hey, why don't you call Dupree and get the 411?" He walked back to the M&M machine and pulled the arm for another hit.

She rubbed her face, brushed her hands through her hair, and said, "Let's go talk to the widow and to Dupree."

As they drove north from the city, Frank smirked and said, "What's the report on the Professor?"

"He is very nice. We're just friends."

"Like I would date my enemy. C'mon just among us girls."

"In case you haven't noticed, you're not anatomically correct to be one of the girls. If you must know, we are going to see a play on Saturday night."

"You know, you might have to put a dress on for that. That's why he asked you to go there. He wants to check the landing gear out."

"You know, you are a pig. I have several dresses."

"You might check the hemline to see if they are still in style."

"Maybe we can stop and pickup a copy of Cosmopolitan for ideas."

They knocked on the condo door for Marge Kress. She opened the door, her eyes swollen and red. It looked like she had not slept in a long time.

Kate said, "Marge, I am very sorry about Max. He seemed fine the other day. Maybe a little flat, but not on the precipice of life."

"Thanks. Please come in. It's so hard. I still loved him and cared for him."

The light was subdued for so early on a clear sunny day. Kate wanted to open the blinds to brighten the mood.

"I know it's tough."

Her mind drifted back to how she missed Jake, even to this day, and the difficulty of getting past the loss of a loved one.

"Kate, I know you are one of the few people that would understand. This brings back all sorts of terrible memories. He could be so tender and caring. Jennifer's death just caused a cascading effect on a lot of people."

"In what way?"

"The murderer was killed. He took my daughter and my husband and ruined my life, and I guess you can throw Luke in there as well."

"Luke? You mean the kid down the street? I saw him the other day."

"He was a good kid in a bad family. His father was abusive and alcoholic. His mother died when he was young. Luke would spend a lot of time with us. We became a surrogate family. Max became the father he didn't have. He was smitten with Jennifer. You could just see it in his eyes. He adored her. We all did. I just don't think he had the courage or the confidence to ask her out. They were more like brother and sister and that's the way she treated their relationship. I think he would have taken it to a higher level. He took it hard.

An accident killed his father. Ran off the road. Drunk. Luke had aspirations of going to college and joining the military. Talked about the Naval Academy. After her death, he withdrew just as Max did. The day after graduation, he came over and said he enlisted in the Army and was going to make Jennifer proud. He had the funds to go to school. He just didn't care anymore. He was going for the Rangers. He hurt his knee in jump school, and he washed out with a disability. He tore the ACL, MCL and, I think, torn cartilage and his kneecap was dislocated."

The detectives both grimaced at the magnitude of the injury.

"He still walks with a slight limp if you watch him, or if he gets tired. He enrolled in St. Leo's and decided he wanted to be a priest. I don't know what happened, but he quit school midway through his second semester. He has just been a wanderer ever since. He has been watching out for Max. They were good for each other. They were always close."

"Do you think they were ever intimate?"

"I don't think so. It was like puppy love. They would giggle and wrestle around, but I don't think it ever went past that. She liked him, but I think she was concerned about ruining their relationship as it stood. I don't think they realized they were in love."

The ringing telephone interrupted them. Marge excused herself and answered the telephone. It was the funeral home. Kate regressed to the time when she was the one making the funeral arrangements for a spouse. Her mind wondered back to Luke. He could be the suspect. She looked at Frank. He nodded, as if he knew exactly what she was thinking.

Marge dabbed her eyes with a Kleenex after hanging the phone up. She said, "I'm sorry about that. What were you saying?"

"What is Luke's last name, and do you know where he lives?"

"It is Luke Shugard. I don't know where he is living. He said he lives in a mobile home. He sold his parent's home down the street as soon as he left for the Army. It was just too many bad memories."

"Do you know what he drives?"

"I'm not good with cars. A smaller silver car."

"Did Max let him use his car?"

"Oh sure. Luke did a lot of things for Max. He would drive to different appointments and just keep him company. Most of Max's friends lost interest. No one wants to hang around with a clinically depressed friend. One of our friends said it was like watching Tigger turn into Eeyore."

"Did Max have an emotional attachment to Wilderness Park?"

"No, not that I know of. I don't know that he ever went there. At least not with me."

"How about parks in general?"

"He was more of a water person like at the beach or maybe the river."

"How about Luke?"

"I don't know. He used to be a big runner until the knee injury. He ran track in school."

"Marge, again I am sorry. I can honestly say I know what you're going through. If you need anyone to talk to let me know, or if you have questions, don't hesitate to call me. Here is my cell number."

Marge touched Kate's knee and whispered, "Thank you, Kate. You believe it was a suicide?"

"It certainly could be. He was suffering from depression. He may have had no reason to live."

"If only I stayed with him." She dabbed her eyes with a tissue.

"No. You may have relieved some of his burden by moving out. He may have suffered a great deal of anxiety and argued with you when you were there. You were still close to him. Don't blame yourself."

"Thank you, Kate."

"Oh, one more thing. Would you mind if we looked through his things at the house?"

"The sheriff's office already did that."

"I am sure they did, but I would like to look myself," She paused just a moment while she came up with an excuse that might make sense to Marge, "Just to rule out foul play since he lived in the city."

"Oh, ah sure, I guess that would be all right. Would you let me know if you find anything?"

"Absolutely."

"This is a spare key. You can just leave it on the kitchen table. You go through the side door of the garage when you leave. The door self locks."

"If you don't mind signing this consent to search form. It gives us the authority to search the house."

"Oh, sure."

Chapter Sixty

As they made the short drive from the condominium to the house, Frank said, "I guess Luke moves up the list now."

"Yep. I would say so. I think we should give him a shake and see what falls off the tree. The house might be interesting. We'll see what secrets the house would like to unveil. I'll keep my options open, but Luke looks better and better. The witnesses all describe a younger male involved with the ATM shooting, the storage facility and the customer at the clothing store."

While on their way back to Max's residence, Kate called Warren Dupree of the sheriff's office. He was in a meeting, and she asked him quickly if he would mind them looking through the house. She did not want to step on their toes, especially a murder or suicide investigation, and ruin anything they were working on. She explained to him they were looking at him as a suspect in three homicides. Dupree gave them carte blanche to have a look.

Kate and Frank drove into the circular drive and pulled up to the front door. Using the key from Marge, Kate opened the massive leaded glass double doors. They stepped into the tiled entryway. Kate recalled the last time she stepped into this entryway was to deliver the crushing news of Jennifer's murder. The two parents wailed and collapsed to the floor.

As they moved further into the house, she thought of the happiness that possessed this home just a few years earlier. A booming business, the epitome of affluence, and a wonderful daughter. A single judge's decision forever changed a beautiful family. Now the judge's life was also in ruin. Was Max or Luke the architect of her misfortune?

The house seemed dark and foreboding compared to years in the past. The A/C was off. Not only was it warm, but the air smelled stale. Her shoes echoed in the neglected home as she walked to the thermostat to turn the A/C on to move the air. She paused, looking at the rippling water of the kidney shaped swimming pool.

"Frank, why don't you look in the master, and I'll try to find the office that I think is back by the spare bedrooms."

He grunted his approval.

She walked to one door and opened it to reveal what must have been Jennifer's room. The room appeared to be a memorial to Jennifer without being disturbed since her death. Lilac tones decorated the room. A poster of a tennis star and a movie poster of *Harry Potter* adorned the walls. There was an assortment of stuffed animals and a couple of china dolls. Shelves displayed trophies and ribbons from various activities.

She located the office. Lined with bookshelves, the room hosted a large desk overlooking a garden in the backyard. His engineering degree hung on the wall from Georgia Tech, along with a baseball team photo from college. There was one action photo of a college aged Max winding up to throw the ball with his left hand. She thought about how he seemed so full of life at that age. Your whole life is ahead of you, and you are so excited about the future. You do not know what catastrophes may befall you. He couldn't predict the hardships ahead. Nor could she have at that age. She thought about how the future would judge her legacy and her life. It certainly would not be fair to Maximilian Kress.

The top of the desk resembled his disheveled life. Mail piled up unopened and several bills were past due. A yellow dusty coffee cup with dried coffee stains said, "Lefties are Right." She went through each of the drawers and the papers on the desk. She found the notepad. Written on the pad was "Wilderness Morris Bridge Rd." She thought it was odd to write down where you were going to go to commit suicide.

She found the bank statements. As she perused the account, they reflected a sizeable sum of money. She noticed quite a few cash deposits for what appeared to be small amounts. They were in odd amounts, like $101.86, $62.23, and $266.99. They occurred almost on a weekly basis. Why would he make such deposits? He received no income other than from investments, and that appeared to be set up on direct deposit from the broker. She noticed an amount deposited and the exact amount went out to MasterCard two days later. The purchased were six months earlier.

Frank entered the office and said, "I guess this is where he keeps his secrets. The bedroom looked abandoned. I am sure he had a maid, otherwise the rest of the house would look like this."

"Help me find all the MasterCard bills."

"Find something?"

"Maybe. I found these different small deposits almost every week. They could be anything, but I see large deposits from his broker from dividends and interest. Normally, brokers pay quarterly, as with the bank. Not several times a month."

"Okay, Nancy Drew, what is your hunch?"

"I'm thinking that Luke is using Max as a bank. So, what if Luke uses Max to buy different items, and he pays him back in cash or checks so the purchases can't be traced back. I'm looking for the February bill. It was $1,336.33."

"That's not a small amount."

"There is a deposit for that amount, and two days later, a check for the same amount goes to the credit card."

"It could be he has another account or Marge is transferring."

"It could be."

"Ding ding ding. We have a winner here it is." He raises his hand.

"Let me see."

He turns his hand in a halting motion. "Just stand back, little lady. I found it."

"Did you say $1,336.33?"

"Yes. What is it.?"

"It's not here. No, just kidding. The charge is from Tampa Bulls Eye Shooters Paradise."

"Are you serious?"

"Yes, Nancy Drew. If you would like, I will call Bob Littleton. He is one of the owners. Retired from TPD several years ago. Real barrel sucker. Good guy, but he just loves those guns."

"Start dialing baby."

He picked up the phone on the desk and began dialing from memory. He remembered the business phone number corresponded with a word "shooter."

"Hey Bob, this is Frank Duffy. I'm doing great. No, she is not. No, it's cancer. Thanks. Hey, listen, I'm a little under the gun, no pun intended, but I'm trying to track down a sale you made in February for $1336.33. On the 12th. No, I don't think it was a Valentine's present. Okay, here is my cell number. Yeah, it was. Later."

"He'll call back. He has to look it up."

They continued to sift through the reams of paper, looking for anything unusual or any notes to show why he killed himself. Kate flipped through the dusty and yellowed Rolodex. Under "L," she found Judge Levy's name and address. Kate turned on the computer, hoping it was not password protected. She was relieved to get to the window screen saver. A family photo of happier days. She went into the email box. Sixty-four new messages. He apparently didn't care to return emails. Most of the emails were spam relating to great can't miss investments, Rolex watches for sale, and Viagra sales. The address book was empty.

Frank's cell phone rang, and he answered it, but began cocking his body and trying to form a human antenna. He asked the caller to hold on as he shook his head in disgust and walked towards the front of the house.

He returned to the office and said, "That was Bob the barrel sucker. It was a Colt Python .357 caliber stainless steel with a 4.25 barrel for $1,275. He picked it up in an estate sale. They also sold a box of Winchester jacketed hollow point 158 grain ammo."

"Does he remember the buyer?"

"He said it was father and son and it appeared the son knew more about it. Said his father needed it for protection and wanted something reliable, accurate, and deadly."

"Wow. All we know is that Max bought the gun. My bloodhound meter is sniffing towards Luke."

Chapter Sixty-One

T hey left Max's house and Kate reached Warren Dupree with the sheriff's office. He was just finishing up at the medical examiner's office with the autopsy.

They drove into the parking lot of the M.E.'s office. The lanky detective stood in the parking lot in a short-sleeved white shirt. He tapped a cigarette on his watch, put it into his mouth, lit the end, and sucked. He exhaled a plume of smoke that drifted upwards. His short, dark hair did not need a comb.

He nodded in recognition as the Ford entered the parking lot and found an empty spot. As Kate and Frank walked toward him, he took one last draw of the cigarette and dropped it to the ground. With the heel of his foot, he squished it like a bug. His lungs exhaled the final cloud of smoke upward like a wayward balloon. He offered a Tic Tac to refusals and tossed a couple in his mouth.

Kate said, "Didn't your mother tell you those will stunt your growth?"

"No. I wished she did. Could you imagine I might have been tall enough to play forward for the Orlando Magic? Just don't report me for smoking to the sheriff. He frowns on smoking."

"I heard."

"How is business in the city?"

"Busy. How'd the autopsy go?"

"He's dead for sure."

They all grinned.

"Large caliber through the right temple. Contact wound. Went right through the driver's side window. We found a .357 Colt Python in the car."

Kate said, "We found he bought it at Tampa Bulls Eye. Who found him?"

"Uniform's responding to a 911 call. Anonymous. Sounds like a black male. I have a recording if you'd like to listen?"

They walked over to his silver Chevy Impala. He opened the door. The car smelled like a stale ashtray. He sat down in the cloth seat and opened an email with an audio file, and turned up the volume. Alexander and Duffy leaned into the doorway to listen.

A female dispatcher's voice said, "911, what's your emergency?"

The caller said, "Yo baby. Some dudes been shot in Wilderness Park parking lot."

Dupree closed the file at the sound of a dial tone and said, "That's all of it."

Kate said, "Did you do a swab of his hands?"

"Yep. But keep in mind if someone else killed him inside the car with the confined space, he would have trace elements on his hands."

"True."

"There was no note. He used bolt cutters to get past the gate. I'm thinking that was a lot of trouble to go through to kill himself and not write out a note. The 911 call came from a pay phone down on Fletcher at a gas station. Pay phones are like dinosaurs. The caller did not want to be tracked. I'm not ready to call this a straight up suicide yet."

"Is the phone booth yours or ours?"

"Ours."

"Have you printed it yet or DNA?"

"I asked crime scene to swing by there after the park. I am not too optimistic about recovering anything useful. Like swabbing a public toilet."

"Warren, I just thought of something." Kate said. "I don't think he killed himself. You said his right temple?"

"Yes."

"I saw a coffee cup that said something about left-handers. This reminds me that my husband said that Max was a great southpaw, drafted out of college, but he hurt his elbow or shoulder. There was a photo in the office of him pitching the ball, let me see," as she simulated the photo throwing the ball, "Yep, he was throwing left-handed."

"Son of a bitch. The lefty would have used his strong left hand, not the right. Why couldn't it have been a simple suicide? Now it is a homicide. I guess I better go back in and let the M.E. know."

Frank said, "Just like sneaking out early on a Friday. Something always happens. It is never simple. That's all I ever want is simplicity in life."

Warren said, "Frank, you're just a regular Socrates."

Kate said, "We think this all goes back to Judge Levy."

"How so?"

"She let this mope, David Stilts, slide. He kidnaps and kills Jennifer Kress. We were thinking the father was out for vengeance. You know, let the judge feel the same pain. This Luke Shugard was her boyfriend and lived down the street. He has remained close friends with the parents. He became a caretaker for Max. The elevator doesn't reach the top floor with Luke either."

"It would fit."

"Luke had to have parked his car somewhere. Either in the parking lot or near the pay phone."

Warren said, "We can check with the businesses around the pay phone to see if any video has his car sitting there unattended. There are a couple of motels, the gas station, and a Wendy's. He could have had Max come pick him up. Could have said his car broke down and needed a jump. Pick him up near the phone, go to the park, cut the lock, pull in, and bang. I'll check with patrol to see if anyone saw him walking along. What is he driving?"

"He drives a small silver car. Maybe a Camry. Did Max have a wallet?"

"Yes. That made the ID quick."

"Can I get a list of the contents? I'd like to know what credit cards were in the wallet and if he had a Master Card with him. In his house, I found a notepad that he scribbled Wilderness Park, Morris Bridge Road. How many suicides will write the location of where their life will end?"

"Good point. I'll email the contents of the wallet when I get back to the office."

"Thanks Warren. We'll talk." They separated and Warren extracted another cigarette from the flip-top box in his pocket.

Chapter Sixty-Two

K ate and Frank made the drive to the parking garage attached to the Blue Monster. She sat down at her desk and made a spot to look through the MasterCard statements. She became convinced that Max was so despondent over his daughter's murder that he was exacting revenge on the judge and her family. Now her prime suspect was dead and the trail instantly turned to Luke. He made a very grievous error, not realizing the right-handed attack on Max revealed a murder instead of a suicide. Now the game was on. A human chess match. It was still possible that Max was involved or had some knowledge, but she felt certain that he did not kill himself and did not kill Lori Applebaum.

She perused each credit card statement to see if anything would jump out at her. She examined the statement from ten months earlier. Two weeks before the accident of Rachel Applebaum, there was a charge from Delta Airlines. On the day after the accident, there was an entry for Calhoun's of Knoxville for $25. She remembered that while attending a cross-country meet at the University of Tennessee that she ate some great BBQ at Calhoun's Restaurant. It was located right on the river across the street from the University. A puzzled look highlighted her face as she saw the charge for Rocky Top Body Works, Alcoa, Tennessee for $2800. She went on the airline's website and checked the airfare from Tampa to Knoxville. About the same. She checked nearby airports. Orlando to Knoxville on Delta was also the similar in price. She checked Google Maps and found Alcoa was just south of Knoxville and close to the McGhee Tyson Airport in Knoxville. Finally, there was a charge of $640 at Volunteer Rental Cars. She became ecstatic. She could feel the adrenaline rush. She plotted the trip driving from Tampa to Knoxville. Eleven hours and fifteen minutes.

She leaned back, smiled, and thought up the scenario. Luke flies to Knoxville. He gets a month long rental and drives down to Tampa. Maybe he has already done his homework, or he stalks Rachel Applebaum. He runs her off the road and heads straight for Tennessee. He gets there around ten or eleven in the morning and heads to Calhoun's setting up an alibi. Luke drops the car at the body shop. They wouldn't look for the wrecked car in Tennessee. If Knoxville got a message on the hit and run, they would have filed it on some clipboard or the trash can. No one would have paid much attention. She thought he probably did not wear his disguise because he wanted people to verify that he was there. Someone might recognize his photo.

She jumped up, pumped her hands in the air, and said, "Yes! I have got you on the ropes now."

Alfonso peered out of his office with an alarmed look, and Bridges looked up from the Tribune. She waved like a frantic traffic cop for them to have a look, and her smile almost touched her ears. The two curious detectives walked over.

She said, "Look at this."

Kate systematically explains the accident reports and the association between the credit card, Luke and the gun purchase. She explained her Knoxville theory, and how she feels confident that Luke was the shooter.

Bridges gnawed on his cheap pen, nodded his head in agreement, and said, "Aha, very interesting. Yep." He walked back to his desk and picked up the newspaper.

Alfonso chuckled loudly as Frank walked back into the office, sipping a Diet Pepsi and said, "What I miss?"

Stewart said, "Kick Ass has done it again. She has solved another whodunit."

Frank responded, "You don't want to play her in Clue. I can't believe she solved it while I was out."

Kate, still beaming, looks to Alfonso and said, "I have to go to Knoxville and prove he is the one that drove that vehicle."

"Hold on there, little lady. This police department is so tight it might take a jackhammer to chisel the funds free. I could see them saying just get Knoxville Police to conduct the interviews."

"Like they don't have enough of their own work."

"I understand, but the powers to be will look at every way to keep from paying for this trip."

"This is no run-of-the-mill gang-banger murder. This is a Judge's daughter, or should I say daughters."

"That is the sole reason they will open their wallet. I can guarantee if it was someone else, the executive floor would never pay it."

"This would be embarrassing to have another department conduct our investigations. NYPD and LAPD would never do that."

"No, but TPD would. I am just playing devil's advocate. Budget crunch makes it tough. This conversation may be for naught. I am just preparing you. The first hurdle is Rizzo."

"Just don't tell her it's me. She'll never let me go."

"You might have a point. Let me see what I can do. I'll tell her Frank is making the trip. Then claim he had a conflict and send you. By that time, we'll have approval, maybe."

"I think either the judge or her husband is next. If Luke killed Max, he did it to put us at ease that Max took all the secrets to the grave and everything is ok. He is going to believe we'll close the case and blame everything on Max."

Frank said, "Luke underestimated Kick Ass."

He put his arm across to her right shoulder, pulled her in towards him, and shook her about, beaming like a proud father.

Kate said, "I have run Luke every way to find out where he is resting his head, but I have come up dry. But I know he'll be at the funeral."

Frank and Alfonso said in unison, "Yeah." In a tone like why didn't they think about that?

"I won't have enough to arrest him, but I can put the fear of God in him. I would rather wait until I can prove the case, but with him still looking to settle a score, I want to rattle him. Put him on notice that he is under the magnifying glass."

Alfonso said, "You're probably right. We'll have to cover the judge and her husband. Oh boy. I need some Advil. I have to sell this to the Lieutenant somehow."

"Thanks, Sarge."

Chapter Sixty-Three

K ate said to Frank, "Let's take a drive into the country."

"Why, I thought you would never ask."

Kate and Frank drove north on I-75 to the sleepy hamlet of San Antonio, Florida. San Antonio was just up the road from St. Leo University, a small Catholic school about thirty-five miles north of downtown Tampa. The Spanish influenced campus overlooked beautiful Lake Jovita. The Spanish moss blew like a wispy beard dangling from stately oak trees that cast large enough shadows to hide from the heat. It was something out of a postcard. The rolling hills gave a sense of being somewhere other than Florida. They turned into the entrance of St. Leo's that had a simple, understated entrance. They made their initial contact with the public safety department, who reported no incidents were on file for Luke Shugard.

The detectives determined that Monsignor Hugh Muldoon was his academic advisor. Luke's major was religion. A pleasant-looking woman in the office of the religious studies department greeted them. After introducing themselves, she instructed them to take a seat, and she called Monsignor Muldoon.

A few moments later, an older gentleman with snow-white hair and a red hued face entered the waiting room. He would have looked like Johnny Cash dressed in black, but the priests' collar gave him away.

He said, "I am Monsignor Muldoon and I understand you are with the Tampa Police. If you're looking for our excellent criminal justice program, you're in the wrong place. If it's religion you are looking for, you have found your way to the right spot. How can I help you?"

Kate said, "We wanted to talk to you about one of your former students."

"Let's go to my office."

They entered a small office adorned with enough Notre Dame memorabilia to open a booster club.

"Do you remember Luke Shugard?"

His face tightened. "Did he do something wrong?"

"Possibly."

"I am sure he is mixed up in some trouble for you folks came up here."

Kate asked, "What can you tell us about him?"

"He was a troubled fellow. He had been in the Army and injured his knee. He was out on a disability. Apparently, he had a girlfriend murdered that he never got over. His parents were both deceased and apparently, he did not have a good relationship with either, but in particular, his father. There may have been abuse. I think he was looking to God and religion for comfort, like so many people in crisis. He had aspirations of becoming a priest. But his interpretations of the bible were confused and diabolical."

"How so?" asked Kate.

"This has always been the case of heretics. Whether it is David Koresh or Jim Jones, they use their bible interpretations to legitimize their conduct and beliefs that contradict established religious doctrine and teachings."

"Do you think he is dangerous?"

"I think he has a lot of rage built up inside."

"Could he be dangerous?"

He shrugged, "I suppose. He appears to be gentle, but when he discusses his bible interpretations, you can see the devil possesses him. He can become quite animated and anxious. I asked him to leave and asked him to get some counseling to get past these issues. I gave him some recommendations."

"How did he take it?"

"No emotion. He told me I was wrong, and that God had spoken to him. This was what he needed to do. I realized he had some mental health issues."

"Does he possess good planning abilities?"

"I would say yes. He could complete his assignments, and they were always thorough. He just had such a convoluted view of the bible and life."

"Were you scared of him or did you have concerns about your safety?"

He creaked back in the chair, "Oh God, no. He has a dark side. I left it open for him to return once he got his life in order."

"Can you provide some examples of his views?" asked Kate.

As he was thinking, he looked and rubbed his chin. "He was always obsessed by secret societies and how the Crusades cleansed the world of evil. He would spin this to the

Trilateral Commission running the U.S. When I asked what his plans were, he said he was preparing himself for his future. That everything he had experienced was his preparation for his legacy. I asked him what his legacy was, and he said it was following God's path."

Kate said, "Sounds scary."

He nodded. "His thoughts were."

"How about any students that he hung out with?"

"He was a loner. I was as close as a friend he had. Once he started talking of his beliefs, they would gravitate away."

"Thanks for your time, father."

"You're welcome. Good luck and God bless."

As they sauntered back toward the car, Kate said, "I wouldn't mind living up here. In some ways, it reminds me of North Carolina. Mayberry RFD. As opposed to flat as a ruler in Tampa. Take a sniff of the fresh air up here."

"It's too country up here. Too quiet. I have played golf down the street at Lake Jovita and it is one of the nicest courses, but it's so far from anything. The movies, Publix, or Lowes. Nothing out this way. I don't want to pack a lunch to buy groceries."

"But it's nice."

Chapter Sixty-Four

T he two detectives parked on the street at one meter in front of the YMCA. Duffy and Kate strode across Franklin Street to the narrow three-story red brick building. The gold script writing of Hattrick's with the green shamrock was on the front and side of the building. It was a lonely building surrounded by parking lots. Frank pulled open the old glass paned wooden door and allowed Kate to walk in first.

Kyle Bridges was sitting on a stool at the long wooden bar, stirring the cubes in a Crown and Coke. Duffy rested his foot on the brass foot rail and leaned with his right elbow on the edge of the bar. The well-endowed bartender walked toward the new customers.

Duffy said, "Two Shock Top." The bartender turned back to the tap station. Kate said, "What, no Guinness tonight?"

"No, I am trying to be light. I need to lose a few pounds. I am just not in the mood for Guinness tonight."

Frank turned towards the dining room and looked around at the sports memorabilia hung on the red brick walls. The exposed pipes in the ceiling and the worn painted floors provided an antique ambiance.

"I love the character of this place. You can't decorate character."

"I'll be sure to get you a subscription to Coastal Living Magazine."

"You know I would read it."

"I'm not surprised. You are an enigma."

She reached into the bowl of peanuts on the bar.

"Don't you know how unsanitary that is?"

Bridges slurped the rest of his crown and coke, stood up, and said, "You can add the bottom of woman's purses as being unsanitary. Have a good night."

"You too."

Kate said, "What are you talking about?"

Frank said, "Look at that guy walking into the restroom. Imagine he is walking up to the urinal, unzipping his pants, pulling it out and releasing the stream. Now count thirty seconds for the average piss."

They paused while Kate watched her sports watch count down the seconds.

"Okay, thirty."

"And now he will shake 2.5 times, pull it back in, and zip it up. He'll either flush or pass, walk over to the mirror and check himself out. Now, just like flushing, he won't wash his hands if he is solo inside. So, he should walk out about now." Just then, the customer walked out. "Now he could just as easily walk up to the bar and grab a handful of nuts and infect the bowl."

"No, you wouldn't want him to grab a handful of your nuts."

They both laughed. They lifted the frosty mugs, leaving a moist ring on the bar and clinked them in unison and said, "Slainte."

"Duffy, is this a scientific study you're going to publish?"

"Human nature. I am a student of life. Did you know that Walt Disney handed out candy bars and determined most people discarded the wrappers between thirty and fifty steps? Hence, all garbage cans in the Magic Kingdom are within fifty steps. He studied human nature."

"You're a piece of work. You're like Cliff Clavin from Cheers."

"All three of my girls say the same thing."

"Hey, I hope you don't mind. I invited Trent to join us."

"You two have become quite an item. Good for you, Kate Alexander. No, I don't mind." He smiled at her, changing facial color from pale to crimson. "Nothing more exciting than love, except maybe putting someone in jail."

"You still get the rush of the hunt, don't you?"

"Henry David Thoreau said, 'Do not hire a man who does your work for money, but him who does it for the love of it.'"

"Wow, quoting Thoreau."

"You like that, huh?"

"I'm impressed."

"When I started this job, I hated for my weekends to come up. I may not have quite the fire. I hate the bureaucracy and the idiot bosses, but I still love the job. When I get to the point of not liking the job, I'm gone. I'm a couple of years from the KMA club."

"KMA?"

"Kiss My Ass. I can tell those gutless wonders to pound sand anytime and walk out with a smile." He looked outside and said, "Here is the professor."

She turned her attention to the door. Trent's face lit up as he made eye contact with Kate.

Frank said, "Why don't we grab that table?" He left three fives on the bar. He winked at the bartender as she nodded back.

Frank grabbed the seat across from his partner, forcing Trent to sit closest to Kate. Another well-endowed, perky waitress approached the threesome.

Trent said, "How about a pitcher of Shock Top?"

"Anything to eat?"

Frank said, "You should try the shepherd's pie. It is the best I have had outside my kitchen."

Trent said, "Sounds good. I'll take one. Kate?"

Kate said, "Chicken Caesar please."

Trent said, "Frank, how about you?"

"No doctor. One and done for me. I need to get home."

The waitress delivered the Sheppard's pie in its own little black skillet. A thick, crusty layer of cheddar cheese covered the potatoes.

Trent pointed at the entrée and said, "My, that looks good."

Duffy said, "I know my food. All right, I have drained this beer to the bottom, so I am going to fly. Good to see you again, Doc. And you two behave yourself." He winked, and Kate's face blazed crimson again as she looked down at the salad.

Trent said, "Do you come here often?" As he pierced the cheese and potatoes with a spoon, steam billowed out.

"Not that often. Maybe once a month. Back when I was single, I could see myself stopping in here all the time." The patrons erupted in a chorus of sighs at one of the televisions, which aired the ball game. The Rays scored a run over the Yankees. "As Duffy says, it's got a lot of character."

"How about you? Have you ever been in here?"

"Once, before a Lightning game."

"So, you're a hockey fan?"

"If I had the money, I would buy season tickets."

"Once the season starts, maybe you can take me."

"It's a date. So, you don't hang out here much?"

"Being a single parent and working the crazy hours that I do, I just want to get home and spend time with Britney. My mom is good company. She would like to see me get out more."

"So, would I."

He put a mouthful of meat in his mouth. He quickly opened his mouth like a large-mouth bass and tried to aerate the burning food.

"Hot?" she asked.

He sipped on the beer and answered, "Yes. You're right. It is important that Britney knows she is important, and that is your comfort zone."

"*But*. You're going to tell me my mental health is important and that my hierarchy of needs must be met?"

"You paid attention in psych 101."

"I just want you to understand that I am damaged goods. I come with baggage."

"It doesn't have to be that way."

"I was devastated after Jake's death. Every time I go to a homicide, I can identify with the survivors. Maybe that makes me better than the guys. I love my job, but it also provides a distraction from life."

"Or a stone wall to loneliness."

"I won't argue with that."

"Outside of work, Britney is my life. She is all I have left of Jake. Some people say, oh what a shame that you are a widow with a child. I couldn't imagine not having a part of Jake. Now and then she'll do something or some mannerism and I think to myself, Jake would have done that."

"If you would like, I could see about a third ticket for the play Saturday?"

"No. Maybe it's time I step out from behind that stone wall." She winked.

"All right, I'll pick you up at five and we will have dinner at the Columbia first."

"Sounds good. I love their sangria."

"Oh good, I can get you all liquored up."

"Remember, I have my black belt in judo."

"I guess you could beat me up."

"What about you, professor? Why no wedding band?"

She looked at his comfortable style. He wasn't trying to impress anyone. Trent was no Jake. He was just Trent. Mr. Nice Guy, Mr. Dependable, and Mr. Easy Going. She would like to spend more time with him. She intently listened and leaned closer. She could smell his cologne. A woody musk with a hint of spice. He had an air of confidence. Not in a cocky way, but in a subtle way.

"I was married to the books. I have had a few interests over the years. A few near misses. No one willing to share me with the books."

"Perhaps I have finally met my intellectual equal."

They both laughed.

Chapter Sixty-Five

With Hattrick's in his rearview mirror, Frank drove south instead of north. He had a look see at something. A personal errand. Well, sort of. He felt a certain exuberance, like a kid peeking over the neighbor's fence to watch the big sister next door sunbathing in a bikini. He turned off Gandy Blvd. into the heart of South Tampa. The area once blighted by old homes was now the chic place to live. Things were definitely going upscale. He loved it for surveillance. No gated communities to fight with the guards and plenty of on the street parking to blend in. He pulled over on the side of the curbless road as the tire dropped in a pothole. He pulled out the binoculars and peered out the windshield. A broad smile came across his face.

"I'll be damned. This is too good to be true."

He chuckled and then laughed hard and loud. Tears came to his eyes. He started the car and eased past Lieutenant Robin Rizzo's nicely restored ranch home. Two Fords sat in the driveway. Her gold one closest to the single-car garage. The second one was Dietz's white city car. Frank opened the cell phone, scrolled through his phone book, and found his old friend, Reese Crenshaw, from the Tribune.

"Hello Reese, baby, it's Frank Duffy."

"Duff, to what do I hold this distinctive pleasure?"

"I am going to drop a bomb in your lap."

"How about we meet at Four Green Fields?"

"No, too many witnesses. Make it The Retreat in fifteen minutes."

"This must be good. I love a little drama. See you there."

Duffy knows that if he can get Reese to snoop around Rizzo, maybe she will get nervous and back off. At least she would have to be careful of her covering for Dietz. She was very concerned with upward mobility and wanted no obstacles that would detract from her rise in power.

The Retreat was one of those obscure bars just across the bridge from downtown on Kennedy Boulevard. Home of the Guinness Book of World Records for the most draft beers sold and serving since 1938, it was a favorite among the downtown crowd and students at the University of Tampa around the corner. Not a place to impress a date, but it had its own comfortable character and wall mural of caricatures of some of the original regulars. Every visitor was greeted with classic rock music as they walked through the door.

Reese rubbed his meticulously trimmed beard and said, "I have not seen you at Four Green Fields lately?"

"Bridget has been sick. You still play golf?"

"Every chance I get."

"You need to get me out there."

"Are you any good?"

"I am a McDonald's golfer. McDonalds was built upon consistency. That's me. I am very consistent." Frank leaned back with a smile.

"I don't know many golfers that are arrogant enough to say they are consistent."

"Oh, I am. I am consistently horrible. I have three rules."

"What are they?"

"One, you can't count a stroke when I miss the ball. The second is we have to have fun, and the third is you're buying."

"What do you mean I'm buying? I am okay with the first two."

"When you hear what I have to say, you will gladly buy."

He leaned forward. "Is it scandal? I love scandal."

Frank also closed the distance. "Yeah, it's scandal. In addition, I am giving you the scoop. You're going to pickup the tab and buy me one and done."

"Love them and leave them."

"I am going to give you the quick down and dirty and you're on your own. Do you know Robin Rizzo?"

"Your lieutenant?"

"Yep, and you know Conrad Dietz?

"He's working the ATM shooting?"

"Yep. Well, let's just say they are doing more banging than a screen door in a hurricane."

"Really?"

Duffy slid a slip of paper to Reese and said, "Yep, and they are at it as we speak. You can go drive by her house at this address and confirm for your records. Another thing, I'll bet that if you check their cell phone records, you'll find that they are chatting up a storm. The city cell phones are public record."

Reese said, "I'll make a note of that. This goes back to President Clinton. Who cares about their personal lives?"

"Stay with me. I'll explain. I suspected something was going on. She has been like a piece of gum stuck to the bottom of a shoe. She is always in the way. She has pulled the carpet from under Kate Alexander on the motel shootings and despite one screw up after another, she is waving the flag for Dietz."

"So, what? She is playing favorites."

"Listen to me here. I can't tell you everything yet, but I will. Kate has traced the suspect of the motel shootings to the Judge. The Judge apparently released some mope that went out and killed the suspect's girlfriend. The girl's father just committed suicide in the park, but it's looking like a murder. One of those where the suicider shot himself in the head with his weak hand. This suspected shooter is a real wackadoo."

"I remember that case when Judge Levy released him."

"You know her nickname is Levy-them-out-of-jail."

"Yes, I've heard that. I was there in court that day. One cop got a lecture from the judge. She took some heat over that case when he went out and killed that girl and she blamed the State Attorney and the cops."

"Well, Dietz initially put out that the shooter at the ATM was black when he was white. He had a name of a recent parolee working in the area and went off like a bull in a china shop trying to build the surrounding case. My sources tell me he goes out with Canseco and tries to find this guy. The parolee takes off like a gazelle and runs. They lose him. He has yet to pull video from the ATM or area businesses. Rizzo has signed off on carte blanche overtime for her boy toy, but not for the motel robberies. Dietz couldn't investigate his way out of a wet paper bag with both ends open. When Al Stewart went to have him removed, she jumped his ass and blamed him for not supervising him correctly."

"You don't like her, do you?"

"Reese, I have never given you bad info. To answer your question, no. I have no use for her and the feeling is mutual. You ever hear of Irish Diplomacy?"

"No."

"It is the ability to tell someone to go to hell in such a manner that they look forward to the trip. I have told her in my own way to go to hell quite a few times. She is smart enough to realize after I gave the jab. You can throw Dietz in the same bag. He is an incompetent blowhard who thinks he is smarter than everyone. He is a constant embarrassment. I personally don't care what they are doing unless it adversely affects me and the job I am trying to do. You'll see."

A mixed group of coeds and frat boys rolled through the front door laughing and enjoying their youth. Frank's mind flashed back to his college days and jealous of their innocence.

Reese said, "Is it because she is a woman?"

"To be honest with you, if I am going into a bar-room brawl, I might be a little apprehensive with a female, but on domestics and as investigators, they are every bit as capable. Kate Alexander is phenomenal and I WOULD go to a brawl with her. She has earned her nickname of Kick Ass. Speaking of nicknames, you know what they call the Lieutenant. When she worked the street for the short time she was there, they called her Gobbler. She made friends with the right people. Again, I don't care about that. I am happy where I am. So, I don't care if she becomes mayor as long as she doesn't cause me problems."

"Why not go to the chief?"

"I would get my wings clipped for jumping out of line on the chain of command. They might slap Rizzo's hand and that would be it. I am all for diversity. I have two girls of my own. I was a foster parent for a Cuban American and my mother was an immigrant in a group that was heavily, I mean heavily, discriminated against. I am Mr. EEO and all that, but I am also for paying your dues and being competent."

"You're just a regular United Nations diplomat. Are you hitting on Alexander?"

"No. I look at her as a daughter. For crying out loud, you know Bridget and I are inseparable."

"Just checking. I feel a little dirty with this. Are you using me?"

"Absolutely. I am giving you scoop here because you're one of those Joe Friday types. Just the facts, ma'am. You always give me a fair shake."

"You're a suck up. What do you want me to do?"

"I will not tell you how to do you job. You're a professional. Rattle her cage. Put her on notice. Maybe she'll back off. When the story comes to a happy ending, I'll give you the full Monty. You know my word is good."

"I'll swing by the house. Next time, take me someplace where you can order beer table side and pay for it."

"Four Green Fields next time and golf is on you."

"You got it."

Chapter Sixty-Six

D uffy opened the trunk to his car and rooted through the equipment that was stored there. He lifted his ballistic vest and found a small red plastic case. Inside the case were some bare essential tools that he needed from time to time. He pulled out the needle-nose pliers. He tossed the case back in the trunk. He picked up a black t-shirt with his free hand, closed the lid, and jumped back in the car. He waited a few more minutes to give Reese a head start. He pulled his necktie off, removed his white dress shirt and t-shirt, and replaced it with his black t-shirt.

As he pulled out into traffic, his thoughts reflected on the case. It was one of the most bizarre cases that he had worked. Revenge was one of the primary motivations behind murder. Add that to jealousy and greed. He could almost sympathize with Max being the killer. He thought if something happened to one of his daughters, he might not be able to control his anger. This Luke kid was just off his axis. To go after the family of a judge? That is just crazy. She was doing her job regardless if you agreed with her. To kill her kids? Nuts. He and Kate had to get enough evidence to stop this guy.

He returned to the Lieutenant's house, making sure that Reese was no longer in the area. He stepped out of the car and walked nonchalantly up the street like he was out for an evening stroll. His eyes peered around, making sure no other cars or people were walking about. As he approached Rizzo's house, he made a quick dart towards Dietz's car. He ducked down on his right knee by the right rear tire. He looked around, as his heart pounded like a jackhammer. Using his fingers, he spun the tire stem cap off as he peered through the car windows at the front door. He took the needle-nose pliers, grabbed the top of the valve stem, and twisted and spun it until it came off. The air hissed out of the stem. Duffy dropped the cap and stem next to the tire so there would be no doubt this was deliberate. A warning that the cat was out of the bag.

Frank stood and rushed away for a time and then resumed his nonchalant stride back to his car as he whistled with joy. He sat in the driver's seat, wiping the sweat off his forehead and from under his eyes. He looked back to make sure no one was outside.

Starting his car, he looked again. He noticed Dietz's car listing toward the flat tire, as he laughed and drove away. Frank thought he would love to have been out there when the two lovebirds discovered the tire. Once locating the valve stem, a smart person would know their tryst was public. They weren't the brightest bulbs on the block and might have trouble putting it together.

Chapter Sixty-Seven

Kate put her shoulder into the front door of her home and nudged it open. One of these days, she was going to fix it and eliminating it from sticking. The cool air of the house felt good. Britney stretched out on the sofa while watching *Harry Potter* with a throw blanket pulled over her. Kate's mother sat in the recliner crocheting a light blue blanket. Kate came in and reached down to plant a kiss on her daughter's forehead. Britney gestured for her mother to move so that she could resume the view of her favorite show.

"Well, excuse me for coming home."

"Shhhh."

Kate reached into the blanket and started tickling her ribs. She burst out in laughter and feigning unsuccessfully to push her mother away. Kate finally stopped and reached over to kiss her mother.

"I'll be right back. Hold a spot for me."

She thought about Jennifer's room and the *Harry Potter* poster. The books and movies had impacted two girls. One was dead and one was the daughter of the investigator. The same detective was trying to capture the boyfriend of the dead girl.

Kate returned in shorts, a gray t-shirt and barefooted. She punched in the code to set the alarm system and then eased into the corner of the couch, picking up Britney's head and placing her head on her lap. Kate gently stroked and brushed Britney's soft hair with her slender fingers.

Kate turned to her mother and said, "Momma, you need to set the alarm when you're inside. That's why we pay for it."

"I set it when we're gone. I just have to keep turning it off and on when I go out to the garage or something."

"I know, but it is just one more layer of safety."

"This is a friendly neighborhood."

"Nicole Simpson lived in a nice neighborhood. We are isolated out here. You never know when someone is passing through with evil intent."

"All right. I get the message."

She loved her mother, despite her stubbornness. When the movie was over, she escorted Britney to her bedroom and helped her pick out her clothes for the next day and into her pajamas.

She looked at Britney. How fast they grow up. It seemed like yesterday she was burping her up on the shoulder. Now she was eyeing boys. Remembering something Trent had said piqued her interest. She decided on a test.

"Let me ask you a question, Brit?"

"Sure."

"What would you say if I said I was going to quit the police department and go back to work at the bank?"

"Why would you do that? You have a really cool job Mommy. You put bad people in jail and make us safe? Nobody else in school has a parent with as cool of a job."

"I was just asking. Don't you get upset when I work late?"

"There is always the weekend. You spend a lot of time with me. I love you."

"I love you too, kiddo. Give me a big ole hug and then go brush your teeth, say your prayers, and I'll come in and tuck you in, sweetie."

"Okay, Mommy."

Kate rejoined her mother, watching TV. Kate plopped down with a sigh. Her mother looked over and said, "Tired?"

"I suppose."

"I worry about you."

"I'll be all right, mama. I'm careful."

"I'm not talking about safety, although that concerns me every waking moment that you're gone. I just don't know what I would do."

"Nothing is going to happen."

"The hours you put in. Britney is getting to the age she needs her mother around."

"I'm not the only single working mother."

"No. But others aren't getting called out in the middle of the night and dealing with death and violence and the associated long hours."

"I'm getting close on this one, so I'll have more time after."

"Until the next one."

She glared. "What am I to do? It's not every day you can go out and find a job that pays my salary with all the benefits."

"You could get reassigned to another section."

"Like crime prevention and hand out coloring books or dress up like McGruff, the crime fighting dog."

"If it provides stability. Hon, I know you love your job, but it's not just about you. It's about your daughter. We as mothers have to make sacrifices and life is not always fair."

"Don't I know that? I didn't ask for Jake to be killed. Just like these two people didn't ask to die. They were deprived of leaving their legacy."

"You have done enough. You have put enough people in jail. Let someone else steps in. Be a mother."

She paused and took a deep breath. She said, "I can't believe you just said that. I have tried to be the best mother I can be to Britney. Just like you have been to me. I want to show her how you meet challenges head on and don't take the easy or easier way out. You know me, momma. I have always put forth the best effort I can, whether it was cross-country or school. Some days, my best wasn't good enough. But I can look at myself in the mirror and know I tried my best."

"I know it's tough. You have done a marvelous job. I am just saying you need to put Britney's needs ahead of yours."

"Momma, I just asked her what she thought about my job. She thinks I have a cool job. She showed no animosity towards my career. I am tired and I have a hard day tomorrow. I think I am going to go to bed after I tuck her in."

"Kate, I am sorry. I didn't mean to upset you."

"I know Mom. I am just trying the best I can. Just maybe I can remove one more person who could prey upon someone else's family or our family. Good night, momma."

Her mother stood up to meet her and gave her a hug. As Kate turned away, she wiped a tear that dribbled from her left eye.

Her mother said, "Good night, sweetie. I love you, Kate."

"I love you, too."

After tucking Britney into bed, Kate walked into her own bedroom. She turned off the lights and climbed under the covers of her bed. Her bare feet enjoyed the comfort of the soft cotton. Her head dropped into the pillow as tears rolled off her face.

Chapter Sixty-Eight

TUESDAY

T he alarm clock displayed 5:30AM. The radio played country music. Kate reached over and hit the snooze button. She lay there for a few minutes and contemplated the day. The funeral of Max was something she dreaded. Duty calls and all that, but she would rather have a wisdom tooth pulled without Novocain. She finally forced herself out of bed. She stared at the mirror and looked at her hair. The pillow had won the fight, and her hair was the victim.

She needed coffee. She shuffled into the kitchen. Thank you, mom. She had set the timer the night before. A full pot was waiting for her. She poured the coffee, added half-and-half and a dribble of honey. She smelled the robust aroma and felt the warmth of the blue stone mug in her hands. She pursed her lips and took a sip. It tasted so good. She took a few more sips. She checked on Britney and watched her sleep with contentment on her face. Oh, if only she could sleep with the same contentment and enjoy life as much. She gently kissed her daughter on the forehead and quietly pulled the door closed.

Now she could take a very hot shower, escape the world, and wash the cobwebs away. Tuesdays were her normal running days. Not today. She thought too much when she ran. The shower summoned her.

The steam-shrouded bathroom provided warmth as she stepped out of the hot shower. She took a washcloth, wiped the steam off the mirror, and looked at the reflection. She thought she was still attractive, but some of her youth had been lost over the last few years. She thought about Marge, perhaps feeling relieved that her husband's life was over, and freed to a better place to reunite with their daughter. Kate only felt despair over her husband's death. She resumed putting on her makeup and covering her anguish.

As she stepped outside from the house, she could hear the songbirds chirping and calling into the darkness. She looked towards the east as the sun made its first appearance of the day. To Kate, it looked like the five fingers of God's hand bathed in magenta reaching skyward. She was leaving this peaceful image to come face to face with evil. She opened the dew-covered car and prepared for her journey.

Chapter Sixty-Nine

I n the homicide squad room, Frank said, "Hey Luster, I thought you were going to slide by Hattrick's."

"I was. I pulled into Publix. I needed to pick up a couple of things."

"Let me guess. A cheap bottle of wine and a box of condoms."

"Duff, man, that hurts. I was sincere. I had my little green hand basket with an expensive bottle of merlot and a loaf of bread when I fell in love."

"Love?"

Pointing with both hands, Rollins said, "Dude, I am telling you this woman was unbelievable. Not to mention, I threw out one of the best lines of my career. Listen up and take notes. I spot this cute little philly pushing her basket. I said to her I couldn't help but notice her basket was lean, mean, and lonely. She asked me what I meant. I said that because of my advance knowledge and observation skills of human interaction amongst a socially driven economics environment, I could ascertain a great deal about people by the contents of their shopping cart, just like I could tell a lot about what they drive."

"Do girls really fall for that nonsense?"

Rollins nodded, "She said, what do you mean? I said you eat healthy because of the yogurt, cereal, fruit, and whole grain pasta, but it was obvious she was shopping for one and therefore the cart was lonely. She asked me to predict her car. I said well one would immediately suggest a sleek black BMW 300 series because of her beautiful looks, but that being she was cautious and conservative, she was probably driving a more modest Asian import or domestic vehicle that gets good gas mileage. Perhaps she bought the car used as a better investment to save on the depreciation. She asked how I made that judgment. I said she was buying Publix brand products instead of name brands and her choice of clothes was again conservative, not impressed by designer labels, and her teacher's ID hanging from her purse was another clue on her intellect and indicative of her cautiousness."

The war story of love captivated Frank. He had never heard a line like this before. "Then what happened?"

Lester pulled on his suspenders, leaned back in his chair and said, "I asked her if I could buy her a coffee at the Buddy Brew. One thing led to another. Then Ms. Brenda Taylor provided the key to her heart and her phone number. She only needs to reel me in. She has caught me on the hook. I am done. Stick a fork in me."

"I can't believe it. Luster, the one-woman man."

He rubbed his goatee and said, "I know. I wouldn't believe it either. Hey, have you seen Dumb and Dumber?"

"Like most of the time, they are MIA."

"I've been told to get up with Dietz and see what *HE* needs. That condescending prick, one of these days I'm going to bust him right in the mouth."

"I hear you, man. You never know when fate will catch up with him and even the playing field."

Chapter Seventy

S ergeant Stewart came out of his office, sliding his jacket on over his large frame. "You ready Frank?"

"I am ready. I'll drive. I told Kate we would meet her there at the funeral home."

Alfonso, Frank and Kate met in the parking lot of the Pleasanton Funeral Home. Kate was in the parking lot waiting for them when they arrived.

Kate looked up at the imposing sergeant and said, "My feeling is that Luke feels like he is in control. He'll think he is in the clear and he can put everything on Max. Once he feels everything has blown over on Max, he can resume his plan of torture. I'll bet my paycheck he won't run and won't get an attorney. He thinks he is smarter than us."

"No arguments here."

Duffy said, "How do you want to do this?"

Kate said, "We'll walk out behind him and if he wants to run, and I assert he won't, the sergeant can relive his football days and make a game saving tackle."

Stewart said, "If I can get my hands on him, we're good, but I have seen you run, Kate. I don't think he'll get far. Duffy, you can just shoot him if he does something stupid, just don't hit me."

Duffy gave the evil grin and winked. He grabbed Kate by the elbow and escorted her inside the funeral home. Traditional décor and depressing music accented the decor. The assignment board showed Max was in the Roosevelt Room. Kate thought it sounded more like a name for a ballroom. No festivities here. They assumed their watch from the back row. The fifty chairs were sparsely populated. No one was interested that Max withdrew from life. Five years earlier, it would have been standing room only. Now most people had forgotten Maximilian Kress. Luke was sitting in the front row next to Marge. She looked tired. The casket was closed. That happens after a head shot from a .357.

Kate walked up to Marge, who stood. Kate embraced Marge and reiterated the phrase she had heard herself so many times. "I am so sorry for your loss. If you need anything, call me." Marge smiled and thanked her for coming.

When the service was over, they waited for Luke to walk outside. Kate tapped Luke on the upper arm.

"Hi Luke. I don't know if you remember us..."

"Yes ma'am. I met you at Max's house."

"That's right. We would like to talk to you about Max and clear up some issues that are not resolved."

"We are all servants of God. I would be in your debt to assist you."

Kate listened and thought, why it is the nuts always embrace religion?

"Would you mind accompanying us to our office? We will give you a lift back to your car."

Smiling like a kid, he said, "Sure. Like Greyhound, leave the driving up to you."

On the way back to the Blue Monster, they talked about everything and anything other than the case. They also wanted to give him a sense of relaxation and not be too concerned about their true objectives. The two detectives wanted to get him into the interview room, where they could control the session.

Chapter Seventy-One

R ollins and Bridges were following up on a request from Dietz. Dumb and Dumber had not followed up on canvassing the neighborhood as ordered. Rollins and Bridges parked in the area around the Plant Bank ATM shooting. They knocked on the doors to all the residences in the area and local business. Most of the residences were void of occupants. The few homes that someone answered were asked the standard questions like did you see anything, see anyone suspicious lurking around, or unusual vehicles? No one saw anything or chose not to volunteer any information. People are afraid to get involved.

They walked into the office of Dr. Mario Marko's, an obstetrician. The two detectives received curious stares from the ladies in the waiting room with rounded stomachs. Rollins did the talking and asked to speak with the office manager. Ms. Theopolis, the plain looking, mid-forties office manager, was dressed in pink scrubs.

Rollins said, "I am Detective Rollins, and this is Detective Bridges. We are investigating the homicide up the street."

"I know. What a shame. That poor girl and her family. What a tragedy."

"It certainly was. We wanted to know if anyone here might have seen anything or if you have a surveillance system?"

"Yes, we do."

"Yes, you do what?"

"We have a surveillance system. The neighborhood is improving, but Dr. Markos had it installed when one of our patients had her car broken into. It also helps when winter comes and it is dark. We can see if anyone is lurking about. Oh my gosh, we might have recorded the killer! I never thought about that. I guess that's why your detectives?"

Her slender fingers motioned for them to follow her. They joined her at the rear of the records room and gathered around her as she showed how the system operated. After receiving their lesson, they went to work rewinding the digital recording to an hour before the killing.

They sat there like two kids at the matinee, transfixed by the screen, looking at the images around the time of the shooting. They could see a dark-colored vehicle pull into the parking lot. The view cut out the driver's side of the car. The vehicle backed into a vacant slot and sat. They focused on the activities of the car, that appeared to be a black or blue Cadillac. They could not read the license. The resolution was not clear enough. Finally, a white male walked around to the passenger side, opened up the passenger door, and pulled out the yellow hooded sweatshirt. The figure turned slightly towards the camera as if to tease, but then turned his back to the camera and pulled the hoodie over and walked away from the camera and out of view. A few minutes later, he returned much faster than he left, but not enough to draw attention. It was definitely him, but as in the artist's rendition, he was wearing the hood and sunglasses with a thick, bushy mustache.

Rollins said, "Cool, that's him. Let's back it up and start over."

As they watched it for the second time, they both edged up on their chairs and stared at the screen.

After the second look, Bridges pushed up his glasses on his nose and said, "No tattoos."

"What?"

"The suspect that Dietz is looking for, Troy Unger has a tattoo of a snake on his right forearm. No tattoo on this one."

"Let's look again."

They replayed for the third time.

"Your right, no tattoo. Man, that was a good pickup. This ought to blow away Dumb and Dumber."

"Right is right and wrong is wrong."

"That was deep."

Rollins said to Ms. Theopolis, "If I wasn't on duty, I'd plant a big ole kiss on your cheek."

A grin erupted across her face. "Now let's not let business get in the way of love."

"Ain't you something. I might take you up on that as a rain check. Can we make a copy of that?"

"Sure, I'll copy it over to a thumb drive and it's all yours."

"This has been a big help. Thank you."

Turning towards Bridges, he said, "Come on, Kemosabe. Let's jump on Silver and head back to the Monster."

"You know Kemosabe means faithful friend. It comes from the Potawatomi Tribe. They are First Americans, who generally live in the Michigan and Ohio area. Up from where I am from."

"You are a useful man to have around, Kemosabe."

Chapter Seventy-Two

Troy Unger followed Melvin Storms like a dependant duckling into the homicide squad room. Rollins said, "Melvin, start franchising. You have so much business. What, are you handing out welcome home packages to all the jail birds?"

"Detective Rollins, what can I say? When you're good, you're good."

"Counselor, I'll give you that. To what do we owe the pleasure?"

"I have escorted my client, Mr. Troy Unger. I believe Detective Dietz has been trying to catch up with Troy to ask him a few questions."

"I am waiting for him myself. I'll call down to Starbucks and see if I can get him over here. You can wait for him in the interview room."

As Rollins picked up the phone, Dietz, out of breath, hurried to his desk to pickup the case file. Rollins called to him, "I got something for you, Big Man."

"I don't have time. Have you seen Canseco?"

"Check Gold's Gym. Can you handle the interview alone?"

"Up yours."

"I need to talk to you!"

Dietz ignored Rollins with a dismissive wave and entered the small interview room to join Storms and Unger.

Storms said, "You guys really need to do an extreme makeover on these rooms."

Dietz sighed and said, "This is not the Ritz. I am going to advise you of your rights, Mr. Unger."

After the obligatory reading of the rights, he said, "Where were you on the day of the ATM shooting?"

"I was working."

"What time?"

"7AM until 6PM."

"Where were you at 1PM?"

Storms spoke up and said, "Detective, perhaps I can make this easier for all concerned. Mr. Unger had taken one car for a test drive. He, unfortunately, was going a little too fast on the Selmon Expressway and was pulled over."

"We have no record of him having any activity with TPD."

"It was the Florida Highway Patrol. Here is the copy of the citation." He handed a copy of the ticket to Dietz.

"Maybe he was trying to get away."

"Examine the time, Detective Dietz. The newspaper reported the shooting occurring five minutes after the ticket. My investigator checked the distance and determined Unger would have had to have driven to the next exit and returned in excess of 120 mph."

"That is, if the trooper used the correct time."

"Take it to court, Detective."

"Do you know Thomas Maguire?"

"I knew a Maguire in Starke."

"What was your relationship with him?"

"I saw him around. We weren't buds, if that's what you're getting at."

"Did you know Seamus Joyce?"

"Nah."

"Didn't you work at the carwash?"

"Yes."

"Did you ever enter the Lucky Cabaret?"

He sat straight and said, "No, I wasn't going to violate parole the first week. If I were out just to have a drink and look at some naked girls, I would rather go to the 7-11 and buy a six-pack and a Playboy. I wouldn't get violated that way. It's not very Christian, anyway. Looking at naked women is against the beliefs of God."

Dietz started waving his hands around. "So, you are telling me you worked one block from the cabaret? After being in prison for six years, and the closest you have come to sex is with your right hand, and you're giving me this crap about you have been saved?"

Storms interjected, "I believe that's what he said."

"We have an employee of the Lucky Cabaret say she saw you in there."

Storms smiled and said, "Detective, we all know how unreliable those photo pack identifications are. He has already denied being there."

"So, you're denying that on behalf of Seamus Joyce you did not kill Thomas Maguire?"

Unger scooted his chair forward, leaned across the table, and said, "No, I did not."

"Why did you run from me?"

Storms put his hand on his client's shoulder and said, "Again, Detective, he did not know you were police officers. There are several witnesses that know he received a strange telephone call and then a speeding car pulls into the lot. Two large men with guns jump from the car and call his name. He was in fear of his life."

"Whatever you say."

"We can play it in front of a jury of his peers."

"Where has he been?"

"He was in such fear of his life that someone was trying to kill him. He kept a low profile. It was only when he called the Reverend at the Tabernacle Church that he found out the police were looking for him."

"Mr. Storms, you don't come cheap."

"Is that a statement or a question?"

"Question."

"It's none of your business. Let's just say I like to give back to my community, especially to individuals that I feel are being railroaded."

"There was a lot of evidence pointing in his direction."

"Not anymore. I believe it is time to leave."

"I would love to let you leave, but Troy, there is a minor problem with a parole warrant."

Storms smiled as if he was holding the biggest surprise until the end. He seemed to be enjoying dismantling Dietz's case. He said, "It's been recalled. Detective, we just left the parole officer's office. I showed him the ticket, and the three sworn statements that no one heard you announce yourself as police officers. The parole officer has good judgment and decided to have the warrant recalled."

"Just keep your seat for a few moments longer."

"I don't think so. I have cleared this matter up. Unless you can show me irrefutable evidence that you are prepared to arrest him, we are leaving."

Dietz said nothing. Not even a stammer. Storms waved with a smile and said, "Have a nice day, Detective."

Canseco approached the interview room. His face was red and perspiration was still beading on his forehead. He said, "What's going on? I just saw our suspect walk past me."

"Where have you been Slick? I needed you."

Dietz provided the Cliff Notes version of what happened. Leaving out the part where Storms baited him and trapped him.

Chapter Seventy-Three

D umb and Dumber returned to the squad room with a depressed look. Sergeant Stewart yelled from his office and then walked out to the squad room.

"Gentlemen, let's have a little meeting. First, I think Luster has something to show you."

They all gathered around Rollin's desk. He pulled up the images from the surveillance video.

Rollins pointed with long slender fingers and said, "Here is the vehicle parking. The suspect steps out of his car and we pause right.... here. Look at this profile of his arm. As our distinguished colleague Detective Kyle Bridges so keenly observed, the alleged suspect here is missing a tattoo. Mr. Troy Unger, the focus of your investigation, had some prominent body art displayed. I think he just walked out of here a free bird."

Bridges hinted an almost never seen grin. Dietz swallowed hard. Rollins said, "I'd say that would put you back to square one, boys. Hey, does that also mean you have to payback all that overtime for being unproductive?"

"Screw you."

"Not a chance. They say profanity is the language of ignorance."

"Screw you!" A spit came out of his mouth.

Stewart called Dumb and Dumber into his office. Canseco now wished he had stayed longer at the gym. The girl on the elliptical was a knockout.

They walked in and sat down, both looking very uncomfortable. All they could hear was the bubbling of the aquarium.

Stewart broke the silence and said, "I don't need to tell you how badly you screwed this case up. This was a high-profile case, and you both allowed your egos to get in the way. A child died. Someone's child died. I don't care that she was a judge's daughter. She was someone's daughter. Because of your total incompetence, we are way outside the window to solve this quickly.

"But..."

"Do not interrupt. I am writing you both up for insubordination. The Lieutenant will try to squash it, but I will go over her head. I don't care if you are counting hubcaps in the property room on the midnight shift. I am reassigning this case to Bridges and Rollins. Now leave my office. You are to clearly document every misstep you made in the murder book."

"Yes, sir."

"One more thing. Give me your cell phones since neither of you seems to answer them."

"But I did." Canseco said pleadingly.

The hand of the traffic cop went up. "Do not think I am stupid. I know everything. I mean everything." As he glared at Dietz.

"Yes, sir."

"Prior to leaving this office, you will ask my permission. That goes for both of you."

They walked out of his office like two scolded puppies.

Canseco said, "Nice going. Now we're in deep trouble."

"Rizzo will fix his wagon."

"I am not sure this time."

Canseco could feel the ship going down. He calculated how he could cut his losses and cover his ass. He was afraid he had sailed this ship too long and there were no lifeboats left.

Chapter Seventy-Four

L ieutenant Rizzo answered her phone with authority and confidence.
"Lieutenant Rizzo, this is Reese Crenshaw at the Tribune." Lieutenant

"Yes, Reese, I am not the PIO."

"I know that. I just want to give you an opportunity to provide a comment about a story I am working on."

"Which story is that, Mr. Crenshaw?"

"The killing of Ms. Applebaum. I understand the case has been severely compromised."

"I don't know where you are getting your information, but..."

"I know Melvin Storms just left with the prime suspect and the case against him had been mismanaged."

Rizzo said, "We are not infallible. When we deem corrections are in order, we take appropriate action."

"You mean you would discipline one of your detectives who had made gross errors?"

"I don't know what you are talking about concerning gross errors, but sometimes newer detectives need closer supervision and tutelage."

"I guess that would explain why Detective Dietz was at your personal residence last night."

Silence.

Reese said, "Are you still there?"

She leaned forward towards her desk and said, "Yes. What makes you think he was at my house?"

"Because I observed his city car parked in your driveway."

"We were discussing the case as a matter of fact. I was just imparting my experience and knowledge upon him."

"Why wouldn't his sergeant, an experienced and respected homicide detective in his own right, provide that instruction?"

"I can't say for sure."

"In the chain of command, isn't Sergeant Stewart first in line?"

"Yes, but sometimes there are personality conflicts and I have an open-door policy."

"Speaking of an open-door policy, are you having an inappropriate relationship with a subordinate?"

"Why would you jump to that conclusion?"

"Lieutenant, you didn't answer the question. I can request your emails and cell phone bills that are public records. I can also interview your neighbors to see how often Dietz's car is in your driveway."

"Mr. Crenshaw, you know how the game is played. I have no further comment and I would suggest you contact the PIO in the future. And one other thing, Mr. Crenshaw, stay away from my house."

"I won't need to go by your house anymore. I have all the information I need. Good day."

She hung up the phone with a look of sheer panic and grabbed the edge of her desk for support.

Chapter Seventy-Five

Kate and Frank huddled together to discuss their strategy with Luke. He would read the rights as the Joe Friday type. She would develop the rapport and ask the questions. When needed, Frank would drop the hammer as the heavy.

Alexander and Duffy sat down inside the interview room in the wobbly chairs. Luke was smiling like a kid with not a worry in the world. He was sitting on top of his hands and lifting his feet. Frank read Luke his rights. He advised Luke he was not under arrest and was free to leave. They just wanted to let him know he did not have to answer questions or if he needed an attorney. To minimize the impact, Frank told him it was just a formality required by law. Sometimes reading the rights was like asking a girl out on a date. You didn't want to act like your entire life resulted in a yes, but you didn't want to sound devastated if you got a no. It was a gigantic game of cat and mouse. Luke eagerly agreed to waive his rights and talk without an attorney. Just like Kate had predicted. The two detectives were relieved. They traded smirks.

Kate started, "How long have you known the Kress family?"

"Since I was a child."

"What was your relationship?"

"They were my adopted family. I loved them more than my own. They were amazing people. So, kind and giving."

She wanted to ask open-ended probing questions. She delivered them as softballs. She wanted him to commit to a story without realizing he had. Her style elicited information in a relaxed manner.

"What was your relationship with Max?"

"He was like a father to me. He never got over the murder of Jennifer. I helped him with different tasks."

"Like what?"

"Mostly keeping him company. I would drive him on errands. Sometimes he was medicated, and sometimes his frame of mind wasn't good."

"What do you mean, frame of mind?"

"He was very depressed. He spoke of suicide to end his misery. When he got really down, he didn't care about anything. Simple things like shopping, or haircuts. I would force him to get out."

"So, you would drive his car?"

"Sometimes."

"Did you ever drive his car without him?"

"Oh sure, plenty of times. If mine was acting up or I was running an errand for him."

"So, you handled his day-to-day affairs?"

"You could say that."

"Did you pay his bills for him?"

"Sometimes. Sometimes I would pay them and he would pay me back."

"Did you know who the landscaping crew was?"

"The same crew he was using since the beginning."

"Did you know Thomas Maguire?"

"Nope."

He was projecting a nonchalant attitude. No worries. At least on the surface. Slumped in the chair, his arms folded across his body. People suffering from mental illness often have a different baseline of what are the truth and the consequences to their actions. Their world is their reality.

"He was on the landscaping crew."

"Then I probably saw him around."

"You would have no reason to kill him or hire an attorney for him?"

"Nope."

"Whoever paid for his attorney paid in cash and dropped it off in an envelope. Obviously, the attorney deposited the cash, but maintained the letter and envelope."

She paused to let this sink in. He presented a poker face. She continued, "Would there be any reason your fingerprints or DNA would be on those pieces of evidence?"

It was a bluff that worked sometimes. You never knew if an examination of the letter could develop latent prints. The author of the note could have used gloves.

"Nope."

Either he didn't touch it or he was an excellent poker player.

"Did you help Max buy any weapons?"

"Yes. I went with him to a gun shop. I was in the army, so I had some knowledge of guns."

"Why would a man who was depressed care about owning a gun?"

"He was also a little paranoid. It scared him that the man that killed Jennifer was coming back. I tried to convince him he was dead."

"Did you know it prohibited him from owning a weapon because of his mental state?" She knew unless adjudicated mentally ill, he could still possess firearms. It was a bluff.

His hands dropped into his lap. "No, not really. I knew he wasn't a convicted felon. He kept it in the box. I would take it out, shoot it, and oil it for him otherwise, it was like everything else in his life." He shrugged. "You know, collecting dust. He would focus on something. In a few days, he would move on to something else. Like the gun. We got it and a week later, he wouldn't be able to find it. In fact, the bad part about this is that I took the gun out to the range the morning before he killed himself and put a case of bullets through it. I took it back to his house and cleaned it. I can't believe that's the gun he killed himself. I had just cleaned it."

"Where did you shoot it?"

He smiled and nodded, as if he was expecting the question. "Precision Guns. I know they have cameras to deter robbers. I am sure you can verify that."

She knew he was a calculating adversary. To avoid the gunpowder residue examination, he went shooting to cover his trail.

"I'm sure they can verify. We'll call them. Did he own any additional guns?"

"If he did, I wasn't aware of them."

"Since you were close to Max, where were you when he was killed?"

"Around."

"Around where?"

"I went for a run and worked out."

"Where?"

"I actually did calisthenics in the garage and took a quick run through Tampa Palms. I came back and showered and left."

"Where did you go?"

"I drove out to Clearwater Beach to enjoy God's serenity. Then I went and stayed at a motel in Pasco."

"Is that where you stay?"

He shrugged his shoulders. "I float. Like a vagabond. As a soldier, I was used to simple accommodations. Sometimes I stayed with Max. Sometimes I would sleep in a park or on the beach. I would hang my hat wherever I got tired."

"Where do you keep your clothes?"

"Some at Max's and some in my car. I travel light. As a soldier, I only had my pack."

"Do you keep anything in one of those storage facilities?"

"Nope."

She could see he was feeling confident. He was sitting up straight and speaking with more authority.

"Do you have any reason to go to a storage place?"

"Nope. It sounds like someplace in a movie."

"You stay around at different places. You ever stay at the Pirate's Cove?"

"Nope."

"Where was Max when you were doing your fitness?"

"He said he was going over to Marge's house. I thought maybe they would work out their problems and get back together. He seemed a little up beat. I guess I didn't read the signs that he was looking forward to the end of his life."

"What was your relationship with Jennifer?"

"We were great friends. She was like an angel. God sent her to us and called home to serve all of us as an angel."

"Did you have a relationship with her?"

"We were best friends."

"Did she have any other boyfriends or ..."

He leaned towards the table and he pointed his finger at Kate. "How dare you impugn her reputation. Jennifer died a virgin, just as Mary was when she gave birth to Jesus. She is serving God as we speak."

Kate softened her voice. "I didn't mean to offend you ..."

"You did. She should still be with us."

Kate noticed a twitch in the left side of his mouth that she had not noticed before. The same twitch described by Lashondra from Boyz N Girlz Hip Hop Fashions. The stress was now removing his armor. She was ready to turn up the heat.

"Murder is not always discriminating." Kate said.

"The killer should have been safely behind bars."

"How is that?"

Luke became more animated. "That judge should have found him guilty. She let him out, and that animal killed poor Jennifer. Max was the last one to talk to her. He had just talked on the cell phone with her. She told him she loved him and said goodbye. He never saw her alive again. Did you know she died the day before Max's birthday? They found his birthday present in her closet. If you go into the house, you will find that present. It was a couple of men's polo shirts. He would not allow anyone to alter that room and left it as a shrine to her."

She thought back to Jennifer's room with the stuffed animals and the Harry Potter poster. It was as if Max was waiting for her to come home.

Kate continued, "Everyone has their own way of grieving. Some people like to plant a tree, or a roadside sign, but it's their own way. How about you? How did you get past her death?"

"I found comfort in God. The Lord has a map for all of us. I believe he took her to show the inadequacies of our justice system."

"Did you love her?"

"Do you know what it's like to lose someone that you love?"

"Yes, I do."

Kate knew exactly what it was like to lose a loved one. She did not intend to share her inner emotions.

"You don't know what it's like to see your entire world lost. She was a wonderful person. I love all humankind, as God does. Love always protects. It allows us to trust, gives us hope. It is the same as God. You must love God and have faith. Without faith, you have no hope, and you are left with despair."

Kate recalled Marge uttered the same saying.

Frank sighed, rolled his eyes, and said, "You didn't answer the question. Did she know the feelings you had for her?"

"Oh, sure she did. Our love was reciprocal."

Luke removed his watch and placed it on the table with the face aiming towards him.

Frank asked, "What's with the watch, pal?"

"I am watching time pass. Time is a precious commodity. Once it is gone, it never returns. Benjamin Franklin once said that lost time is never found again. "Veritum dies aperit"

Frank said, "Time discovers the truth."

Luke looked surprised. "Oh, you are familiar with the works of Seneca?'

"No. Just Latin."

"He was a fabulous philosopher and writer in Rome whose great works predated Shakespeare. Seneca was a part of the stoicism mood in Rome that adhered to the educated elite. He believed all men were the offspring of God and, therefore, brothers. As a result, each person deserved compassion and justice. I live by his teachings in that I get contentment from thrift rather than a ceaseless passion for wealth. Seneca wrote in *The Madness of Hercules* that bloodied tyrants will one day face judgment."

Kate resumed, "Do you think that Judge Levy is a bloody tyrant?"

"She has blood on her hands for the countless individuals she let out of jail with her indignant dispersal of her own agenda of justice. Those evil doers she let go are now free to continue destroying lives and creating mayhem in our society. Do not judge, or you too will be judged. For in the same way you judge others, you will be judged, and with the measure you use, it will be measured to you. Blessed are those who hunger and thirst for righteousness, for they will be filled. You have heard that it was said an eye for eye, and a tooth for tooth?"

Kate saw a smile on Frank that she recognized. She knew he was now taking the fuzzy sweater off and was going to get in his ass. Frank said, "You didn't finish. You are quoting the book of Mathew. That quote is often mentioned and misquoted. The full quote is, 'Do not resist an evil person with an eye for an eye and a tooth for a tooth.' In Romans, it says, 'Do not repay anyone evil for evil. Be careful to do what is right in the eyes of everybody.' God is the ultimate judge, not you, Luke."

"God has entrusted me as one of his soldiers on earth. God is not satisfied with our sinful ways. His soldiers will bear arms like they did during the Crusades and fight for his Kingdom."

Frank continued, "Why do you think you are a soldier?"

"We are all put on earth for a reason. Sometimes it takes a while to find your righteous path. Let each one deny himself and take the Cross! God wills it." Frank glared, "Hey, I hate to shatter your world, but this is not the Crusades."

"If you realize it, we are in a holy war."

Kate asked, "Do you speak with God?"

"We just have to listen to him. We all hear God. Some listen and some don't. Sometimes we are not aware we are following his direction."

Kate knew that quite often a schizophrenic would go off on tangents in their own real little world. They needed to convince everyone it was true. She needed to keep him on target. She resumed her questions. "Do you follow directions from God?"

"Yes. Being given trust, I must prove my faithfulness. "

"Do you hear voices or see visions?"

"Only that of God."

"If God told you to kill me, what would you do?"

"He would not do that because you also are servants of God."

"What about Judge Levy? Isn't she a servant of God?"

"She is full of hypocrisy and wickedness. God will judge her for her misdeeds." He twitched again.

"Did you kill her daughter?"

He sat on his hands and started swinging his legs. "We are guided on a path from God. I do not know what he has in store for me tomorrow or next week. I merely put my faith in God. Everything happens for a reason. I believe that Jennifer's death was for a reason. I have come to terms with that."

"Did you kill the Judge's daughters?"

"That was God's decision."

"Did God tell you to kill her?"

"It was God's choice."

He picked up the watch and said, "Time is God's way of keeping everything from happening at once. We must be patient."

"Have you ever received mental health counseling?"

"My counseling, I receive from the Bible."

"Did you kill Max?"

"Max died a long time ago, after Jennifer's death."

Frank said, "Here is a quote for you pal, In Romans, 'Paul says to not be overcome by evil, but overcome evil with good.' You are a sick piece of garbage. You are no different from Bin Laden or David Koresh in wrapping your evil in the cloth of God. You are despicable. Even Shakespeare said, 'The Devil can cite scripture for his purpose'."

"Only God will judge me, not you, not ever!" His head bobbed and accented every word as spittle came from his mouth.

Frank stood, pulled his waistband up, and pointed at Luke. "Let me tell you how God judges you. You are a failure. A miserable loser. You hurt yourself and the army threw you out. St. Leo's threw you out of school because of your religious interpretations. Your parents ignored you. Poor Jennifer didn't love you any more than as a brother, certainly not as a future husband. You went out there and started killing to make up for your failures. You will burn in hell with all the other pieces of crap I put in jail for murder."

Luke's eyes narrowed and his lips tightened. The twitch returned.

Frank continued, "You are not as smart as you think you are. You have made a lot of mistakes. Max would have used his left hand to shoot himself since he was a lefty. You forgot that, didn't you, pal?"

Luke's grin dropped like a car going off a cliff. His eyes looked at the floor and then looked directly at Frank and stared with seriousness.

After several moments, Luke spoke flatly, "God has spoken to me. Judge Levy will be punished for her abuse of power. She sits all high and mighty, with no one to answer to."

Kate said, "Perhaps she rules by an indignant dispersal of her own agenda of justice, as you described. Her children should not have died anymore than Jennifer should have died."

"It is God's plan. Not mine."

Now Kate was going to switch sides. She would sound like she was on his side. She said, "I know you loved Jennifer and love God. It must have been excruciating to know that Judge Levy had let the man go that killed Jennifer. I too knew Jennifer. She was a wonderful person from a wonderful family. You watched her die and the family fall apart while that evil person, Levy, continues to hurt society and release people that God has brought before her for judgment. She is the extension of God on earth. She should render punishment. She has ignored his direction. It is your responsibility to work as a soldier of God, just like the Knights in the Crusades. You are right, the three of us are all servants to God. Why did God ask you to remove those people?"

"It was his will."

"Did you follow his will and remove those people on his behalf?"

"We all operate under the direction of God, whether or not we know it."

He picked up the watch and studied it.

"I believe my time here was not very productive and will be lost forever."

"No, I think it would be better if some doctors spent some time with you."

"You think I am crazy?"

"I think you need some help."

"People thought Albert Einstein was crazy. The school kicked him out too. He visualized his theory by riding on a wave of light. I must carry on with my mission."

"What mission?"

"God's mission."

"Can we help you with the mission?"

"No. Only God has entrusted me. He has selected me as the noble servant. Don't you realize Judge Levy is part of a secret society?"

Frank fidgeted in his chair, sighed, and asked sarcastically, "What secret society?"

"She is an object within an essential nature of the being of the society."

"Who else is in this society?"

"It reaches the uppermost crust of the power grid of this country. They are the front people for the Council on Foreign Relations, the Trilateral Commission, the Bilderbergers, the CIA, and even the Vatican. The President has no control. The Trilateral Commission pulls all the strings and the Secret Society does the dirty work. That bitch Levy is part of the society."

Kate asks, "Why do you say that? What proof do you have?"

"I don't need proof. I know it right here." As he closed his fist and patted his heart. "Read the book and you'll see for yourself."

"If the Vatican is involved, why are you conflicting with God's teachings by targeting the people involved?"

"The Vatican has been corrupted and they are not aware yet. I know."

"Why did you kill the daughters instead of Judge Levy?"

"I never said I killed them. It was God's path."

Kate says, "We are going to get you some help."

"That is fine. It is a momentary diversion. This will strengthen my standing. The psychiatrist will determine and vouch for my stability so people will be required to accept what I say is the truth. I am prepared to embark on this journey."

"We'll be right back Luke."

The two investigators stepped out of the interview room into the hallway.

Kate said, "It impressed me with your knowledge of the book of Mathew."

"I went to Xavier High School in New York that was run by the Jesuits. Father DeJulio made me hand write those ten times for seeking revenge on Horace Jacobs. He was a nerdy kid that was talking down to me. He put me down in class. I punched him in the stomach after class. Father DeJulio saw me."

"That's not like you to get caught."

"I have learned a few lessons since then."

"What do you think?"

Frank pointed to his head. "He is as crazy as a bedbug."

Kate nodded. "Absolutely. Remember Lashondra at the clothing store said the buyer had a twitch?"

"Yeah?"

"When we jabbed him with Jennifer, maybe having another boyfriend, he began that twitch she described. It was then he unraveled. He went off on the whole crusades tangent."

"Never underestimate the observation skills of a woman. That's why girls focus on the face and eyes. Men focus on the boobs."

"A study in human nature again?"

Frank just smiled.

Kate said, "We need to get him Baker Acted and over to the mental health clinic. That ought to tie him up for seventy-two hours. That should buy us enough time to get him jammed up."

"Girl, the clock is ticking. Let's move." He tapped his watch.

Chapter Seventy-Six

WEDNESDAY

K ate and Frank strolled up to the Starbucks Kiosk in the Hilton. Kate said, "Can I buy you a coffee?"

"You'll have to order it for me as well."

"What do you mean?"

"Coffee lingo. I hate the language. All I want is a regular coffee, no steamed milk or whipped cream. It's the same way with these restaurants with cute names on the bathroom doors. Think which one is the ladies. There is a real problem if you have had a drink or two."

"Okay, I'll order a small regular coffee."

"Fine."

The barista, dressed in black with an earring on his left brow, said, "Next in line, please."

"Yes, I'll take a vente vanilla latte and one tall regular coffee."

"No, no, I wanted a small."

"Frank, tall is small."

"See what I mean."

She shook her head in feigned disgust and handed the coffee to Frank. He took a sip through the lid and said, "It's okay coffee, don't get me wrong and thanks for paying, but you get better coffee for half the price down the street. I admire the Starbucks business model. They have a created a destination for overpriced coffee. It's the place to be seen and to hold court."

She smiled in amusement. Frank was always good at picking up her spirits. They walked the few blocks to County Court House and badged their way through the magnetometers and past all the worried faces waiting for their day in court. The repeat offenders were relaxed.

Kate and Frank snuck inside Judge Levy's courtroom. Sitting down on the hardwood bench, Kate noted the coolness from the wood. She gave a slight shudder from the chill. The temperature variant from the hallway to the inside of the courtroom was extreme. She noted that all the employees were dressed for the weather. The bailiff wore a long sleeve shirt. The clerk was wearing a high neck sweater. Judge Levy was not on the bench.

Kate whispered to Frank, "Who is that?"

"Some pinch hitter."

"Let's go to her office."

As they stepped out, Kate said, "You could hang beef in there."

"Did you ever hear the story of her?"

"No."

"They call it the Levy Ice Vault. A couple of years ago, they were working on the A/C for the building. She called the contactor into her chambers and told him it was too damn hot and she was tired of her panties sticking to the crack of her ass. She warned the contractor that when he completed the project and if her panties continued to stick to the crack of her ass, she would make sure he never worked in this town again."

"You're not serious?" as she touched his arm.

Frank shrugged his shoulders and said, "That's what I heard. I don't know if it is true, but it is an icebox and she is not complaining."

They entered the reception area for the judge's chambers. Again, they felt the chill. Kate noticed the receptionist had a space heater plugged in with its elements glowing red. She was wearing pants and a long sleeve blouse. The plain-looking receptionist told them the judge was still out of the office because of the death.

Kate called Bridges on the cell phone and asked him about the Jewish burial customs. She figured since he wrote obituaries, he would have more knowledge than anyone would. The burial was on Thursday afternoon after the morning autopsy. The family would follow a strict, ritualistic seven-day mourning period.

After retrieving Frank's car from the garage, they drove to the Hyde Park home. Judge Levy answered the door. The grieving mother escorted them into the living room in bare feet. The childless mother removed her glasses and, without smiling, said in her New York accent, "Yes, officers?" Her eyes were flat and cast down.

Kate started and said, "Our condolences to you."

"Thank you. What can I do for you?"

"We believe that you and your husband may also be in danger."

The judge leaned back. "I thought this was a random street crime?"

"I am not so sure. Do you recall the case of David Stilts?"

Judge Levy cocked her head with a puzzled look.

Frank said, "You set Stilts free a few years ago..."

Her eyes locked on Frank and didn't allow him to finish. "I didn't set him free. The prosecution had a weak case. I had no choice. How does that affect me now? He went on a crime spree and was killed a few days later by a deputy."

Frank continued, "Not just a crime spree, but a murdering rampage."

"He had an addiction to drugs. That case before me was insufficient and should never have been prosecuted."

Kate spoke. "I am not here to question the outcome of the case. Stilts killed a young girl by the name of Jennifer Kress. She was not much younger than your daughter, Lori. We believe a boy named Luke Shugard had a strong bond with Jennifer Kress. He may hold you accountable for her death. He may have hired a Thomas Maguire to help him and he killed Maguire after he became unreliable. In the process, he accidentally killed a second person. We strongly believe he killed your daughter and may have something to do with the accident that killed your other daughter, Rachel."

Judge Levy's brown eyes widened and her right hand covered her opened mouth. She took a quick breath and sat down for support.

Kate continued, "We think he wanted you to suffer the same devastation he felt."

"I received a Christmas card and birthday card each year addressed to the girl in care of me."

"You mean Jennifer?"

"Yes, I suppose I should give her the decency of calling her by her name. There are a few like that. I don't waste my time with them. I just threw them in the trash. This is not like TV where everything is clear-cut. The law is not always black and white, but many shades of gray. Just like TV we don't always see the cascading effects of rendered justice."

"Your decision and I am not saying you were right or wrong, because I wasn't on the case, but that innocent girl was brutally attacked by someone that you decided was innocent."

"I didn't say he was innocent. There was just not enough to convict."

Frank said, "Innocent or not guilty, it doesn't matter to these people. In their eyes, you are responsible for the death of Jennifer Kress. This is no excuse for the horrible pain you have endured. No parent, and I mean no parent, should have to go through what you are experiencing."

"Thank you for your concern."

Kate said, "Her father, who I knew as a great person, died from what was initially viewed as a suicide after a steady spiral downhill, but it now appears he was probably killed by Luke. Her boyfriend Luke has killed four, maybe five people because of that decision and those families have all suffered from the same loss that you currently are experiencing. Just be careful."

"My God, I can't believe this."

Kate pulled a piece of paper from her pocket and said, "I was checking on the internet and since 1970, ten state and federal judges have been murdered, seven of them in job-related incidents. Be careful. Luke Shugard is definitely disturbed. We just Baker Acted him."

Judge Levy's face looked like she had been embalmed said, "Well, ah, thank you for coming in ah... thanks."

"If you need anything at all, I would call the police chief. She can make things happen. I am sorry that initially the investigative thrust on Lori's death was misguided and resources were misdirected."

"Are you saying there were mistakes?"

"No. I am not saying that. We were not involved, so I can't say what my responses would have been. We were working an ancillary investigation that forked back down the highway toward Lori's case. Timing is everything. We just happened to be in the right place to pick up a few leads."

"Thank you for your efforts and your concerns."

"One more thing. Could we get a copy of the Stilt's case file and have it delivered to my office? I would like to review it."

"Yes, ah I'll call my ahh receptionist.... this is unbelievable."

As they walked towards the door, Kate looked back and noticed Judge Levy looked defeated. She didn't look tough any more. She felt sorry for her. She could even see in the face of the hard-edged Duffy that the obvious pain the Judge was suffering moved him.

Chapter Seventy-Seven

S ergeant Stewart called Kate and Frank into his office upon their return from the Judge's home and said, "You can knock me over with a feather."

"What do you mean?" said Kate with a quizzical look.

"I just went up to Rizzo's office. Normally, I would rather go to the dentist."

"What words of wisdom did she share?"

"I asked for the approval to send you to Knoxville. She said yes."

"She said yes?"

"Not only yes, but then she said that perhaps she may have made a couple of errors in judgment and that she wanted the full court press. She said she had even spoken with the Chief and got her blessings. She asked me to stay in touch with Judge Levy to keep her apprised of the progress of the investigation."

"Wow. Someone must have spiked her coffee with feel good drugs."

"I don't know. Something must have happened."

"Thanks. I'll make travel arrangements."

"Good luck and happy hunting."

Frank and Kate walked back to their desk. Both were wearing a look of surprise. Frank said, "Remember what Forrest Gump said about life and a box of chocolates? This place never ceases to amaze me. You never know when people will see the error of their ways."

"Maybe it was the trip to the Judge."

"Could have been." He grinned as if he just swallowed the canary.

"Frank, could you be a sweetheart and start preparing a subpoena for Luke's military records in St. Louis? I don't think it will be a quick turnaround, but at least we'll have them for trial."

"I am going to call an old friend of Jakes, who is at Ft. Benning. Maybe I'll get lucky and he'll remember Luke."

"It's a small world sometime."

He grinned and winked.

Kate sifted through her email contacts and came to a stop under "C." She stared at the entry for an eternity. Trying desperately to suppress the memories of her past. It didn't work. It never worked. Her mind drifted back to water skiing, the drinking, and the laughter. She dialed the phone number. On the second ring, she answered the phone.

"Major Chamber's office. Can I help you please?"

"Yes, this is Kate Alexander calling. Is Major Chambers in please?"

"Hold the line, please."

A deep masculine voice answered, "Kate! How are you? It's been a long time. Janice and I were just talking about you the other day. Your ears must be burning. How's Britney?"

"Bill, she is growing up so fast. She is taking riding lessons. She is quite the adventurer. Just like her dad and looks like him, too."

"That's great. Kate, it's good to hear from you. You need to come up and visit us. We would love to see you."

"You know, maybe I'll just do that. I need your help on a case I'm working on down here."

"Wow a murder. I get to play Kojak."

"More like Barney Fife. I have a suspect that may have been in Ranger School and blew out his knee in jump school. The injury was severe enough to wash out of the Army. Probably around three years ago. His name is Luke Shugard. I am just looking to see how competent he was as a soldier and how stabile mentally he was."

"You've got it Kate. I'll make some calls over to the jump school and see what I can dig up. What's a good number to call you back?"

"I'll give you my cell."

"Okay. I'll call you back."

"Thanks." She hung up the phone and her mind wandered. She turned to a more productive outlet. Kate pulled out the murder book and began the laborious updating concerning the motel murders when her cell phone rang. She answered, "Hello."

"Kate, it's Bill."

"That was quick."

"For an old friend nothing is too quick."

"You're sweet."

"Here is what I found out. Shugard made it through basic and advanced infantry. He came here for jump school before going off to Ranger school. I called over to the 507th

Infantry Regiment and talked to one of the black hats over there that was an instructor when he came through. This black hat remembers him so well because he would put him in the excellent category on everything. Very focused and very intense. On his last jump, he landed the wrong way. He had too much speed. That can happen even to an experienced jumper and he blew the knee. That was it. He was out. I asked him about Shugard's mental state. He said Luke was rock solid, very serious not a jokester. Not very friendly, kind of a loner, but a very competent soldier. After the injury, this black hat went to see him in the hospital. Shugard was reading the bible and broke down in tears when he saw the instructor. It's a shame that now the guy is a killer."

"Truth is stranger than fiction."

"I hope this helps."

"Definitely."

"When things calm down, I'll have to come up and see you and Janice."

"It's a date."

Chapter Seventy-Eight

T hat afternoon, Frank walked into the mental health facility and approached the receptionist's window. The receptionist was on the telephone with a friend. She ignored Frank standing there. He looked at the mission statement of the facility. The CEO, Kimberly Annanert, signed it. It was framed and hanging above the window. He cleared his throat. She continued to ignore him as she talked about some gossip with a friend. He reached to the small of his back, pulled out his handcuffs, and tossed them on her desk. She jumped and yelped at the thud.

She told the caller, "Girl, I got to go. I'll call you later." She gave Frank an indignant look. "What is this about?"

"I'll tell you what this is about. I am going to use those on you when I report you to Ms. Annanert, the CEO of this place that you are defrauding the hospital of salary by conducting personal phone calls on the clock."

She rolled her eyes. "What do you need?"

"I need to see someone's records."

"Try first floor patient records."

"He is a current patient."

"Oh. Have a seat. I'll get somebody."

A young woman with long curly black hair and a big nose walked out wearing a white lab coat. She reminded him of Cher, but shorter and no voice for singing. Without identifying herself, she said, "Do you need something?"

"Yes. I have a patient release to review his medical files."

She looked at the form and with disgust said, "This was signed yesterday."

"Yes."

"He was in the midst of a crisis."

"What do you mean?"

She folded her arms and said, "He was Baker Acted. He was a danger either to himself or to others. Therefore, he was in a crisis mode and had impaired judgment."

"Is that what you call it? A crisis?"

Her hands moved to her hips. "Yes. He was emotionally detached. Because of mental illness, he could not make an informed decision. His judgment was clouded."

"Are you an attorney?"

"No, a social worker."

"Figures. While you are doing your group hugs and finger-painting to determine his self-awareness and inner discoveries, he may be responsible for several deaths. I just hope you don't get on his bad side. Can I have the proper spelling of your name?"

"Why?"

"Because when he gets out and kills someone, I want the newspaper to know you obstructed this man's intention to cooperate and, as a result, there are additional bodies to account for. I call it CMA. Cover My Ass. But it will expose yours."

"Sheila Schwab. The attending physician has not examined him yet. I looked at his file. There is nothing in his file outside his initial intake evaluation."

"Sheila, thank you for your cooperation." Frank whistled no particular tune as he walked outside the clinic.

Chapter Seventy-Nine

Kate called Trent in his office and described the entire interview to him and her impending trip to Tennessee.

Trent explained, "The Kress's were a surrogate family to him. He was probably at a minimum emotionally and physically abused by his biological father. He found some comfort and normalcy with Max. Remember that often abused children grow to be abusive parents. It is a pattern of acceptance. That was normal. He obviously had a thing for the girl, but because of a low self-esteem, he was reluctant to risk damaging the relationship he has with her and her family. When Jennifer was murdered and Luke sees his surrogate father spiraling down, he begins again to accept violence as a solution. He is reaching out for guidance. His real father is dead, his surrogate father is dying, and he lacks inspiration. He seeks God for his comfort. He seeks revenge for the perceived ills against his loved ones and he can now justify his actions as a warrior for God."

Kate said, "It's a shame he has probably lived with these demons for a while."

"These demons are real to him. He believes everything he tells you."

"In a way, I feel sorry for him."

"He was just a spectator in his life. He didn't have much control."

"I feel the same way sometimes."

"I think we all do. Certainly, you have situations occur out of your control. When do you get back from Tennessee?"

"Either late Friday or Saturday morning."

"Maybe we can go horseback riding."

"Sure. Did you take out some life insurance?"

"Since last Saturday, I have become quite proficient in the saddle. I know it's only been four days, but I can tell you I am so sore from the hours I spent riding yesterday."

"You're pulling my leg."

"I'm serious. I spent hours at the Wal-Mart. Do you know how many quarters it takes to keep the horse going up and down? The manager had to ask me to dismount because of the line of kids waiting to use it."

"You're a mess. I'll call you on Saturday when I get home. I am looking forward to the performance Saturday night."

"So am I. I'll talk to you later. Be careful."

"Always, bye."

She hung up the phone and sighed with a contented look. She looked up at the ceiling and whispered to herself, "I hope you're all right with this. I hope you understand. I love you and always will." She picked up the priorities photo of Brittany and beamed with pride.

Chapter Eighty

THURSDAY

Dietz was leaning over his desk drinking a black coffee and eating a lemon poppy seed muffin. Crumbs dropped on his desk. Canseco was sucking the red straw of a protein shake. The summer college intern with floppy hair walked in carrying a large manila envelope. Conrad looked up at the intern and said, "Who are you looking for, Slick?"

The intern looked at the black specks in between Dietz's teeth and said, "Detective Alexander?"

"She is not in. Is that something for her?"

"Yes. It was sent over from the clerk of court's office."

"Well, Slick, I'll take it from you."

"Ah, I guess."

"Hey, we're all cops."

"Here you go."

After the intern walked out, Dietz turned and said, "I wonder what gem this is. Oh, look here, the flap on the envelope isn't sealed too well." He pulled the papers out and quickly flipped through them like a deck of cards. "What is she going to learn from the court file of an old case? The lefty judge releases the bad guy. Badda da bing. He gets out, so what? So, do a lot of other criminals. HCSO kills this guy a few days later. Case over. Why waste your time reading old files? She thinks she is so smart. Kick Ass my foot. More like Kiss Ass."

He tossed the file in his in-basket and resumed gnawing on his muffin. Canseco gurgled the bottom of the shake, nodded and stood up.

Kate stepped off the flight and entered the terminal for the McGhee Tyson Airport in Knoxville. She walked with impatience, bobbing and weaving around the less hurried. She slowed long enough to enjoy the indoor stream that rolls over rocks in the center of the concourse. She thought not only was this cool looking, but even in her anxious mood, she found it soothing.

Tennessee Bureau of Investigation Special Agent Smokey Walters was smoking a cigarette, leaning up against an unmarked white Ford Taurus parked at the curb. He had a thick head of brown hair and a thick neck that wore a thinly groomed beard like a scarf. Kate met Smokey a year earlier at a Vernon Gebreth Homicide Investigators class in Orlando.

His face portrayed a pleasant recognition. He blew smoke upward, tossed the cigarette toward the curb, and popped a piece of Dentyne in his mouth. "Madam, can I give you a lift?"

"Yes sir, if you're going my way.""I am going anywhere you want to."

"How about Calhoun's?"

"I was just thinking of some BBQ."

Kate gripped his hand with firmness and Smokey pumped her hand up and down and said, "Kate, it's sure nice to see you again. Never thought business would bring you up this way."

She threw her carry-on into the trunk, slammed the lid closed and said, "You never know where crime will take you." She jumped into the passenger seat. The interior had an underlying odor of stale smoke covered by the pine scented tree air freshener dangling from the rearview mirror. Old Spice cologne became the overpowering scent once Smokey sat down. She told him about the case and they had caught up on each other's lives since attending the conference. He told her he had checked for any police activity on Shugard with all the departments in the area. There was nothing under Luke's name or under the name of Al Lias.

He parked in the long narrow parking lot of Calhoun's Restaurant, which was across the street from the University of Tennessee. The diners enjoyed a panoramic view of the Tennessee River.

Smokey asked for the manager, Travis Boyd, in his soft comforting southern twang. They introduced themselves to the boss, who stood a full head taller than Kate. She showed Travis the MasterCard bill and asked if he could locate the original receipt and identify the waitress that took the order. Travis said he would review the records and see if he could find the transaction.

They had lunch while they were waiting. A college student working as a hostess escorted them to the enclosed deck overlooking the river. Kate ordered the smokehouse salad and Smokey selected the ribs. They were still waiting for the meals when Travis walked towards their table followed by an attractive tall brunette whose hair flowed over her shoulders.

Travis said, "Today is your lucky day. Not only did I find the original receipt, but Rosemarie here took the order." He held up the receipt in a plastic bag. Kate and Smokey had a look of surprise. Travis explained, "I used to be a deputy with Knox County, but the money is better in the restaurant business. I have already made a copy for my records. Here is my card if you need anything else. If you need some privacy, you can use my office."

Kate said, "Since no one else is out here right now, we can just knock it out right now. Thank you, Travis."

"I know it's important if you came up from Tampa. Good Luck."

"Thanks."

"Hi Rosemarie, I am a detective from Tampa. My name is Kate Alexander, and this is Special Agent Walters from TBI. Do you remember the ticket?"

"Not really. Travis showed it to me. That was some time ago. We get a lot of customers every day."

"I am sure you do. Can I show you a group of photographs and see if you recognize anyone?"

She showed the six portrait size photos. Rosemarie studied them intently. Pointing to the fourth, she said, "I remember this one. I can't say he was the one that placed this order, but I definitely remember this guy. He asked me what church I attended. I've had all kinds of pickup lines, but that was different. I told him I didn't go because I worked late on Saturday. He started giving me this story about being children of God and he would be disappointed in me for not going. I told him my kid would be more disappointed if I didn't put food on the table."

"Did he say why he was in town or where he lived?"

"I think he said he was from Florida and he was visiting. He was kind of creepy."

"Creepy in what way?"

"He was just odd. He kept looking at me. In fact, the next few nights, I was careful about going out to my car. He just gave me the heebie jeebies."

"Thank you very much, Rosemarie. Could I get you to circle his photo on this Xerox copy and sign and date? You have been a big help."

"Can I ask, what did he do?"

"We're not sure yet. He may have been involved in some serious issues. He is back in Tampa and is actually locked up, so don't worry about him coming back."

Rosemarie left and their waitress returned with their lunch.

As they left the restaurant, Kate slid her sunglasses on her face. Smokey hit the tooth-pick dispenser and began picking his teeth. They ambled back to the car. Smoky Walter's beige sport coat looked older than his onset of middle age. The buttons would never fasten again and the breeze caught the jacket lifting the opening like a kite. Smokey said, "Have you ever heard of the Body Farm?"

"Is that where they conduct the studies on the decomposition of the bodies in natural settings?"

"Yep. I thought if we had time, I would take you by, but I saw the director flying out this morning. Going to some conference. It really is fascinating to listen to him explain how they can determine the time of death according to parasitic infestation and breakdown of the body. Great subject after eating, huh?"

"We are in the wrong business if you have a weak stomach."

"Ain't that the truth?"

They headed out towards Alcoa, a community southwest of the airport on Rt. 129.

"I guess we can stop at Volunteer Car Rental. It's one of those off property, independently owned rental agencies." Smokey said. "They get their cars from big agencies after they get too many miles and charge a lower price than the big boys. I checked it out for you. Alyssa Stryder is the owner's name."

As they approached the front door, they passed a 1971 Cadillac El Dorado convertible painted bright orange. The sign on the windshield advertised the weekend game special. 'See inside for details.' Smokey walked up to the counter, identified himself, and asked for Ms. Stryder. The young black man wearing an orange polo shirt and short-cropped hair greeted them at the counter with a friendly smile. His nameplate identified himself as Todd. He answered the inquiry.

"I am very sorry. Alyssa is traveling back today from out of town. She should be back in tomorrow. Is there something I can assist you with?"

"Are you in charge?"

"Yes sir, I am."

"First of all, what's the price of the Caddy?"

"500 a day, 3 days minimum, and the horn plays Rocky Top."

"Too steep for my paycheck, but I am sure someone will rent it."

"It's booked a year in advance for each home game."

"Wow."

Smokey's nickname endeared him to his beloved University of Tennessee Volunteers, as he earned the nickname from the gray patches in his hair. He liked the nickname and preferred it to his first name of Jerome. The team mascot, an old hound dog, was also named Smoky.

Smokey continued, "Hey we are trying to find out who rented a car here on this date under this transaction." Smokey leaned over the counter and showed Todd a highlighted credit card statement.

"I'll have to check with the billing department. That is offsite."

"Can you search by name or vehicle type or pull up all the rentals on that day?"

"Give me a name."

"Last name Shugard, first name Luke."

Travis typed on the keyboard and pointed at the screen and said, "Yes, sir. Right here. Rented a Yukon in May of last year. He returned it thirty days later."

"Does the record have the credit card number?"

"Yes. I can print out the entire record for you."

"That would be great. Is that car here, by any chance?"

"Let me see..." as he scanned the monitor and hit some keys. "No, it is due back tomorrow."

"You have been a big help."

He seemed to stand a little taller and his smile was wider.

As they walked towards the car, Kate asked, "What was the total mileage on the car when it was returned?" Smokey handed her the printout. She looked down and read, "1425 miles. It is 1350 round-trip from here to Tampa."

They headed out SR 35, N. Hall Road, towards the Rocky Top Body Shop. Smokey eased the car into the parking lot of the body shop. Looking bored, numerous parked cars waiting for the restoration of pride sat idle under a layer of dust and rust. Six men occupied bays, generating more noise than a rock concert with a steady sound of pneumatic tools, saws, and grinders. The eager looks of recently restored cars waited on the side of the building for their owners.

One of the dark blue uniformed workers with mangled gray hair pushed his goggles up on his head and walked out to greet the visitors. "Howdy, can I help ya?"

Smokey said, "Russell Rhodes?"

"Yep. Unless your process servers." He cupped his hand over his eyes to deflect the sun.

Smokey and Kate introduced themselves and asked if he could look up the charge in May of last year.

"Nope, can't help you today. Everything over one-year-old, I keep in storage. I live out towards Greenback. If you leave me the information. I can get it for you tomorrow morning."

"All right we'll see you tomorrow."

Kate's cell phone rang, and she stepped away, allowing Smokey to finish with Russell. She answered, "Hello?"

"Kate, it's Frank."

"Hey Duff, how are you?"

"Not so good and you won't be after you hear this."

"Okay, I'm game, what?"

"They let Luke out."

"What? How?"

"Keep in mind the Baker Act only says that they must be examined by a clinician within seventy-two hours. It doesn't say they have to keep them that long. Once the clinician makes the decision that the patient is not suicidal or homicidal, they really cannot keep them unless they show they cannot care for themselves. They are short on hospital beds and he has no previous history of being Baker Acted. Even if they don't think he can't take of himself, they can't keep them unless they go to court."

"That's bullshit!"

"I know Kate. I know you're pissed. They didn't notify us until after he was in the wind. I told them he was homicidal, but they had their head too far up their asses to figure it out. They told us that if we felt that way, we should have charged him instead of using the mental health system to do our work. We are going up on protective surveillance on the Judge and her family 24/7 and we put out a pickup on him. If we get him, I'll come up with something. How close are we up there?"

"I got him renting the car. It fits the description given by the witnesses of the accident. I have him eating at the restaurant. The body shop guy needs to check his records. We'll see him tomorrow. Wow, I can't believe he walked."

Frank said, "We showed his photo spread to Lashondra and the storage facility. I guess with the oversized aviators, they focused on that. They couldn't pick him out. I got a subpoena today for his military records in St. Louis. I am faxing it out this afternoon. We have to keep after it. We can't feel sorry or get mad. We have to kick it into overdrive and find him."

"All right Frank. Thanks for the great news. What would I do without you?"

"Probably sleep better tonight."

"I'll get a glass of wine, or maybe two or three."

"It doesn't work. I've tried it before."

"Give me a call night or day. Scratch that. I forgot my charger for the cell phone, so I'll turn it off in the room. I am staying at the Marriott next to the University."

"I'll find you and, in the meantime, we'll keep looking for him."

"Thanks."

Kate relayed the frustration and bad news that Frank had provided to Smokey. He listened to her diatribe about the shortcomings of the mental health system. After he was sure she had exhausted her thoughts, he asked Kate if she wanted to do dinner. She told him she was tired and just wanted to grab a sandwich and relax in her room. They arranged to meet the next morning. He dropped her at the front door of the hotel.

Chapter Eighty-One

S he walked into the tall atrium of the Marriott's lobby, across the tile floor, past the piano to the registration desk. Her stride had less enthusiasm than her walk off the plane just a few hours earlier. What started as an encouraging day transcended into frustration and a sense of despair at the news that Luke was out fulfilling his mission. After checking in, she asked the front desk clerk where the workout room was located.

She went to her room, dropped her bags, and changed into her workout clothes. She dragged herself back to the lobby workout room, craving a shot of adrenaline. Fellow travelers occupied all the aerobic machines. Must be a conference. She hit the weight machine for a quick pump. With her stagnant body now revitalized, she wanted to continue. She walked outside to the heat and scorching sun of Knoxville and decided to take a run outside down along the river to the UT campus. It was nice to be alone with her thoughts. No one to bother her. She looked at the students as she passed them. They looked so young and innocent. Who knew what was in store for them? Success or failure? Joy or grief?

She remembered the less hectic days of running on this very campus as an athlete. She herself was a few years past her nineteen-minute plus collegiate times. Today was not for speed. Today was for therapy.

She had an uneasy feeling, a sense of anxiety and was hoping the long run would help to relieve her jitters. She couldn't explain it, a sudden feeling of dread oozed through her like syrup. Kate looked back over her shoulder just as a shadow closed the distance behind her. She gasped and stopped short, digging her foot into the soft turf for balance. She prepared to strike with the heel of her hand. The streaking shadow blasted past her without pause. Kate took a deep breath after realizing the shirtless athlete was running wind sprints.

She completed the five-mile run and felt relaxed returning to her room, laughing at her brief scare. She called room service for a turkey sandwich. She decided that while she waited for dinner, she would step into the shower and embraced the heat and steam as it invigorated her body.

She wrapped a towel wrapped around her head, just as she heard the knock on the door. Assuming it was room service, she pulled the door open and looked at the room service attendant carrying the silver domed tray. She signed for the meal, put the privacy sign out, and set the tray on the bed. She peeked under the tray like a kid, picked up a French fry, and stuck it in her mouth. Kate sat Indian style on the soft bed and watched reruns of Seinfeld. She needed a laugh. After inhaling the contents of the tray, she dabbed her mouth, carried the tray, and placed it outside her door while hanging the "Do Not Disturb" sign on the door.

She picked up her cell phone and looked at the energy level. It was only down one bar. She called home. She gave her mother the contact number for the hotel and explained she would turn her phone off because she had left the charger at home. Britney got on the phone, "Hi mommy."

"Hi, sweetie. I miss you."

"Mom, you just left. How could you miss me so quick?"

"I can still miss you. I should be home either late Friday or Saturday morning. I am going out Saturday night with..."

"On a date with Trent?"

"It's not a date. It's just a friend's thing."

"Whatever."

"Listen to you. How about Busch Gardens on Sunday?"

"That's sounds good Mom, but we have a hurricane coming. It's called Alex."

"Don't worry, sweetie, Grandma is with you."

"I'm not worried Mommy. I'm a big girl. I just worry about the horses."

"They'll be okay."

"When do you take your judo test?"

"The next Saturday."

"Good."

"Well, I guess I'll let you go, sweetie. I don't want to drain the battery. I love you and I'll talk to you tomorrow."

"I love you, too, Mommy."

She ended the call and turned up the volume on the TV and thought of hurricanes and Luke. Both had the potential for violence.

Chapter Eighty-Two

FRIDAY

In the morning, she was standing in front of the triangular shaped hotel waiting for Smokey. The Taurus lumbered around the corner. She watched the plume of smoke pour out the driver's side window and the cigarette flipped out to the pavement. He popped a Dentyne in his mouth as he put the car in park. She hopped in and smelled the Old Spice. It brought back memories of her dad. She often wondered if her dad were still alive, if he would approve of her life, and would he be proud of her. He had always been strict and quiet, but had an underlying compassionate streak not always noticed. The cool air conditioner chilled her. She closed the vent closest to the door.

They made it back to the Rocky Top Body Shop. The two investigators approached Russell, who was surveying the damage on a small import. They waited patiently until he provided a written estimate of the bad news to the owner.

Russell motioned for them to follow him into the office. The inside of the office was as gritty as the outside. "Have a seat."

Kate said, "I've been sitting all morning."

"Well, I found the file. I stopped by FedEx Kinko's and made copies. Inside are the estimate, work agreement, and the final bill. There are also before and after pictures."

"Pictures?"

"Yep, you never know when someone claims we did shoddy work, or you get subpoenaed to court. When the attorney's start calling and find out I have pictures, I can usually get a higher fee from them."

"When was it brought in?"

"On May 10 of last year."

She looked at Smokey and said, "That was three days after he rented it." Turning back to Russell, she said, "How about mileage?"

"Oh sure, I record that and the level of gas. People accuse us of joyriding around or siphoning gas. Like we actually drive one of these wrecks around. Let's see, he had half a tank, and the mileage was 28,610."

She looked up to the calculator in the sky and said that was 1410 miles. "Let's look at the damage."

"Not too bad. It needed a front quarter panel and door."

"Did he say how it happened?"

"For court, I always put that line on the estimate even if they don't have it repaired here."

Kate's eyebrow pitched upward.

He continued, "Yes, ma'am, I watch *The Lincoln Lawyer*. I know how these attorneys operate. He said someone hit it while parked and I noted EV. That is my shorthand for evasive. I can tell you most times the damage will occur on the drivers' side of a parked car unless it was in a parking lot. This wasn't the typical damage from the parking lot. If you look at the photos, you can see the transfer of red paint."

"Mr. Russell, you may just have to come testify in Tampa."

"I have only two conditions. Not during football season, and I prefer the winter."

"You and all the snowbirds. They do have televisions to watch the games."

"I have season tickets to the Vols."

"I am sure we can work it out. You have been a big help."

"I'm not finished." He dangled a baggie containing red paint chips. "I scraped these off the car. I don't always do that, but this whole thing didn't smell right. That dog just didn't hunt. I knew there was more to it."

"You, sir, have made my day. I can't believe it. Most *COPS* aren't as thorough."

"I used to drive a tow truck and had to watch the cops work these accidents. I watch all the cop shows like CSI."

"Well, you have done well, Russell."

He wiped his hand on his pants and shook hands with the two investigators.

As they drove away, Smokey said, "Well, that was positive."

"It certainly was."

"On to the rental car."

Chapter Eighty-Three

Kate and Smokey returned and met Todd once again.

"The car is ready for you. I have it parked out back."

Kate asked, "I thought of this last night. Did Mr. Shugard report the car as being involved in the accident or as stolen and recovered?"

"No. Neither one."

"Thanks."

They walked out and Smokey clicked a digital photo.

Kate said, "Let's go through it and see if we get lucky and find anything. He may have left in the car that was not by the hurried cleaning crew on each turnover. "

Smokey took his sport coat and left it in the car, exposing his gun and badge on the belt. They were not optimistic about finding anything left in a car rented ten months earlier, but Kate wanted to give it a shot. They looked with the care of a neurosurgeon during brain surgery. They painstakingly looked under the seats, floor mats, glove box, and trunk. They checked any crack or crevice that a receipt or business card may have fallen. No luck. Smokey grabbed a hand towel from the trunk of his car and dabbed the perspiration.

"Todd, thank you very much for your help. It sure is nice to show this out-of-town detective how the volunteer spirit is interwoven in the fabric of all the outstanding citizens of Knoxville. I bet they ain't this way in Tampa, are they, Kate?"

"Not always. Todd, thank you."

Perspiration was again beading up on Smokey's face as they stepped out of the office. Kate slid her sunglasses on her face. Smokey plopped into the seat of the Taurus and turned the A/C on max high. The vents spewed an initial blast of heat from the vents that quickly changed to soothing cool air. Kate adjusted the vent to blow into her face.

"Lunch and then go hunting for his kinfolk?" Smokey asked.

"Sounds like a plan."

***

After lunch, they parked in front of the plain white wood framed fixer upper that sat in the long shadows of Interstate 40. They stepped up on the porch and swatted away mosquitoes as they stood at the door. Smokey rang the doorbell as they listened to the steady hum from the traffic on the interstate.

A teenage boy with no shirt and plenty of bones answered the door with a nonchalant "Yeah?"

Smokey said, "We're police officers. Mom or Dad at home?"

"Nope, they are at work."

"Where do they work?"

"My momma cleans homes and daddy drives a truck."

"You have any way of getting in touch with them in case of an emergency?"

"No, sir."

"Cell phones?"

"No, sir."

"Are you sure?"

"I don't have the phone numbers."

"What time do they get home?"

"My mother gets in around 4 or 5 and my dad around 6."

"Do you know Luke Shugard?"

"Yes sir, he's my cousin."

"When was the last time you saw him?"

"About a year ago. Maybe a little less. He stayed with us for a spell. Slept on the couch. Is he okay?"

"We just wanted to confirm he stayed here. Tell your folks we will be back around six."

"Sure will. See ya."

Kate said, "I don't guess he wanted us to talk to his parents."

"No, but it's probably better to talk to them together in person."

Kate went back to the hotel to get a workout in and allow Smokey a chance to go to his office for some paperwork.

He picked her up for an early dinner and drove to the award-winning Tomato Head restaurant in the historic Market Square downtown. The buildings dating back to the 1800's provided an eclectic mix of restaurants and shops. Kate enjoyed the Tuscan chicken sandwich with a side of fruit, and Smokey went for the four-cheese pizza. Kate agreed with the diners' choice of voting the restaurant tops in the city.

They returned to the tired house. Kate checked her watch. It was 6:30PM. A white Pontiac and a battered red pickup now occupied the previously vacant driveway. They rang the doorbell. A hardscrabble thin man holding a can of Budweiser answered the door. When he spoke, it was obvious he spent more on beer than dentists. "Can I help you?"

"Yes, sir, we are police officers. Are you Billy Cannon?"

"Yes sir. The police?"

Smokey asked, "I understand Luke Shugard is a relative."

"Yep, he sure is. He ain't in any trouble, is he?"

"That's what we're trying to find out. I understand he stayed here with you for a little while?"

"Yep, hang on. Hey, Sue, when did Luke stay with us?"

Sue, with short blonde hair and wearing a too big t-shirt, came to the door, wiping her hands with a dishtowel. "I'd say about a year ago. What's this all about?"

Smokey said, "We're with the police. How long did he stay with you?"

Billy said, "What, I guess maybe three weeks? Right there on that couch in there. We just didn't have another bed for him. He said he was used to sleeping in terrible places with the army. I'll tell you this, that boy ain't right in the head."

Smokey said, "How so?"

"He was always reading the bible. Nothing wrong with that, but he was always going on about different verses and how he was reincarnated."

Sue said, "Remember, hon? He thought he had been a knight and was now a warrior. I remember when he was just a kid, he was just as good a kid as you would find. That father of his beat him silly."

Billy said, "Yep, like an old yard dog. I knocked his father on his drunken ass one night. Told him I wouldn't put up with that crap in my presence." Billy took a swig of beer.

Sue said, "His father was married to my stepsister. She died from a broken heart. He totally dominated her. Luke seemed to shine like gold. Just a good kid. I think after that poor girl was murdered; the beatings finally caught up. Then he got hurt in the army. He started college, but I don't know what happened there. He dropped out."

Kate said, "Did he mention anything about a judge?"

Sue said, "That one that let that killer go free? He hated her. He would go off like a crazy man. His eyes would bug out. If we were watching some legal show on TV, he would get up and go for a walk or sit on the porch."

Kate asked, "Did he ever say anything about hurting her or her family?"

"No, he would get wound up, but he was gentle deep down."

"Why did he come here?"

"He just wanted to visit. He had left school and said he needed to smell the fresh air of the Smokey Mountains. His rental car had been wrecked, and he was waiting for the car to get fixed."

"Do you know how the car got wrecked?"

"He said it was parked over by the river and someone must have hit it and run off."

"Did he say anything about what was happening in Tampa?"

"Nah."

"When was the last time you spoke to him?"

"A couple of months. Sometimes he might just show up for a few days. Outside of his old neighbors, the Kresses, we're his only family. They were good people to him."

"Did you go down there much?"

"To Tampa? Once every few years."

"We just didn't fit in. Luke's father, William, always looked down on us. We might not have much, but we're honest, and what you see is what you get. He was rotten to the core. Struck it rich. What is that saying, you can slap lipstick on pig, but it's still a pig? We weren't in his class."

Kate said, "Maybe he should have spent more time with real people like you."

"Probably so."

Smokey said, "If you hear from him again or if he drops in, could you call us immediately?" He handed a business card to Billy.

"Sure can. What kind of trouble is he in?"

Kate said, "All I can say is he is a person of interest in the death of two of the judge's daughters and the death of Max Kress."

Sue said, "Max Kress? Oh, he wouldn't hurt Mr. Kress."

Kate said, "Like you said. He ain't right in the mind. He is very confused. I tried to get him some help at the mental health facility, but he didn't go for that. Now, I don't know where he is and I would like to get him help before he hurts someone else or himself."

Sue said, "I doubt he'll come here, but if he shows up, we'll holler at you."

"Thank you. Have a good night."

As they drove away, Smokey turned the headlights on. Kate said, "They seemed like good people."

"Yep, simple, but good."

Smokey said, "Can I give you a lift to the airport in the morning?"

"No way. I don't want you coming in on a day off. I'll just grab the shuttle or a cab. I'll voucher the cost. I just hope this Hurricane Alex doesn't affect my flight going back to Tampa. I don't like the idea of being out-of-town away from my mom and Britney, when one of those things swirls in the Gulf."

"We have tornados and you have hurricanes. If you get stranded, let me know. I'll have you out to the house."

"I hope not. You have been a great help, Smokey. People say this all the time, but I mean what I say. If you ever, I mean ever, need anything down my way or anything in the State of Florida, I'll hook you up."

"I know you will. You didn't wear out your welcome, so as they say in these parts, y'all come back now ye here."

"I will. Maybe I'll come here to Dollywood with my daughter."

"It's a fun place."

He pulled up to the front of the hotel. Both officers stepped out of the car and Kate gave a big hug to the bear of a friend. They separated and went in different directions, not knowing if or when they would ever see each other again.

Chapter Eighty-Four

SATURDAY 3:30 AM

F rank sat in the driver's seat sipping coffee from the black lid of a stainless-steel thermos. The coffee aroma filled the inside of the car. Lester was in a reclined position in the passenger seat with his head against the headrest sucking on a toothpick. They were both in jeans and very casual attire.

They looked at Judge Levy's quiet home. The warm humid air created halos around the street lamps. The lights dimly lit the area, as the canopy of trees reduced the natural light. Most of the homes projected more illumination from the porch lights and landscape lighting.

Frank looked at the darkened house. He had no love for this judge. She was never considered "Cop Friendly." She was still a mother and her two children were dead. He put himself in that position and having two girls of his own made it easy. What if someone hurt his family because of someone he arrested or did not arrest? He knew the devastation the judge must have been feeling. In that position, he would hunt down that sick bastard and kill him. Every parent's nightmare is to outlive their kids. Here she and her husband worked hard to get to this station in life. They have great jobs with respect and admiration in the community. They have two beautiful girls on the road to success. Then the rug is pulled out from under them. Just as Max Kress never recovered, nor would the Levy family ever recover from the murder of their two girls.

Lester said, "Hey Duff, man, you better ease up on the java or you'll be pissing the night away."

"That could be a problem for an old dude."

"Man, you got that right. I hate surveillance. You sit here, bored out your ass and think, I got me a college degree, and here I sit in a dark car, on a dark street, alone with another dude, talking about the size of our manhood and knowing ain't anything going to happen."

"Hate is such a strong word."

"Your right. I should have used disliked."

Frank pointed towards the police radio and said, "Turn up channel one, it sounds like somebody's got something going on." Lester turned up the hand-held police radio and they listened to a street crimes unit jump some auto burglars in Ybor City. The youths ran to a waiting car that sped off, striking a couple of parked cars. They listened to the broadcast of the suspect vehicle as it successfully eluded capture. The bad guys had escaped the army of officers normally working the night shift in the Ybor nightclub district.

Lester said, "It sounds like some youths have beaten the long arm of the law for the time being."

"You grew up in Central Park. You could have been just like those fellows running from the poleece. How did you escape?"

"My mother, Billy Tubbs, and baseball."

"How so?"

"My mother would whoop my ass for almost anything. She made me go to church every week. No excuses. Billy Tubbs gave me the job at the Zoo and believed in me. He was the father I didn't know. Baseball gave me a way out of the neighborhood and away from the bad influences. Of course, with these good looks and brains, I would have been all right any way."

"Still go to church?"

"Not as much as a kid, but I still go. When I miss, momma gives me a hard time."

"Was she one of those displaced when they tore down Central Park?"

"Nope. Moved up to Seminole Heights. I helped her get into a nice little bungalow fixer upper. Needed a lot of work, but I was on nights and I would go over there after a few hours of sleep and work like a madman. What I couldn't do myself, I'd find some firefighter to help. You know, those guys all work some scam on the side. The price has doubled from what I paid. Add that to my condo on Harbor Island that I bought before the investors drove up the price. I'm doing ok."

"You should have gone into real estate." "I will when I retire. I'll have a nice pension from here and I can get my license. Yep, you'll see my smiling white teeth on billboards all over town. A face you can trust. What about you, Duff? You can go soon."

"I still enjoy the hunt. When I get sick of it, I'll go and maybe I'll write some books. Be a crime fiction writer."

"Go figure. You'd have enough material."

The radio traffic increased. Another unit found the suspect car on Kennedy and was in pursuit. The stolen car crashed, and the occupants jumped and ran in four different directions. The helicopter was en route and K-9 and every other unit in the area was swarming like bees towards honey.

Lester said, pointing at Franks silk shirt, "Duff, is that a Tommy Bahama?"

"It was a gift from the girls."

"For a white dude, you always look good, even when you don't need to."

"Thanks. Coming from you, I take that as a genuine compliment. You are a clothes whore as well."

"You can look bad or you can look good. It takes about the same time to get dressed and not a lot more money if you're smart. Look at poor Kyle Bridges. He looks like he shops at a second-hand store."

"Can you imagine the conversation in that car with Bridges and the Sarge?"

"Poor Sarge. It's like listening to the wallpaper dry."

Frank said, "At least we have a similar interest in jazz. Ole Kate and that whiney ass country. It's like scratching across the chalkboard. Who is that?" As he pointed to the radio.

"Mindi Abair. She's from St. Pete. Before that was Eric Darius. He is from here. Went to Blake High. I am always partial to the sax. I played a little sax in high school. There is nothing like a good sax."

"No kidding. I call the sax the greatest sex toy in the world." They both laughed together.

"I also played a little violin."

"Really? You don't look like the classical type.""Yep. Check my play lists. I have some Bach and his violin concertos.

Deep down, I was a band geek."

"Who knew?" Lester adjusted the A/C vent and said, "I'll tell you with that hurricane spinning in the gulf, it sure has kicked up the humidity. It is hotter than black asphalt in the dessert. It was days like this that I hated being in uniform. You'd have that vest on and you could ring that t-shirt out at the end of the shift. I enjoy having it in the back seat and not wearing it."

"Now they have that Under Armour stuff that wicks the sweat away."

"You would need a drain tube for me to wick it away."

Frank said, "Speaking of hot. I can't believe that Luster Rollins has collapsed and fallen in love."

"I know, man. I am seeing Brenda tonight. She has got me hook, line and sinker." They listened to the dispatcher broadcast, "Any unit that can handle a prowler call near 9th and Delaware?"

Nothing but dead air.

Duffy said, "That's just a few blocks over. We could shake it and get back in just a couple of minutes."

"Sure, why not? Since half the city has ganged up on the perp on foot."

"Let's run it by the Sarge first."

"Al, are you guys monitoring the patrol channel?"

"10-4."

"We thought we would run up really quick and shake the prowler call. If it turns into something, we'll get patrol over there."

"Go ahead. Just be careful and make sure radio is aware you are plainclothes and they tell the caller the same thing. In fact, put your raid vests or jackets on, so there are no mistakes."

"Good idea. That's why you're the boss."

"Now you sound like Dietz."

They stepped out into the humid air and slid their mesh police marking vests on.

Rollins said, "Hey, what about our ballistic vests?"

"Too hot. Besides, it's probably some teenage peeper."

"Yeah, you're right."

They informed communications of their response, and to call the complainant to inform them they were responding in plainclothes. Duffy eased the unmarked car to the curb a couple of houses from the supposed activity. Most prowler calls were nothing but animals rummaging for scraps and insects. Occasionally, you would get lucky and find some peeping Tom or a teenager coming home after curfew.

Chapter Eighty-Five

T hey stepped out of the car and quietly pushed their doors closed. It was always fun to sneak up on someone and surprise them. Even if it was an animal, it was still fun. Neither detective had jumped a call like this in years. They approached the huge three-story red brick home. The white trim and the dormers pierced the darkness. They cut up between the knee-high brick wall that surrounded the house like an empty moat. They split up and headed to opposite sides of the house. They would both meet up in the back. Duffy took the shorter distance to the left and Rollins went to the right.

Duffy had his pistol in his right hand and a black flashlight in his left. He crept up along the hedges, staying away from the lighted driveway portico. Lights were not good for cops lurking at night, as they made them easy targets and eliminated the element of surprise.

Rollins eased around the right corner of the house and let his eyes adjust to the lack of moonlight between the homes. He eased around the impeccably groomed hedges. An armadillo was rooting through the shrubs. The suddenness of his appearance startled the foraging mammal. The runt of an animal rumbled away. Rollins shined the flashlight at the fleeing armored sloth. He then heard the crackling of bushes further down the side of the house, no doubt the mate.

He shined the flashlight towards the sound. He had no time. He saw the blast of fire from the barrel of a pistol and the explosion of sound and the almost simultaneous feeling of a sledgehammer hitting his right chest. He collapsed in a motionless heap.

Duffy, who was warily walking along the opposite side, heard the unmistakable sound of a single shot of gunfire. He pulled the radio off his belt and barked into the mike, "Nine-oh-five shots fired!"

The words no cop wants to hear. He ran around the rear of residence and saw a dark figure running from the opposite side.

He yelled, "Police halt!"

He hesitated, not knowing if it was Rollins. A motion-sensored spotlight illuminated the yard, bathing Duffy and the fleeing target in light. The sudden brightness blinded him and silhouetted the target as a shadow. His heart was exploding in his chest. He was now in a full sprint toward the running figure, shouting to stop. He could see the figure slow, turn, and fired three shots.

Frank fell to the ground and heard a ping sound off the metal framing of the screen enclosure. This was not his partner. He pointed the barrel toward the figure and fired four shots.

Chapter Eighty-Six

S tewart's head jerked as he heard a single gunshot in the distance. Then he heard the hurried broadcast of Duffy shouting on the radio that shots were fired. Now he listened to a succession of shots fired a few blocks away. A gun battle had erupted. He quickly spoke on the radio that additional shots were being fired, get some help, and he was en route with his partner in plainclothes. There were a steady series of unit announcements barking they were on the way and heading towards the trouble. A family member from the Thin Blue Line was in trouble.

The gunfire stopped. Frank could smell the odor of gunpowder from his pistol. Duffy had fired seven rounds at the figure. He could no longer see him. He called out to his partner and received no response. His radio had fallen a few yards behind him. He could hear sirens in the distance. Frank focused into the darkness, looking for the assailant. The figure was no longer visible. Was he waiting for Duffy to get up? He had no choice.

He slowly stood into a combat stance and raced between the two homes towards his partner. He waited for additional shots. None came. He saw the slumped figure of Rollins. He ran towards him and kneeled down, hoping he had fallen and gotten hurt. His worst fears became reality, as he put his hand on his partner and felt no movement. He glanced back in the attacker's direction to make sure the suspect was not returning to kill both of them.

Frank picked up Rollin's radio and yelled, "Nine-oh-five, multiple shots fired. Officer down critical. Suspect in dark clothing fled westbound behind the victim's residence. Suspect may be injured."

He could hear the sirens getting closer. He knew the feeling like a parent who hears the blood-curdling scream of their child in the backyard and they are in the front. Its panic and helplessness. He checked the carotid pulse. It was weak, but there was a pulse.

"Hang in there, buddy. You're going to make it. Listen to me. You are going to live. Fight it, baby. Don't you give up on me. Fight it. Come on."

He felt Rollins's back and could not find any wounds. He slowly rolled him over. Despite the dark sky, the streetlights allowed him to see the dark wet spot on the maroon t-shirt. He could hear a sucking sound and shined the flashlight on the spot on the right chest. He pulled out his pocketknife, cut the t-shirt, and could see the frothy blood leaking from just below the right nipple.

Duffy's brain recalled all those useless first aid classes he took. He knew this was a sucking chest wound, where air was getting into the chest cavity. Frank also knew it could jeopardize the lung and it could collapse under the lack of pressure. He looked around as he heard the first racing engine of the cavalry screaming down the street. He pulled out his wallet, grabbed his Hillsborough County library card, and placed it over the wound.

Stewart and Bridges were running with guns drawn. Duffy yelled, "Bridges, get some crime scene tape out of your trunk. Al, watch our back. The shooter could come back."

Frank peeled off his mesh vest, rolled it up and placed it under Rollin's feet to elevate his legs to treat for shock. Bridges returned with the roll of yellow crime scene tape.

Duffy asked Bridges to pull off a long strand and said, "Help me wrap this around him over the wound."

He exposed one corner of the library card against the wound so some exchange of air would occur.

The arrival of the first marked unit interrupted the darkness with his red and blue lights flashing. Several more marked units converged on the scene.

Duffy yelled, "We can't wait for the EMT's. Let's load and go. Call TGH and tell them we're on the way."

Five cops, one on each extremity and one on the head, loaded the unconscious Rollins in the back seat of the marked unit. Duffy stayed with his wounded comrade as the uniformed officer jumped in the driver's seat. The siren wailed. The deep-throated engine sped the two minutes to the level one trauma center where miracles occurred daily.

The ER staff anxiously awaited their arrival. They lifted Lester onto the gurney and hurried him inside. Duffy took a deep breath and bit his lower lip, trying to control his emotions. The younger officer, who drove the fallen detective, patted Duffy on his back. They gave a silent nod to one another, knowing Rollins' fate was out of their hands and rested upon the surgeons.

Chapter Eighty-Seven

Back at the scene, Alfonso called out for units to set up a perimeter while the helicopter cruised over the top with its powerful searchlight and its heat sensing imagery. The K-9 officer arrived with his eager companion. The neighbors began circulating outside with the block bathed in a sea of blue flashing lights and the squawking of the police radios. The crime scene tape, initially used to save Lester's life, now set up a visual reminder of the expansive crime scene.

A gentleman with a long white mane and sleep still in his eyes shuffled out in bare feet while he clutched his bathrobe with his hands. He said to no one in particular, "What in the hell happened here?"

Bridges asked, "Who lives here?"

"I do. Melvin Storms."

"A police detective was shot. He was responding to a prowler call."

"My god. It must have been one of my disgruntled clients."

"Were you involved in the David Stilts case several years ago in which he killed a girl?"

"Yes, I was the defense attorney. I don't understand. He was killed."

"We think the boyfriend of the girl that was murdered by Stilts is dispensing his own justice. You must be on his list."

"Oh my God. This is terrible. This scares the hell out of me."

Alfonso, overhearing the conversation, was shocked that after hearing a police officer was shot in his front yard and with an army of police officers out front, all Storm's was concerned about was his own safety. The thankless job of being a cop. It would be nice to grab this obnoxious soul and scream at him, but it probably wouldn't do any good. He walked away and wondered why he had not thought of this angle of Storms being a target. Now, one of his detectives and a friend were fighting for his life. He had no time to dwell on mistakes. There would be plenty of time later. He concentrated on the job. He wanted to go to the hospital, but he had no choice.

Storms continued his inquiry. "I hope this maniac doesn't come back. Who was the officer?"

Bridges, being the consummate professional, politely answered, "Lester Rollins."

"I know Rollins. I just saw him yesterday. This is unbelievable."

"He is fighting for his life at TGH. He was trying to protect you. Anyone else that worked on that case that should be worried?"

"Wendell Holmes was the State Attorney on the case. He is one of my partners now. He lives over on Davis Island."

Stewart called dispatch to have another unit check the welfare of Holmes and maintain security at the residence. He also directed another unit to sit on Judge Levy's house in case this was a diversion. The chances were that he was long gone, not expecting a gun battle and a police dragnet.

Stewart remained at the scene, waiting on the crime scene unit to arrive. The first of the media began showing up like vultures circling the carcass. This would be the lead story for the viewers, still a few hours from waking up. He assigned the case to Bridges. There was no way he would call Dumb and Dumber.

The K-9 handler returned and said to Stewart, "We followed the trail over to Newport Street. It looks like he had a car parked there. We also found a couple of drops of blood. We're knocking on doors in the area to see if anyone saw what kind of car was there or anyone looked suspicious the last day or two. The blood is being collected by crime scene."

"Good work. We also need to contact area hospitals. I doubt he'll show up at TGH with it, looking like a precinct house. We'll need to change the BOLO from an unknown subject to Luke Shugard. We had one out on him as a suspect in the shooting of the Judge's daughter and Max Kress. Now we can add the shooting of a police officer. Approach with caution. Presumed armed and dangerous."

Alfonso knew that adding the last information on armed and dangerous would give every officer a justification to shoot, unless Luke threw his arms in the air to surrender. Cops didn't like when one of their own brothers was shot. Luke had also killed the children of a judge. This was Tampa, and no one would ask many questions.

Chapter Eighty-Eight

A dditional units began showing up at the hospital. Duffy never liked hospitals. Nothing but bad news. He hated the medicinal smell of the hospitals and the utter chaos in the emergency rooms. The nurse in blue scrubs walked out towards Duffy. He stood up apprehensively, not wanting the news. He tried to read her face. She looked tired after a long night working in a level one-trauma emergency room. He never cared for poker, trying to read faces. Her hospital ID badge displayed her name was Sharon Benson.

She asked, "Did you bring in the police officer?"

Frank said, "Yes."

"He is in surgery. The surgeon said who ever used the library card to seal the wound may have saved his life. We washed it off and put it in a bag. It's in here with all his other personal effects."

"That's my card. The Hillsborough County Library pays dividends!"

She smiled and said, "You must have paid attention in first aid class or you watch a lot of *Gray's Anatomy*."

"I have spent enough bad times in hospitals, so I never watch medical shows."

"You did well."

"Thank you, Nurse Benson. What are his chances?"

"Torso wounds are difficult. You never know where the bullet travels. He has good chances, having survived to this point."

"Let me know if he needs blood. We'll have the entire Blue Monster standing in line."

"We'll keep that in mind."

Duffy looked in the clear plastic bag with a drawstring and looked at the Rollins belongings and found his cellphone. Frank knew the passcode and opened the recent calls. The last one was to Brenda Taylor. He hit the call button. He heard the ringing of the phone.

A sleepy voice answered, "You better have a good reason for calling me."

"Brenda, this is Frank Duffy. I work with Lester."

"Is everything okay?"

"No, Brenda. I am sorry to say there was some trouble and Lester got hurt. He is at the hospital. He is tough, and he is hanging in there. I know he just met you, but I know he cares for you."

"How bad is it? What happened?"

"He was shot. He is alive, and he is in surgery."

"Oh, my gosh."

"If you give me your address, I'll have a unit come and pick you up and drive you to Tampa General."

"No. No, that won't be necessary. I'll drive myself. Thank you for calling."

Frank rubbed his burning eyes and took a deep breath. He looked at the uniforms, wanting to help, but feeling useless. He said, "We need to have someone pickup Lester's mother and call dispatch and get in touch with the Baptist chaplain and Sister Anne as well. She is always a big help."

One of the younger officers Frank did not recognize said, "Will do, sir."

The Chief walked in wearing plain clothes and a ball cap to cover her disheveled hair. Sleep had not completely departed her eyes. She recognized Frank and asked for an update and a synopsis. The Chief told Frank that Becky Godfrey, the PIO was on her way, as was the mayor. Frank always respected the Chief, who had risen through the ranks. The Chief was now in charge, taking control of a chaotic situation. Frank felt comfortable releasing the leadership reigns to someone that lead by example.

Frank slipped over to the side and called Reese Crenshaw from his cell. As promised, he gave him the scoop and returned to the gaggle. The Chief was comforting Rollin's mother. Frank noticed a beauty queen pretty girl standing off to the side with a lost look.

He walked over to her and said, "Brenda?"

"Yes, Detective Duffy?"

"Yes, have a seat over here."

Frank explained what had happened and released the intimate feelings that Lester had for Brenda, just in case he didn't make it. He didn't want it to look like contrived if he didn't make it. Then he introduced Brenda to Mrs. Rollins, knowing this introduction would absolutely sink Lester into matrimony if he survived.

Frank saw Lieutenant Rizzo wandering around, not sure what to do or what was expected. He kept his distance. He figured she was probably worried about her upward mobility. Now she had to go into damage control after undermining the motel shootings that tied back into the Levy-Applebaum shootings. She would have to explain how Dietz, her lover, misled her. Somehow, it always seemed that these types of politicians had a way of surviving.

As word spread and more of Lester's friends came in for the vigil, they began swapping 'Luster' stories. Even in these dire circumstances, the stories often resulted in laughter and lifted the spirits.

Reese Crenshaw arrived. Frank stood up and said, "Excuse me, Lieutenant, this is Reese Crenshaw from the Tribune. Do you know where the PIO is?"

She glared at both of them. She said nothing and pointed in the direction. "Thanks, Lieutenant."

The TV in the waiting room was providing the weather updates on Hurricane Alex. It had slowed in the Gulf and now appeared to be turning away from Tampa and instead heading towards the Texas coast. Frank thought Tampa had dodged another bullet. Too bad his friend wasn't as lucky.

Chapter Eighty-Nine

SATURDAY

F rank sat there amidst the pandemonium in the waiting room. News trucks parked outside. Laughing and crying. It dawned on Frank he had forgotten to call Kate with all the hysteria. He dialed her number.

"Hello, you have reached Detective Alexander. Please leave a message after the tone."

"Hey Kate, Duffy here. Ah listen, we had a problem on surveillance this morning. Rollins got hurt. Shugard got away. Call me as soon as you get this. Thanks."

Because of the hurricane activity, Kate's flight arrived thirty minutes late. As she waited at the carousel for her luggage, she pulled out her cell phone. She dialed home, and the phone went dead. No juice. As she contemplated looking for an archaic payphone, if one even existed in the airport, her bag arrived. She just wanted to get home and see Britney and her mother. She knew Frank was probably at home in bed after pulling the midnight shift. When she arrived home, she would call dispatch and find out who was working the day shift and call them for an update.

As Kate drove past the orange groves, she thought that as much as she enjoyed the mountains and hills of Tennessee, this was home. She parked in the driveway and gathered up her stuff. She was halfway to the door and was surprised that Britney did not come running out, but sometimes they would surprise her inside with a cake or balloons.

She tried the front door, and it was unlocked. She nudged the door open with her shoulder. Not only was the alarm not on again, but the door was unlocked. She was really going to give her mother a talking to now.

With her hands full carrying a garment bag, purse, and a messenger bag, she shuffled into the house, calling out, "Hi, I'm home."

No answer. She pushed the door closed with her left foot. She entered the family room and looked up as her entire life drained from her body.

Chapter Ninety

D uffy called Kate's cell phone and reached the voice mail again. He looked down at his watch. Thinking she should have landed. Maybe she forgot to turn her cell phone on. Then he remembered she had said she forgot her charger and perhaps the battery was dead. He said aloud, "I hate these things." He relaxed. Then he dialed her home number, but it also went to voicemail. He hung up. He thought that was odd. The Chief walked up to him to ask additional questions from the scene.

Kate's mother had duct tape across her mouth and her hands bound behind her. Luke stood there with a smirk, holding a pistol to her head. Her mother looked terrified.

"Hello, Kate," said Luke.

"I'll kill you."

"I would not do anything foolish. Your daughter is safe in her bedroom."

"I want to see her."

"Kate, I am sorry you are not in control. I am. You know what I am capable of doing. She is in her bedroom. Your mother can nod her head to show if Britney is good or not." Her mother's head went up and down. "Britney is spunky and intelligent like you."

"You didn't hurt her?"

With his free hand, he pointed toward the ceiling. "I promise you, under the watchful eye of God, I have not hurt her. I have no plans to hurt you, either."

"If anything happens to me or my family, I can assure you that the entire weight of the Blue Monster will crush you. They will be on your ass. I guarantee you."

"The Blue Monster?"

"The Tampa Police Department is the Blue Monster."

He looked around and smiling, said, "I don't see the Blue Monster around here. Now, you will follow my directions. You will walk away from your luggage. Is your gun on you or in the messenger bag?"

"In the bag."

"I want you to get on your knees in front of your mother, facing her. I want you to put your hands behind your back so that I can cuff you. If you do anything stupid, you will witness your mother die."

Kate wondered if he was going to shoot her. She thought, if he wanted to kill her, he would have shot her when she walked in the door. The same for her mother. Her daughter was kept in another room, so Kate would be less inclined to resist not knowing the situation.

"Point the gun at me."

"No. That won't work. Now lean into your mother's knees."

Luke moved around her rear. He placed flex cuffs on her wrists and pulled the plastic snug against her wrists.

"If you like, you may sit next to your mother."

"Actually, after the long flight, my legs tend to cramp. I don't want thrombosis to develop. So, I'll stand."

"Not likely. Sit next to your mother. How was your trip to Knoxville? Did you find any evidence on me?"

"I found the rental car that you used to kill Rachel Levy and the body shop that repaired it. I also spoke with your Aunt Sue. Sure, is a nice person."

"That's very interesting. Speaking of nice, I have been chatting with your mother. She really is a nice person. You are very blessed to have her. It is a shame that you are such a young widow. My hat is off to you. Your husband was in special ops. He was the real deal. There are so many wannabes and imposter warriors. Your husband was a brave warrior and so are you, whether you realize it. Here you are carrying on as a hero, protecting our city and community, while raising your daughter as a single mom. I admire you so much that there is nothing I would not do to protect you and to help you. I do not intend to hurt you. I still have a mission I must accomplish. You are the only one who can stop me. You and that Duffy. Although, after last night, I am not too sure how much help he'll be."

"What happened to Frank?"

"You didn't hear? They must have gotten wise. They almost caught me at Storm's house. That poor black detective. Nothing against him. He was just in the way. All I could see were the whites of his eyes when I shot him." He chuckled to himself.

"You shot Rollins?"

"That's not all. I was just trying to get away. Duffy and I got into a little firefight. He winged me in the leg. I don't know if I hit him, but I sure scared him." The chuckling resumed. "They were preventing me from accomplishing my mission."

She became concerned that her two friends were hurt. She did not know the status of her daughter. She had to think. This man was very capable of killing. He was a sociopath who had no conscious.

"Why Storms?"

"He was the attorney for David Stilts. You didn't know, did you? Perhaps I overestimated you. I thought you were a challenging adversary."

"Why me? Why my family?"

"The other day when you were walking out of the hospital, you told me good luck. I knew you were endorsing my plan. I can't tell you how much that meant to me. You had finally embraced my plan. It brought a certain peace to me. When the doctor let me out, that was divine intervention. I knew you were the only one who could stop me. Until last night, when those two detectives almost caught me. My training and instinct took over. I tell you what, I don't want any more miscalculations. Why don't you lay on the ground so I can search you?"

"Sure."

While still sitting, he patted her waist and legs. She thought, what would Jake do in this situation? How would he handle this deranged man with his family held hostage at gunpoint? Then an epiphany occurred to her. Jake was not in this situation and never was in any situation like this before. The real question was what Kate would do? How was Kate going to handle this? She realized she had to control her emotions.

Use your training and the psychology that you know. Use your interviewing skills. Keep him as your ally, but don't get too close. Wait for an opportunity and seize the moment. Do not hesitate. You cannot hesitate. Even if he hurts you, you must save your mother and daughter. Kate could not bear to think of her daughter living without both parents. She had to block that thought out. She had to focus on survival. Not her survival, but her mother and daughter. Never underestimate the willpower of a mother.

With her hands still bound behind her, she stood up and asked, "What is the rest of the plan?"

"Sit down, Kate!"

She complied. She now knew the amount of energy needed to stand and how quickly she could stand.

He said, "You really don't need to concern yourself with the plan. You know, when I looked into your eyes the other day, it was like looking into a mirror. I could feel a connection. Not in the physical sense, although you are very attractive, but in a spiritual sense. I don't want to hurt you or your family. You are too formidable of an opponent. I need you out of the way until I can accomplish my mission."

"I told you good luck with getting your life together. I was hoping the hospital would help you."

"They helped. They said I wasn't crazy. They validated my mission and my sanity."

Chapter Ninety-One

D uffy dialed Kate's number again. Once again, voicemail. He hung up. He thought her mother or Britney would answer. Unless they were on the phone and didn't want to answer the call waiting. Something was not right. He called Verizon and asked if they had trouble with any of their lines going to Kate's area. Verizon advised there were no reported outages. He thought for a moment and called the sheriff's office.

"This is Frank Duffy. I am a homicide detective with TPD and I was involved in the shooting this morning with that BOLO suspect, Luke Shugard. I am concerned that my partner, Kate Alexander, is not answering her home phone, and neither is her family. She is not answering her cell, either. Could you send a couple of units out there? If Shugard has found her, they will have a fight on their hands."

"We'll send two units and a supervisor. We won't put it over the air. We'll send it to their terminals."

"Thanks. Call me as soon as you hear."

"Ten - Four."

Luke said, "My original plan was to kill that bitch's husband while she watched. I would have come back to kill Storms and Levy several months later. I wanted her to know why everyone around her died. I wanted her to experience the same grief she had bestowed upon everyone else. Max, Marge and me. All of Jennifer's friends and relatives. Max is free of his grief. He gave up on God. That is why he was in despair. He lost all faith. My faith only strengthened. I helped Max as long as I could. I made the toughest decision of my life to let him go. Like a child disconnecting the life support to a parent. He was no longer alive. He was breathing and his heart was pumping, but he died a long time ago. I united their spirits' together. Max was my real dad. He encouraged me, gave me shelter, and love and recognition."

"Why kill Levy's children?"

"I never said I did."

"Admit you did. Why are you continuing to deny it?

"You put the evidence together."

"Storms has a job to do."

"Storms is a whore. He would defend the lowest of low life if it put money in his pocket. He deserved a slow death."

"You hired him to defend Maguire?"

"I wanted to make sure he was still a whore."

"Why did you kill Maguire?"

"I didn't say I did. I thought I could use him to help and do some work for me. After his arrest, I knew I made a mistake. He was a weak link. He jeopardized the entire mission. It was a shame he met such a tragic death. Drug deals go wrong all the time."

"That was no drug buy gone wrong. You killed him."

"It was a shame that the girl died. It was God's will. She was cheating on her husband. She was coveting her neighbor and deserved to die. That bullet was her penance for her sin. Her husband is free to find a worthy spouse."

"Why the storage facility?"

"I don't know what you are talking about."

"That was a pretty nifty alarm system you set up."

"I deny your accusations. The government's provided me great training. The one thing they taught me was operational security. I really don't want to continue chatting and answering your questions."

Kate could hear hoofbeats. She was at first puzzled and then realized what she was hearing.

Luke said, "God has spoken to me. When my plan is complete, the world will be better off. Jennifer and Max's death will not have been in vain."

She could see that Luke could hear the hoof beats as well. He was now listening and focused on the sound.

They both heard the Professor yell out, "These Wal-Mart horses sure are fun!"

She tightened the thigh muscles like a tightly wound rubber band to give her the power she would need to react.

Luke looked towards the window to see Trent pulling the reins to slow the horse. She saw Luke move the gun off target just a little as his focus turned towards the window. She had to seize the moment. No hesitation. Instinct took over. She exploded from the sofa and kicked with all her ability and strength into Luke's maimed left knee. The pistol discharged with a loud explosion inside the house. Luke screamed in agony. With her hands still bound behind her, she lowered her shoulder, took two steps, and drove into his sternum. He fell backwards into the wall. His head bounced like a soccer ball. Luke collapsed to the ground, writhing in pain. She drove another kick into his face. Blood spurted from his mouth and nose. He slumped to the floor, unconscious, as the gun fell to the carpet. Still within his reach, she pushed it away with her foot.

As the professor stepped into the house, he said, "What the hell is going on?"

"Pickup his gun down there on the floor. Trent, the scissors in the butcher block in the kitchen. Get them so you can cut us free."

Trent picked up the gun with both of his hands. He fumbled with the gun, as he was unsure of the grip. Clutching the pistol, he pointed the barrel toward Luke and stepped toward the kitchen.

Luke groaned and stirred. He raised his head and said, "Please kill me."

Kate said, "Not a chance."

"Please."

"By the way, never come between a mother and her child again. You have just experienced the Blue Monster."

Trent backed up and kept the barrel pointing towards Luke. After retrieving the scissors, he reached down and cut the duct tape from Kate's mother. He went to Kate and cut the plastic restraints from her hands. She went to her messenger bag, opened it, and pulled out her handcuffs and gun. She handcuffed Luke, who was still writhing in pain.

She told Trent, "If he tries anything, shoot him in the other knee. I want him to suffer the same pain as everyone else. Mom, call 911."

"He cut the phone line."

"Use your cell phone."

She ran to Britney's room. The door was closed. She took a deep breath, turned the knob, and pushed it open. Just then, she heard her mom yell the police were on their way.

She entered her daughter's room. Britney was hunkered on the floor. Cartoons on the TV. Tears free flowing and the muffled sounds of sobbing.

"It's okay, sweetie. Mommy is here."

She peeled the tape off her mouth, pulled the sobbing girl in her arms, and consoled her.

"Everything is okay. We are all safe. Gramma is all right. The bad man accidentally fired the gun. No one is hurt. Except for the bad man. Are you okay? I am so sorry. I am so sorry." Kate wiped tears off her own cheeks and then said, "I promise it's okay. Let's get these flex cuffs off your hands." She could hear the comfort of sirens as she patted her daughter's back.

Chapter Ninety-Two

F rank's cell phone rang, "Hello."

"Detective Duffy?"

"Yes, this is Debbie, with county dispatch. We just received a 911 from a cell phone requesting help at Detective Alexander's residence. There was also a report of shots fired. The caller said everyone was all right. Deputies are within one minute. I'll give you a status update as soon as I hear."

"Thank you."

His heart sank. Kate was like a part of his family. He spent more waking hours with Kate than with his own family. They shared thoughts, feelings, and laughs. He couldn't stand to hear she was in peril or her family. Their families socialized on birthdays and holiday cookouts. Never in all his years had he been through anything like this. It was bad enough that his friend Lester suffered a gunshot wound, but now his closest friend was in peril.

The deputies arrived in tandem. Kate walked outside with her badge held up and carrying Britney, who clutched her in a death grip. She gave the deputies the quick overview, and they went in and relieved Trent of his guard duty. The third vehicle, carrying the patrol sergeant, killed his siren as he turned into the driveway.

The deputies escorted Luke out of the house, hobbling on the bad knee. His face was covered in blood and was already bruised. He said nothing and with each step, he grimaced as if he was passing a kidney stone. Kate glared as the car door slammed.

Trent enveloped Kate and Britney in his arms. Kate said, "We're all right." She broke the grip and turned to her mother. She embraced her mom, who broke down and wept.

"Thank you, Kate. Jake and dad would have been proud. You saved us."

"It wasn't about them. It was about you and Britney."

"I love you."

"I love you too Mama."

She heard the horse whinny, and she turned to Trent and said, "What did you say about the horsy rides at Wal-Mart?"

"I sure got my money's worth."

"You rode in here like the Pickett's last charge. How did you learn to ride?"

"Lessons."

"I can't believe you did that."

She hugged him and finally kissed him, not on the cheek, but on the lips.

"You're a tough broad to earn a kiss from. I hope I don't have to do this again for another kiss. I thought Homicide wasn't dangerous?"

She smiled and shrugged her shoulders.

The Sergeant walked up and said, "Ma'am I have Detective Duffy on the line." He handed her the cell phone.

"Frank?"

"Kate, are you okay?"

"I am now, thanks to the Professor."

"What?"

"It a long story over a lot of beers. Everything is okay. Luke is in custody. What happened to Lester?"

"Another long story over more beers. The surgeon came out and said he was going to survive. I guess it was close. He'll be off for a while."

"I tried to reach you on your cell phone."

"I know the battery died."

"I hate those things."

"I know, simplicity in life."

"You got it. Hey, I am on my way out to you with Al and the Chief. We'll be there in thirty minutes."

"Thanks."

Chapter Ninety-Three

MONDAY

On Monday morning, it startled Dietz to see Kate leaning back in his chair with her feet up, resting on the desk. She was reading a file.

"Can I help you?" Dietz asked.

"Nah, I think it's too late for that."

"Well, why don't you vacate my seat?"

"Some things never change. You know what this is?" She patted the file.

"Let me see. A file, duh."

"This was a file that Judge Levy sent over concerning the trial of David Stilts. He was the one that killed Jennifer Kress that started this whole fiasco. It's a shame you didn't give it to me or to someone that knew how to pull their head out of their ass."

He stammered and said, "I meant to."

"In here was listed the defense attorney who played a part in getting Stilts off. That defense attorney was none other than Melvin Storms. With him being hired to defend Maguire on a simple probation violation, *we, not you, but we* could have figured that Storms would have been a likely target."

Panic flooded his face. "I... ah... ah..."

"Don't speak. You were so caught up building a case around Unger, you didn't want to share any info. If we had seen that file, we might have caught Shugard at Storm's house. Rollins is in the hospital and my family is terrorized because of your incompetence. Here is your desk."

He was stunned. Frank, who was sitting behind his desk, chimed in and said, "I can't get you two straight. Are you Dumb or are you Dumber? By the way, I wouldn't go crying to Rizzo. I think the milk train has dried up. Her stock is plummeting."

Dietz jabbed his finger toward Frank. "I knew it was you that flattened my tire."

Frank nodded and grinned. "I know nothing. Let's just say she didn't get the name Gobbler for nothing. There could be a lot of jilted lovers left in her wake."

Dietz's shaved head turned crimson.

Bridges now piled on and said, "As Zig Ziglar once said, 'Failure is a detour, not a dead-end street.' In your case, you might need to stop and ask for directions."

Dietz stormed out.

Kate said, "You know she got the name Gobbler for eating turkey sandwiches. She carried her own lunch bucket." Frank looked at Kate in disbelief. She said, "Yep, the truth."

Frank responded, "You see how tales sometimes grow their own legends? I still don't like her."

Kate walked out of the squad room after telling everyone she had a quick errand to run.

Frank picked up the telephone and called a number from one of his post-its. The female voice answered, "Hello?"

"Judge Levy, this is Frank Duffy from TPD."

"Detective Duffy, I was just composing a letter to the Chief concerning the actions of you and Detective Alexander."

"Oh. Thank you, your Honor. I just wanted you to know that in court, I have always looked at trial as a chess game involving real people. This past week brought home to me the reality of the impact on those chess pieces as real people. I may have come across a little abrupt with you during your time of mourning. I was playing Joe Friday and stating the facts without concern to what you and your husband had suffered. Generally, I have empathy for my victims' family. As I sat outside your home the other night, I couldn't fathom the depth of despair that I would go through if my two daughters died within a year. All because I was doing my job, and some psycho did not agree with my actions. I am genuinely sorry."

"I know you are. Like you, I detach emotion from my decisions. Thank you for your call, and I hope Detective Rollins has a speedy recovery."

"Good bye, you Honor."

He hung up the phone, peeled the post-it off his blotter, and tossed it into the trash.

Kate strutted into the mental health clinic and asked the receptionist for Sheila Schwab. When the Cher look-a-like in casual clothes walked out to the lobby, Kate said, "Are you Sheila Schwab?"

"Yes?"

"I am with TPD and I would like to speak with you and Dr. Shabaz."

"Wait here."

A few moments later, a man with his hands tucked into the pockets of his lab coat and straight black hair followed Sheila Schwab.

He said, "Yes, what is it?"

Kate said, "Hello Dr. Shabaz, I am Detective Alexander. I just wanted to meet with both of you to see you face to face. I understand psychiatry is not an exact science. In fact, that was my minor in college."

The doctor said, "Yes, Detective, get to the point. I am in a hurry."

"Yes, I am sure you are. You assessed Luke Shugard the other day. You determined he was not a danger to himself or to others."

"Excuse me..."

"No excuse me! After completing that assessment and letting him out, he shot and severely wounded a police detective. He attempted to kill an attorney. He begged me to kill him. To end his life. That was after he took my mother and young daughter hostage at gunpoint. I guess you missed the diagnosis. I hope you have an excellent attorney. Because you're going to need one when all the victims get in line to sue your ass."

She turned and headed to the door with no reflection of emotion.

She could hear the receptionist tell the doctor, "Dr. Shabaz, a reporter from the Tribune, is on the phone and would like to speak to you."

Now Kate smiled.

Chapter Ninety-Four

K ate walked back into the squad room and hurried as she reached for the ringing phone. She picked it up on the fourth ring.

"Homicide, Detective Alexander."

"Detective Alexander, this is Fire Investigator Rex Chandler. "

"Yes, Rex."

"I just read the newspaper story. Are you all right?"

"I am fine. My family is fine. Maybe a little shaken. Thanks for asking."

"I just received the report from the crime lab concerning the results from the storage facility fire. Everything latent wise was smudged, but they were able to retrieve two usable prints on the plastic bag. They ran it through AFIS and identified the print, but you're going to have to prove the suspect was responsible for everything."

"I understand Rex. Who did the prints come back to?"

"One came back to a Luke Shugard. No criminal history."

"This is great. Hang on a sec Rex." She covered up the phone and said, "They found Luke's fingerprint on the shopping bag from the clothing store. That's the last nail in his coffin. We have him buying the costume used at the storage unit and the killing of Lori Applebaum."

Frank's telephone rang. She uncovered the mouthpiece and said, "I am sorry Rex, you said there were two prints? Did the other come back to a Lashondra Watkins, the clerk?"

"No. They came back to a Marjorie Kress."

"What?"

"Marjorie Kress."

"My God. Are you sure? Oh, listen to me, of course, you're sure. You didn't just make this up. Could you email me a copy of that report?"

"Sure will."

"Thanks, Rex."

Kate hung the phone up and sat there in disbelief.

Frank said, "Hey, you, ok?"

"Ah yeah. You will not believe it, but another print on that bag came back to Marge Kress."

"That fits with the last call I just received. It was Warren Dupree from HCSO. He said they went around reviewing video at all the local places near Wilderness Park where they found Max's body. Neil's Quick Stop has a video that covers the pumps and the front of the store, including the payphone. They have Luke making the 911 call. They also have him as a passenger in a Jaguar. A female was driving. An hour prior to the 911 call, the Jag pulls in. Luke makes a call, probably to Max, asking for the help. The driver gets out of the car and goes inside. The plate comes back to Max Kress. He pulled the D.L. photo of Marge Kress and showed it to the attendant. He identified her as coming inside to buy coffee and a lottery ticket."

"A lottery ticket? Unbelievable. She is about to have her husband killed and buy a lottery ticket." Kate said.

"Hey, her life went in the tubes, too. Her only child is gone. Her husband falls apart. It costs her the affluent lifestyle. The humiliation of her husband's declining state. It's tough to go to the country club to play bridge and tennis, knowing everyone is gossiping about you. Now she collects on life insurance and moves back into the house. Marge might be in cahoots with Luke. He could be the loyal soldier carrying out orders. She would have been able to manipulate Luke. She also could put it back on her ex, and claim he pulled a Kevorkian to look like a suicide."

"I am shocked. I just never suspected, but it all makes sense. Hell, hath no fury like a mother scorned. I know better than anyone."

"I would agree with that assessment. I told Warren we would meet him out at his office. He is going to have Marge come in under the pretext of identifying some of Max's property so they can give it back to her."

Chapter Ninety-Five

K ate and Frank arrived at the homicide squad for the sheriff's office on Falkenburg
Road. The expansive pale one-story building was nestled conveniently next to the
razor wired compound of the jail. They met with and discussed the case with Warren. Kate
agreed to start the interview with Marge because of her relationship with Marge. Warren
would come in with the heavy hand if necessary.

Marge entered the interview room, and Kate was waiting. "Oh Kate, I didn't expect to
see you. I was so worried about you. I couldn't believe that Luke went that far over the
side. He was such a nice boy when we knew him."

"Marge, how did he know where to find my house?"

She shrugged. "I am not sure. Probably from Max's computer or on the internet."

"No, I went through his contacts and my name was not there. I sent you a bereavement
card. Do you think he might have seen that?"

"I'll bet you're right. He stopped by and browsed through the cards. It must have been
scary to be held hostage with your family."

"Yes, it was, but I am sure you can sympathize with the judge after going through the
murder of Jennifer and watching Max fall apart. I am sure you have a picture of Jennifer
in your purse or on your phone to this day."

"Oh sure, I miss her so much." Marge leaned over, pulled the wallet from her handbag,
and set it on the interview table. Kate noticed a slight tremble in Marge's hands as she
opened the wallet and showed several pictures in their plastic inserts of Jennifer. She held
up her phone, displaying the home-screen image of a once happy family.

Marge said, "You know, I felt so frustrated by her death. She was beautiful."

"She was. She's still is in my heart."

Kate pointed to the money in the billfold and said, "Is that a lottery ticket?"

"Yes, it is."

"Quick pick or do you pick your own?"

"Pick my own."

"What numbers?"

Marge pulled the ticket out, showed it to Kate, and said, "They are a combination of Jennifer's birthday and my wedding anniversary."

"Dates of happier times."

"If we could only rewind the clock."

"Do you always pick the same numbers?"

"Twice a week. No luck so far."

Kate grinned and thought about how Marge's luck was going to run out. She knew Marge was conspiring with Luke. She cringed at the thought of how she manipulated him.

"You seem to be coping with Max's death."

"The separation made it easier, and he had been hurting for sometime."

Kate leaned forward and said, "You wouldn't have helped him commit suicide?"

Her mouth opened with surprise and she said, "Ah, what would ever give you that idea, Kate?"

"So, you're saying you had no involvement with his death?"

Her face displayed revulsion. "Why would you say that?"

Kate could see she wasn't denying her involvement. Marge was answering with a question.

"Marge, you almost had us fooled. You bought a cup of coffee and a lottery ticket at Neil's Quick Stop when you were waiting for Luke to call Max. He called him to come help him at the park."

"I don't know what you are talking about. Kate, how dare you."

Kate noticed Marge was rubbing her trembling hands as if she was washing dirt off them.

"We have video of your Jaguar and of Luke and you. The clerk identified you buying coffee and the lottery ticket. Every ticket has a sequence of numbers on the lottery ticket. The ticket gives a precise date and time sold and identifies a terminal code. We can go back to that terminal and search the time you were there and find your Lotto numbers that you selected. The same numbers you play twice a week."

"Lots of people play the same numbers for various reasons."

"Not your numbers at the same date and time and at that same location. I'll bet we can even find the discarded ticket from last week in your trash at home. We can get a search warrant. Marge, the clerk identified you. Your numbers match. You know Luke has also given a statement. It's over."

She was bluffing. Luke, despite not liking attorney's, invoked his right not to speak and desired representation. He even called Storms, who quickly declined to represent him.

Marge said, "Luke is crazy. You know it."

"Crazy or not, his story corroborates what the physical evidence shows. I know what it's like to lose someone in their prime. I lost Jake, but that pales to your loss. No mother should out live her child. Jennifer was just becoming a lady who you could share so many things. Deprived of watching her graduate from college, the grand wedding, and you becoming a grandmother was terrible. All because the judge let that piece of garbage out. I met her last week. They call her courtroom, 'Levy's Ice Vault.' Her nickname is 'Levy-them-out of-jail'. So, I can understand. I have been to parties at your house. You were both so much in love. Jake and I were envious of the love you and Max shared and we hoped to have the same love at your age. You had the perfect family. Until that judge destroyed your family and your life. Now she shares in some of the same grief. Max is free. He is in a better place. You can get your life back together. Maybe move back into the house. Collect the life insurance. They owe you that much. You earned it. I know you didn't take Max's life. You're not like that judge. You only helped Luke put Max out of his misery. No different from flipping the switch off on the life-support machine at the hospital. You and Luke were helping him. No one can blame you. In fact, many people would hail you as a hero. We know you didn't harm Max. Luke will probably plead insanity, and he'll be all right after a little help. That's all you were doing was helping. You were helping Max and helping Luke, isn't that right?"

Kate leaned forward and touched Marge on the shoulder. "It's all right Marge. You just helped, didn't you?"

Marge's head dropped, and a couple of tears sprinkled the thighs of her slacks. She sniffled and said, "Yes." She paused and said, "It wasn't fair."

"I know it wasn't. You only drove Luke, right?"

"Yes." She sniffled again and rubbed her nose with the back of her hand.

"You knew Luke was going to end Max's misery and allow him to be reunited with Jennifer?"

"Yes. Oh God, what did I do?"

Kate hugged Marge while she sobbed, and she patted her back and comforted her. Kate handed her some tissues. She thought about how wrong she had been. Maybe if she had looked at Marge sooner, Max would still be alive and Rollins would not have been shot. Guilt crept into her own conscience.

"I am going to be outside. Detective Dupree is going to take a statement from you and clarify a few things."

Chapter Ninety-Six

K ate walked outside. Frank patted her shoulder, and he said, "That was great. You have her on a conspiracy to commit murder. You did great breaking her open. Luke would have gone to his grave with that secret."

"No, it's not great. It sucks. Let's go."

He pulled her arm, "Hey, hey you put this one to bed."

She turned, "Frank, I missed it. I never suspected Marge."

"Nor did I. A nurse friend of mine once told me a wise old doctor taught her when you hear the thundering of hoofbeats, look for zebras. In other words, look for the out of the ordinary."

She nodded slightly and said, "Yeah."

Frank said, "Keep in mind the female mosquito is the one that stings, but we swat at all of them. Marge fooled all of us, but like that nagging mosquito, you caught the right one."

She nodded again and clenched her lips.

On the drive back, Frank said, "Let me buy you lunch. The Columbia, okay?"

"No thanks, Frank. I'm not very hungry and I wouldn't be very good company. I have a peanut butter and pretzel sandwich at the office."

"I understand. Hey, I almost forgot. How was the play Saturday?"

"I couldn't find a dress." They both smiled.

Frank said, "The Professor must have been heartbroken."

"No, we're going camping this weekend."

"With or without Britney?"

"Without."

"That a girl."

"Do you have like a camouflage nightgown that you wear?"

"Or nothing at all."

"TMI, TMI."

They both broke into laughter.

Frank dropped Kate at the corner of Lykes Park so he could pick up his shoes from Reina's Shoe Repair.

She walked across the park and looked up toward the old tiled Blue Monster. Somehow, the tiles looked cleaner and shinier. Her smile broadened as she once again entered the mouth of the monster.

The end.

I want to thank you for taking the time to read this book. If you liked this book, I would be extremely grateful if you would be kind enough to leave a brief review on Amazon. This will help to enlighten other readers and spread the word. I am humbled that you spent your time with Kate and Frank and my fictional tale. My Amazon Author page is: https://www.amazon.com/Mike-Roche/e/B00BHEIF78?ref=sr_ntt_srch_lnk _1&qid=1661706928&sr=8-1I left a taste of the the next Kate Alexander adventure below. Please stop by my website at: https://mikeroche.com/ to join the mailing list and receive a free Detective Kate Alexander short story. Thank you!

Cheers, Mike

A Taste of Coins of Death:

Sunday 2:02AM

Looking for danger, Alex Diaz sat alone in the darkness. The dispatcher's mundane voice assigned units to disturbances, drunks, prowlers, and alarm calls. Alex sat in the driver's seat, sucking on a Marlboro. He blew a cumulus cloud of smoke out the open window and watched it hang in the heavy humid air of October. He took another sip from the can of Coke and watched a black Ford Explorer drive past. A grin creased his face as he spotted the burned-out rear taillight of a passing car.

He flicked the cigarette out the open window and turned on the ignition. He increased the volume of the radio to listen to the dispatcher as he shifted the gear selector into drive and depressed the gas with his foot. The Crown Victoria emerged from the darkness through a curtain of streetlights. He hesitated at the avenue, looked right and left, and punched the gas. The car accelerated down the street like a hunter after the prey. Alex loved the adrenaline rush of catching up to violators. He could feel the excitement of the engine as it increased in speed. He always had a sense of self-importance and an ego boost when he pulled over cars.

Alex easily caught up to the unsuspecting violator. He was now close enough to read the license plate, but not too far that the driver would entertain running. He flipped the switch under the dashboard and engaged the blue LED lights affixed to the windshield. He flipped the second switch for the strobes in the headlights. The left brake light of the SUV illuminated bright red. Alex chuckled quietly, knowing the driver was scared to death. The Explorer slowed down and pulled towards the curb.

Alex brought his car to a rest behind the violator. The blue lights echoed off the surrounding buildings, providing a brilliant light show in the darkness. He stepped out on the asphalt and strutted towards the offender. With both hands, he grabbed his belt and pulled the leather up. The badge, hooked to the belt just in front of his holstered gun, glistened in the light. His left hand grasped the black metal flashlight as he aimed the bright beam at the driver's window. The driver's door opened, and the driver stepped out of the car with his hand raised to his midsection in a surrender position.

The driver said, "Did I do something wrong, Officer?"

Before Alex could respond, he heard movement behind him.

Available exclusively through Amazon.

About Author

While working as both a local cop and a federal agent, Mike Roche has spent four decades chasing bad guys and conducting behavioral assessments of stalkers and assassins. He is also an adjunct college instructor. Mike enjoys the serenity of spending time with his family in sunny Florida.

Acknowledgments

I have to start as most authors, by thanking my family for all their support. They sacrificed many hours as they watched me hunt and peck on the keyboard. Many times, I would ask for five minutes of typing that would turn into sixty. Many instructors at writers' conferences shared their knowledge and taught me the craft of literary fiction. I would like to thank the writers that became my friends. To Dr. Cichon and Dr. McBath, who kept me alive, and to my wife and children who would not let me give up. To Adele Brinkley for her editing and Stuart Bache, the artist who created the cover of this book and especially to all of you readers who spent your money on my ramblings, thank you.

Also By

Coins of Death

Backstabbers

Karma! (Young Adult Fiction)

Non-Fiction:

Face 2 Face: Observing, Interviewing and Rapport Building Skills: an ex-Secret Service Agent's Guide

Mass Killers: How You Can Identify Workplace, School and Public Killers Before they Strike

Afterword

This book was set in and around Tampa, Florida. The primary characters in this book of fiction are employed by the Tampa Police Department. Other characters work for the Hillsborough County Sheriff's Office. My experience with both departments is that they are extremely professional and well trained. As in all departments, there will always be bureaucratic obstacles, morale issues, and personality conflicts. Cops are cops. Tampa is merely the setting for my stories. I took literary license of procedures for reasons of creative flow.

In my forty years of law enforcement, I have encountered and worked with many officers and departments. I write and share with my readers the amalgam of these experiences. I hope I have accurately portrayed what it feels like to be a cop in an urban police department. Each city has its own inherent issues, as do most departments.

The nobility of the profession attracts many cops. As careers progress, the nobility often tarnishes and is often questioned by individual officers. It is this process and the subsequent transformation of the maturing officer I strive to capture. I hope you can feel the experience and escape on the journey through the eyes of my characters. Thank you for taking a chance and buying my book.

Made in United States
Orlando, FL
28 February 2023

30517563R00193